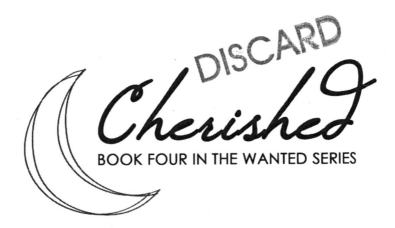

Cherished

BOOK FOUR IN THE WANTED SERIES

FROM *NEW YORK TIMES* AND *USA TODAY* BESTSELLING AUTHOR

Kelly Elliott

Cover Designer: Angie Fields, i love it design studio,
www.facebook.com/iloveitdesign

Editor and Interior Designer: Jovana Shirley, Unforeseen Editing,
www.unforeseenediting.com

Photography by Angela King-Belleville,
www.angelamichellephotography.com/

Visit my website at http://www.authorkellyelliott.blogspot.com

ISBN-13: 978-0-9913096-1-0

Other books by Kelly Elliott

Wanted Series

WANTED

Saved

faithful

Believe
a novella

Cherished

Full-length novels in the WANTED series
are also available in audio.

Broken Series

BROKEN

# Dedication

*This book is dedicated to my husband, Darrin, and my daughter, Lauren.
Thank you both for loving me and letting me live out my dreams.*

Contents

Prologue: Scott 1
Chapter One: Jessie..5
Chapter Two: Scott..9
Chapter Three: Jessie 15
Chapter Four: Scott 21
Chapter Five: Jessie....................................25
Chapter Six: Gunner................................31
Chapter Seven: Ellie................................... 39
Chapter Eight: Ari.................................. 43
Chapter Nine: Jeff................................... 51
Chapter Ten: Scott................................... 55
Chapter Eleven: Jessie 61
Chapter Twelve: Scott 73
Chapter Thirteen: Jessie 81
Chapter Fourteen: Heather...................... 85
Chapter Fifteen: Josh........................... 95
Chapter Sixteen: Scott 99
Chapter Seventeen: Jessie....................... 103
Chapter Eighteen: Scott 109
Chapter Nineteen: Jessie 119
Chapter Twenty: Heather...................... 127
Chapter Twenty-One: Scott................... 135
Chapter Twenty-Two: Jessie.................. 143
Chapter Twenty-Three: Josh 151
Chapter Twenty-Four: Scott................... 155
Chapter Twenty-Five: Jessie 159
Chapter Twenty-Six: Lark 167
Chapter Twenty-Seven: Scott................ 173
Chapter Twenty-Eight: Jeff 181
Chapter Twenty-Nine: Ari 185
Chapter Thirty: Ellie 189
Chapter Thirty-One: Scott.................... 195
Chapter Thirty-Two: Jessie.................. 207
Chapter Thirty-Three: Scott 211
Chapter Thirty-Four: Gunner 217
Chapter Thirty-Five: Jessie 223

Chapter Thirty-Six: Scott 229
Chapter Thirty-Seven: Jessie 235
Chapter Thirty-Eight: Jeff 241
Chapter Thirty-Nine: Ari 245
Chapter Forty: Jessie 251
Chapter Forty-One: Josh 257
Chapter Forty-Two: Scott 261
Chapter Forty-Three: Jessie 265
Chapter Forty-Four: Scott 271
Chapter Forty-Five: Scott 277
Chapter Forty-Six: Jessie 285
Epilogue: Jessie 289
Seven Years Later: Alex 293
Sneak Peek: *Unconditional Love* 299
Thank You 305
Playlist 307

Prologue
Scott

High School

I'd gotten tackled four fucking times during football practice because I couldn't take my eyes off of Jessie Rhodes sitting in the bleachers.

Damn it. Why does she affect me the way she does? I could have any girl in this school. Why Jess?

Dewey walked up to me and hit me on the shoulder. "Hey, asshole. Stop eye-fucking my sister, or I'm going to kick your ass," Dew said before he started laughing.

"Fuck off, dickhead." I put my helmet back on and tried to forget that Jessie was sitting there, watching me.

I looked up a few minutes later to see Michael Smith talking to her on the sideline. I instantly felt anger building inside me. *That asshole only wants to get into Jessie's pants. She is way too good for him. Stupid-ass baseball player doesn't even deserve a second look from her.*

Jessie pulled her beautiful blonde hair back into a ponytail before turning and sitting back down with her friends. Once coach got done talking, I stalled for as long as I could until I saw Dew heading into the locker room. Jessie was standing up to leave, so I ran over toward her, calling out her name.

"Jess! Jessie, hold up. Hey, can I talk to you for a minute before you go?" I flashed her the smile that I knew made all the girls melt—well, all the girls except for Jessie Rhodes. I could never read her—*ever.*

She turned and nodded her head. As she made her way down the bleachers, I walked under them to meet her on the other side. She walked up to me, and she gave me that sweet smile of hers that made my stomach do all sorts of messed-up shit.

"Hey," she said.

"Hey, I, um...I wanted to ask...do you have the notes for the history test next week?"

I watched as her expression fell for a second. *Shit. Was she expecting something else? Could Jessie actually like me? Shit, just do what you've wanted to do for the last three years.*

"Um...yeah, I have them. Did you want to borrow them? Or are you gonna try to cheat off my paper again?" she said with a wink.

I watched her lips as she talked, and I instantly felt my dick jumping in my pants. *I've had a crush on this girl for as long as I can remember.* I looked up into her eyes, and I swore they turned gray. I moved my eyes down to watch her chew on her lower lip. She had the most beautiful bee-stung lips, and I had to fight the urge to stare at them every time she talked.

"Scott? Are you okay? If you want the notes, they're at home, so you'll have to swing by my house."

I didn't even know what she was saying. I couldn't pull my eyes from her mouth.

"Scott?" She walked up to me and snapped her fingers in my face.

I shook my head and tried to calm my beating heart. *What in the hell is this girl doing to me? I can't even think when I'm around her.*

I quickly glanced back to her eyes. They seemed so different, and I couldn't really pinpoint what her eyes were trying to say.

"Jessie…I…"

She looked at me and tilted her head. "You, what?" She let out a giggle. "Scott, what's wrong with you? Did you get hit too many times out there today?"

Nothing came out. I couldn't talk.

"Okay…well, I'm going to take off. You know where the notes are if you need them."

I watched as she turned to leave. *Fuck. It's now or never.* I ran after her and grabbed her by the arm. I turned her around and slowly backed her up against the bleachers. I dropped my helmet and cupped her face with my hands as I leaned down and lightly brushed my lips against hers. She let out a soft, sweet moan, and my whole body shivered.

Oh God…what would she taste like?

I slammed my lips to hers and kissed her with as much passion as I could. When she reached up and ran her hands through my hair, something instantly happened. I wasn't really sure what it was, but it scared the shit out of me.

I pulled back and looked into her eyes. *What is that look in her eyes? It almost seems like…love?*

She smiled slightly, and then it hit me full force. I felt things for Jessie that I'd never felt before.

What is happening to me? My hands started shaking, and I felt like I couldn't breathe.

I looked up and saw Chelsea Mason walking by. She licked her lips with her tongue, and she smiled. She'd been trying to get me to sleep with her for the last few weeks, but I hadn't been the least bit interested…until now.

I quickly glanced back down at Jessie, who was just about to say something.

I smiled and said, "Thanks for the kiss, Tiny." I backed away from her as I reached down and grabbed my helmet before turning and walking toward Chelsea. "Hey, Chels, wait up."

As I turned away from Jessie, I felt sick to my stomach. I'd seen the look in her eyes after I kissed her. She liked me just as much as I liked her, and she must have felt the same connection I had. She'd smiled that sweet smile, and I'd just walked away, like a prick.

I tried to clear my head. *What did I just do? What am I so scared of?*

Chelsea skipped up to me and glanced over my shoulder. "You and, um…Jessie Rhodes got something going on?"

I quickly turned back and looked at Jessie standing there. *Oh shit. Are those tears rolling down her face? Oh god…Jessie.* I started to head back over there when Chelsea grabbed my arm and pulled me to her.

She leaned up and whispered in my ear, "I'm not wearing any panties under this skirt."

I snapped my eyes down to her, and she wiggled her eyebrows up and down.

Last thing I'm going to do is sleep with Chelsea.

I glanced back to see Jessie walking away as fast as she could. *Motherfucker. I just hurt the one girl I didn't ever want to hurt.*

I watched as Jessie walked up to Michael. They'd been talking earlier, and the way he'd kept touching her arm had driven me mad. After she said something in his ear, he reached out, grabbed her, and spun her around. He set her down, and she gave him a weak smile before they walked away together with his arm draped over her shoulders.

What in the fuck? Is she leaving with him?

I quickly turned back to look at Chelsea, and I smiled. "Let's go. My parents are out of town for two days." I grabbed her hand and practically pulled her to my truck.

It didn't take me long to get Chelsea back to my house and up to my room where I fucked her hard and fast.

I'll do anything to forget how I just hurt the girl of my dreams.

After we were done, Chelsea quickly got up and gave me a full-on smile. She said, "That was so worth the wait. I think I'll go take a shower. Feel free to join me if you'd like."

I smiled, but then I got up and began to get dressed.

I walked down to the barn and sat on a hay bale where I cried for the first time since I was six years old.

What did I do?

Oh god…what did I just do?

I pulled over on the side of the road and jumped out of my car. I couldn't even see enough to drive because I was crying so hard. I frantically wiped the tears away as I looked up to the black sky and screamed, "Why?"

Oh my god. How could he do this to me? I thought we were happy? I was going to move in with him. We talked about marriage and new puppies and babies.

"Oh god! How stupid are you?" I screamed out to no one.

I felt my legs slowly giving out on me, and I fell to the ground. I pulled my knees up to my chest and cried. I closed my eyes, and all I could see was Chelsea fucking Scott. I shook my head as fast as I could. I'd never be able to erase that image from my head. *Never.*

Then, my phone went off. I pulled it out of my pocket.

Scott. How dare he call me!

Then, a text message came through…and another…and another. I opened the first one.

> *Scott: Jessie! It's Bryce. I NEED to talk to you. Please let me explain.*

Ugh. He had his brother send me a text message?

I backed out of it before I read any more.

My phone started ringing again. I stood up and looked out into the open field before tossing my phone as far and as hard as I could.

Fuck you, Scott Reynolds. I hate you. I'll never forgive you for this. Ever.

I stood up taller and wiped the tears from my face. I slowly turned and walked back to my car. I got in and made my way to Aaron and Jenny's house. They were expecting their first child, so there was no way I was going to let them know what was going on. I wasn't even sure if they were home yet. They had gone to the hospital to be with Emma and Jack.

As I pulled up, I saw Aaron's truck. I took a deep breath and walked into the house. All the lights but one were turned off. I quietly made my way to my room and reached under the bed for my suitcase. I threw it on the bed and started packing up my clothes.

I stopped packing and looked all around my room. *Where in the hell am I going to go?*

Away—as far away from Scott Reynolds as I can get.

I walked to my closet and reached up for my old shoebox. I had been saving money since I was fourteen years old, so I could start my own veterinary clinic one day. Every spare dime had gone into this shoebox. I brought it over to my bed, sat down, and opened it up. I felt a tear roll down my face. *So much for buying the local vet clinic in Mason.*

There was no way I was staying in this town now. I shook my head as I got up and placed the shoebox in my suitcase.

I reached in my pocket for my cell and closed my eyes as I whispered, "Fuck!"

I hadn't even thought that I'd had everyone's numbers on that stupid phone. I knew the number to the vet clinic by heart, and I silently said a prayer that I had backed all the numbers up on my Google Contacts. I reached for the landline and waited for the clinic's answering machine to pick up. By the time I was done leaving my message, I was in tears again. All my dreams were gone because of one guy—one guy who I'd thought loved me with his heart and soul.

I quickly wrote a note to Aaron and Jenny. I told them the truth. I was leaving because Scott was an asshole and a cheating bastard. I didn't tell them where I was going because I had no clue where I was going. I left the note on the kitchen table and looked around one more time before I walked out the door and to my car.

As I drove toward Austin, I cried off and on. One minute, I was so pissed-off, and the next, I felt like curling up into a ball and just crying.

I found myself pulling into Brad and Amanda's driveway at five thirty in the morning. A light was on, so I got out of my car, walked up to the front door, and lightly knocked. I was just about to turn away when Amanda opened the door.

"Jessie! What in the hell are you doing here this early in the morning?"

I tried to talk, but I broke down, crying. Amanda immediately pulled me into her arms.

"Oh my god! Gramps!" Amanda called out.

I pulled back and shook my head. "Oh god, no! I'm so sorry. No, Amanda, this has nothing to do with Gramps. When I left last night, he was in stable condition and doing well. He was even kidding around with Gunner, saying he had just tripped," I said with a small giggle.

Amanda grabbed my arm and pulled me into her living room. "What is going on then, Jessie?"

I shook my head. "I can't talk about it right now, but I need a favor." I looked up to see Brad standing there.

"Jessie, we're here for you, sweetheart. You know that," Brad said with a smile.

I took a deep breath and looked between the two of them. "Can I leave my car here for a few weeks? And can y'all drive me to the airport?"

Amanda snapped her head over toward Brad and back at me. "Why? Jessie, you're really scaring me. Please tell me what's going on."

"Scott...well, he..." I shook my head as I wiped the tears away. "He doesn't love me. He doesn't want to be with me." I let out a laugh. "History is repeating itself really. I was just stupid enough to think he loved me."

Amanda grabbed my hands. "Jessie, he does love you, baby. I know for a fact that he loves you very much."

I started shaking my head. "No, Amanda, he doesn't. He cheated on me. I can't...I just..."

I began crying again as Amanda pulled me into her arms.

"I just need a few weeks away to clear my head. *Please.* Please just do this for me," I said with pleading eyes as I looked between Brad and Amanda.

Brad nodded and reached for his keys. "I'm heading into Austin this morning anyway. Let's move your car into the garage."

I smiled as I hugged Amanda. Then, I walked over to Brad and whispered, "Thank you."

Brad pulled up to the Austin-Bergstrom Airport and jumped out to help me with my bag. "Do you even have a ticket, Jessie? Where are you going?"

I shrugged my shoulders. "Will you do me a favor? I know I'm asking a lot of you."

Brad nodded.

"Please don't tell anyone you brought me to the airport—at least not for a few days."

Brad's mouth dropped open. He slowly shook his head. "Jessie, I can't make you that kind of a promise. If people ask, Amanda and I are going to have to tell them that I brought you to the airport. I mean, if I don't know where you're going, then I can't really tell them any more than that."

I nodded. "That's fair enough. Hell, at this point, I don't even know where I'm going." I gave Brad a weak smile and thanked him for the ride.

"Jessie, Amanda said you threw your phone in a field. Will you please buy a new phone? Then, let us know when you get to where you're going. Please."

I couldn't help but laugh at my own stupidity. I nodded. "I'll buy another phone and get in touch with y'all, I promise."

"You better. Your father and brothers are going to freak the fuck out when they find out you've just up and left without any word on where you're going."

I laughed as I hugged Brad good-bye.

I turned and walked into the airport with the worst feeling I'd ever felt. Something was telling me that I was making the biggest mistake of my life. At first, I didn't even try to stop the tears. I finally got them under control as I walked up to the ticket counter.

I sat down in my seat on the United flight that was taking me to Houston and then on to Ambergris Caye, Belize. I asked the flight attendant for a drink before takeoff.

"What would you like, dear?"

I just stared at her. "I don't care. Something to make me forget a guy."

She winked and nodded. "Oh, I know just the thing."

As the plane took off, I grabbed the arms of my seat and closed my eyes.

Never will you make me feel like a fool again, Scott. I'll never waste another tear on you for as long as I live.

2 Scott

Jesus H. Christ. I woke up to damn horses sniffing around my face. *Where in the fuck am I?* I tried to stand up, and immediately, I fell back down to my ass. *Holy hell, my head is pounding. How much did I have to drink last night?* I slowly stood up and looked around. I was in Gunner's stable. *Why in the hell am I in here?*

I couldn't even remember anything that had happened last night. All I remembered was playing tag football and drinking. *Yep, I did a lot of drinking. Oh shit!*

I reached down into my jeans pocket and let out a sigh of relief when I felt the ring box in there. I reached in and pulled out the box. I opened it up and smiled at the engagement ring I had bought two days ago. I was going to ask Jessie to marry me at my parents' anniversary party on Christmas Eve. That was the whole reason I'd drunk my ass off last night. Gunner had said it was nerves.

I walked out into the sun and let out a few curse words. As I made my way back to Gunner's house, Dewey, Aaron, and Drake were standing there, talking to Gunner. Drake turned and started toward me.

Shit, he looks pissed. Where's Jessie? Damn, I'm never drinking again.

As Drake walked up, I held out my hand to shake his, and before I knew what was happening, he reached back and punched the fuck out of me. I fell backward, and I swore I saw my future flash before my eyes. Gunner yelled out and ran over as I slowly got up and wiped the blood from my mouth.

"What in the fuck, Drake?" both Gunner and I said at the same time.

"You son of a bitch, what did you do to my daughter?"

I looked at Drake like he was crazy. I glanced over toward Dew and Aaron, and they both looked like they wanted to kick my ass.

I shook my head. "Wait…wait just a second. I just woke up in Gunner's fucking barn, for Christ's sake. I can't even move my head, and thanks to you, I think I might have ruptured something. What are you talking about? Where is Jessie? I don't remember anything that happened last night."

Drake looked at me, confused, and then he looked at Gunner.

"Scott, do you remember most of us leaving because Gramps had a heart attack?" Gunner asked.

My heart stopped, and I put my hands on my knees. "What? Oh my god, Gunner! Is he…"

Gunner held up his hand. "He's okay. He's doing good, but he'll be in the hospital for a few days."

I let out a sigh of relief, and then all of a sudden, I was taken over with a sick feeling.

Jessie…

"Where's Jessie?" I asked as I looked at Drake.

He ran his hand through his hair and waved for one of the boys to come over. Aaron walked up to me and gave me a dirty look as he handed me a piece of paper. It took me a few minutes to focus on the paper, but once I did, I felt my legs slowly about to give out. Gunner and Aaron both reached out and grabbed me before I fell.

"What does she mean…she's leaving? Where in the hell is she? Why in the hell does she say I'm cheating? I'm not cheating! I just bought her an engagement ring. I was going to come talk to you today, Drake, about asking her to marry me."

Dewey started laughing. "Is that right?"

I shot my head up and looked at him as I reached into my pocket and pulled out the ring. I opened it up. "I've been carrying it around with me the last few days. I was going to ask her at my parents' anniversary party." I started shaking my head. "I don't understand. Why would she think I'm cheating?" I glanced up at Gunner with tears in my eyes. "Gunner, I swear to God, I've never been unfaithful to her. I would never hurt her. I love her more than anyone. She's my whole goddamn life."

Gunner hit my back as he guided me into his house. "I know, Scott, I know."

We all sat down at the kitchen table.

All I could do was put my head in my hands and cry. *She left me? Why would she leave me?*

I reached for my phone to call her. "Where in the hell is my phone?"

"Don't bother. We've been trying all morning. It just keeps ringing," Aaron said as he looked over at Jenny, who had just walked into the kitchen.

I threw my hands in my hair and then dragged them down my face. *Maybe she's hurt? Fuck! What if she's been trying to call me? Where in the fuck is my phone?*

"I gotta get home." I got up and started making my way out to my truck.

Gunner called out to me, "Scott! Your brother took your truck home last night. When he couldn't find you, he thought you'd left with Jessie. I guess he didn't think you would be passed out in the barn."

"Can I use your phone, Gunner?" I let out a long sigh.

I made my way to the phone and dialed my home number.

When Bryce answered, he sounded panicked. "Hello?"

"Bryce, it's me. Hey, do you have—"

"Holy fucking shit. Where have you been? Oh my god, Scott, I'm so sorry. Jesus, I've been trying to call her all morning."

My head was already spinning, and now, my brother was talking so fast that I had no idea what in the hell he was saying.

I tried to get him to calm down. "Bryce. Bryce! Jesus H. Christ, what in the hell are you talking about? Have you talked to Jessie?"

"Wait—you haven't talked to her? Where are you?"

"I'm at Gunner's. Somehow, I managed to pass out in the barn last night. After I woke up, Drake knocked the shit out of me, and Aaron showed me a note that Jessie had left for him. She said that I'm a cheating bastard, and she was leaving town."

"Oh fuck. Fuck! Fuck! Fuck! This is all my fault."

When my brother began crying on the other end of the line, my heart started beating faster. I glanced up toward Gunner and then Drake.

"What do you mean, Bryce? How is all this your fault? What in the hell happened?"

Bryce took a deep breath and slowly let it out. "Last night, Jessie asked me to make sure you got home 'cause you were drunk. She was going to the hospital. She was panicking about Gramps."

I shook my head. "I know all this shit. What is all your fault? Cut to the fucking chase."

"When I got to your house, I saw your phone sitting on your passenger seat, so I grabbed it to bring it in. I saw a BMW parked in the driveway, but I didn't really think anything of it. Then, as I got closer to the front porch, I saw Chelsea sitting there. She said she'd been locked out of her house, and she had nowhere to go."

I started to get a sick feeling in my stomach. *What in the fuck did Chelsea do? And how was my brother a part of it?*

"Anyway, I invited her inside, and we got to talking. Then, we had a few drinks, and man, she started coming on to me like crazy. She got up and said she had to make a call on her cell phone. When she got back, she was naked, and then she began walking toward your bedroom. I was pretty trashed. I wasn't thinking clearly. We ended up in your bedroom…in your bed."

I started shaking my head. "You fucked my ex-fiancée, Bryce? And in my own goddamn bed? You couldn't at least go to another room?"

"Jesus, Scott, I've been cursing myself all night. At any rate, Chelsea had the whole thing planned out. She was on top, going hard and fast, and the next thing I heard was Jessie saying, 'Oh my god.' Then, Chelsea told her something about waiting on her before we started without her. Chelsea had blocked me from Jessie's view. I tried calling out, but Jessie slammed the door, and then Chelsea was laughing. I pushed the bitch off and got dressed. I tried to go after Jessie, but Chelsea stopped me, and by the time I got outside, Jessie was gone. I ran back into the house to grab your phone. I remembered setting it on the foyer table, but it was gone."

Jesus, no wonder she thinks I cheated. Why would Chelsea do this?
Oh my god…Jessie.

"I asked Chelsea if she had taken it, and when she started laughing again, I lost it on her. I grabbed her and began screaming at her, asking her what she did. She ended up telling me that she had just happened to stop by, and she had been waiting for you to come home. When I got there and said I couldn't find you, I guess she made a phone call to a friend of hers who had been at the birthday party. She told Chelsea that you were trashed, and the last she'd heard, you were passed out somewhere. So, Chelsea sent a text to Jessie, saying you were waiting on her to come home."

"Motherfucker," was all I could get out.

"She'd set it all up, Scott, and if I hadn't been such a prick and fucked her, it would have never happened. My god…I'm so sorry. I've been trying to call Jessie ever since she left last night."

I need my truck. I have to find her. "Bryce, I'm heading home to get my truck. Call everyone you know. Tell them to be on the lookout for her."

I hung up and turned to everyone. They were all staring at me.

"Well?" Dewey said as he gave me a pissed-off look.

"Short version—Bryce and Chelsea were screwing in my bed, and Jessie walked in. She thought it was me. Chelsea had set it all up. I need to find Jessie. I need to get home and get my truck."

Drake looked at me and nodded. "I'll take you home."

I turned to Gunner and asked him to start calling everyone in case Jessie called anyone. I started to make my way to Drake's truck. I couldn't walk fast enough.

"Scott…Scott, let's calm down and think this through. I'm sure we will find her, and everything will be okay. All we have to do is explain to Jessie what happened," Drake said.

I turned and just stared at him. "How, Drake? None of us know where in the hell she is, and she thinks I fucked Chelsea. She thinks I hurt her . She has to be devastated, Drake. I have to find her." I felt tears falling down my face. "I have to find her, Drake. *I have to.* She's my whole life. I don't want to live if she's not in my life. She's…she's…" I started shaking my head. "She's my whole life."

Drake nodded and put his hand on my shoulder. "We'll find her, son. I know Jessie, and she wouldn't just leave without telling someone where she's going."

I nodded in agreement, but something deep down inside was screaming that she was gone and was never planning on coming back.

Jessie…baby, please come back to me. I love you, baby. Please just come back to me.

3 Jessie

I woke up to the sound of Scott calling out for me, begging me to come home. I looked around the plane and grabbed my stomach. I felt so sick. This just didn't feel right, running away like this, but I couldn't chance seeing him.

Oh god, Scott, why? Why did you sleep with her? Drunk or not…how could you hurt me like this?

After the long flight, I was finally walking up to my cabana. I couldn't help but smile at the thatched roof. The view to the ocean was breathtaking.

Scott would love it here. I felt tears coming again.

Scott had been asking me so many questions about what I wanted to do when we got married. He'd asked if I wanted a big wedding with lots of guests or a small one with just family and where my dream honeymoon would be. I had told him I always wanted to go to Belize. Belize would be my dream honeymoon, and here I was, standing outside a beautiful cabana. I was all alone and totally heartbroken, feeling like I was flying in a free fall.

I took a deep breath and made my way up onto the small porch that looked out to the ocean. I glanced over to the beach and saw a man around my age walking alone. I wasn't sure why I stopped and watched him, but I couldn't pull my eyes away from him. He looked up, and our eyes caught. I tried to smile as I gave him a wave, but he must have been able to tell that I'd been crying. He frowned and then smiled as he continued along the beach.

I turned and opened the door. I walked into the room where I was planning on spending the next few weeks…alone. I just needed time to sort through things and figure out what I was going to do now that I wouldn't be buying the vet clinic in Mason.

Where will I go? What will I do?

I sat at the small table for two at the Mesa Café and waited on my shrimp burger. I'd tried to call my father's house to let him know I was okay, but I couldn't get the stupid phone in my room to work. I just hoped that Amanda and Brad had let everyone know that they had seen me. I didn't want my dad to worry about me.

Oh shit…he's going to kill me for running off and not telling him where I was going. Double fuck!

"Long time no see."

I looked up and saw the same man I'd seen earlier walking on the beach. He was peeking down at me with a drop-dead gorgeous smile. I couldn't help but notice those deep green eyes, and his dark brown hair had that perfect messy look to it. I smiled back and nodded.

"Hi, um…I just got here today, so you're actually the first person I've talked to…well, besides the hotel staff and the waitress here." I let out a giggle.

Oh, for the love of God, what is wrong with me? I just made an ass of myself.

He glanced down at the empty chair and lifted his eyebrows. "Tell me why a beautiful woman, such as yourself, is here alone."

My smile slowly faded before I managed another weak smile. "It's a long story."

He nodded and said, "Mending a broken heart?"

My mouth dropped open, and I just stared at him. *Am I that obvious?* "Um…"

He started laughing. "Don't be too shocked, love. I'm here for the same reason."

I lifted my eyebrows with a questioning look.

"Yep. I was left at the altar…literally. I was standing there, waiting for her to walk down the aisle. She never made it, and I was left with two plane tickets to Belize and a broken heart bigger than the size of Texas. So, what else could I do? I made the trip with my best friend. He just left yesterday."

"I'm so sorry. That must have really hurt. I'm glad your friend was able to make the trip with you though. Did y'all at least get to have fun while he was here?"

He smiled. "Oh, hell yeah. It was nothing but getting drunk and then waking up the next day to go sightseeing before getting drunk again. That was our routine for two weeks. By the way"—he extended his hand out to me—"the name is Trey Walker."

I placed my hand in his and smiled. "Jessie Rhodes. And yes, I'm mending a broken heart, but I'm not really ready to talk about it, so…"

Trey held up his hands and smiled bigger. I wasn't sure what made me do it, but the next thing I knew, I was inviting him to sit and have dinner with me. I couldn't believe how easy it was to talk to him. I actually laughed a few times. I also found out that he was a lawyer from Dallas, Texas.

Huh…I would have never pegged him as a lawyer.

"You've got to have the key lime pie gelato. Oh man, it's to die for."

I smiled. "Share it with me?"

"I was hoping you'd suggest that," he said with a silly grin.

My stomach did a funny little dip. *What in the hell was that?*

I instantly felt guilty for even having dinner with Trey, and now, we were going to share a dessert. Then, I closed my eyes and saw Chelsea riding Scott, like the whore that she was, and I quickly pushed those feelings aside.

Besides, the last thing I wanted was another relationship. *Men sucked.*

Trey was telling me how he and his best friend had ended up falling off a pier a few days ago, and I couldn't help but laugh at how animated he was. It was so nice to finally not think about what had happened to me. To be able to laugh felt so good.

"Sounds like y'all had an interesting few days," I said.

Trey nodded his head and smiled. "May I walk you back to your cabana?"

For a few seconds, the guilt from wanting him to walk me back filled my whole body until I quickly pushed it aside.

"Yes, I'd love that. Thank you."

As I walked up to my cabana, I turned to face Trey. "How much longer are you here for?" I asked.

He let out a long sigh. "I'm not sure. I'm, uh…I'm kind of afraid to go back, so I took a leave of absence. I'm thinking maybe another two months. I love the lifestyle down here. I just need…time. Does that make sense?"

I caught my breath because I felt the same way. I slowly nodded as I bit down on my lower lip. He reached up and pulled it out of my teeth.

There goes those butterflies again. I smiled and felt my face blush.

"Trey, I'm not looking to…you know." I peeked up at him.

When my eyes caught his, I swore his eyes twinkled.

He gave me the cutest crooked smile and let out a small laugh. "Believe me, love, I'm not interested in a relationship either…but since we're both here, we might as well enjoy each other's company. How about I show you around tomorrow?"

I smiled and nodded. "I'd like that."

He took a step backward and gave me a thumbs-up. "It's a planned event then—not a date but a planned event."

I let out a giggle. "Sounds great. What time should I expect you?"

"Eight thirty. We have a ton to see."

We said our good-byes, and then I walked into my empty cabana. I leaned back against the door and smiled. There was something about Trey that just made me feel comfortable. I couldn't put my finger on it, but he made me feel…happy.

I'm not going to feel guilty. If being friends with Trey will make me feel better and forget about the hurt for a few hours, then so be it.

I started stripping out of my clothes, and then I put on a T-shirt. After I sat on the bed, I pulled my knees up and set my chin on them as I listened to the sound of the ocean. I couldn't help but think of Scott. *God, I miss his touch already.* I missed his breath on my neck as he would whisper how much he loved me and only wanted me. I put my hand up to my neck and could almost feel the warmth. I took a deep breath and let it out as I lay down.

After four hours of just lying there, I finally fell asleep. I dreamed of Scott walking along the beach with me. We were holding hands…and then someone came up behind us and pulled our hands apart. When I turned around to see who it was, I saw deep green eyes looking into mine.

I sat up quickly in bed and looked at the clock. It was eight on the dot.

"Shit!" I jumped up and started getting ready.

For ten minutes, I tried to get my hair to look decent before I ended up pulling it into a ponytail.

Shit, I never called anyone. I made a mental note to look for a cell phone.

I quickly walked up to the lobby of the hotel and noticed a pay phone. I had to laugh. I hadn't seen one of those in years. I pulled out my credit card and hit zero. I gave the operator my credit card number and Amanda and Brad's phone number. I didn't think I could talk to my father just yet. The call was full of static, but I heard Amanda answer.

"Amanda! Hey, it's Jessie."

"Jessie! Thank God! Scott's…insane…mistake…Chelsea…Bryce."

"Wait—what are you saying, Amanda? I have a terrible connection. I'm only getting every other word. Can you hear me?"

"Yes! You…come…quickly…he's…bad."

"Okay…sweetie, I can't understand you, but listen, I hope you can hear me. I'm fine. I'm going to stay here for about three weeks. Please let my dad and brothers know that I'm okay…Scott, too, I guess…if he even cares."

"No! Please…Scott…he…talk…right away."

"Ugh…Amanda, this connection is driving me nuts. I'll give you a call in about a week or so. Tell Gunner I'm praying for Gramps. Bye, sweetie!"

"Wait!"

I hung up the phone. There was no sense in trying to piece together the conversation. I glanced up at the clock to see it was eight thirty.

Oh shit! Trey!

Right as I made it back to my cabana, I saw Trey walking up with the biggest smile on his face.

"Are you ready to see the sights of Ambergris Caye?"

Seeing him instantly made me feel better. All thoughts of Scott were pushed aside as I looked into the most beautiful green eyes I'd ever seen.

I nodded and smiled. "Yep, let's do this!"

Trey held out his arm, and I took it as we made our way into town. Only about one minute into our walk, and I was already laughing my ass off.

Oh yeah…Trey is just what the doctor ordered for me to forget about Scott.

4 Scott

"Sir, believe me, I understand your frustration. But if Ms. Rhodes is not a missing person and you don't have a warrant, there is no way I can look at the security cameras to see what airplane she got on. Do you know how many cameras we have? Or how long that would even take?" the Austin-Bergstrom security manager said.

I nodded. "I understand. I'm just desperate. I need to find her before I lose my mind."

"I wish I could be of more help to you, sir. Do you share a credit card with her? She might have charged the ticket."

I shook my head. "No, she only has one credit card, and it's in her name, so I can't check it. Thank you so much for your help. Have a good day."

As I walked out of the airport, my cell started ringing. I didn't even want to answer it. When Brad had called me yesterday and told me he'd brought Jessie to the airport, my heart had broken all over again. I couldn't believe she had been mad enough to get on a plane and leave.

I pulled the phone out of my pocket to see that it was Amanda calling.

"Amanda! Have you heard from her?"

"Yes! Oh my god, she just called me, Scott! I could hear her, but she said she was only getting every other word of what I was saying. I tried telling her that it wasn't you and that it was Bryce, but I don't think she got any of it."

My heart was pounding in my chest. "Did she say where she was?" *Please, God…please let me find her.*

Amanda paused for the longest time, and I already knew the answer before she started talking again.

"No. I'm so sorry, Scott. The number didn't show up either. She only said she was okay and would be staying about three weeks."

"Three weeks!" I stopped and had to lean over. *I. Can't. Breathe.*

"Scott? Scott, are you okay? Scott…please say something," Amanda pleaded.

"I can't talk right now. If she calls again, please try to find out where she is."

"Of course I will, Scott. Don't worry. When she comes back, she'll find out the truth, and it won't be long before she's back in your arms."

I tried to talk, but nothing would come out. I just hit End to disconnect the call. I walked back to my truck and slowly crawled in. My legs were like iron. My chest hurt, and it felt like someone was sitting on it.

Three weeks? Jessie, please don't do this to me. I need you.

I sat at Gunner's kitchen table and watched Ellie moving around while she made homemade marinara sauce. Every now and then, she would look at me and smile.

I couldn't go home. It had been a week since Jessie left, and I'd only been home once. I had asked Bryce and Jeff to get rid of my bed. I was going to buy a new one. There was no way I'd ever sleep in that bed…or let Jessie sleep in it. *That is, if she ever comes back.* I'd noticed that Doc had put the vet clinic back up for sale. Jessie had left a message for him, saying that she was no longer interested in buying the practice.

Please just call me, Jessie.

Fuck! If she would just call me…

Ellie sat down and reached for my hands. The moment I felt her hands touch mine, I jerked.

Ellie jumped and let out a giggle. "Holy hell, Scott, you scared the shit out of me."

I smiled at her. She was so sweet. I kept noticing how she would place her hand on her stomach. Gunner was beyond happy that Gramps was okay and home and that Ellie was having a pretty easy pregnancy so far. She'd hardly had any morning sickness. My smile slowly faded as I thought of Jessie and how much I wanted to have children with her.

"Ells…I miss her so much. I have such a bad feeling, and I can't shake it. What if she meets someone else? What if she doesn't believe me when I tell her it wasn't me? *Oh god…*what if I never see her again? I want to marry her and have children with her. I don't want anyone else, Ellie. I only want her."

I couldn't believe what a pussy I'd been during the last week, so I wasn't surprised when I started crying again. My whole world felt like someone had just ripped it apart.

"Scott, I know you're worried about her and things seem like they are really bad right now, but in her mind, she thinks she saw you and Chelsea having sex. That probably really upset her beyond belief. She just needs time…that's all. Just be patient, and wait for her, sweets. She's going to come back, Scott, because I know how much she loves you."

I shook my head. "If she thinks I cheated, Ellie...she's not going to forgive me. I know her, and the last time I walked away from her for Chelsea, it devastated her."

I looked up when I saw the back door of the kitchen open. Gunner walked in with Jeff, and they both gave me that look. Everyone was feeling sorry for me, and I wasn't helping anyone by sitting here and moping.

"Hey, dude. How are you doing?" Jeff asked as he reached out and shook my hand.

"I feel like someone keeps punching me in the gut." I let out a small laugh.

"Ari made your favorite dessert—apple pie. She's bringing it over tonight for dinner." Jeff gave me a weak smile.

Everyone was going to come over to Gunner and Ells's place for dinner to celebrate Gramps being okay. Even Josh, Heather, and the twins would be here. Everyone would be here.

Except for Jessie.

I smiled and tried to look as happy as I could even though I was slowly dying inside. I was supposed to head to Kentucky to look at a horse today, but I'd called and told them I would have to come in a few weeks. There was no way I was leaving and missing Jessie if she decided to come back early.

Gunner walked up to me. "You need to take a ride. Get some fresh air, Scott. You look like shit."

"Gunner!" Ellie said as she punched him on the arm.

I threw my head back and laughed. "Leave it to you to keep it real, Gunner." I stood up and smiled. "I think a ride is exactly what I need— open space to clear my thoughts. You need me to check on anything while I'm out?"

Gunner looked over toward Jeff.

"You know, the south pasture fence line hasn't been checked on in a few days. Would you mind?" Jeff asked.

"Done!" I said as I hit Jeff on the back.

I made my way out and down to Gunner and Ellie's barn. When I stepped inside, six horses all turned and looked at me, each pleading with me to pick them.

I smiled as I made my way to Rose. "Hey, beautiful. You ready to go for a run, girl? Just you and me...and the open sky."

She started bobbing her head up and down, and I couldn't help but laugh.

Once I had her saddled up and out of the barn, she was practically begging to run. We walked a little ways until I came to an open pasture. All it took was one squeeze of my legs, and she was off in a full run. The feel of her running under me with the wind in my hair was exactly what I needed.

I wasn't sure how long I'd let Rose run, but she ended up stopping on her own. I jumped off and walked her up to the river to let her get a drink. I sat on the bank of the river while Rose patiently stood by and waited.

I fell back and looked up at the blue sky. I let out a scream, and I was pretty sure I sounded like a girl, but I didn't care. I needed to get it out. It was either that or beat Bryce's ass. I couldn't even think of looking at Chelsea. I hated her more than ever now.

"Jessie, baby, please come home to me. I'm hurting so bad without you. I can hardly breathe with you being gone. I love you, baby. Please…"

I lay there for a few good minutes, just staring up at the blue sky, willing Jessie to come back to me. As I prayed for her to come back to me, I fought the sick feeling in my stomach that I hadn't been able to shake for the last week.

I had the strangest feeling that I was losing her…and there wasn't a damn thing I could do about it.

5 Jessie

I couldn't pull my eyes from the sky. It was so blue and beautiful, and it just held my gaze. I closed my eyes, and then I quickly opened them. Every time I closed my eyes, I would either hear Scott or see his smile.

I felt something cold dripping on my stomach, and I sat up quickly. Trey was holding a beer over me, laughing.

"Damn you! That's cold, you ass!" I said as I swatted at his leg.

He jumped and laughed. He sat down next to me and let out a long sigh. I glanced over and watched him take a drink of his beer. I smiled and shook my head. Trey and I had spent practically every waking moment together, touring the island. We had taken a hike yesterday, and I'd ended up throwing up twice. The guide had said that I was probably just not used to the salt air. I'd been feeling like the flu was coming on for the last two days.

Trey bumped my shoulder and smiled at me.

Shit! There goes that damn dizzy feeling in my stomach. I wasn't even sure why Trey was having such an effect on me. I was clearly only interested in a friendship, but I was slowly starting to think that he was hoping for more from me. Last night, he'd leaned down to kiss me good-bye, but I'd turned away.

"You look amazing in that bathing suit. Have I told you that?" he asked with a wink.

I let out a giggle. "Yes. Yes, you have, Trey—about four times now."

"Can't blame a guy, Jessie. You've got two really good things going for you."

I took a drink of my beer. "Oh yeah? What are they?"

"Well, for one, you're from Texas. And the other one is that you have an amazing fucking body."

I felt the blush move up my cheeks, and I actually had a moment of need between my legs. *Oh god. Jessie, what's wrong with you? Friends. Trey is only a friend.*

I quickly turned away before he could read my eyes. I looked out toward the water. "Well, thank you so much for that compliment. So, what are the plans for this evening?"

He fell back onto his elbows, and when I glanced at him, our eyes met. His eyes were full of lust. At least to me, they looked like that. I slowly turned away again and downed my beer.

"Well, my love, I actually think you need some rest. We've been going and blowing way too much with all the hikes and tours, and it's taking a toll on you."

I nodded in agreement. "I think you're right. I'm so tired, and honestly, I don't feel very well. I thought lying out here in the sun would make me feel better, but it kind of makes it worse."

Trey sat up and peeked over at me. "Maybe you should go in and take a nap. I'll take care of all of this."

Oh man, a nap sounds like heaven right about now. I'd been having such a hard time sleeping. I still couldn't shake the feeling that I was making a mistake by staying away for so long, but I just brushed it off as wanting to see Scott.

"You know what? A nap sounds like a great idea. Will you make sure I'm up in time for dinner?" I asked with a wink.

Trey smiled as he stood up and held out his hand. "You better believe I will."

As he helped me up, I started to feel dizzy, but I didn't say anything. Just as I was about to turn and make my way to the cabana, I felt like I was going to faint.

"Um…Trey…I don't feel right…"

The next thing I knew, Trey was carrying me in through the door and laying me down on the bed.

He ran to the sink and wet a washcloth. He came back and placed it on my forehead. "Jesus, babe, you're burning up. Maybe I should call a doctor?"

"No. No, I just need rest. Please…just let me rest."

"Jess, maybe I shouldn't leave you alone."

"No, really, it's okay. Just go clean up and come back in a few hours. I promise, I'll be fine."

Trey stood and shook his head. "Damn stubborn girl. Alright, but don't get up. Just rest. Do you hear me?"

I smiled. "Yes, dad."

It didn't take long before I was drifting off to sleep and was dreaming.

I was walking up to the river, and I saw a man standing there. He was holding something in his hand. The closer I got, the more the image became clear. Someone was next to him. It was a young child. I called out for them, and as the man turned around, I sucked in a breath of air.

Scott.

Hey, baby, we've been waiting for you to come back to us.

I glanced down and looked at the beautiful little girl holding Scott's hand. She had curly blonde hair, and her smile was exactly like Scott's. I smiled as I looked back up at Scott, but he was starting to fade away. The little girl started calling out for him to stay, but he kept fading away. She pulled on my shirt, and I looked down at her to see a tear trailing down her face.

Why did you leave him without talking to him first? You killed him. You killed him by leaving him all alone.

My eyes instantly flew open. *Holy fuck!*

I sat up quickly and instantly felt sick to my stomach again. I barely made it to the bathroom before I was puking. I sat on the cold floor and leaned up against the wall. I put my head on my knees, and I felt the sweat just pouring off of me.

Oh my god. What in the hell kind of dream was that? What did I eat that's making me so sick?

I just sat there and thought about the dream I'd just had.

Who was the little girl? Why did she tell me I killed Scott? What did she say? I should have talked to him first? What if…what if what I saw wasn't really what happened? Maybe…

Oh, Jesus H. Christ, Jessie. You saw Chelsea fucking Scott…in his bed. I closed my eyes and felt tears stinging them. *I never actually saw Scott though…but I heard him call out after me.*

I hate that bitch more than the air I breathe. I hate Scott for doing this to me again. I started crying. *Fuck, I'm so sick of crying. I just want to forget. I need to forget!*

I heard a knock on the door, and I figured it was Trey as I stood. I quickly rinsed out my mouth with mouthwash and then splashed water on my face.

I headed toward the door and opened it. Trey was holding a huge bouquet of flowers.

"How are you feeling?" he asked with that sweet smile of his.

I smiled back. "So much better now that you're here."

Trey's smile faded for a brief moment as he took a step closer to me. I instantly felt the heat between us as he reached his hand up and placed it on the side of my face. It was nothing like when Scott touched me though. When Scott touched me, my whole body would shiver. But Trey's touch…helped me to forget…even if just for a moment.

"Jessie…you're so beautiful."

I closed my eyes and saw Scott. I snapped them open, and before I knew it, I was walking into Trey's arms. He gently began kissing me, and he let out a small moan, which caused me to open my mouth to him. Our tongues began exploring each other as he brought me closer to him. He pulled slightly away from my lips.

I whispered, "Trey…help me forget. Please help me forget him."

As he slammed his lips to mine, I felt his erection pushing into my stomach. I ran my hands up and into his hair. I gave it a hard tug, causing him to let out another moan. He slowly reached down and picked me up.

He carried me over to my bed. As he gently laid me down on the bed, I started to panic.

What in the hell am I doing? I need to stop this now.

Trey moved his hand up my shirt. He slipped it under my bra and started playing with my nipple.

Oh god…that feels so good, but fuck, my breasts hurt like a son of a bitch.

I let out a moan as he moved his hand down. He started to unbutton my shorts.

Stop this, Jessie. You don't want to do this.

Ah…feels…so…good.

The moment he slipped his fingers inside me, I almost came undone.

He stopped kissing me. "My god, Jessie…you're soaking wet, love. I just want to bury myself in you."

He started kissing me again, but this time, our kissing turned frantic. It was almost like if we stopped, we knew we wouldn't start again. He quickly moved and started taking off my shorts and panties. He licked his lips as he looked at me. I quickly sat up and pulled off my shirt as he pushed my bra up and over my breasts.

I need to forget…I just need to forget him.

Trey slowly bent down and started kissing me again as he moved his hand and placed his fingers inside me.

"Ah…" I cried out as I felt the pressure building inside me.

"Jesus…I just want to fuck you."

I closed my eyes and held back the tears. *That's what we'd be doing— fucking, not making love. We'd be fucking the people who hurt us out of our heads for just a few brief moments.*

He started fucking me with his fingers as his thumb began its assault on my clit. It wasn't going to take long now before I just fell apart.

"That's it, love…let it go. Let me make you forget all about him. Let me in, and I'll make you forget all about everything."

I looked away and over toward the window, out to the ocean. My mind drifted away from what was happening, and all I could think about was Scott. Then, I saw the moon in the sky, and I heard Scott's voice.

I love you to the moon and back.

He'd said it to me all the time, and that was all I could hear now, over and over in my head.

I love you to the moon and back, Jessie—always.

No…no…something about this feels all wrong. I can't do this. Stop! Please stop!

I looked back at Trey as he was sucking on one of my overly sensitive nipples. *Jesus, it feels so good but so wrong at the same time.*

I began pushing him away. "Stop. Please stop, Trey."

He stopped moving his fingers and looked up at me. "Jessie…please let me do this for you."

I shook my head, and I felt tears falling down my face. "I can't do this. I need you to get off of me, please."

Trey immediately jumped up and turned away. I quickly pulled my bra down and reached for my panties. I slipped them on, and then I began putting on my shorts and shirt as I looked at Trey pacing back and forth. He was breathing so heavily, and I knew what I had just done was such a shit-ass thing to do.

When I walked up and touched him on the shoulder, he jumped.

"Please don't touch me. It's taking everything I have not to try and convince you to let me make love to you, so please don't touch me."

"I'm so sorry, Trey. I thought I wanted to…but I can't. It just feels so wrong. I still love him."

Trey spun around and looked at me. "What? After you caught him fucking his ex, you can stand here and say you still love him?"

I nodded as tears began to fall harder. "I can't help what my heart feels. I just…I love him so much, and I…I need more time."

He ran his hands through his hair and let out a long, drawn-out sigh. "Jessie…I know you only want to be friends, and I'm trying…really, I'm trying, but I want to be honest with you. I think I'm falling for you, and I want to move this on to something other than friendship."

My heart dropped to my stomach. "Trey…I just…I can't—at least, not right now."

He slowly smiled. "Well, I guess that's better than a flat-out no."

I tried to smile, but I could only manage a weak grin. "Yeah, I guess," I said. I turned and looked down at the necklace Scott had given me right before all hell had broken loose. I reached down, picked it up, and held it in my hand.

"I'll take it, and I'll be patient, love. I'll be content with being friends— for now."

I turned and nodded. "I think I need to eat. I'm feeling a little dizzy again."

Trey gave me a weak smile as he opened the door and waited for me to walk out.

As we made our way to the restaurant, neither one of us talked. I had the most uncontrollable urge to turn around and take a shower, so I could scrub every inch where Trey had touched me. I didn't understand why I felt like I did because it wasn't like I was cheating on anyone. I'd left Scott…because he had been with Chelsea. And now, I was…alone. What had happened between me and Trey still felt so wrong, and the feeling in my stomach only grew worse and worse as the night went on.

Oh, God…please forgive me. What did I just do?

# 6 Gunner

I walked into the barn and nearly fell over. *What in the hell?*

"Um, Gramps…what are you doing?"

Gramps turned and looked at me. He smiled, and I couldn't help but smile back. I silently said a prayer and thanked God for not taking him from us.

"What does it look like I'm doing?" he said as he turned back and adjusted the saddle on Big Roy.

I took a deep breath and pushed my hand through my hair. "It looks like you're going for a ride. Can I join you?" I asked.

He turned and flashed me that smile of his. "I don't know, son. Can you?"

I let out a laugh and shook my head as I reached for my saddle and walked up to Firelight. I gave her a few strokes and grabbed a handful of oats for her.

"*May* I join you?" I asked with a chuckle.

"Yes, I'd love to shoot the shit with you for a bit."

Gramps and I rode in silence for a good fifteen minutes before he finally started talking.

"How's Scott?"

I let out a sigh and thought back to last night when Scott had broken down. "Scott has been spending more and more time at our house. Last night, he and Ellie were sitting on the back porch, and he just lost it. I think what is killing him the most is not having a clue as to where in the hell she is."

"And she hasn't gotten in touch with her daddy? That doesn't sound like Jessie," Gramps said with a shake of his head.

"She called Amanda, but the connection was bad, and Amanda said Jessie was only getting every other word. Jessie said she'd be home by now, but…"

"You know, Gunner, women are a strange group."

I let out a laugh. "Yeah. Yeah, they are, Gramps."

"Here's what I'm thinking—Jessie is so deeply hurt by what she thinks is a betrayal by Scott. For her, maybe the easiest thing to do is stay away, and by staying away and not talking to anyone, she can't be reminded of that hurt. You and I both know that is not a good way of handling things, but right now, her heart is so broken that she doesn't know what to do."

"But, Gramps, if she would just fucking call someone, we could tell her the truth—that it wasn't Scott she saw that night. How can we help her if she won't let us?"

Gramps turned and looked at me. "That's the problem—she doesn't want help. She doesn't want to talk to anyone—maybe for fear of asking how Scott is or of someone telling her that he's with that bitch."

I snapped my head over toward Gramps. "Damn, old man. Don't hold back."

"I never did like that girl. I'm not trying to be judgmental 'cause you know I ain't that way, but there has always been something about her that I just never cared for. I saw the way she would look at you while she was on Scott's arm. I never did care for those who carry a cheatin' heart."

I looked straight ahead and did what I'd been doing for the last couple of weeks. I tried to figure out how in the hell to find Jessie.

"How's my granddaughter?"

I smiled, and my heart started beating harder. "She's doing wonderful. She walked yesterday!"

"No!"

I threw my head back and let out a laugh. "Yep! Ells and I were sitting across from each other, and Alex just started walking toward me. It was one of the best moments of my life...and I've been having a lot of those lately."

"Did you cry?"

I slowly looked at my grandfather. I tried to picture him during the first time his sons had taken steps. *I would bet the ranch that he cried like a baby!*

"Okay, I'll be a man about it. Yes, I cried...a little."

"Yeah, the first steps your father took were toward me. I cried like a dam had broken. Emma laughed and told me that was one of the reasons she would love me forever." Gramps let out a chuckle.

I looked down and then back up at the clear blue sky. It was a beautiful Texas day in December. It couldn't have been more than sixty-five degrees outside.

I closed my eyes and took in a deep breath before slowly letting it out. "God, I love it out here. I never want to be anywhere but here," I said.

"Drew..."

I opened my eyes and saw something I'd never seen in my grandfather's eyes before—*fear*. "Gramps...are you okay?"

He smiled slightly and nodded. "I am, son. I truly am. It's just...when the whole heart attack happened...well, I've never been so scared in my life."

I nodded. "Yeah, me, too."

He stopped Big Roy, so I did the same with Firelight.

"It's gonna happen someday though, son. I'm not a young stallion anymore," he said with a grin.

My heart dropped to my stomach. *Is something wrong? Oh god, please no…not with the new baby coming. Please…no.*

"Jesus, Drew. Stop thinking so hard. I see your wheels spinning in that head of yours. Nothing is wrong. Matter of fact, I'm probably more fit now than I have been in a long time. The ticker is tickin' just fine. It's just…I was thinking this morning. Someday, I will be gone. I sure as hell hope I got at least another ten years or more, but—"

"Gramps, why are we even talking about this? I don't want to talk about how you're going to die someday. I know that."

"Because I want you to know something. I want you to know that I couldn't be more proud of you, son. You've done an amazing job, taking over the whole ranch with the help of Jeff and your father. To look out my window and see you and your father walking together with smiles on your faces…it makes my heart swell like you wouldn't believe. If I had died—"

"But you didn't!"

Gramps gave me a look. "Don't interrupt your elder, boy. It's rude."

I tried to hold in the smile, but I couldn't. "Yes, sir. I'm sorry."

He nodded. "If I had died, I would have died as the happiest man on Earth. I have a woman who has loved me beyond my wildest dreams, two sons whom I've never been more proud of, and my grandchildren and great grandchildren…well, hell, they're the best blessing of all. I just want you to know…I've lived a very good life." He slowly smiled. "A very good life indeed."

I smiled, knowing he was thinking of Grams. "Gramps, I bet your story with Grams is probably the best love story ever."

He looked at me and raised his eyebrows. "It is. Someday, I'll tell you how I had to fight like hell to win that woman's heart."

I laughed. "Really? I figured Grams just took one look into those baby blues, and that was it."

"Shit, I wish. That woman made me work my ass off to win her love, but it's been a forever love."

I started laughing as I noticed my father quickly riding up.

"Hey, y'all," he said as he stopped his horse on a damn dime.

I had yet to ever win a race with this man.

"Ells? Alex?" I asked, trying not to sound panicked.

"They're fine, but I got a call from Jeff. He's with Scott at the Wild Coyote Bar. Scott is pretty drunk, and Jeff said—and I quote—'Tell Gunner to get here before I punch the living shit out of Scott.'"

I rolled my eyes and shook my head. "Damn it." I turned to Gramps and tried to give him a small smile.

"Go, Drew. Your friend needs you. Just be patient, and try to understand what it would be like if Ellie had left you and you had no idea where she was while she thought the worst of you."

My heart dropped to my stomach. *I'd rather die.*

"Thanks, Gramps. Let's do this again, okay?" I turned to my dad and smiled. "Thanks, Dad. You should finish out the ride with Gramps. He's being all emotional and shit." I turned to look at Gramps.

His face fell. "You little shit."

I laughed as I gave Firelight a good kick, and she took off.

I walked into the Wild Coyote Bar as Miranda Lambert's "Baggage Claim" was playing, and the first thing I noticed was Scott dancing. I had no clue who he was dancing with, but I could immediately tell that he was drunk off his ass. I looked around and saw Jeff sitting at the bar.

I walked up and slapped him on the back. "I heard there was a problem," I said with a wink.

Jeff rolled his eyes. "That motherfucker is gonna kill me!"

I sat down and ordered a beer as I looked back out at Scott. He was all over the girl.

"What's going on?" I took a sip of my beer.

"For the last hour, I've been fighting with that little ho-bag out there on the dance floor." Jeff looked out at the girl dancing with Scott.

I couldn't help but start laughing. "What's she doing?"

"Trying to get Scott to leave with her. I won't let him do it, Gunner. I don't care how upset he is. He's drunk, and he's hurting, so I won't let him be unfaithful to Jessie…even if she thinks he already has been. But the fucker is starting to piss me off. He just wants to leave with this girl."

The song ended, and they both came walking up to the bar. I smiled when I got a better look at the girl.

"Lucy…I don't think your husband would like knowing his wife is out trying to pick up men."

Lucy was married to a friend of mine who was in the Army and just happened to be deployed. My heart instantly broke for him, and I made a mental note to let him know that his wife was at the bar today.

Scott spun around and looked at Lucy as she shot me a dirty look.

"Fuck off, Gunner," Lucy said.

Scott instantly removed his arm from her shoulder. "You're married?" He shook his head. "Fucking women—you're nothing but a bunch of deceiving, lying bitches."

Lucy gave Scott a good push, causing him to fall toward Jeff and me. We both reached out and grabbed Scott before he fell to the floor.

She threw her hands on her hips and gave Scott a dirty look. "Asshole. You just keep crying over the girl who walked out and left your ass. You probably deserved it."

I grabbed Scott and made him sit down. "What in the hell are you doing, Scott? You can't drink or fuck her out of your mind…or heart."

"Ain't that the truth? Been there and done that." Jeff took a drink of his beer.

Scotty McCreery's "The Trouble with Girls" started playing, and Scott put his head in his hands.

"Perfect-ass song. I can't take it. I'm going crazy. I have to know where she is! What is she doing? Who is she with? What if she meets someone and falls in love with him? She obviously doesn't give a fuck about me or anyone else back home."

Jeff shook his head and put his hand on Scott's shoulder. "Scott, she's not going to fall in love with someone else in a little over a month. She told Amanda three weeks, so she'll probably be here any day."

Scott started shaking his head. "No, I feel her slipping further and further away. I can't explain it. I just feel it in my heart. I sure hate my brother and Chelsea right now."

"You don't mean that, Scott," Jeff said as he glanced over toward me.

"I do mean it. It's because of them that I lost the only girl I've ever loved…the only girl I'll ever love. I hate them both."

I took a deep breath and pulled out my phone. Ellie had sent me a text, asking how Scott was. She also wanted me to stop and pick up Alex's birthday cake.

"Scott, let's get you to my house, so you can sleep this off. Stay with Ellie and me for a few days. You can help me get the house ready for Alex's first birthday party. How does that sound?"

Scott looked up at me, and the tears in his eyes about gutted me.

I don't ever want to know how he is feeling right now. My heart was physically hurting for him.

He slowly smiled and nodded. "I can't believe Little Bear is going to be one. You're so blessed, Gunner." Scott snapped his head and looked at Jeff. "Both of you. You're so damn blessed. Jeff, how is Grace?"

Jeff smiled the biggest smile I'd ever seen. He'd been on cloud nine since Grace was born.

"She's growing fast. I do believe she's already got me wrapped around her little finger—just like her mama."

Scott let out a small chuckle. "Yeah, I bet. Listen, I'm sorry y'all had to come down here and deal with me. I'm not sure how I'm gonna drive home or get my truck back to my house."

Jeff started laughing. "Dude, I drove. We came here together, you stupid fuckwad."

"Oh…well, okay. I'm not feeling so well. Maybe I should head home. Bryce is there though, and I don't really want to see him."

I stood up and threw some money onto the bar. "Come on, Scott, let's get you out of here."

After getting Scott into the truck, I turned to Jeff and shook my head.

"Jesus H. Christ. Gunner, I'm really worried about him. I've pretty much been running his breeding business the last few weeks. He also just bought a Thoroughbred, sight unseen, for a small fortune. I'm praying to God that the damn horse is fast and can get him his money back. If Jessie would just fucking check in with someone…I mean, this is destroying him. I've never in my life seen anyone just give up like this."

I looked around the parking lot and then back at Jeff. A part of me was so pissed-off at Jessie for doing this. It was hard to be mad at her because of what she thought she'd seen, but the fact that she'd just up and left with no word to anyone in the last few weeks just wasn't like her.

"Dude, why are you looking around the parking lot like you're fixin' to say something top secret? Do you know where Jessie is?"

"What? No. Shit, I would never do that to Scott. I've been thinking though. Do you think she could have met someone?"

Jeff looked down at the ground and kicked a rock before glancing back at me. "I've already thought about that. It's just weird that she would tell Amanda she was only going to be gone for three weeks, and it's been almost five weeks now. Christmas is in a few days. Is she really not going to come home for Christmas? Or even call her dad? I get that she's trying to just avoid it all, but this is just insane. If she were my daughter, I'd be losing my goddamn mind."

I glanced back at Scott in the truck. He was passed out cold.

Turning back to Jeff, I said, "I don't know, Jeff. I know Jessie has been in love with Scott since high school, and the same goes for his feelings for her. He hurt her so bad in high school though, and I know it was a huge leap of faith for her to trust him not to hurt her again. And now, in her mind, he did. I can't even begin to imagine how she felt when she walked into that bedroom. I think she panicked more than anything. The only thing she knew to do was run away—just like she had done after high school when she'd left for college and avoided Scott like he was the plague. The only thing we can wish for is that she comes to her damn senses and comes home. I just can't see Jessie not even calling her dad on Christmas. All we need is for someone to tell her what really happened."

"Yeah…let's hope." Jeff took a deep breath and let it out. "Anyway, Ari wants to know what she can do to help with the birthday party."

I smiled and shook my head. "Nothing…just bring Luke and Grace and a big appetite 'cause I think Ellie ordered enough food for a small army."

Jeff smiled and said, "Alright. I'll talk to ya later."

"Later, dude," I said.

Jeff and I each got in our trucks. I glanced over and looked at Scott sleeping. I had a strange feeling that Jessie wouldn't be coming home next week or letting anyone know where she was anytime soon.

7 Ellie

I stood on the back porch and watched as Scott and Gunner made their way toward the barn. Gunner had insisted on building a barn by the house, and now, I was wishing he never had. If we hadn't built that barn, Scott wouldn't have fallen asleep in there that night, and Bryce would have found him.

"Ellie, you're so deep in thought, sweetheart," Grace said from behind me.

I placed my hand on my stomach and turned to smile at her. "I was just thinking that if we had never built that barn, then…" I shook my head. I couldn't even finish my sentence.

I took a deep breath and held it for a few seconds before slowly letting it out. Everyone would be here soon for Alex's first birthday party, and I couldn't help but think that it didn't feel right, not having Jessie here.

Grace walked up and put her arm around me as she looked out toward Gunner and Scott. "I know, honey, but the barn is not to blame for what happened. Honestly, I'm so shocked Jessie has not gotten in touch with anyone. Drake is about to go crazy with worry. My heart hurts for him and for Scott."

"I've never in my life met anyone like Chelsea. I mean, I thought Rebecca was bad, but this girl makes Rebecca look like an angel. I just can't believe she lured Jessie over there, and then she was able to talk Bryce into having sex with her, for Pete's sake."

Grace let out a small laugh. "Well, Bryce is a man, and sometimes, men make poor decisions because they don't know how to think with anything but their dicks."

I snapped my head over and looked at my mother-in-law. "Grace! Oh my god!"

She rolled her eyes and sat down on one of the rockers. "Oh please, I've heard you and your friends talk. Just because I'm in my forties doesn't mean I can't say the word *dick*."

I let out a giggle and put my hand on my stomach as I felt the baby move. She'd been moving for about a week now, and every time she moved, I felt my face blush because I thought back to the night she'd been conceived. I was almost positive I knew which night it had happened. When I'd told Gunner about this, he had laughed at me. He'd said we made love too much to know when she could have been conceived, but I knew. I had known it the moment we were done making love.

"Grace, can I ask you a question?" I asked as I sat down in the rocker next to her.

"Of course you can. You can always ask me anything," she said with a smile.

I smiled back at her. "Did you ever think that you knew the moment when you'd conceived Gunner?"

She looked out toward Gunner. I slowly followed her gaze, and I couldn't help but smile. Just the sight of him caused me to catch my breath. I didn't think it was possible to be so in love with someone or to feel this way after being married for a few years, but with Gunner, I swore that I fell in love with him more and more every day.

I glanced back at Grace and watched as the smile grew on her face. It was followed by a blush of her own.

"Grace, you're blushing!"

She let out a small laugh and threw her hands up to her cheeks. "Am I?"

I nodded and settled in for a story.

She looked at me and made the cutest face before she started talking. "Well…Jack and I had been fighting. I mean, knock-down fighting. We didn't talk or see each other for probably almost three weeks."

"*What?* Wow. I could never go without seeing Gunner for three weeks. I'd die."

Grace started laughing. "Trust me, if you were as mad as I was, you might think twice about that."

I set the baby monitor I had been holding in my hand down on the side table, and then I crossed my legs. "Oh, this sounds good. I wish I had popcorn."

Grace shook her head. "It started off at a Thanksgiving Day party. One of Jack's friends invited us over to his parents' house. Everything was nice—the dinner, the people. It felt like home. It was probably one of the best Thanksgivings we had spent together since being married."

"What happened?" I asked.

"Jack flirted with his friend's sister. I mean, he *flirted*, and she was just as guilty. Oh, I was so mad that I couldn't even think straight. Listening to the two of them made me sick to my stomach. I asked to talk to Jack outside, and I told him that his flirting was getting out of hand and that he needed to stop."

I let out a gasp. *Jack flirting…in front of Grace?* "Jerk! What did he say?"

"Well, he said he wasn't flirting. He was just having a bit of fun. I told him it was the same thing, and I asked him how he would like it if I did that with his friend. He laughed and told me I was just being jealous. That was the last straw. I gave him a look and said if he did it one more time, I was leaving. He'd also been drinking, and when he drank, he acted like an ass sometimes."

"Good for you, Grace. Gunner must have inherited that from Jack." I glanced over right as Gunner threw his head back and laughed at something Scott had said.

Grace grinned and shook her head. "Yes, Gunner does act just like his father when he's drinking. Anyway, when we walked back in, Jack's friend's parents and everyone had started decorating the Christmas tree. I was so excited. You know how much I love Christmas and decorating the tree!"

I rolled my eyes and nodded. Grace loved decorating for Christmas more than anything. When she decorated for Christmas, the little cabin would be so full of white and green lights that it was almost blinding.

Poor Jack. His back has to kill him after hanging all those lights.

"They started playing Christmas music, and my favorite singer ever came on. Nat King Cole was singing "The Christmas Song," and I looked around for Jack because everyone started dancing. He knew how much I loved that song, and he always danced with me when it would come on. Well, I found him…dancing with her. Gesh…I can't even remember her name anymore, but he might as well have kicked me in the stomach. He knew how much I loved Nat and that song."

She started shaking her head. "I called a friend to pick me up a few blocks down from the house, and then I grabbed my coat and purse and left. I stayed with my friend for almost three weeks. So, a part of me understands Jessie's need to just get away. I mean, what she thinks she saw is ten times worse than what Jack had done."

"Did you tell Jack where you were?"

She looked at me with a sad face. "No. I didn't talk to him for two and a half weeks. Nothing. Not a word. My friend had begged me to call him and at least let him know I was okay, but I was so mad at him that I wanted him to worry. I wanted him to think about the idea of losing me."

I peeked down at the ground. "Wow. I'm not sure if I could ever do that. I mean, I guess if I were mad and hurt enough, I could, but—"

"Oh, believe me, at the time, it made perfect sense to me. Today, I see what a terrible mistake it was. I could have driven him into that tramp's arms. One time, I drove by our place. I almost died when I saw her standing on the porch, talking with Jack. My heart broke, and I spent three days wondering if she had just stopped by…or maybe she was leaving after they had just had sex. I about drove myself mad before I broke down and called her. I told her to tell me the truth."

I sat up straighter. "You called her? Look at you, you gutsy bitch. Ari would be so proud!"

Grace giggled. "I guess so."

"What did the tramp say?"

Grace winked at me and said, "That she had stopped by to see if she could help in any way because she felt guilty. She had liked the attention Jack had given her, and she'd egged on the flirting. She had asked him if she could help with trying to find me."

"Gasp! What did you say to that?"

"I asked her to please leave my husband alone. Then, I told her that I really hoped when she married the man of her dreams someday, some little bitch would do the same thing to her. I hung up, and then I picked up the phone and called Jack. The moment I said his name, he broke down, crying. My heart had never beat so hard in my chest like it did in that moment. He begged me to come home, and he promised to never hurt me again if I would just come home."

"Jack cried? Hard-core Jack from the Army?" I raised my eyebrows.

"Yep, that same Jack. I asked my friend to give me a ride home, and when I walked through the door, he pulled me to him and kissed me like I'd never been kissed before."

Her cheeks were stained a beautiful rose color as the memory must have been coming back to her.

"One thing led to another, and…well…" She looked over at me and smiled a huge smile. "I'd never felt so loved in my life as I did when Jack made love to me that afternoon. Let's just say that afterward, something told me that we had just made something magical together. Nine months later, Drew was born."

She felt it, too. I smiled and nodded. "Gunner thinks I'm crazy, but I know when the baby was conceived. I just felt it afterward one night. Everything was just…perfect. It was…"

Grace and I both said, "Magical," at the same time.

We looked at each other and started laughing.

"Grace, thank you so much for always being here for me. I'll always appreciate how you treat me like your daughter."

I watched as Grace's eyes filled with tears.

"Ellie, you *are* my daughter, and I love you more than life itself. Thank you for loving my son and for being an amazing wife and mother. I watch you, and you just amaze me."

My eyes betrayed me as I struggled to keep the tears from falling. We both stood and hugged each other before I heard Alex laughing over the monitor.

Grace hooked my arm with hers and said, "Come on, let's get the birthday girl ready for her big party."

"Luke…please get Grace's foot out of your mouth."

I reached down and picked Grace up and out of her bouncy chair.

I looked over toward Josh and Heather. Heather was holding Will and laughing at something Jeff was saying. Josh was holding Libby and dancing with her as he sang in her ear. My heart just melted.

Damn that boy. He sure has Gunner beat in the whole romance department.

Then, Gunner caught my eye. I smiled as I watched him run after Alex, and then he grabbed her. He brought her face up to his and smiled. I thought that even his one-year-old daughter was smitten with him.

Stupid good-looking bastard.

I watched Gunner smile at his daughter as she grabbed his face and practically bit him while she was trying to give him kisses. With the way he was looking at her, I just knew there wasn't a thing he wouldn't do for her.

Poor thing. I sure feel sorry for her when she starts dating.

Jeff walked up to me and kissed me on the cheek. He took Grace from my arms and walked back toward Heather and Josh. I sat there and watched my husband with our daughter. I'd been through a flood of emotions the last few months—overwhelming happiness to sadness to nothing but anger. During the last two weeks, I'd finally felt normal. I thought back to when my mother and I had had lunch a month after Grace was born. She'd insisted that I had postpartum depression.

I shook my head and took a deep breath. I couldn't pull my eyes from Jeff. Luke came up and started pulling on my shirt, trying to get my attention. I leaned down and whispered for him to go attack Gunner.

When I looked back up, I saw Jeff walking with Grace. He was talking to her, and she was just staring back at him.

What is he saying to her?

I watched him walk away from everyone. I quickly glanced over to Gunner and saw him chasing Luke and Alex. I started to make my way over to where Jeff was sitting on the tree swing with Grace. I snuck up and stood behind another tree as I listened to him talk to her.

"Oh, Grace Hope, I don't think you'll ever know how much I love you and how you'll always be my baby girl. Your mommy says you've already got me wrapped around your little finger, and even though I'll never admit it…you do. You're so precious, and you look so much like your mommy.

Your mother is so beautiful, Grace, and she takes my breath away with just one look at her."

Oh. My. God. My heart was beating so hard, and I felt the tears beginning to sting my eyes.

"Even when she leans over in the morning with her terrible, yucky bad breath as she says good morning to me, she still captivates me."

Bastard!

"I love her so much, and I love you and Luke so much, too. The three of you are my whole world, but you…you are my special little gift. Your big sister brought you to us, and I know she'll always be with you—just like she's with your mom and your big brother and me."

I grabbed my angel necklace as I put my head against the tree, and I just let the tears fall.

"You see, Grace, I made a terrible mistake one day, and I walked away from your mommy when she needed me the most. I'll never forgive myself for that. Your mommy has…but I won't."

No…oh, Jeff, no. I felt my heart slam in my chest, and I placed my hand over my mouth to keep from crying harder. I looked back up and continued to watch Jeff talk to Grace.

"Then, you came along. And just with that first sight of you in your mommy's tummy, I had the strangest feeling come over me."

Jeff held Grace out in front of him, and she just stared at him, like she was looking into his soul. It was all I could do to just stand there and watch it all unfold.

"You healed me, Grace Hope. Mommy says everything happens for a reason, and I think she's right. But shhh…don't *ever* tell her I said that. It'll go to her head."

I grinned as I watched a little smile move across Grace's face. I sucked in a breath of air. If I hadn't known any better, I would swear she knew what he was saying.

"Now, this might be a little too early to talk to you about this, but someday…" He started to shake his head as he sat Grace down on his lap. "Someday, some nasty boy is going to come along and try to take you from me, and you're going to want to go with him. It's going to break my heart for sure, but I'm going to have to let you go. I can only hope that you have the heart of your mother."

He let out a laugh as Grace started hopping up and down, making noises.

"Oh, Grace…your mother is a firecracker. She's tough as nails, but at the same time, she's the sweetest angel from God. I pray every night that you'll be like her. Don't ever take any crap from anyone. If a boy ever makes you feel less than what you are, walk away. No…first, kick him in the balls for making you feel that way, and then walk away."

I held my hand tight against my mouth. I was unsure if I should be crying harder or laughing.

"You need someone like Gunner. Your Aunt Ellie is so lucky to have your daddy's best friend as her husband. He loves her so much, and he treats her so good. He is just a good ole country boy. I'll never, ever tell him this…but I admire him. He makes me want to be a better father and husband. But the stupid bastard is overly romantic, and sometimes, I'd like to knock the hell out of him. And now…now, Josh is the same way." Jeff took a deep breath and let it out slowly. "But I love them both like brothers, and I know they would kill anyone who hurt any of y'all."

Grace let out another little laugh. Jeff stood up as he brought her up to his chest, and he started slowly dancing with her. I couldn't possibly love him any more than I did in this very moment. As he started to sing "My Little Girl" by Tim McGraw to Grace, I slid down the tree. I buried my face as I listened to my husband serenade our daughter, and I fell more in love with him as the seconds passed by.

"I think we should get back to the birthday party. What do you say? Your mama is gonna wonder where we went."

I stood and wiped the tears from my eyes. I watched as he started to head back toward the house. I tried to call for him, but nothing would come out.

"Jeff!" I finally shouted.

He jumped, and Grace started laughing, thinking he was bouncing her.

"Motherfucker! Ari, you scared the shit out of me," he said.

I walked up to him, and then I reached up and smacked him on the head. "Don't swear in front of her like that! You want her to walk around, cursing like Luke?"

Jeff shook his head and gave me that smile that still made my knees weak.

"Jeff, I love you so much, and right now, I just want to go home and make love to you."

Jeff's smile dropped as Grace started leaning out for me to take her. Before I could reach for her, Jeff put his hand behind my neck and pulled me closer to him. He brought his lips down to mine and kissed me. I felt like I was floating on a cloud just from his kiss. As he slowly pulled away, our eyes caught.

"I love you, Ari."

I shook my head and smiled. "I want you, Jeff. I need you."

He closed his eyes and licked his lips.

Oh god…I just want those lips all over my body.

"There y'all are! Your father and I have been looking everywhere for you. Now, give me my granddaughter, so I can love on her properly."

I looked around Jeff and saw my mother walking up to us. I smiled at her and watched her take Grace from Jeff's arms. As she made her way back toward everyone else, I glanced back at Jeff. He had the biggest grin on his face, and I followed his eyes as he looked over toward the barn.

I laughed and shook my head. "No! Are you kidding me? Everyone is just right here. No. I'm not having sex in Gunner and Ellie's barn."

"Oh, come on, baby. Just think of the last time we had sex in a barn." Jeff wiggled his eyebrows up and down. "The barn is far enough away from the house that no one could possibly hear us. I mean, you'll have to keep your screams of pleasure down and all."

I instantly felt the wetness between my legs. I quickly looked back at the house before turning and walking toward the barn.

"I'm so going to hell for this," I said as I heard Jeff say, "Oh, hell yes!"

I hadn't even walked into the barn before he grabbed me and spun me around. He pulled me to him and lifted me up as I wrapped my legs around him. He backed us up and leaned me against the wall. His hand moved up and under my shirt. The moment I felt him push up my bra and then squeeze my nipple, I almost came on the spot.

"Jeff…*oh god*," I whispered.

He slowly let me down to unbutton my jeans.

"Jesus, Ari…you drive me crazy. Do you know that?" he asked.

I watched him pull my pants and then my panties down. I lifted each leg as he took my sneakers off, and then he pulled off the pants and panties. He quickly undid his pants, and I felt my breathing pick up as I watched him push his pants down, his erection springing free. I licked my lips and looked up into his eyes.

"Fuck…" Jeff said as he picked me back up.

I wrapped my legs around him again. In one movement, he slammed his dick into me, and I let out a small whimper. I threw my head back and bit my lip… attempting not to yell out in pleasure. Nothing felt as good as having Jeff inside me.

"Ah…Ari…baby, come on," Jeff said as he moved in and out of me.

I tried so hard to hold off, so I could just enjoy the feel of him inside me.

"Baby…"

That was it—his pleading voice was my undoing. I snapped my head forward, and our eyes met.

"Jeff…I'm gonna come."

He let out a grunt and whispered, "Yes."

I bit hard on my lower lip as Jeff closed his eyes. I swore I could feel every ounce of him pouring into my body. I'd never felt so damn sexy in my life as I did at this very moment with my husband holding me up after making such passionate love to me. He stood there, panting to catch his breath, still inside me.

I smiled as I leaned in and grabbed his lower lip with my teeth.

"Ah hell, Ari. I could totally do that again if you'd just give me a few minutes."

I started laughing and then instantly stopped. I could hear someone talking.

I looked at Jeff as we both said, "No fucking way!"

Jeff dropped me and pulled up his pants. Then, he reached down and grabbed my pants, panties, and shoes before quickly taking my arm and walking me over to Big Roy's stall. He opened it and pushed me inside.

"Get down!" he whispered as he zipped up his pants.

"*What?* I'm half-fucking-naked in a horse stall, and you want me to get down?"

Just then, we heard Garrett call out, "Ari? Jeff?"

Jeff turned back and pushed my head down before spinning around and walking away.

Big Roy walked up to me and kept trying to nudge me with his head.

I looked at Big Roy as I tried to get him to stop. "Stop it, boy. No! We aren't going for a ride." I rolled my eyes and hurried like hell to get my clothes back on.

Big Roy took a few steps back, and I was finally able to get my panties on. I heard Jeff talking to Garrett, but I couldn't tell what they were saying.

How does this man always know when we're having sex?

Just then, Big Roy pushed me hard on my back, making me fall forward…right into a pile of horse shit.

Jesus, Mary, and Joseph, that did not just happen to me!

I turned and looked at him. He was moving his head up and down.

"It's true—y'all are nothing but big fucking dogs! You're supposed to be on my side, you bastard—not standing there, laughing at me in your horse way," I whispered.

Then, I heard them talking.

"Ellie was looking for you and Ari. They're fixin' to sing 'Happy Birthday' to Alex, and Gunner told me to check the barn for you and Ari," Garrett said.

I slowly got up and moved away from the giant pile of shit as I shook my head. *Gunner! Oh…oh…your ass is mine.* He must have seen Jeff and me heading down here.

"Awesome! Thanks, Garrett. Yeah, I, um…I've been looking for Ari. I'll give her a few minutes, and if she doesn't show up, I'll head on up."

Garrett said something else to Jeff that I couldn't make out. I closed my eyes and began to plot my revenge on Gunner.

"What in the fuck?" Jeff said.

I looked up at him. I was itching everywhere, and I had horse shit all over my shirt. My warm and happy just-fucked feeling was gone, completely and utterly *gone*.

"Yep. I was trying to get dressed, and this little fucker here pushed me into his own shit! My warm and happy just-fucked feeling is gone!" I yelled out.

Big Roy started bouncing his head up and down again.

I jumped up and said, "Look! He's laughing at me. I swear to you, he did it on purpose."

Jeff looked toward Big Roy, then down at the shit, and then back up at me. He busted out laughing. I just stood there with my mouth hanging open, wearing a shit-covered shirt and red polka-dot panties, while my own husband laughed at me.

"You think it's funny?" I asked.

He started to nod. I reached down and picked up my shoes. Jeff opened the stall door, still laughing his ass off.

"I'm sorry, baby, but I can't let you near the kids with horse shit all over you!" Jeff said as he placed his hands on his knees and continued to laugh.

Uh-huh, I see how this is going to be. "Is that a fact? You think this is pretty funny, huh?"

"Holy shit, Ari! Oh man," Jeff said as he wiped away the tears.

Tears! He is laughing so hard that he has tears.

I slowly smiled and started laughing.

"See! You can't help but laugh, too," Jeff said.

I quickly walked up to him and slammed my body against his. I wrapped my arms around him and held on for dear life.

"What in the hell, Ari? Get off of me!"

Jeff tried like hell to get me off of him, but I was holding on like my life depended on it. We ended up losing our balance, and we fell to ground where I crawled on top of him and pushed his hands down and over his head. He slowly smiled as I felt his erection up against me.

He said, "He's ready again."

I couldn't help but smile back as I rubbed myself against him. *Oh god…I could totally—*

"Ari…what in the hell are you doing?"

I snapped my head up and saw my father standing there with his hands on his hips, looking rather pissed.

Jeff pushed me off of him. He jumped up and took about three steps away from me.

Pussy.

"Dad, um…I was…well, we were…"

I looked at Jeff, who was clearly not going to offer to help me out with an explanation. It was then that I realized I was standing in my panties. *Shit! Shit! Shit!* I quickly pulled on my jeans and slipped my sneakers back on.

The whole time, my dad was giving the dirtiest looks to Jeff. I couldn't help but giggle.

"Jeff and I came down to see the horses, and I…I, um…"

My dad walked closer and stopped right in front of me. "Is that…horse shit on you?" He looked over at Jeff. "And why in the hell is it on you, too? What in the world were you two doing?" He instantly stopped talking.

He closed his eyes and let out a breath as he shook his head. "Okay, I understand you're married with two kids now…but really? Sex in the barn…at your niece's first birthday party?" He turned and looked at Jeff. "What in the hell is wrong with you, Johnson?"

Jeff's mouth dropped open, and that was when I knew I was in trouble. *Don't talk. Just don't talk, Jeff.*

"What? Why do you always assume it's *my* fault?" Jeff asked.

I stepped in between Jeff and my father. "It's okay, Jeff. Let's just head on back up— "

My dad gently pushed me out of the way as he pointed his finger at Jeff. "Because, nine times out of ten, it is your fault."

"Oh…oh, real nice. Well, it just so happens that it wasn't my fault this time," Jeff said.

I tried desperately to get him to stop talking. "Jeff, it's okay, really. I'm sure Ells and Gunner can give us a change of clothes, and—"

"Why do you both have horse shit on you? And why was my daughter sitting on top of you, half-naked, you ass?"

Oh shit. Jeff has that look.

"First off, it was your daughter who propositioned me for sex in the first place."

My mouth dropped open, and I couldn't move. *He did not just say that!*

"Being the good husband that I am, I wasn't about to let her down, so I brought her to the barn."

Stop. Talking.

"We heard Garrett, and Ari was half-naked, so I pushed her into Big Roy's stall before Garrett walked in. Roy was obviously in a playful mood, and he nudged Ari. She…well, she…she lost her balance and went into the…"

He's gonna start laughing! Oh my god. He's actually going to start laughing again.

Even though he tried to contain it, Jeff let out a small laugh. I didn't know what to be more pissed about—the fact that he'd just told my father we'd fucked in the barn or that he was laughing because I had fallen in horse shit.

My dad stood there for a second, just staring at Jeff. "Jeff...son...there are some things you just don't tell the father of your wife. You'll start to understand this more when Grace grows up, but in the meantime, from now on...let's just keep you and my daughter's sexual encounters to yourself, shall we?"

My father turned and walked away. I put my hands on hips and gave Jeff a what-the-fuck look. I shook my head as he shrugged his shoulders.

"What? The man scares me. He's threatened my life before, so excuse me for panicking. I felt the best thing to do was to come clean, but..." Jeff took a deep breath and quickly let it out. "But I see I was wrong."

"Ya think? Dickwad."

I started making my way out of the barn and up toward the house. I walked up to Ellie, who was standing on the porch.

She just looked at me. "What happened?"

"Trust me, you don't want to know. Have y'all sung 'Happy Birthday' yet?"

Ellie smiled and shook her head. "Why don't you go take a quick shower and change into something of mine?"

"Oh god, thank you, Ellie. This horse shit stinks. Jeff will need to take a shower, too, and borrow something of Gunner's."

"I don't even want to know," Ellie said as she looked over at Jeff.

"No, you don't, but I will say that your brother sure can make me happy one minute and so pissed-off the next."

Ellie put her fingers up to her ears. "Eww...eww...stop! Yuck!"

I started to walk away when I heard Ellie say to Jeff, "Oh no, you horny ass. You go shower in the guest bathroom. I'll bring you a pair of sweats and a T-shirt."

I turned and looked over my shoulder at Jeff.

He smiled and winked at me. Then, he mouthed, *Sorry*.

I couldn't help but laugh. *Yep. Stupid, romantic dickwad.*

9 Jeff

I sat on Gunner and Ellie's back porch and watched Ari run around, chasing Luke. I couldn't help but smile when Luke would scream every time Ari grabbed him and swung him around. I glanced over and saw Ellie with her hand on her stomach, gently moving it up and down. Gunner was holding a sleeping Alex in his arms as he talked to Brad.

Ellie glanced over and smiled at me. I held up my beer to her, and she winked. She said something to Gunner and Brad, and then she made her way over toward me.

"Have you talked to Mom?" Ellie asked as she sat down next to me.

I smiled and nodded. "I did. I still can't believe she's moving to Mason."

Ellie let out a giggle. "I know. What about being engaged to Philip?"

I smiled as I watched Ellie getting all excited from just thinking about it.

She started shaking her head. "I mean, her life has changed so much, and her dreams are finally coming true. She's getting a nursing job at Mason Memorial Hospital, and Philip asked her to marry him." Ellie turned and looked at me. "She's gonna be here for the birth of the baby! I mean…she'll be here for everything this time."

A tear slowly rolled down her cheek. I reached over and wiped it away.

"I know, Ells, I'm excited about it, too. I'm even more excited that she's going to be here during this pregnancy."

Ellie nodded and put her head back against the chair. "I think it's a boy."

I started laughing. "And what makes you think that?"

"He moves a lot, like he is always twisting and turning in there."

I glanced over toward Gunner, who was still talking to Brad. Amanda was now sitting in a chair with Maegan on her lap. They were laughing at something they were doing.

"Has Gunner mentioned wanting a boy?" I took a drink from my beer.

Ellie shook her head and smiled. "Nah, he just always says he wants the baby to be healthy, but I think he wants a boy deep down inside."

I heard Luke call out as he ran by, "Daddy!"

I jumped up, grabbed him, and gave him a hug and kiss. He pushed me away. As soon as I set him down, he took off running again. Now, Mark was chasing him. As Mark ran by, he shot me a dirty look. Smiling, I turned to walk back up onto the porch, and I sat down.

Ellie started laughing. "So…sex in my barn, huh?"

I smiled as I put my lips up to the beer bottle and took another drink. "Blame it on your sister-in-law."

Ellie snapped her head over and looked at me. "You two are something else. Why was Mark giving you the death stare?"

I shrugged my shoulders. "Probably because he walked in on Ari sitting on top of me, grinding and—"

"Stop! Just stop talking. Ugh…poor Mark."

Ellie stood and smacked me on the back of the head before walking over to Gunner. She took Alex out of his arms and made her way into the house.

"Hey, handsome," Ari said as she walked up. She leaned down and kissed me.

"Who has Grace?"

Ari rolled her eyes. "Who else? My mother. She is currently telling Grace all about Katharine Hepburn. She's making plans for a K.H. movie marathon when Grace reaches the age of five."

I shook my head as I handed Ari my beer. "Five, huh? I'm impressed your mom is holding off for that long."

"Don't be. I walked in once and saw Grace in her bouncy chair, sitting in front of the TV, watching *Bringing Up Baby*."

I let out a laugh as Ari giggled.

"I swear…the first string of words Grace will say will be a Katharine Hepburn quote," she said.

"Probably. So…when can we leave? I really want to finish what we started earlier."

Ari giggled. "What did we start earlier?"

I gave her a smirk. "Oh please…like you don't remember rubbing that fine body on me, getting me all worked up."

Ari bit down on her lower lip and smiled. "Hmm…I don't really remember that. You might have to remind me."

I instantly felt my dick growing harder. "Come on, let's go."

I stood up, and Ari went to go say something to me as she glanced over my shoulder.

"I think my wife needs to get back that warm and happy just-fucked feeling."

Ari slammed her hand over my mouth as she looked at me with horrified eyes. I closed my eyes as she slowly removed her hands.

I opened my eyes and whispered, "Your dad is behind me, isn't he?"

Ari nodded. I turned around to see Mark standing there, holding Luke. He shook his head, and if looks could kill, I swore I would have fallen over on the spot.

"Sometimes, I lie in bed and just ask God...why? Why Jeff Johnson? Why?" Mark said as he looked up toward the sky.

"Oh, Daddy, knock it off."

Ari walked past me and went to reach for Luke, but Mark held up his hand.

"Your mother wanted to bring the kids home with us. Maybe you could pick them up tomorrow evening?"

Ari stopped dead in her tracks. "You want to take both kids...for the night? Why?"

Mark laughed. "Because I hardly ever get to see them, and Matthew needs to spend some time with them. Grace is growing up too fast. It would be nice to just spend some time with Luke and Grace. Matthew would love it."

Ari turned and looked at me. She smiled the biggest smile I'd ever seen. Before she turned back, she put on a serious face.

"Oh, I don't know, Daddy. Are you sure y'all want them both? I mean, we could come first thing in the morning."

Mark turned and looked at me. Daggers could have been coming out of his eyes with how he was staring at me.

"I'm sure your husband wouldn't mind some time with his wife— seeing as how he feels the need to sneak you down to a barn for some...alone time."

I just smiled and made a mental note to make sure my life insurance was up to date.

"Well...if you don't think it would be too much trouble?" Ari said.

"Trouble? My grandchildren? *Never.* Y'all just plan on having lunch at our place tomorrow. Your mother is already putting Grace in her car seat as we speak."

Ari put her hands on her hips and tilted her head. "What if I had said no? What if I didn't want the kids to leave for the night?"

Mark laughed as he threw his head back. "Please...Miss Polka-Dot Panties, I know better."

He turned and walked away as Ari's face turned ten shades of red.

I walked down the stairs and stopped next to Ari. "Yep, I'm gonna say your dad saw you grinding on me." I followed Mark to his car, and then I looked back at a stunned Ari.

I couldn't help but laugh as I ran to catch up with Mark, so I could say good-bye to the kids.

Oh yeah, I'm gonna make sure my wife gets that warm and happy fucked feeling back tonight...and more than once.

10 Scott

"I'm about to lose my goddamn mind, Drake," I said as I paced back and forth.

Christmas was in three days, and no one had heard from Jessie.

"Scott, I came over to tell you that I got a postcard from her today."

I stopped dead in my tracks. "What? Where is she? Is she okay? Who's she with? Did she say when she was coming home?"

Drake held up his hands and started to shake his head. "Scott…settle down. I know you want to know the answers to all those questions, so here you go." He reached out and handed me a postcard.

I took it from his hand.

He said, "Read it for yourself. She pretty much just says that she's fine."

My heart skipped a beat when I recognized her handwriting. I looked at where it was stamped. *Florida? She's in Florida!* I tried to keep the tears from falling as I began to read what she had written.

Post Card

Daddy,

I'm so sorry I haven't gotten in touch with you. I'm fine, I promise. I'm not in Florida. I asked a friend to mail this for me when she got back home. I just need more time.

Daddy, please understand. My heart is so broken, and I just can't risk Scott trying to find me. I need to get him out of my mind, and most importantly, out of my heart.

Tell the boys I love them. I'll try to call you on Christmas, but I'm going to stay through New Year's. I've met a friend, who has helped a lot. He's been a real support for me. He's helping me get over Scott. I love you, Daddy. Talk to you soon.

Jessica

I slowly sat down on the sofa as I let the postcard fall out of my hand. *I've met a friend. He's been a real support for me. He's helping me get over Scott.*

Oh my god, she's met someone else. She's with another man.

Drake sat down next to me and put his hand on my shoulder. "Now, Scott, don't go jumping to conclusions. She said he was a friend, that's all."

"Oh god, she's with another man. She left me, and she's with another man in God knows where." I stood and started pacing.

My phone began ringing, and when I pulled it out of my pocket, I saw that it was Chelsea. She'd been calling for the last week.

Fucking bitch. I hate you!

I threw my phone as hard as I could against the wall. I looked around for something else to throw, and I saw a picture of Jessie and me. I walked over, picked it up, and threw it. I didn't know what was happening, but I just snapped and started throwing everything I could get my hands on.

The next thing I knew, Drake and Aaron were both holding me back, and I felt my knees slowly giving out.

I lost her. I lost the only girl I've ever truly loved, and I never even had the chance to fight for her.

Oh god…I can't live without Jessie.

I sat there in the middle of my living room…crying…as Drake and Aaron tried to tell me it was okay.

"It isn't okay. It'll never be okay. I lost her, and she's moved on with someone else."

Aaron bent down and hit me on the arm. "Damn it, Scott. Don't…don't give up like this. She's gonna call Dad in three days. He can tell her everything, and she'll be on the first flight back. I promise you."

I felt tears falling down my face, but I didn't even care. I just needed a drink. I needed to forget about Jessica Rhodes…like she'd forgotten about me.

He's helping me get over Scott.

"Hey, Scott. Fancy meeting you here at the Wild Coyote. What are you drinking?"

I slowly looked up and saw Karen standing there. I couldn't even remember her last name. She had been a friend of Jessie's in high school.

"Why are you here on Christmas Eve, Karen? Shouldn't you be at home with your family?" I asked as I looked her body up and down.

She certainly looks good. Not as good as Jessie, but who the fuck cares? Jessie has moved on with a friend. She doesn't want to be found. Maybe they've been friends this whole time, and that's why she hasn't come home.

Karen sat down next to me and asked for a Bud Light as she nudged me with her shoulder. "I live in New Orleans now, but I'm home, visiting my parents. They were driving me crazy, so I came down here for a couple of beers," she said with a wink.

I looked down at the cream corset-type shirt she was wearing. Her breasts looked amazing in it. I slowly moved my drunk eyes up and looked at her lips. The moment she licked them, I put my hand behind her neck and pulled her closer to me.

"What the hell are you doing, Karen?"

She let out a laugh. "Isn't it obvious, Scott? I came out for a little bit of fun. When I walked in and saw you sitting here, I thought I'd come check you out and see if you're still single. I heard about you and Chelsea."

I watched as she slowly took her left leg off her right. She spread her legs open before crossing her right leg over her left.

I didn't feel a fucking thing. Here was this beautiful woman flirting with me with her fucking tits just staring at me, and I didn't feel shit.

"You married, Karen?"

She shook her head and smiled. I grabbed her hand and led her out to the dance floor. I pulled her to me and pressed our bodies close to each other. She started moving her hands up and down my back before she placed them on my ass and pulled me even closer to her. She looked up at me and smiled. I began to feel my dick coming to life.

She's with another man. She's forgotten about me.

I couldn't pull my eyes from Karen's lips. She was biting down on her lower lip so hard that I swore it was turning white. I backed her up into a corner that was fairly dark. I put my hand behind her neck and pulled her up for a kiss. The moment our lips touched, she let out a long, soft moan. I felt her hand on mine, and she moved it up her skirt.

"Touch me, Scott…oh god…please touch me."

I quickly stopped my hand and moved it out from under her skirt. Instead, I started to feel her breasts. As badly as I wanted to touch her, it felt so wrong.

She threw her head back and whispered, "Yes. I'm so wet for you, baby. I've always wanted to be fucked by you." She snapped her head straight and looked at me. "Fuck me, Scott. Right here…in your truck…in the restroom…I don't care. I just want you to fuck me hard from behind."

For one brief moment, I wanted to pick her up and take her to the restroom to do just that. I could fuck her so hard and fast that I would surely be able to forget about Jessie…at least for a little while.

"Scott…" She reached her hand over and squeezed my dick. "Take me. I'm yours for tonight, Scott."

I closed my eyes, and all I could see was Jessie's smiling face. *No. I won't do this. I can't do this. I love Jessie. I'll always love Jessie.*

I pulled my hand away from her and took a few steps back. "Um…I'm sorry, Karen. I'm in love with someone else, and I won't be unfaithful to her, no matter what."

Karen's face dropped. "What? You're gonna feel me up and then tell me you're in love with someone else? What would she think if she knew you were about to fuck me?"

I shrugged my shoulders. "Probably nothing since she's fucking someone to forget about me." I turned and walked away.

I saw Jeff and Gunner walking in with Josh following close behind. I smiled, knowing they were only here to check up on me.

Thank God I came to my senses with Karen before they walked in and saw us.

I walked up and shook Josh's hand. "Dude, what in the hell are you doing in Mason?" I asked.

Josh gave me a quick hug. "Heather and I decided to take Gunner's offer to stay with him and Ellie, so we could celebrate Christmas morning with the Mathews."

I smiled as I nodded. Gunner and Ellie had invited me to stay with them, but I'd turned them down.

"Scott, are you sure you don't want to stay with us tonight? Ellie and Heather are in a baking mood, and I swear that we have enough baked goods to feed a small army," Gunner said with a laugh.

I shook my head. "I appreciate it, Gunner, but I think I'll just head home and go to bed. I was planning on asking Jessie to marry me on Christmas Eve at my parents' anniversary party tonight, so I kind of just want to be alone."

Jeff hit me on the back and smiled. "Come on, dude. Let's settle up your bill, and I'll drive you home."

"Did you get a new phone yet?" Gunner asked as we walked out to the parking lot.

"Yeah, I got it, but I haven't turned it on. I'm not in any real rush to use it."

"I am. I've been getting a ton of calls about a horse you wanted. I guess you gave them my number, Scott, and I knew nothing about it," Jeff said.

"Damn…sorry, Jeff. It's just…I can't think about anything. I can't eat, I can't sleep. She's gone, and she's using some fucker she met to forget about me."

Gunner let out a long sigh. "Scott, you don't know that. She's gonna call Drake tomorrow, and then we can get this whole damn thing settled.

Just hang tight, dude. One more day is all you've got to wait, and then Jessie will know the truth."

I shook my head. It felt like I had a hundred pounds sitting on my chest. I just needed to get home and go to bed. I felt so tired for some reason.

I held my hand out to shake Josh's and then Gunner's hands. "Thanks, guys. Thanks for having my back. I really do appreciate each of you and your friendship. I don't know how I would have done this if I hadn't had your support."

"Always, Scott. We're always here for you," Josh said.

Gunner told Jeff he would follow him to my house since Jeff was driving my truck for me.

As I made my way to the passenger side of my truck, I felt sick to my stomach. It didn't even matter that she was calling home tomorrow. In my heart, I felt like she was already gone. She'd met someone else.

He's helping me get over Scott.

"Scott, she's gonna call. She wouldn't let her dad down by not calling, and I know she still loves you. It's almost over, dude. It's almost over," Jeff said with a weak smile.

I leaned my head back against the headrest and tried to smile. "I hope you're right, but I have this sick feeling that everyone is wrong. Jessie has spent the last five weeks moving on. I feel her in my heart, but she's slowly fading away."

I looked over toward Jeff. He was just staring at me. He turned and started the truck before pulling out of the lot to take me home.

I closed my eyes and took in a deep breath as I pictured her in the arms of another man.

Jessie…please come back to me, baby.

Trey and I had been dancing for the last five songs, and now, we were dancing to Britney Spears's song, "3." The more his hands moved across my body, the more I yearned for Scott. I knew Trey wanted to take our friendship to another level, and I was starting to wish I was going home tomorrow instead of on New Year's Eve.

"Oh god, Jessie…your body drives me crazy," Trey said as he pushed his erection into my stomach.

The twists and turns of emotions were driving me crazy. I enjoyed Trey's friendship so much, and he'd helped me so much the last few weeks.

Do I want more than friendship with him? No…at least, not now anyway.

Everything was so raw, and the hurt in my heart was still so strong. The last thing I wanted or needed was to fall for someone else. Plus, I was still in love with Scott…even though I tried to fight that feeling with everything I had.

"Don't Let Me Be Lonely" by The Band Perry began playing. Trey pulled me closer to him, and we began to slow dance. My head was spinning, and I felt so sick to my stomach.

"Trey, I think this is my last dance. I'm not feeling very well, and I just really need to rest."

He reached his hand up and ran his knuckles down the side of my face. When he touched me, I couldn't deny that I felt something. It was nothing though compared to when Scott had touched me…or smiled at me…or told me how much he loved me.

Scott…why did you have to hurt me again?

"Smile, my love. I hate it when you have such a sad look in your eyes," Trey said with that sweet smile of his.

I looked into his green eyes, and I couldn't believe his fiancée could ever walk away from such an amazing man. I returned a weak smile. "I'm just not feeling well."

"Is it your stomach again? Maybe you're eating something here that doesn't agree with you."

I shrugged my shoulders. I knew it was most likely just nerves. I had been such a nervous wreck and so stressed out that I hadn't even had my period in two months.

Trey leaned down and lightly kissed my lips. I wanted so badly to open myself up to him more. I just wanted to be held in someone's arms tonight. But what I wanted most was to be in Scott's arms.

"Jessie, don't spend Christmas Eve alone. Stay with me tonight. Please. I know you're leaving in a few days to be home by the New Year, but please…let's just spend this next week together."

I let out a small laugh. "Trey, we've pretty much spent every waking moment together. I don't think we could spend any more time together."

He shook his head and kissed my lips again. This time, he gently bit down on my lower lip and pulled it with his teeth. I couldn't control myself, and I let a small moan escape from my lips.

"Trey."

"I don't mean, hang out like friends, Jessie. I want to be with you. I want to know how you feel and what you taste like. I want to touch every inch of your body and cover you with kisses."

Oh god…I want that, too.

But I want it from Scott. Only from Scott.

"Once we leave this island, if you tell me that this is it and there could never be anything else, I promise you that I will totally respect that. It's just…I've never felt this way with anyone…not even with Renee. I was going to marry her, and I never wanted her like I want you right now."

A part of me wanted to go back to his cabana. I could just close my eyes and dream I was with Scott, but I'd never hurt Trey that way.

I placed my hand on his chest and smiled at him. "Trey, I'm not going to lie and say that I don't feel a connection to you because I do. I feel it when we touch and when we kiss, but—"

He started shaking his head. "No…don't say but, Jessie."

I took a deep breath in and quickly blew it out. "But it's not fair to be with you when I'm still in love with Scott. I can't change what my heart feels, and yes, I know, he hurt me. Please don't keep reminding me."

"I'm sorry, Jessie, but he did hurt you, and that bastard doesn't deserve your love."

"Trey, I keep having this dream. It's about Scott and a little girl, and she keeps telling me that I didn't even give him a chance to talk to me before I ran away. She told me I killed him."

Trey rolled his eyes and let out a sharp breath as he shook his head. "A dream? That's what has you so upset? Jesus Christ, Jessie. It's a damn dream that doesn't mean anything. You didn't kill the asshole."

"I haven't even talked to my father in over a month. I gave the lady I met at lunch one day a postcard I'd bought in Texas to mail to my father. I'm hiding from my own family and friends, but mostly, I'm hiding from Scott. I have to keep asking myself why. Why am I so afraid to talk to or see him?"

"Because you know the moment you see him, you'll forgive him, Jess. You'll fall right back into his arms, just waiting for the next time he hurts you."

I shook my head and turned to walk off the dance floor. I went back to our table and had to put my hand up to my mouth. *Oh god, please don't let me get sick here. Shit!*

I grabbed my purse and headed for the door. *I need fresh air. I can't breathe.* As soon as I got outside, I took a deep breath and felt the cool, crisp air hit my lungs. Then, I noticed the wind. *Holy shit.* It was so windy that it almost knocked me over. I felt dizzy, and I tried to get my balance when I felt Trey grab my arm.

"Jessie, don't run away from me like you have with everyone else."

I spun around and looked at him. The anger began building, and all I wanted was my father right now. *I need to get home.*

"How can you stand there and say that to me of all people? Did you not run away with your best friend and come here after Renee left you at the altar? You're not going home because you don't want to face everyone asking you what happened, right? How dare you say that to me."

"Jessie, you deserve to be loved and taken care of. I can do that. I would never hurt you. You would never have to run away from me."

Oh god. I never even gave Scott a chance to talk to me before I just ran away from him. What am I afraid of? Finding out the truth? What if I was wrong all along?

Then, something hit me like a brick wall.

"What if it wasn't him?"

Trey just looked at me. "What? Who in the hell else could it have been, Jessie? You're talking crazy."

"No...I've been fighting this sick feeling in my stomach since I got on that plane. It was like...like I was making one of the worst mistakes of my life. There's a reason my love for him is so strong still." I shook my head. "I need to get back to my cabana."

As I started practically running, Trey ran up and grabbed me.

"Jessie! Listen to yourself. You didn't imagine seeing him screwing his ex."

I closed my eyes and thought back to the night I'd been trying to push out of my memory for the last month and a half. I opened them quickly and looked at Trey. "No...I don't think it was him. The more I think about the voice calling out after me...the more I realize that it wasn't Scott's. I *know* it wasn't Scott." My heart started pounding. "I'm going to call him."

Trey threw his head back, and I knew he was upset.

"Fine. Let me walk with you then since it's dark."

I nodded and began to run back to the cabana. The wind was getting worse, and it was starting to sprinkle now. Just before we got to the door, a bolt of lightning struck somewhere close by. I screamed, and Trey took a hold of me.

"Holy shit! That was close. Is there a damn tropical storm coming in this late in the year?"

The wind was blowing so hard that chairs were flying down the beach. *Where in the hell did this storm come from?*

I ran into my cabana and went straight to the phone. I picked it up and started telling the operator that I wanted to make a call to the U.S. I reached into my purse for the calling card I had bought.

"Jessie, please don't do this right now. It's Christmas Eve."

I smiled. "All the more reason to call him."

After I gave the operator all the information, Scott's phone rang once and then went straight to voice mail. My hands started shaking, and I felt a lump in my throat.

Shit. Maybe I should have called my dad first.

When I heard the beep, I took a deep breath. "Scott, um…hey, it's Jessie. I, um…I really need to talk to you. I don't have my phone, so I'll try to call you in a few minutes or so. I, um…I love you, Scott. I love you, and I just need to talk to you."

I hung up the phone and then cursed. *Shit! Shit! Shit! I didn't tell him where I was.* I picked up the phone again, but another bolt of lightning hit, and then all I heard was a loud crash.

Trey took the phone out of my hand and hung it up. "Come on, we need to get to the main hotel, Jessie. This storm is getting worse."

"No! Wait! Let me just call him back and let him know where I am, Trey!"

Trey tried to pull me away, but I used all my might to yank my arm out of his hand. I picked up the phone, and it was silent.

No! Oh no! God, please don't do this to me.

Just as I was about to tell Trey I had no dial tone, there was a knock on the door. Trey opened it, and it was one of the hotel employees.

"Miss Rhodes, Mr. Walker, I need you both to come to the main hotel."

"What happened to the phone lines?" I asked in a panicked voice.

"They're probably down from the storm."

"I thought we were out of storm season!" I yelled over the increasing wind.

"It is very rare for a tropical cyclone to develop this late in the year, but it's not unheard of."

Trey and I both said at the same time, "What?"

"A tropical cyclone? I knew there was a tropical storm out there, but the front desk clerk said it wouldn't develop into anything. Oh my god!" I said.

"Miss Rhodes, it's okay. It is a category-one cyclone, and it developed rather quickly throughout the day. We put a notice on your cabana doors. Neither of you got it?"

I looked at Trey, and we both shook our heads.

"We've been sightseeing all day," I said.

"Please come now, and let's get to a safer location."

I grabbed a sweatshirt, and then I followed Trey and the hotel worker out of my room. I didn't even have time to take anything else.

By the time we got to the hotel lobby, everyone was sitting around, talking, as the employees did their best to keep the guests calm and comfortable. I walked up to the front desk and noticed the girl was on her cell phone.

Oh my god! She has a signal in this mess?

She hung up and turned to face me. "Miss Rhodes, how are you?" she asked with a smile on her face.

Jesus H. Christ, how does the staff stay so calm?

"Honestly, I'm slightly freaked, but I've been told the storm is only a category-one cyclone, so..." I rolled my eyes.

She laughed. "We locals are used to storms like this although it is very rare to get them this time of year."

"I couldn't help but notice you were talking on your cell phone." I looked at her with pleading eyes.

She glanced around quickly and motioned for me to follow her into the office. "I'm not sure how I've managed to keep a signal, but my husband is in New York City on business, and I was able to call him. Is there a loved one you want to try to call?"

I jumped up and down. "Yes! I would be forever grateful to you if I could call him."

She handed me her cell, and I saw she still had a signal. I quickly tried Scott, only to get his voice mail again. I left him a quick message, telling him I was in Belize and that I would be coming home in a few days. Then, I tried Daddy.

"Hello?" he answered.

The moment I heard his voice, I began crying. "Daddy?"

"Oh my god, Jessie! Thank God. Oh, baby, we've been worried sick. Scott is about to go crazy. Jessie, why?"

"Daddy, I can't talk long. I'm in Belize, and we are being hit with a tropical storm."

"Jessie, you're going in and out. I think you said you're in a tropical storm? Baby, where are you?"

"Belize. Dad, I called Scott, but his phone went to voice mail."

"Jessie, I'm only getting a few words here and there, but if you can hear me...baby, it wasn't Scott who was with Chelsea. It was Bryce, Scott's brother. Baby girl, Scott didn't cheat on you. God, Jessie, can you hear me? Jess, have you met someone new? Scott is not doing very well after your postcard."

I almost dropped the phone. *I knew it. I knew deep in my heart that he would never hurt me.* "Daddy, I hear you! I hear you. Please tell him to call me. I'm at the—"

Then, I heard a beep. I pulled the phone away from my ear and looked at the screen.

No service.

I slowly handed the phone back to the front desk clerk.

"The signal is gone," I whispered.

"Ah…Miss Rhodes, I think you better sit down. You don't look so good."

I glanced up and noticed her name was…Chelsea.

Oh god…I think I'm going to get sick. "I feel sick."

Chelsea ran and grabbed a small trash bin. She held it as I started puking into it. Then, the dry heaves began.

"Ugh…I'm so sorry, Chelsea. I've been feeling so bad the last few weeks. I'm not sure what it is."

She smiled and sat down. "It's okay. I just hope you are not getting the flu or something."

I nodded and tried to remember what my father had said.

Baby, it wasn't Scott who was with Chelsea. Jess, have you met someone new? Scott is not doing very well after your postcard.

Why in the world did he ask me if I've met someone new? What did my postcard have to do with—

I threw my hands up to my mouth. Chelsea jumped back up and grabbed the trash can.

What did I write? Oh god…did I write about meeting someone new?

"Oh my Lord, Miss Rhodes, you don't look so good. Should I get a doctor?"

I stood up and started pacing. *Think, Jessie! Think! What did you write? I told him I was fine…I'd call…*

Oh. My. God.

I told him I'd met a friend…and he was helping me get over Scott.

"No…oh no! No! No! Oh my god, what did I do?"

Then, I thought about my dream.

You left him. You killed him.

I heard Trey asking Chelsea if everything was okay.

I turned to face Trey. "I'm the one who hurt him. He thinks I've found someone new. He thinks I've…" I started shaking my head violently from side to side.

"Mr. Walker, I really think she needs a doctor—now," Chelsea said.

"No! Oh god...no...Scott. I need to get to Scott!"

I started to make my way out of the office when Trey grabbed me.

"Jessie, there's a storm out there. You can't get to Scott right now. No one can talk to anyone unless that person is on the island."

I could hear the wind outside, and things were banging against the building. "You don't understand. I have to leave. I have to leave now!"

Trey placed his hands on my shoulders and looked into my eyes. "Jessica, you can't leave. There's a storm outside, love. Come on, I'll hold you if you feel sick. Everything is going to be okay."

The sick feeling in my stomach was more than I could stand as everything hit me all at once. I looked up at Trey and shook my head. "No...just please let me have a few minutes. I just need a few minutes alone."

"Jessie—"

"Trey, please!" I shouted.

Trey took a step back. I watched as he turned and headed out of the office.

"Chelsea...can you please give me a few minutes alone?"

Chelsea nodded and left. She shut the office door behind her. I sat there for a few minutes, trying to process everything.

It was Bryce? Why Bryce? Then, who sent the text from Scott's phone, telling me to meet him at home? Why were Chelsea and Bryce in Scott's bedroom? She said they had gotten tired of waiting for me. Did she mean she and Bryce or—

Oh my god. Oh god...I'm so fucking stupid! Chelsea set me up. Somehow, she must have sent the text...or maybe Scott sent it and passed out...or...

My head was spinning, and I felt like I was going to get sick again.

I just need to talk to Scott. I need to tell him that I'm not in love with anyone else, and I could never forget him. I could never stop loving him.

I thought about how much time I'd spent with Trey, laughing and enjoying the islands, while Scott had been back home...scared to death and worried about me and what I was doing.

I put my right hand on my stomach and my left hand over my mouth. *I almost slept with Trey.* I closed my eyes and thought back to the night I'd let Trey finger-fuck me and how much I had just wanted to orgasm to forget about Scott. I could almost feel Trey's hands on my body. I reached up and touched my still tender breasts as I felt tears rolling down my face, knowing that I'd let another man suck on my breasts and touch my body.

I opened my eyes and sat up. I stared straight ahead for a good two minutes before I stood and walked to the office door. I barely opened it, but I could see Trey standing on the other side of the counter. He stood up taller and smiled when he saw me. I tried my best to smile, but my heart was pounding so loud that I could hear it in my ears.

"Um, Chelsea? May I speak with you...in private, please?"

Chelsea smiled. "Sure."

After she walked in, I slowly shut the door. The winds seemed to be dying down outside, but I could still hear things blowing around and hitting the building.

I didn't even know how to ask for what I needed, so I just went for it. "Chelsea, I need to take a pregnancy test."

The smile that spread across her face caused me to smile.

"Does Mr. Walker know?"

My smile disappeared, and I felt sick to my stomach. "Mr. Walker is just a friend. We're just friends and nothing more."

"I'm so sorry, Miss Rhodes. I just assumed because the two of you are always together and all."

I tried to smile. "I can understand that, but I have a boyfriend back home, and I, um…well, it would be his baby."

"I see. And he's okay with you spending so much time here with Mr. Walker?"

I felt my cheeks instantly flush. I could see how people would assume Trey and I were together. Almost every day, we'd spent breakfast, lunch, and dinner together. We'd walked on the beach and taken tours together…danced together…and kissed on more than one occasion.

I wiped away the tear that had rolled slowly down my cheek. "No…he doesn't know I'm here or that I've been, um…spending time with Mr. Walker. But I have not slept with him—at all," I said as the guilt began to eat away at me.

For over a month, Scott has been back home, worried about me, and I've been…having a grand old time, running around Belize with another man.

"Well, I'm not one to judge anyone, Miss Rhodes. I do believe we sell them in the gift store. Would you like me to go and buy you one?"

I slowly nodded. "I left my purse in my cabana. Can you charge it to my room?"

She gave me a pitiful smile and nodded as she opened the door.

I said, "Two. Please get two."

My hands were shaking as I held up the pregnancy test. *Two lines. Pregnant.*

I immediately opened the other test and repeated the whole process, crying the entire time.

I waited five minutes and held it up. *Two lines. I'm carrying Scott's baby.* As I placed my hand on my stomach, I practically let out a scream. I sat there, rocking back and forth. I'd let another man touch me while I was pregnant with Scott's child.

Oh god...Scott, please forgive me.

He's never going to forgive me. He's going to hate me forever.

Every time I closed my eyes, all I could see was Trey sucking on my nipples...the same nipples my child would touch.

"No! Fuck! Fuck! *Fuck*! Why did I let him touch me? Oh god, why did I ask him to touch me? *Why*?" I yelled out.

In that instant, I had more hate for Chelsea than I'd ever had.

There was a knock on the restroom door.

From the other side, Trey asked, "Are you okay?"

"I'm fine. I just need a few minutes. Please just give me a few minutes." I got up and pulled my jeans back up. I wrapped both tests in toilet paper and put them into my back pocket as I left the stall.

I heard the restroom door open, and I spun around to see Trey standing there.

"Jessie, what in the hell is going on? Please tell me. You're scaring the shit out of me."

I pushed past him. *How dare he come into the restroom when I asked him to wait.* "I talked to my dad."

Trey looked at me, confused. "How? When?"

"Earlier. I saw the front desk clerk, Chelsea, talking on her cell. I asked if I could use her phone. I tried to call Scott, but it went to his voice mail again."

I noticed how Trey seemed to be relieved when he found out I hadn't talked to Scott.

"But my father answered when I called. He couldn't really hear everything. He said I was breaking in and out, but I did hear him tell me that it wasn't Scott with Chelsea. It was Scott's brother. Scott never cheated on me."

Trey's whole body slumped. "Well...I mean, are you sure Scott is not just lying to your father?"

I nodded my head. "Yes! I know now that the voice I heard was Bryce and not Scott."

"Wait...Jessie, the whole thing just doesn't make any sense. How do you know your dad wasn't just saying that to get you to come home?"

I hadn't even thought of that. *Would my father lie to me?*

I shook my head. "No, my father wouldn't lie to me like that, Trey."

"Jessie, if you were my daughter and I had no idea where you were, I'd tell you whatever I thought you wanted to hear to get you to come home to me."

I stood there, staring at Trey. *I'm so confused.*

"Baby, your dad knows you're fine and safe now. Let's get through this storm and spend the last few days together, just you and me, and then we will both fly back to Texas. Hell, I'll even fly home with you if you need me to."

"No…wait…my head is spinning. I'm so confused. Trey, you're confusing me. I have to talk to Scott right away."

Trey was clearly getting frustrated as he pushed both hands through his hair. "Why? Why do you have to talk to that cheating bastard right away, Jess? Why can't we just enjoy what we've started here?"

I looked down at the floor as I reached around and felt the tests in my back pocket. "I have to talk to him, Trey, because I just found out that…" My voice cracked as I looked into his eyes, and the flood of guilt came back full force. It felt like I had a weight sitting on my chest.

Trey took a step closer and went to reach out for me. I held up my hand and stepped away from him. The hurt in his eyes about killed me.

"You just found out what, Jessie?"

I inhaled a deep breath and let it out. "I just found out that I'm pregnant."

Trey's eyes grew bigger, and his mouth dropped open. "Oh my god," he said so low that I barely heard him.

"I know, and I'm filled with so much guilt because I let you touch me. I let you touch me, and we almost…almost…"

I broke down crying again as Trey walked toward me. He pulled me into his arms, and he began stroking my hair as he kept repeating for me to calm down.

"We didn't, Jess…we didn't make love. There was a reason you stopped it, and you didn't do anything wrong."

I looked up into his eyes as I pulled back slightly. "I didn't do anything wrong? Trey…I asked you to have sex with me, so I could forget about my boyfriend."

"Who you thought had cheated on you. We didn't do anything, Jessie. You don't even have to tell Scott about it, love. It can just stay between you and me. I promise you, I'll never tell anyone."

I started shaking my head. "Everyone thinks we're together. Do you know how many times I've kissed you? And I'm carrying another man's child. I…I…"

"God, Jessie, stop this. You didn't know, and we didn't do anything wrong. Most of those kisses were friendly pecks. Please…don't get upset like this. It's not good for the baby. Come on…let's get out of the restroom and find somewhere to sit."

We made our way through the lobby, and Trey guided me over toward empty chairs in the bar area. I looked around at everyone laughing and drinking while a terrible storm was going on outside. I closed my eyes and thought about the terrible storm going on inside me. I sat down in a chair, and he bent down as he pushed my hair behind both of my ears.

He smiled that sweeter than sweet smile at me. "I'm going to get you some water, love. Just try to take some deep breaths, and I'll be right back."

He placed his hand on the side of my face, and I leaned my head into it. His touch had become such a calming force to me. My body betrayed me with the shiver that ran through it. I watched as he turned and walked up to the bar. I noticed all the women looking him up and down. One bitch licked her lips and nudged her friend, who started laughing.

Bitches. He's mine.

I sucked in a breath of air and covered my mouth. *What?* I started shaking my head. *No! No…he's not mine. We're only friends—just friends.*

I looked back at Trey. He was now talking to one of the ladies who had been eye-fucking him as he'd walked up to the bar. The insane jealousy I was feeling was very confusing. All I wanted to do was get to Scott, so I could beg him to forgive me and tell him how much I loved him. Yet, I also wanted Trey to stop talking to this bitch and come back to me. I needed to feel him near me. I needed his touch again.

What is going on with me? Why am I feeling this way toward him? I don't love him. God, please…please just clear my head of these feelings.

I turned away and began watching everyone in the lobby. Little kids were chasing each other as their parents kept telling them to slow down. A little girl with curly brown hair was playing hide-and-seek with a little boy who looked to be about a year younger than her. I smiled, thinking about the child I was carrying.

I'm carrying Scott's child. What will our baby look like? Will she have Scott's beautiful blue eyes? Will she have blonde or brown hair?

I felt Trey touch my shoulder, and it was like a warm blanket enveloped my whole body. I looked up at his tender smile. I couldn't help but glance back at the woman he had been talking to at the bar. She was giving me a dirty look, and a part of me felt triumphant.

As I watched Trey sit down and get settled in the chair, I wondered what his children would look like. Whoever he ended up with was going to be one lucky lady.

"Jessie, I know you don't want to hear this, but I have to say it."

I nodded.

"If it turns out that Scott did cheat—"

"He didn't."

"I know, but if he *did*, I want you to know that it would be my honor to take care of you and your child. I'd do everything in my power to make you both happy."

Tears flooded my eyes as I looked into Trey's eyes.

How can I care about someone so much when I only just met him, not even two months ago?

I got up, crawled onto his lap, and wrapped my arms around his neck. "Trey," was all I could say. Right before I fell asleep, I whispered, "I love Scott. I'll always love Scott." I drifted off to sleep where images of little girls with curly hair took over my dreams.

12 Scott

All I could hear was banging. *What in the hell?* My doorbell was ringing, and someone was pounding on my front door.

"I'm coming! Holy fuck, hold on to your pants!" I yelled out.

I opened the door, and Drake pushed his way past me.

"Well, hello, Drake. Merry Christmas to you, too," I said as I shut the door.

Is it too early to have a drink? I looked at the clock. It was just after midnight.

"Where's your phone? Your cell phone, Scott. Turn it on."

I rolled my eyes and shook my head. "You came over here in the middle of the night to tell me you want to use my cell phone? Buy one, old man," I said with a chuckle.

I made my way into the kitchen. I needed coffee.

"She called."

I stopped in my tracks and turned to look at him. "Jessie?"

He smiled and nodded.

"Holy fuck. What did she say?"

"It was a really bad connection, but she said something about being in a tropical storm."

A tropical storm? "Drake? Are you sure you weren't dreaming or something?"

"Yes, of course, I'm sure. I asked her where she was, and she said something, but I couldn't hear her. She mentioned a tropical storm, and she also said she'd left you a message."

"Did you tell her it wasn't me? Did you tell her I didn't cheat on her?"

Drake smiled and nodded. "I did, but I don't know how much she heard before we were disconnected."

I turned and quickly walked into the kitchen. I reached into my jacket pocket and pulled out my phone. I turned it on and waited for the longest forty seconds of my life for that bitch to start up.

I had twenty voice mails. Jessie's messages were the last two to come through. I hit Speaker and listened to the first one.

"Scott, um…hey, it's Jessie. I, um…I really need to talk to you. I don't have my phone, so I'll try to call you in a few minutes or so. I, um…I love you, Scott. I love you, and I just need to talk to you."

The second message started to play.

"Hey, it's me again. I'm in Belize, but I have a flight coming back on the twenty-ninth. There's a bad storm, so I'll call you when the phone lines come back up. I'm using the front desk girl's cell. I love you, Scott. I love you so much, and I'm so sorry."

I looked at Drake as he stared at me. "Belize?" we both said at the same time.

"Holy fuck. She's not even in the country, Drake. She's in fucking goddamn Belize. And who's the guy she's with?"

"Scott, she said she loved you. Wait—what time did that first call come in?"

I looked at my phone. "Right before nine."

Drake smiled and shook his head. "She called you before me, Scott."

"So? That's supposed to make me feel better when all I can think of is how she has a friend helping her get over me?"

"No, you ass. She didn't know yet about you and Chelsea. She must have either talked to someone else, or she figured it out on her own. Bryce said he'd called out after her. After thinking about it, maybe she realized it wasn't your voice she'd heard."

My heart started pounding. "Do you think? *Fuck.* I can't wait until the twenty-ninth for her to come home. I have to get to Belize."

"Did you not hear that they're in the middle of a tropical storm? No airline is going to fly into that. Let's just wait until morning, and we can call the airlines and see about flights to Belize."

There was no way I could wait, but I nodded my head to reassure Drake. "Okay. We'll wait until morning."

I showed Drake up to one of the spare bedrooms and made my way back down to my room. I crawled into the new bed I had bought, and I lay there, looking up at the ceiling. I wasn't going to be able to sleep. Drake had said Jessie was about to tell him where she was staying when the phone died.

I sat up in bed and grabbed my cell. I wrote down the number that Jessie had called from earlier, and I dialed another number. If there was one person I knew who could help me…it would be him.

I had already had four cups of coffee, and it was only six in the morning. I heard Drake walking into the kitchen. I turned and smiled as I held up my coffee cup.

"Want a cup?" I asked.

He looked down at my bag on the floor.

"You going somewhere? I checked the airlines, Scott. The storm knocked out almost all the power, and the airport is shut down. They don't see it opening for a day or two, if that. How in the hell do you think you're going to get to Belize?"

My phone rang right then, and I pulled it out. I smiled when I saw who was calling. "Lark, what's the word?" I said as my heart started pounding.

Lark was my best friend from college, and he now worked for some hotshot guy who did business all over Central America and God knows where else.

"I can be there in two hours. Perfect." I hung up the phone and quickly turned to rinse out my coffee cup. I reached down and grabbed my bag before making my way to the back door.

"Scott! Where in the hell are you going? Are you going to tell me what's going on?"

"Walk with me, Drake." As I made my way out the door and over to my truck, I started to tell Drake my plan. "My best friend from college works for some guy. I'm not really sure what type of business he's in, but Lark flies him all over the place. I gave Lark a ring and said I needed to call in a favor. I told him what was going on and asked if he could land a helicopter in Belize right now with the storm hitting. He made a call to his boss and asked if he could use the Sikorsky S-92 helicopter to make a run to Belize. I offered to pay for the gas plus some."

Drake grabbed my arm and pulled me to a stop. "Wait." He shook his head. "This *guy*—why in the hell would he let your buddy take his helicopter to Belize just for you to get to Jessie?"

I shrugged my shoulders. "I don't know…maybe he believes in love. I don't really give a shit. I'm paying him enough money to probably buy a new fucking helicopter. I don't care, Drake. I just need to get to Jessie."

I jumped into my truck and shut the door. I started the truck and rolled down my window. "I should be in Austin in two hours. Lark is going to be waiting for me there. He said it was about a four-hour flight to Belize, not including one or two fuel stops. I'll let you know when I get there and find her."

"How are you going to land in Belize?" Drake asked.

I took a deep breath. I didn't really want to tell him that I was going to stay at Lark's boss's house, which had a helipad. "Lark's boss has a house in Belize. He's gonna land there."

Drake started shaking his head. "What in the hell does this guy do, Scott?"

"I've got to go, Drake. Don't worry, it's not drugs." I rolled up the window and took off down my driveway.

Okay…at least I hope it's not drugs. A part of me wondered what in the hell Lark and his boss did for a living.

Lark showed me around his boss's house, and I was dumbfounded. I'd never seen such a big house.

Do I want to know what this guy does for a living?

I was tired, cranky, and just pissed-off. We'd ended up having to land at the airport anyway to go through customs. As soon as the customs people had realized who I was a guest of, they had practically brought out the welcome committee. The tropical storm hadn't been that bad, and most of the airport had opened back up. Once we had flown out to Mr. Martin's house, I was just ready to get to the hotel where Jessie was staying.

"Lark, what in the hell does your boss do for a living?" I asked.

Shortly after one phone call to Lark with the number that had come across on Jessie's first call, Lark had called me back with the name of the hotel where she was staying.

Lark let out a laugh. "He's in communications and a few other things. He does a ton of work down here for one of his…jobs."

I just looked at Lark. "Is it illegal?"

His smile dropped. "Hell no. You think I'd be involved with someone doing something illegal?"

"I don't know, Lark. Would you?"

He sat down on the sofa and glared at me. "Fuck no, I wouldn't, Scott. You just have to trust me. I can't say what all Mr. Martin does, but I give you my word as one of your best friends, it's all legal. He's a shrewd businessman, and he makes good investments."

I sat down in the chair opposite the sofa and took a good look at Lark. He was tall with light brown hair and green eyes. I wondered if the ladies still flocked all around him.

"Good enough for me. Do we have a car, so you can take me to the hotel?"

Lark smiled and nodded. He jumped up and called for someone.

A young kid who looked to only be about eighteen came walking into the room.

"Roads open and clear?" Lark asked.

"Yes, sir," the young gentleman said.

Lark looked at me and raised his eyebrows. "Ready to go and get your girl?"

Lark and I got out of the Mercedes Roadster, and as I looked back at the convertible, I had a very strong suspicion that Mr. Martin didn't make his money in communications only.

"Did you want to wait just in case, you know, I can't find her or something?" I said as the sick feeling in my stomach came back full force.

Lark was looking all around the lobby. It was almost like he was staking the place out. "I actually had Carlos follow us over here," he said as he handed me the keys to the Mercedes.

I just looked at him. *He doesn't think I'm going to drive an eighty-thousand-dollar car, does he?* "Dude, does your boss know you're offering up his Roadster?" I asked with a chuckle.

"Actually, that's my car. I come to Belize a lot when I'm not working with Skip."

"Skip?"

Lark smiled and then watched a girl walk by before he looked back at me. "Yeah, Mr. Martin. His nickname is Skip."

I rolled my eyes. I didn't want to know how or why Lark was the owner of such an expensive car. After college, Lark had spent a year in the Marines as an officer, but he had been medically discharged, and then he'd immediately begun working for Mr. Martin. He never did tell anyone what had gotten him discharged.

"Bring it back with a single scratch on it, and I'll kill you," he said with a wink.

I smiled. "Are you heading back to the house?" I asked.

Lark chortled. "Hell no. I'm going to say hi to that pretty little thing that just walked by." He gave me a wink and turned to walk toward the bar.

I sucked in a deep breath and slowly let it out. I spun around and walked toward the front desk. The young girl behind the desk smiled as I approached. I glanced down to her name tag and felt my stomach drop.

Chelsea. Ugh.

I gave her a smile and watched as her face turned a light pink.

"Good evening, sir. May I help you?" Chelsea asked as she looked me up and down.

"Yes, I got here as soon as I could after I found out about the storm. I'm looking for my girlfriend, Jessica Rhodes."

Her smile faded, and she started looking around before her eyes met mine again. "Um, you're Miss Rhodes's...boyfriend?"

The look in her eyes told me she was surprised.

Ah shit, Jessie must be with her friend.

"Can you tell me what room she's in? I'd like to surprise her."

She looked down at the floor and then back up at me. "Oh...I'm pretty sure she'll be surprised."

My heart dropped to my stomach, and all I wanted to do was walk away and go back to Texas. "Is that so?" I asked with a slightly forced smile.

She nodded and must have realized what she had said. "Oh, I mean, she's going to be happily surprised. Um…she's in cabana seven. Let me show you how to get there on the map. I don't think her cabana was one of those that flooded. It sits back a bit higher than the other ones."

After she showed me how to get to Jessie's cabana, she handed me the map, and I made my way down the path. Everything was still soaking wet from all the rain they had gotten from the tropical storm. I stopped and sent Drake a quick text message, letting him know that I'd arrived safely and I was on my way to Jessie's cabana.

I turned around the bend, and the first cabana came into sight. The small front porches faced out to the ocean. I thought about how nice it would have been to sit and watch the sunset with Jessie. I glanced down at the map and found that Jessie's cabana should be around the next tree.

I saw her the instant I rounded the tree. She was standing in front of a guy who was leaning up against the railing. I stopped dead in my tracks. He had his hand on the side of her face, and she was smiling at him. Her smile almost dropped me to my knees.

He's helping me get over Scott.

He must have said something to her because she let out a small laugh. I was frozen. I couldn't even muster the energy to turn and walk away. I watched as he pushed a piece of loose hair behind her ear before dropping his hand down to his side.

Jessie must have sensed someone watching them because she looked up, and her eyes captured mine. Her smile faded just a bit, and my heart started breaking all over again.

How stupid of me to come here. I knew I could possibly find her in the arms of another man, but now…now, my worst fears have come true.

She just stood there and stared at me. The prick turned and looked at me. One look at him, and I wanted to beat his fucking ass. I turned and started to walk back to the hotel lobby. I just needed to find Lark and have him fly me back to Texas. I would pay twice as much just to get me off this fucking island.

"Scott!" Jessie called out.

I picked up my pace and tried to get back to the car as fast as I could. "Scott, wait! Please wait."

Oh my god. I can't believe how stupid I was. Why did she leave a message and tell me she loved me when she's been with another man this whole time?

I heard her running up behind me. She grabbed on to my arm and pulled it, trying to get me to stop.

"Scott, please stop!"

I turned to see her beautiful eyes filled with nothing but sadness.

"Scott, what in the world are you doing here? How did you find me? I mean…how did you get here with the storm and all? I just called you yesterday."

I glanced up and saw the dirty rotten bastard standing down the pathway. I looked back at Jessie. "I got your message, but I guess I misunderstood."

She looked confused and shook her head. "What do you mean? Misunderstood what, Scott?"

I let out a gruff laugh. "The part when you said you loved me. I've been going crazy, not knowing where you were. When you told me you were in Belize, I knew I needed to get to you, but…" I glanced over to her *friend* and then quickly looked back at Jessie. "But I see your friend has done a pretty damn good job of helping you forget me."

I spun around and walked away as I heard her suck in a breath of air.

"Scott…no. *Please* don't walk away from me."

It sounded like she was crying, but I didn't care. I needed to get away from him…and her. I made my way back into the lobby and into the bar. I saw Lark still talking to the girl who he had followed into the bar.

I walked up to him and smiled at her. "Excuse me. Lark, I'm leaving, and I have no idea how to get back to the house."

"Oh no, dude. Did you find her?"

I nodded and looked away. "Yeah, can we just head back? I'll pay you double to take me back to Texas."

Lark stood up and reached for his wallet. He pulled out some cash and threw it onto the bar as he said his good-byes to the girl.

As we made our way out of the bar, I saw Jessie standing there.

"Scott, please don't leave me. *Please.*"

She walked up to me, and as she reached out to touch me, I took a step away from her.

She instantly threw her hands up to her mouth and started crying as she shook her head. "He's just a friend. Please don't do this. Please forgive me for running away. Scott, I thought that was you with Chelsea, and I just—"

"So, you know it wasn't me?" I asked her, watching as the tears rolled down her face.

She nodded.

"Your dad told you?"

She shook her head. "It just finally hit me. It couldn't have been you because I know you love me too much, and…the more I played it over and over in my head, the more I realized it wasn't your voice I'd heard calling out after me. I think I knew it all along in my heart. It just took my head a bit longer to catch up."

"I'll say, Jessie. It's been over a month. What about the postcard you sent to your dad? You said you'd met someone."

She started shaking her head again as she began crying harder. "No...oh god, no. I didn't mean it like that, Scott. I didn't mean that I'd found someone else. It's just...Trey was here because his fiancée had left him at the altar, and we started up a friendship. We both helped each other forget the hurt for a little while."

I felt the tears burning my eyes, and I did everything I could to hold them back. "How did he help you forget the hurt, Jessie? Did you go for walks along the beach? Or maybe romantic dinners out each night? What about a little bit of dancing under the stars? That should have been you and me, Jessie, not you and him."

The moment she looked into my eyes, I knew she felt more for this guy than she was admitting. I felt sick when I saw that look on her face. I turned and headed toward the car.

"Scott, stop!"

I kept going, but then Lark grabbed my arm to stop me.

"Dude, if you leave, make sure you know what you're walking away from."

I shook my head and went to move again when I heard Jessie trying to say something through her crying.

"Scott, I'm...I'm...pregnant."

I stopped dead in my tracks. *What? Pregnant? Oh. My. God.*

My legs started to buckle out from underneath me. Lark reached out and grabbed me as I tried to get my legs to work.

"Scott...oh my god!" Jessie called out.

I felt my legs go out, and Lark slowly let me go down to the ground. *She's pregnant. With my child or...*

Jessie ran up to me and dropped to her knees. "Scott, are you okay?"

I looked into her eyes, and I couldn't hold back my tears anymore. "Is...is it his baby or...or mine?" I asked.

The look on her face turned to one of pure shock, and then it was replaced with sadness. My whole world just stopped with that look, and all I wanted to do was sleep. I was so tired all of a sudden.

I'm so damn tired.

13 Jessie

The moment Scott asked me if the baby was his or Trey's, I wanted to throw up. *He thinks I've been sleeping with Trey. Oh god.* Then, the guilt of letting Trey kiss me and touch me swept over my whole body, and I was pretty sure Scott noticed it as well.

I shook my head as I felt a tear roll down my face. I tried to talk between my sobs. "It's your baby, Scott. I never…I never slept with Trey. I couldn't do that because…because I love you, Scott. I've always loved you, and I'll always love you. Even when I thought you had cheated with Chelsea…I couldn't. I love you too much."

I watched his face for any emotions of believing me. *Oh god…please believe me.*

"Is that why you called me? Because you found out you are pregnant?" Scott asked.

I watched the tears rolling down his face. *Oh. My. God. His heart has been broken, and it's all my fault because I ran away.*

You left him. You killed him.

"No! I called you before I found out. I called you because it hit me all at once…I knew it wasn't you with Chelsea. I was planning on coming home in a few days, but everything just kind of all clicked, and I had to talk to you. The second time I called you…" I thought about the two pregnancy tests that were still in my back pocket. I smiled and said, "I still didn't know. I just needed to hear your voice…to tell you how sorry I was for leaving…to say I love you."

Scott looked at me, confused. "When did you find out you're pregnant?"

I smiled and peeked up at Scott's friend. "Um…"

"Shit," Scott said as he started to stand up.

He reached his hand down and helped me up. The moment his hand touched mine, I felt that familiar feeling zip through my body. I instantly wanted him. I just wanted him to hold me and then slowly make love to me.

"I'm sorry…Jessie, this is Lark Williams. He's my best friend from college and the reason I was able to get here to you so fast," Scott said as he introduced me to his friend.

I looked Lark up and down. He was a bit taller than Scott and had messy light brown hair. I smiled and held out my hand. He took it and kissed the back of it while giving me a smile I was sure melted many hearts.

"You've had my boy here in knots for the past month, darling."

My smile faded, and I felt like I was going to throw up. I quickly looked at Scott. He was smiling at me with the goofiest smile on his face, and I couldn't help but giggle.

"Well, I guess I have a lot of making up to do, don't I?" I smiled at Scott, and then I turned to look at Lark.

When I glimpsed back at Scott, the look in his eyes caused my stomach to drop. He was looking at me with nothing but pure love…and his eyes were saying how much he wanted me.

Lark started laughing as he slapped Scott on the back. "I think you need to gather up your girl's things and bring her back to the house."

I looked between Scott and Lark. *House? What house? Whose house?*

Lark whispered something into Scott's ear, and the smile that spread across Scott's face made me weak in the knees.

"Baby, how fast can you pack up your stuff?"

I let out a chuckle. "Um…ten minutes? I have to check out though."

"I'll check out for you. Do you need help getting your stuff?"

I shook my head, and I felt my stomach dip when I thought about Trey. I needed to find him and say good-bye just in case I didn't see him before I left. For some reason, the thought of leaving Trey made me feel sad. We'd grown close as friends, and I was going to miss him.

Scott reached up and ran his knuckles down the side of my face. My face was on fire where his hand touched, and the love just poured into my body.

"You want to stay in your cabana?" Scott asked.

The image of Trey lying on top of me in the bed flashed through my mind. "No. No…I want to go somewhere else. I don't want to stay in there."

Scott looked at me with a questioning look, but then he gave me a weak smile. "Okay, baby. We'll meet you back here in ten minutes?"

I nodded. "Give me fifteen."

I reached up and brushed my lips against Scott's. He put his hand behind my neck and pulled me in closer as he deepened the kiss. I let out a small moan.

God, I've missed him so much.

Scott pulled back slightly and smiled against my lips. "God, I've missed you so damn much."

He put his forehead against mine, and I felt the sting of tears building in my eyes again.

I pulled back and grinned. "I'll go as fast as I can."

I took a few steps back and turned. As I quickly made my way back to the cabana, my heart was pounding in my chest. I had to tell Scott about what had happened between Trey and me. *I have to.*

I lifted my fingers and gently rubbed them against my lips. They were still tingling from Scott's kiss. I smiled as I thought about being with him, making love to him again after being away for so long.

I rounded a tree and saw Trey sitting on the steps to my cabana. He jumped up when he saw me.

"What happened?" he asked as he walked up to me.

He went to take me into his arms, but I put my hand up to stop him.

"Trey, please…I have to go pack up my things, but I'm so glad you're here. I wanted to say thank you so much for being such an amazing friend and for helping me these last few weeks."

Trey's whole body slumped. "So, that's it? He comes here, and you're just going to leave with him? Just like that, and what we had stops?"

My whole body started shaking. "Yes! Trey, I love Scott. I've never been dishonest with you about my feelings, especially my feelings toward you."

Trey ran his hand through his hair as he shook his head. "I see how you look at me, Jessie. You say you only want to be friends, but I know you care about me more than that."

I felt heat move up into my face. "Trey—"

"No. I waited for you. You asked for time, and I gave you time. I stayed away from my family and waited. I waited for you to get over that prick, and then he just swoops in here and takes you from me."

The anger I was feeling surprised me. "*What?* I didn't ask you to stay here! I didn't keep you away from anyone. I told you I love him, and yes…yes, he can swoop in here because we love each other, and we're having a baby together. He isn't taking me from you because I was never yours in the first place. I've always been his."

Trey gave me a weak smile. "You got that right." He turned and started to walk away.

I couldn't let him leave like this. "Trey, wait, please."

He kept walking.

"Trey!"

He stopped and slowly turned around. I walked up to him, and I did the one thing I knew I shouldn't do. I reached up and brushed my lips against his. It started off as a simple, innocent kiss, but Trey attempted to turn it into a more passionate one before I pushed him away.

"Trey, *please*…I love him more than life itself." I looked up into his eyes.

He reached down and wiped away the tears rolling down my face.

"I'll let you go…but only because I've fallen in love with you, Jess. You'll always hold a special place in my heart—always. Good-bye, love."

He took a step back and gave me that smile of his. Then, he turned and walked away. I watched him for a few seconds before I quickly ran into my cabana.

I looked around at all the things Trey and I had collected throughout our time here on the island. I didn't need…or want any of it. I reached for my bag and quickly put all my clothes in there. I walked over to the bed and reached under it. I grabbed my shoebox and put it into my bag. I looked around and saw the shell that Trey had bought me sitting on the table. I picked it up. I thought back to the day when we had gone on the tour of the ruins and how much fun we'd had. Trey had found this shell in one of the stores we had gone through. He'd bought two, one for me and one for him.

When you look at this seashell, you'll always think of me and our time here in Belize, love.

I gently set it back down on the table. I looked over at the bed and closed my eyes. *Please don't let Scott hate me. Please, God. Please let him forgive me.*

I put my hand on my stomach and forced the tears to stop. After going into the bathroom, I quickly wiped my face, and then I splashed some water on it. I fixed my hair into a ponytail, and then I went back into the bedroom to grab my bag. I left the room and headed back to the lobby of the hotel.

I didn't look back once. I just wanted to forget that the last five weeks had ever happened. What happened on this island was going to stay on this island.

I was going home with Scott, and we were going to have a baby together. Trey would always have a special place in my heart, but my heart belonged to Scott.

Forever.

I slowly sank down on the sofa and let out a long breath. I turned my head and looked down the hall at Josh sneaking out of the babies' bedroom. When he turned and saw me, the smile that spread across his face instantly caused me to giggle.

I think Josh had more fun today than Libby and Will did.

He walked into the living room, and after he sat down, he pulled my legs over his lap. He took off my shoes and began massaging my feet.

"Ah…god, that feels *so* good." I threw my head back.

Just Josh touching me felt like heaven.

We sat there for a few minutes without saying anything. I finally looked at him and smiled. He smiled back and gave me a wink.

"I think Libs and Will had fun on their first Christmas today. Don't you? I mean, they didn't really know what was going on, but with all the shit Mom and Dad bought for them, I think their little minds were very stimulated." Josh said with a chuckle.

I smiled as I slid my right leg up and began moving my foot across his lap. I slowly licked my lips. "I know something that needs to be…stimulated."

The look in Josh's eyes dropped my stomach in an instant. He pushed my legs off of him, and then he crawled over and began kissing me.

"Jesus, Heather. You drive me insane with lust, do you know that?"

I smiled as I nodded. "I have surprise number two."

Josh pulled back and looked at me funny. "What?"

"Do you remember the first time you ever tied me up? I told you that I had two surprises for you."

He slowly smiled. "Oh yeah…the first one was my parents moving here. I totally forgot about the second surprise. What is it?"

I bit down on my lip, thinking back to that day when Josh and I had played a bit more. He'd tied me up, and he'd even let me tie him up once. I'd had this gift since then, and it had taken everything I had to keep it until Christmas.

"It's upstairs," I said.

He reached over and pulled my lip out from my teeth. Then, he leaned over and kissed me so sweetly.

"One more present for me, huh?" Josh raised his eyebrows up and down.

I let out a small laugh. "Yep!" I said, popping the P.

Josh slowly stood and then reached down for my hand. He pulled me up and into his arms, and he began kissing my neck.

"I've got one more present for you, too, baby," he whispered against my neck.

My heart started pounding. *Ah…the things he does to my body. I can't even control it anymore. I'm absolutely his…body and soul.*

"You want your present first? Or do you want to give me mine?" he asked with such a breathy voice.

The sound of it practically made me tell him to have his way with me right then and there.

I looked at him. "Depends. Will your gift lead to mad, passionate sex?"

Josh's smile grew bigger. "Will yours?" he asked with the cutest damn smile ever.

I nodded. "Oh yeah."

He tilted his head as he closed one eye and stared at me. "Okay…I'm thinking that we just say to hell with my gift and get straight to your gift, princess."

I let out a laugh and shook my head. "No. I want your gift first."

He took a step back, and his smile faded for a brief second. He turned and walked over toward the Christmas tree. He reached in and pulled out a small box. I grinned, knowing he must have hidden that there just today. I'd been searching the tree every day since we'd put it up.

Josh took my hand and led me over to the fireplace. It was slowly going out, but he started to sit down on the floor, so I followed him. When he did things like this, it made me feel like a little girl again.

"Today was probably one of the best days of my life, Heather. I loved spending Christmas with Gunner, Ellie, Jeff, Ari, and everyone else. Then, we were able to come home and spend time with Mom and Dad."

I nodded. "It was the best Christmas of my life. It was our babies' first Christmas."

"It's not over yet, princess. I knew you would be sad with your mom and dad not here, especially with this being the kids' first Christmas."

I looked away as I felt tears building in my eyes. Josh took his finger and turned my chin toward him.

"I wanted this gift to mean something for you. I hope you like it, princess."

As he handed me the gift, my hands started to shake. I carefully untied the bow and then began to take off the wrapping paper. I looked up into Josh's eyes every so often, and the love I saw there just seared into my soul.

I removed the blue velvet box and slowly opened it. I let out a gasp when I saw the necklace. I reached in and took it out. There were three hearts, and each had writing on it. The biggest heart said, *Forever in my heart.*

One of the smaller hearts said, *Will,* and the other said, *Libby.* I moved the smaller hearts to see a small round charm with *J & H* inscribed on it.

"Look on the back of the one with our initials," Josh said.

I turned it over to read, *I'll love you for infinity.*

My heart didn't know whether to be sad or happy. I looked up, and Josh gave me a small smile. He leaned over and kissed my tear-soaked cheek. I tried to talk, but my voice caught in my throat as I gazed into Josh's eyes.

How could I love him any more than I do at this very moment?

"Josh...this is so beautiful, and I don't even—"

"Shh...just tell me you like it."

I peeked down at the necklace in my hand and then back at him. "I love it. Oh, Josh, it's so perfect."

I threw myself into his arms and started crying. He pulled me onto his lap and held me while I let it all out.

Today had been so hard for me. It was our first Christmas as a married couple, the kids' first Christmas, and another Christmas without my parents.

When I finally settled down, I felt chills running up and down my back from where Josh was moving his hand. I instantly thought of his gift, and I could practically feel myself getting wet. I pulled back and looked at him with the most smoldering look I could muster.

"What's wrong, baby? Why are you making that face?"

I rolled my eyes. *Epic fail on the smoldering look, Heather.* I let out a laugh. "You want your gift now?"

"Hell yeah, I do," Josh said.

He lifted me out of his lap. We both stood and made our way upstairs. I set my necklace down on the dresser and turned to look at my husband. He was standing there, like a kid waiting to see what Santa had brought him. I grinned at my thought of Santa.

"Okay, go sit down on the bed and give me a few minutes," I said with a wink.

I walked into the closet and opened up my T-shirt drawer. I pulled out the Santa outfit and smiled. I quickly undressed and started to slip on the red thigh-high stockings. The touch of innocence from the black-and-white bows on the top of each stocking made me smile. I pulled on the red silk panties. The small white trim was perfect on them, and I couldn't believe how sexy they made me feel. Then, I put on the red bustier. The girl at the store had shown me how to get it on without anyone's help, but it was still a pain in the ass.

"Heather? What in the hell are you doing in there? Still shopping for it?" Josh called out.

I rolled my eyes and smiled. "Give me two more minutes."

I put on the black belt, and then I turned and looked in the mirror. The white trim at the top of the bustier matched the white trim on the panties. I slipped on the red high heels and quickly threw my hair up into a sloppy bun with pieces hanging down. I bent down and pulled the box out from behind the stack of blankets. I smiled as I looked at the perfectly wrapped present.

Oh my god, I can't believe I'm going to do this.

When I had asked Ari for her help a few months back, I'd thought she would pass out from screaming for so long. Before I'd known it, we had been sitting in front of her computer, ordering a Dare Me Pleasure Set from Lelo.com.

I took a deep breath and slowly opened the closet doors. Josh was lying back on the bed with his arm over his eyes. When he tilted his head up, his mouth dropped open. I was standing there in my sexy Santa outfit, holding his present.

"Holy shit, you look…you look…"

I tried so hard not to blush…or laugh at his expression. He was speechless, and I was silently thanking Ari for talking me into getting this outfit.

"I look…like what, Josh?" I said in a purr. *Oh yeah…I'm getting this sexy shit down.*

Josh looked me up and down as he licked his lips. "My god…you take my breath away, princess." He stood and walked toward me. He stopped just short of me. "Turn around, Heather," he whispered in a deep voice.

A chill ran up and down my body at the sound of his voice. I placed the gift on the dresser and then slowly turned around, stopping once to look over my shoulder at him, until I came back full circle.

Josh started taking off his shirt, and I began panting heavily as I moved my eyes all over his body. The sight of him with his shirt off still drove me insane with lust. Sometimes, I just couldn't believe he was mine.

He took a few steps toward me. He looked down and smiled. "I like the bows."

I let out a giggle. "So do I."

He glanced up, and his eyes landed on my breasts that were practically falling out of the bustier. He ran his finger in between my cleavage, and I let out a small moan.

"Motherfucker," he whispered.

He reached up, took a piece of my hair hanging down, and ran it along his fingers. Then, his hand went behind my neck, and he pulled me to him as he leaned down and kissed me. The passion in his kiss was pushing me to the edge of pleasure. Both of his hands went into my hair, and he grabbed it before pulling my head back, breaking our kiss.

"Heather, you are so damn sexy. I just want to be inside you and stay there all night."

All I could do was whisper, "Yes."

He reached down and picked me up as he began kissing me again. He walked me over and gently put me down on the bed.

"You look so fucking hot in that outfit, princess…but I really can't wait to slowly peel it off of you."

I rubbed my legs together to ease the throbbing in between them. Then, I remembered the gift. I sat up quickly. "Oh wait! My gift."

I put my finger in my mouth and tried to give him the most seductive, innocent look I could as I walked over and grabbed the present I had set down on the dresser. Then, I came and sat down on the edge of the bed. He dropped to his knees in front of me and put his head on my lap.

"Are you trying to kill me, Heather? Because if you keep doing shit like that, the only thing I'm going to take off is your panties before I bury myself deep inside you."

"Oh, um…Merry Christmas, baby," was all I could manage to get out of my mouth as I handed him the gift.

Jesus, how can things still be this hot between us? I want him so much I can hardly stand it.

Josh looked at me, confused. "You want me to open the gift *now*, Heather?"

I nodded. Josh sat on the bed next to me and started to unwrap the present. First, he picked up the black box that had *Dare Me Pleasure Set* written in white with the word *Lelo* under it. Josh looked at me and tilted his head.

"Open it," I said as I felt my breathing getting heavier.

The moment he opened the lid, I heard him let out a gasp.

"Holy shit…"

He snapped his head at me, and the smile that spread across his face erased all my fears. He slowly started taking the items out of the box. The first thing was silk handcuffs. He looked at me as he raised his eyebrows, and I felt the blush instantly hit my cheeks.

Then, he pulled out the Ben Wa Balls. He peeked back up at me and said, "What in the hell are these?"

I laughed. "I'll show you later."

The next thing to come out was a suede whip.

"I think this is the best Christmas gift I've ever gotten." Josh gave me that panty-melting smile of his as he set the box down. He looked back into the larger gift box and pulled out the last gift. It was a purple vibrator with a clitoris stimulator and a silk blindfold. "Mother of God…this is by far *the* best damn Christmas gift *ever*," he said.

"You like it all? Is it too much?" I asked as I looked away from him and down to the floor.

He reached over and turned my face up toward him. "You just made me the happiest man on Earth. Now, let's get you out of that Santa outfit and play for a bit, shall we?"

I'd never been so damn horny in my life. The idea of Josh using any of those things on me had me wanting to rip off the Santa outfit. Josh got off the bed and kneeled in front of me.

He began slipping off my red shoes. "It's kind of a shame. I like these on you. You'll have to wear them again," he said in a low voice.

My whole body trembled. "Okay," I said, like an idiot.

Josh let out a small laugh. He oh-so slowly started to take off the thigh-highs. "Heather, my goals in this life are to always make you happy…to make you feel safe…and most importantly, to make you feel pleasure beyond your wildest dreams."

Oh my…

"Your love means more to me than anything," he said.

We stood, and he slowly started to pull down my red panties as he covered my body in gentle kisses.

"I need you like the stars need the moon. You're the light in my darkness. You are my inspiration for everything I do in my life. Just one look in your eyes, and I feel your love for me. My heart practically bursts with how much I love you."

My hands started to shake as he turned me around. He took his time taking off the bustier, and he began kissing my back.

"You're so beautiful, inside and out, and I'd be lost without you, princess."

I turned around, and my eyes immediately landed on his lips.

"Lie down on the bed, baby."

I can't breathe. I slowly backed up and sat on the bed before lying down. I closed my eyes and tried to calm my breathing. *God, please don't let one of the twins wake up. Please!*

I kept my eyes closed and jumped when I felt Josh moving the silk cuffs up my body.

"Put your hands up above your head."

"Josh…" I whispered.

I kept my eyes closed as he restrained my hands, attaching the cuffs to our headboard.

"I can't wait to make you come, Heather…over and over again."

I snapped my eyes open and looked at him.

He smiled. "Please tell me you charged this," he said as he held up the vibrator.

My chest began moving up and down. *Oh god.* I was about to come just from the way he was looking at me. I slowly nodded my head.

"I think we'll play with only these two things for tonight," Josh said.

I licked my lips as I couldn't seem to find my voice. Finally, I cleared my throat and said, "Okay."

Josh reached his hand over and began playing with my breast. Then, he turned on the vibrator and touched it to my nipple.

I arched my back and let out a loud moan. "Oh god...Josh...oh my..."

The moment his fingers entered my body, I felt the pressure building.

"Jesus, Heather. You're so wet."

Josh moved up and kissed me on the lips. Our kiss quickly turned more passionate. It was like we couldn't get enough of each other. Josh moved to lie down next to me, and then I felt the vibrator. First, it hit my clit before he took it lower, and then he slowly pushed it inside me.

I pulled my lips away from his and about came off the bed. "Oh my god!"

"Heather..." Josh whispered. He moved his head down and started sucking on my nipple.

The orgasm that was building was unbelievable. *Oh my god.* I could hardly take it.

Josh began moving the vibrator in and out...faster. Then, he turned it up more. I started to pull at the restraints. I needed to touch him.

Oh god. Something about being tied up was making it so much hotter.

"God, baby...you look sexy as fuck," Josh said.

I came undone. I tried to turn my head into my pillow to hide my screams of pleasure. *Oh. Good. God.* I'd never felt such an intense orgasm. *What is happening to me?* It felt like my orgasm was going on forever.

"Josh...oh god, stop. I can't take it anymore," I begged.

Josh slowly pulled out the vibrator, undid the cuffs, and started to move on top of me.

"No!" I yelled out.

He instantly stopped. "What? Oh shit...did I hurt you?"

I smiled as I sat up and slid out from underneath him. I pushed him down on the bed and smiled. *I can do this.* I'd been practicing, so I knew my gag reflex had gotten so much better. I slowly moved into position, and then I saw the look in Josh's eyes when he realized what I was about to do.

"Heather..."

I quickly took him into my mouth, and Josh jumped.

"Jesus, Heather...*fuck.*"

I smiled as I slowly moved up and down. I ran my tongue along him just like Ari had told me to, and Josh kept letting out moan after moan.

"Oh god, Heather..."

As I took him a little deeper, I heard Josh suck in a breath of air. I started to go faster as I moved my hand along the bottom of his shaft.

Motherfucker…my cheeks are starting to kill me! I don't think I can do it much more.

Then, I remembered Ari's tip—*hum…the vibration will drive him to the edge!*

I started to hum just like she'd told me as I exposed my teeth just a little.

"Heather…baby, stop. I'm going to come. Move unless you want me coming in your mouth, baby."

I sucked just a little harder, and then I heard Josh come undone. The moment I felt the warm, salty liquid hit the back of my throat, I wanted to throw up. *Shit! Shit! Shit! Oh god…oh my god! It's nasty as hell. Swallow, Heather…oh god, just swallow it!*

I quickly pulled away and leaned over the bed. I started spitting that nasty shit out. Then, I started gagging. I got up and ran into the bathroom. I quickly turned on the water and started rinsing out my mouth. I heard Josh laughing as he walked up behind me.

"Holy hell. That shit is *nasty!*" I opened up the mouthwash and went to town. *Ugh!*

I leaned down and spit it out, and then Josh grabbed me and turned me around. The goofy look on his face caused me to laugh.

"My god…do you know how much I love you?"

I shook my head. "How much?"

"So much that it's endless."

"Even though I suck at blow jobs? I did get you to come this time though," I said with a triumphant grin.

The look in Josh's eyes turned from excitement to lust. He pushed a strand of hair behind my ear as he leaned down and lightly kissed me.

"I love you, princess. I love you so much."

I smiled against his lips. "I love you more plus infinity. I'm going to go check on the little ones."

"Hurry back," he whispered against my lips.

I went down and checked on the twins, and then I grabbed a bottle of wine and two glasses. I made my way back upstairs, and I smiled the whole time, thinking about Josh using the vibrator on me.

I came to a stop when I saw him standing in the doorway to the bathroom. I looked his body up and down and let out a small moan. *Holy hell, this man is breathtaking.*

Josh walked up to me and took the wine and glasses out of my hands. He set them on the dresser, and then pulled me into the bathroom where he pushed me against the sink. He lifted me up, and I wrapped my legs around him. He brought me down on him, and we both moaned as he slowly sank into me.

He moved his lips to my neck and up along my jawline before stopping right below my ear. "I'm gonna fuck you now, baby."

I threw my head back and closed my eyes. *God, it drives me crazy when he talks like that.*

"Oh...feels so good," I whispered.

I put my hands on either side of the sink and let myself go as my husband took me to heaven and back again. This time, I didn't even care who could hear my screams of pleasure.

15 Josh

I carried Heather over to our bed and gently laid her down on it. She looked spent and kept whispering how much she loved me. I loved it when we made sweet, passionate love, but doing what we had just done was so fucking hot. I couldn't get enough of this woman.

I covered her up and leaned down to kiss her lips. "I love you, princess."

"Hmm…"

I smiled as I grabbed the vibrator. I took it into the bathroom where I cleaned it off and put it up in the cabinet. I shook my head as I thought about my sweet, innocent wife buying a pleasure kit for my Christmas present…and then I thought back to the blow job. I had to laugh, thinking about the look on her face as she'd spat my come out of her mouth. I turned back toward the bedroom, leaned against the doorjamb, and watched her sleep.

Damn, I'm one lucky son of a bitch.

My phone went off with a text message. I looked at the clock. It was almost midnight. *Wonder who that could be on Christmas night?*

I walked over and grabbed my phone. I saw it was a text message from Scott. Drake had told me earlier that he had heard from Jessie and that she was in Belize. Scott knew someone who had taken him there even though a storm had just passed through the area.

I opened up the text and read it.

> *Scott: Got my girl and the most amazing Christmas gift ever. I'll fill y'all in when we get home. Thanks, guys, for always being there for me. —S*

I shook my head. It was about fucking time Jessie had gotten in touch with him, and they'd worked it out. I hadn't thought Scott would be able to take it much longer if he hadn't heard from her soon.

I reached for my boxers and pulled them on, and then I grabbed a T-shirt and made my way downstairs. I walked into the kitchen, opened the refrigerator, and grabbed a beer. Then, I made my way to the twins' room. I slowly opened the door and peeked in. Libby was making the sweetest sounds, so I walked in and looked down into her crib. She was lying there with her eyes wide open, looking up at the stars glowing on the ceiling. I smiled as she looked over at me.

"Hey, baby girl. Can't sleep either, huh?"

I turned and looked into Will's crib. He was out like a light.

That's my boy.

I set my beer down, and then I reached in and picked up Libby. I grabbed my beer and made my way out to the living room. I put the beer down on the end table, and I sat in the chair next to the fireplace.

"You hungry, baby? Or do you just want company?" I asked in a whispered voice.

She let out a giggle that caused a warm feeling to run through my whole body. I looked into her eyes as she stared back into mine. Her beautiful blue eyes caused me to catch my breath every time.

"Do you know how much you look like your mommy? So beautiful. I can't believe you're really mine, little princess. Yep, you're my little princess. Don't tell mommy 'cause she was kind of my first princess."

It was almost like Libby could understand me because she let out another giggle.

"I love your mommy so much. I love you and Will, too, but your mommy…she's my everything. She makes me so happy. Her smile…oh man, her smile is my undoing. If she smiled at me the right way, I think I'd do whatever it was she asked." I laughed and kissed Libby on her forehead. "Kind of like you. I'm pretty sure you're gonna have your daddy wrapped around your little finger."

I got up and started moving around as I kept talking to the other girl in my world. "It's not just her smile. It's her sweet heart. I hope that you get your mommy's heart, Libby. She's so unselfish, and she'd do anything for her friends or me. She amazes me every day. Your grandpa and grandma did such a good job in raising her. I wish we could have met them because I'd love to thank them. If it wasn't for their love, you and Will wouldn't be here, and I wouldn't have the most amazing woman sleeping so sweetly upstairs. Now, don't get worried. You'll always be my number one little girl, I promise…but your mommy…she'll always be my everything."

I slowly rocked Libby, and I could tell she was starting to fall asleep. As I began to dance with my daughter, I tried to imagine what it would be like when she got older. I never wanted her heart to be broken…*ever.* I was going to have to make sure her brother knew how to threaten any boy who even looked at his sister in the wrong way.

I began to hum to her when I heard her little breathing getting softer. I glanced up and saw Heather sitting on the steps. I noticed tears rolling down her face as she smiled at me. I smiled back and started to walk toward her. She stood up and gently put her hand on Libby's back as she leaned in and smelled her. She was always smelling them both. She'd said she loved their baby smell, and she'd even refused to wash a few of their outfits, so she would have the smell always.

"Is she asleep?" she whispered.

I nodded and gestured toward the bedroom. After entering their room, I walked up to the crib, gently laid Libby down, and covered her up. I quietly shut the door and turned, and then Heather threw herself into my arms.

I held her as I felt her sobbing. "Baby, what's wrong?" I moved my hand up and down her body.

She had thrown on one of my T-shirts, and there was nothing sexier than her wearing only my shirt.

"I just love you so much. I love you, Josh Hayes."

She pulled back, and the look in her eyes about brought me to my knees.

"Josh, will you please make love to me?" she asked.

I smiled as I gently picked her up and kissed her. She tasted like heaven.

"Yes, princess," I said as I carried her back up to our bedroom.

After laying her down on the bed, I slowly crawled on top of Heather. I took in every inch of her beautiful body with my hands. I just wanted to touch every square inch of her. I'd never gone so slowly while making love to Heather before, but I just wanted it to last forever. I wanted to stay like this with her, connected together.

Then, she grabbed my arms and threw her head back. I could practically feel her squeezing my dick. I leaned down and took her lips with mine as we both came together. Nothing would ever feel better than making love to my wife and then seeing the love in her eyes as she smiled at me.

"That was amazing, Josh."

I kissed her nose and gently pulled myself out of her. I rolled over and lay next to her. She rolled onto her side and started running her fingers through my hair.

"Thank you," she said.

I looked over at her and laughed. "Thank you, princess. I swear to God, it gets more amazing every time."

She shook her head. "No...I mean, thank you for what you said to Libby."

I closed my eyes and then opened them again. "How much did you hear?"

"All of it. I started to come downstairs, but then I heard you talking to her, so I stopped and listened to you. You're my everything, too, Josh, and I don't know what I would do if I didn't have you and the twins. I feel so blessed that it's not even funny."

I nodded. Then, I thought about Scott and Jessie. I hadn't told Heather that I'd heard from him. "I got a text from Scott. He said he was with

Jessie, and he had gotten the best Christmas present ever. What do you think he meant?" I pushed a piece of her hair out of her eyes.

She took a deep breath. "Probably just getting Jess back, maybe? I just can't believe Jessie left us all hanging like that. I'm kind of pissed at her."

I let out a chuckle. Ari had said the same thing to Jeff and me earlier. Ellie was so mad at Jessie that she'd told Gunner to keep Jessie away for at least a week after she got home.

"I kind of feel sorry for Jessie. Y'all are mad at her. She's not going to get a very good welcome home."

Heather smiled. "No…no, she's not. So, Scott better make sure he gives her one!"

I laughed. "Oh, believe me, I'm sure he intends to."

As Heather snuggled in next to me and drifted off to sleep, I tried to shake the bad feeling I was having. A part of me didn't think that everything would be going back to normal.

I closed my eyes and thanked God for the girl in my arms and for the babies sleeping downstairs. Then, I prayed for my friends to be happy and for the feeling in my gut about Jessie and Scott to be wrong.

16 Scott

Jessie had hardly spoken two words during the entire drive up to Mr. Martin's house. After a quick tour of the house, Lark showed us to the guesthouse, which I swore was almost the size of my house.

I couldn't shake the unnerving feeling I had. Jessie seemed to be uncomfortable around me.

Does she really believe it wasn't me?

Maybe once we were finally alone, it would be better. I shut the door and turned to see Jessie standing there, staring at me. My heart started pounding.

"Did you want to call your dad or anything, honey?" I asked as I noticed the look in her eyes change.

The next thing I knew, she was slamming into me and holding on to me so tightly. Then, she began sobbing.

"Jessie…baby, please don't cry. I'm so sorry all this happened. It took everything out of me not to kill Bryce and Chelsea. I'm so sorry, baby, that she hurt you and caused you to—"

She pulled back and looked at me with tears streaming down her face. She looked down and said, "Run away? Because that's what I did, and I'll never forgive myself for it. *Never.*"

I shook my head and tilted her chin up to make her look at me. "I love you, Jessie. I'm not going to lie and say that the past five weeks were okay because they weren't. I was dying a slow death when you were gone."

She sucked in a breath of air and started shaking her head as she began crying harder. "I'm so sorry. I should have talked to you instead of running away like an idiot and—"

I pulled her to me. "Shh…it's over now, baby. We're together now, and you know the truth. Jessie…as God as my witness, I promise you that I'll never be unfaithful to you…*ever.* I'm yours, body and soul. And now…now, we're going to have a baby."

She buried her face in my chest and just kept repeating how much she loved me. She finally looked up and said, "Please…I just need you so much. I need you to hold me…I need you to make love to me, Scott. I've missed you so much."

My heart was breaking. She looked so sad, and I knew she was feeling guilty for leaving and for being gone for so long. I reached down and gently moved my lips across hers as she let out the sweetest moan ever. Just the idea that she was carrying my child caused my heart to practically burst with happiness.

She reached her hands up and ran her fingers through my hair. She pulled on it as she bit down on my lower lip.

Oh god, I want her so much. "Jessie…I've missed you so damn much," I whispered against her lips.

"Touch me, Scott…please just touch me."

I put my hands on either side of her face and deepened our kiss. I was going to go slow with my lovemaking. It had been too long since I had been with her, and I needed her to know how much I wanted her. She had come back to me, and that was all that mattered right now. I slowly started walking her backward until she hit the bed. The windows were open, and all I could hear were the waves crashing on the shore.

I pulled my lips away and whispered, "I love you, Jessie. I love you to the moon and back."

I watched as a tear slowly made its way down her cheek. I used my thumb to brush it away. I moved my hands and began taking off her T-shirt. She stood there, chewing on her lower lip, and I didn't think my dick could get any harder than it was. Then, I placed my hand on her stomach as I dropped to my knees. I kissed her on the stomach and looked up at her. Her head was back, and she was touching her breasts. I wanted to rip off her damn clothes…but slowly. I needed to go slow.

I looked back at her stomach and said, "Best Christmas present ever."

"Scott…oh god, I love you so much."

I began to unbutton her jeans, and then I slid them down her legs…oh-so slowly. She lifted one leg and then the other as I pulled off her pants. I glanced up her body. She had on a pair of blue boy shorts and a white lace bra.

My god, she's so damn beautiful. The thought of her stomach growing bigger with my child sent shivers through my body.

I began kissing her body as I stood up. She had her hands in my hair, and the little noises she was making were making it harder for me to go slow.

"Scott…" she whispered over and over.

I began kissing her gently as I unhooked her bra and slipped it off her shoulders. I cupped her breasts in my hands and squeezed gently.

"Oh god…they're so tender," she said as she snapped her head straight and looked me in the eyes.

"I want to kiss them, baby…can I kiss them?" I licked my lips.

She smiled and nodded. The moment I put her nipple in my mouth, I reached my hand into her panties and brushed my fingers against her.

My god, her panties are so wet. I stopped sucking on her one nipple and made my way over to the other one. "Jesus, Jessie, baby…"

"Yes…oh god, yes."

I slipped two fingers inside her and started gently moving them in and out.

"Scott…my god…I feel like I'm going to come."

I stopped my fingers.

She immediately grabbed on to my shirt and called out, "No! Please don't stop."

"Hmm…I don't want you to come yet, baby. Lie down on the bed, Jess."

The look in her eyes was driving me insane. She quickly moved and lay down on the bed. Her whole body was shaking. I began to take off my clothes.

Slowly.

She locked her eyes on mine, and I swore she was peering into my soul. I'd never in my life loved her as much as I did at this very moment. As I took off my jeans and boxers, I watched her eyes move down and lock on to my rock-hard dick. When she licked her lips, I let out a growl, and her eyes snapped back up to mine. I gently made my way onto the bed and hovered over her.

"Scott…I want you inside me so badly. I just need to feel you close to me. *Please.*"

As much as I wanted to just slam myself into her, I forced myself to smile and wink at her. "Oh, baby, don't worry…I plan on burying myself so deep inside you that you'll know I've been there for the next few days."

She closed her eyes and lifted her body up to me as she threw her head back. She sucked in a breath of air as she brought her hands up and touched her breasts.

"*Please.* I can't stand it any longer."

A part of me wanted her to beg me. I wanted her to know how I'd felt all those weeks when she had left me alone…wondering where she was and what she was doing…and who she was with.

I moved down and kissed right above her clit. She let out a gasp as she put her hands in my hair and began pushing me down. I couldn't help but let out a small laugh.

"Oh, baby…have you missed my touch?" I asked.

She began thrashing her head back and forth as I started to blow on her clit. I quickly ran my tongue over it, and she let out a small scream.

"Oh god…Scott. *Yes!* Yes…I've missed your touch and your smile. I've missed your laugh. I've missed the way you hold me and kiss me. I've missed making love to you. *Fuck!* Jesus…I've missed being with you…"

That was all I needed to hear. I placed my lips on her clit and began sucking as I put three fingers inside her.

"Ah...oh...oh my god! Yes! Scott...I'm going to come...oh god, yes! That. Feels. So. Amazing." Then, she began calling out my name over and over.

The rush of wetness was more than I could take. I pulled my lips away and took my fingers out. I moved up and barely pushed my dick inside her.

"Scott! Please...oh god, please. More."

I slowly pushed myself into her warm body. I lowered my head and let out a moan against her neck. "Motherfucker...you feel so damn good."

"Oh..." was all she could say as she brought me in closer to her.

It was like she couldn't get me in her deep enough. I began moving in and out, and she let out the most amazing noises.

I began thrusting harder in her. "I missed you, Jessie. Don't. Ever. Leave. Me. Again," I said with each thrust into her.

"Never!"

I'm not going to last long. Oh god, I've missed her.

"Harder, Scott. Please go faster and harder."

I gave her what she asked for. "Talk to me, Jessie...promise me that you'll always talk to me," I said as I slammed myself into her harder.

I wanted her to feel me...to feel how much she was mine.

"I will...I promise. God, I promise you..."

The moment she began calling out my name with her orgasm, I couldn't hold off any longer.

"Jessie...baby, I'm gonna come."

"Yes! Scott...it feels so good."

I swore I could feel every ounce of me pour into her. After I finally caught my breath, I just held myself slightly off her body. I was still inside her, not wanting to move. I just wanted to stay inside her warm body.

"I love you so much. Don't ever leave me again, Jessie," I said as I kissed along her neck.

"Scott, oh god, I love you. I love you so much, and I'm so sorry for everything."

I slowly moved myself off of her, and then I lay down next to her. I rolled her against me, and we faced the giant window overlooking the beach.

I closed my eyes and thanked God for her and for the baby and for finally bringing us together again.

Finally...things are going to be okay because we are together again.

17 Jessie

As I listened to Scott breathing in and out, I was overcome with a sense of relief that we were together again. He had made such sweet, passionate love to me. I reached my hand up and ran my fingers along my swollen lips. I closed my eyes and could practically feel his lips on me.

Then, the sheet of guilt swept over my body. I opened my eyes and looked out to the ocean.

Talk to me, Jessie…promise me that you'll always talk to me.

My heart started pounding in my chest, and I fought the urge to start crying again. *I have to tell him what happened. If I don't…it will eat me alive.*

I slowly moved Scott's arm off of me and rolled over to look at him. *I can't believe he got his friend to bring him here…on a helicopter of all things!* My heart swelled, knowing he had come for me as soon as he'd found out where I had been.

I closed my eyes and thought of Chelsea. I wanted to kill her for doing this to us. She'd pushed me away from him. If I hadn't been so damn scared, I would have called my father weeks ago, and I would have found out the truth, and I would have never, ever kissed Trey…or let him touch me…or let him make me feel the way he'd made me feel.

Oh god, please let him forgive me. Please.

I peeked up and saw it was just after six in the morning. Scott and I had made love three times throughout the night. Each time had been so different. The first time was almost a blur. I just knew how much I'd needed his touch and needed to feel his love. The second time was hotter than hell. I had gotten up to take a shower, and the next thing I'd known, Scott had been fucking me up against the wall with the hot water just pouring on us. The third time was the most amazing. I swore Scott had kissed every inch of my body. He'd moved so slow and sweet while he'd whispered the most romantic things in my ear. I'd never had so many orgasms in one night.

I heard Scott's cell phone buzz on the table. I stood up and grabbed his shirt. I slipped it over my head as I walked over and picked up his phone. I saw it was a message from my dad. I thought about how angry he had been when I'd talked to him last night. *Ugh…I'm going to have to hear it from him when I get back. He's going to lay into me about how I walked away from the vet clinic…and how I could have walked away from the love of my life.*

I moved across the room over to the giant sliding glass door and watched the sky light up. So much had happened in the last two months, and at the same time, I felt like my life had been at a standstill. I ran my hand down my body and felt my tender breasts. Then, I placed my hand on my stomach.

The moment I felt Scott's hands over mine, the butterflies took off in my stomach. I leaned back against him and smiled.

"I missed you," he whispered.

The tears began building. "I missed you, too."

"Did you want to try to leave today? Or would you like to stay a few days?" he asked as he held me closer to him.

The moment I felt his erection pressing into my back, I wanted to tell him to take me again. I wanted to forget the last five weeks and focus on our future together—just Scott, our child, and me.

"I'm not sure. Do you think we can get flights out?"

Scott let out a laugh. "Baby, if you haven't noticed, my best friend has a helicopter, and he can take us home anytime you say the word."

The idea of going home excited me so much. I was so ready to leave and get back. I missed work. I missed my father, brothers, and the girls. I missed waking up every morning, looking at the love of my life.

I turned and looked into his eyes. "I want to go home."

The smile that spread across Scott's face caused me to smile in return. Then, I thought of why I wanted to get off this island so quickly.

I'm running away again—running from the truth.

I took a deep breath and looked away from Scott. "Um…before we leave, I have something I need to tell you," I said as my voice cracked.

Scott took a step back and looked at me. "About what? Is everything okay with the baby?" His eyes were filled with fright.

"Yes. I mean I'm sure everything is okay with the baby. Um…this has to do with Trey."

The second I said his name, Scott's eyes turned to anger…and then sadness.

Oh god. The sadness in his eyes about killed me.

He knows. He must know that something happened.

He took another step back. "Okay…what about Trey?"

I took in a breath and bit down on my lower lip. "Something happened."

"No…oh god. Jessie, you didn't…you didn't sleep with him, did you? You told me you didn't sleep with him," Scott said as his legs began to wobble.

"No! No, of course, I didn't sleep with him. I would never lie to you, Scott, ever."

He threw his hands in his hair and then ran them down his face. I just stood there with tears rolling down my face now.

"Well then, what the hell happened, Jessie? Because the shit that's running through my head right now is driving me fucking mad!" he yelled.

I jumped and started crying harder. "Um…we…um—"

He shook his head. "What? You kissed? Did you kiss him?"

I slowly nodded my head.

His eyes began to turn gray. "How many times?"

My mouth dropped open. "Does it matter?"

He nodded. "To me, it does."

I started biting and chewing on my lower lip. "A few times."

"Friendly kisses or more?"

"At first, it was friendly, but a couple were, um…"

His eyes filled with tears. "Is that it? Is that all you did with him? You just kissed him?"

I shook my head, and then I watched his face drop as a tear escaped down his cheek. He slowly backed up and sat down on the bed.

"What did you do together if you didn't fuck, Jessie?" he shouted.

"Scott…you have to understand that, at the time, I thought you had slept with Chelsea. I thought you'd cheated. I was hurting so bad, and he was hurting, and we both just wanted to forget…and…" I couldn't talk anymore.

His head was down, so I couldn't see his face. When he looked up at me, the hurt in his eyes was more than I could stand. When I started to walk toward him, he jumped up and held out his hand.

"What. Did. You. Do. With. Him?"

"Does it matter?"

He turned and knocked over the lamp on the end table. It crashed to the floor, causing me to jump back and scream.

"Yes! Yes, it fucking matters. You're the one who brought it up, for Christ's sake. I just made love to you all night long. Were you thinking of him while we fucked, Jessie?"

I started crying so hard that I could hardly talk. I began shaking my head frantically back and forth. "Scott…I love you…I only want to be with you."

He walked up to me and grabbed me by the shoulders. "Tell me what happened, Jessie. Tell me!" he screamed.

"Um…he took off my clothes, and…and he touched me."

His eyes filled with anger, and I felt my whole body shaking.

"Where? How?"

I closed my eyes and tried to erase the memory. "He…he kissed on my nipples…while he…while he…oh, Scott, please…I made him stop, and I felt so guilty afterward…even though I thought you had cheated on me. I made him stop!" I shouted out.

"Did he finger-fuck you, Jess? Did you come?"

I couldn't move. I tried to open my mouth, but nothing would come out.

"Jessie!"

"Yes! Yes…he touched me with his fingers, but no…I didn't come. I made him stop almost as soon as he'd started because I couldn't do that to you. I love *you*, Scott. I love you so much, even when I thought you had hurt me. I still loved you too much to do that."

Scott looked down at his hands holding on to my shoulders, and he quickly let go. He started to back up slowly. "He touched you while you were pregnant…with my child, Jessie. You let him suck on your nipples…while you were pregnant with my child." He started to shake his head, and then he looked at me with disgust on his face.

"I didn't know I was pregnant at the time! I would have never let me touch him if I had known, I swear on my life!" I cried hysterically.

Scott reached into his bag and grabbed a pair of jeans and then a T-shirt.

"Where…where are you going?" I asked in a panicked voice.

"I need to go for a walk. I need to clear my head."

I started panicking even more. *He's going to leave me.* "No…please don't leave me. You have to believe me when I say that it meant nothing. I swear to God, it meant nothing. I just want to be with you."

Scott turned and looked at me. "It all makes sense now—the way you were looking at him when I walked up, what you wrote to your dad on the postcard. It all makes sense."

Wait…what is he saying? "No…" I whispered.

"Have you seen him since you told me you're pregnant?"

"Yes. He was waiting for me at my cabana to make sure I was alright."

"Did he ask you to stay with him?"

I shook my head. "He knows I love *you* and *only* you!"

"Oh yeah? Sure doesn't seem like he cares if he's fucking you with his fingers and sucking on your nipples, now does it?"

I felt like I was going to throw up. "Scott…we were both lost and hurting. I would have never…I didn't…I stopped him. All I could think about was you and how wrong it felt, even when I thought you had cheated on me. *Please*, Scott. You have to know that I wish to God it had never happened." I sucked in a breath of air as I sobbed. I tried to keep talking. "If I just hadn't run away, none of this would have happened."

The look in his eyes turned from anger to hurt. "You never even called…you just left. You left me to wonder where in the fuck you were and whom you were with. I was slowly dying with each day that passed."

I sat down on the bed and put my head in my hands. "I'm so sorry! I'm so, so sorry. I never meant to hurt you. I would never hurt you."

I looked up and saw tears rolling down his face. *I did hurt him though. I did the one thing I thought he was going to do to me.*

He shook his head and walked past me. When he opened the sliding glass door, I jumped up and grabbed his arm.

"Wait! Where are you going, Scott? Please don't walk away. Please don't leave me."

He slowly looked up at me, and the sadness in his eyes gutted me.

"I need to be alone for a while. I need to think, Jessica."

I threw my hand up to my mouth and tried to keep the sick feeling I had down. "Let me come with you…*please*," I begged.

"No. I just need some time to clear my head. I can't even really think right now. Every time I look at you, I think of him touching the one thing that I value the most in this world. I think of you, pregnant, with him…" He stopped talking as he turned and walked out the sliding glass door.

I stood there, watching him head toward the beach. I quickly turned and ran into the bathroom where I began throwing up.

Scott had been gone for over thirty minutes. I walked into the kitchen and opened the refrigerator. I found it stocked with bottled waters and every kind of beer I could think of. I grabbed a bottle of water and made my way out to the deck that was off of the main living room. The view was amazing. I looked up and down the beach, but I saw no signs of Scott. I quickly wiped away the tear I felt, and I tried my best to keep from crying.

I was starting to get cold, so I walked back in and grabbed a blanket. I headed back outside. I was so tired, and I fought to keep my eyes open. I was hungry also.

I placed my hand on my stomach, and for the first time, I talked to my child. "Daddy is upset with Mommy, and he has every right to be. I really screwed up…but I thought your daddy screwed up first." I made a face and shook my head. "Not that it really matters who screwed up first. I love Daddy, and I know Daddy loves me and you, pumpkin. Mommy just needs to make him understand that I love him so much, and I would never, ever hurt him. Without your daddy, I'd be…I'd be…" I began crying again.

Jesus Christ. What is with me and all the crying?

"I'm so tired, pumpkin, so very tired."

I leaned my head back and decided I was just going to rest my eyes for one minute. I didn't want to miss Scott when he came back.

As I slipped deeper and deeper into sleep, I began dreaming.

Scott and I were walking in a field, holding hands and laughing. I heard someone calling out my name. I tried to ignore the voice, but Scott kept looking back over his shoulder. I tried to keep him walking straight.

Ignore it, Scott. Please ignore it.

Scott turned around and made a funny face. As I spun around, I saw Trey walking up. He reached out and began pulling me away from Scott. I started pushing Trey away, but he kept pulling me harder and harder.

Don't let go of me, Scott! Please don't let go of me.

Before I knew what was happening, Scott was fading away, and I stood there, crying out his name, as Trey just smiled. I turned to look at Trey, and he smiled bigger.

He said, "I won."

I opened my eyes quickly and sat up. I was sweating, but I was so cold. I shook my head to clear out the dream. *Shit.*

I turned and looked at the clock in the living room. He'd been gone for almost an hour. I held my hand up to my mouth to keep from crying.

"Scott…please come back to me. Please…please come back to me," I whispered.

I closed my eyes and silently began crying…again.

18 Scott

I wasn't even sure how long I'd been walking for. I stopped and looked out at the ocean. I closed my eyes and thought about last night. I saw the look she'd had in her eyes. She loved me, and I knew she loved me. Her eyes had looked into mine so many times last night, and they had been filled with nothing but love.

The baby...I can't believe we're going to have a baby.

I thought back to everything she had said.

I didn't know I was pregnant at the time! I would have never let me touch him if I had known, I swear on my life!

I knew she had been hurting. I knew she'd thought I had cheated on her.

Can I forget that he touched her? Can I forget that she let him touch her? I had almost done the same thing in the bar, but I'd stopped myself.

"Fuck!" I yelled out. "Why? Motherfucker! Why did this happen? Why?" I put my hands on my legs and felt like I was going to get sick. I shook my head as I stood up and took a deep breath.

I loved her more than anyone on this Earth. *I've always loved her, and I won't let some fucking prick, who just walked into her life, take her away from me.* She had come back to me last night, and there was no way I was letting her go. *Ever.*

As I looked one more time out over the vast ocean, a sense of calm washed over me. I turned to walk away, and that was when I saw the prick. He was walking up and stopped when he saw me.

My first instinct was to go up and pound the fuck out of him, but I slowly ran my hand through my hair and took a deep breath.

"Scott?" he asked.

I nodded.

He held out his hand. "Trey Walker."

I just looked down at his hand.

He nodded and gave me a weak smile. "Where's Jessie?"

"She's not your concern. She's mine, and so is the baby she's carrying." I balled up my fists and took a deep, slow breath.

He made a face, and his smile faded. "Alright. But just know that I was here for her when she needed a friend, and that's what I was to her. I helped her for a little while, and she did the same thing for me."

I let out a gruff laugh. "Yeah, you sure were a friend to her, weren't you? Don't know many people who suck on their friends' nipples and finger-fuck them, dude."

He looked shocked for a brief second. "She told you?"

"Yes, she told me, you fucker. That's one of the things about our relationship—we're honest with each other."

He laughed. "Well, she certainly didn't think you were honest when she thought you were fucking your ex...*dude*."

Little motherfucker must want me to pound him in the ground.

"It might have taken her longer than I would have liked, but she figured it out, didn't she?" I said.

His smile faded as he looked down toward the sand. He slowly nodded before looking back up at me. "I love her."

"You just met her." I felt the anger building inside me.

"I think I've loved her from the moment I laid eyes on her." He let out a smile. "I only had one problem...she didn't love me back. All she ever told me was how she just wanted to be friends. When I finally thought I had won her heart, she shut me out and told me she loved you...that she'd always loved...you. Then, when she was trying so hard to get to you the other night...hell, it about killed me to hear her tell you she loved you when she left you that voice mail. I think I knew then and there that I never stood a chance. But that didn't mean I was just going to walk away. Then, she found out she was pregnant. When you walked up to us standing outside, she was telling me about how she'd loved you since she could remember. She was excited about telling you about the baby. Seeing the love in her eyes as she talked about you destroyed me, but I tried to be happy for her."

I thought about walking up and seeing them. I remembered the look in her eyes. *Was she talking about me when she had such love in her eyes?*

"And then, right on cue, there you were, Prince Charming coming in to save her. I know she loves you, Scott. But I also know a part of her loves me as well, and I'll always hold on to that hope."

I wanted so badly to punch this guy. "Well, you're going to be holding on to that hope for a very long time because I don't *ever* intend on letting her go."

He laughed and raised his eyebrows. "If she were mine, I'd be saying the same thing."

"She'll never be yours."

He nodded and gave me a cocky smile before turning and walking away.

I could have sworn I heard him say, "We'll see."

I watched him for a few minutes before I spun around and quickly started running back to the house. The whole way there, I kept replaying everything that had happened in the last twenty-four hours.

We just need to get off this fucking island and get back to Texas.

I stopped running and pulled out my cell phone and sent a text to Lark.

Scott: I'll pay you double what I paid you before if you take Jessie and me back to Austin today.

Lark: Let me get rid of the girl I've got here, and we can leave in thirty minutes. Shit…give me an hour. She's got strawberry-blonde hair. You know how I love blondes. Plus, she gives good head.

Scott: Dude, too much information. Forty-five minutes, and we'll be up at the main house.

I started jogging. Shit, I really walked a long way. Jessie was probably going crazy. I'd gone for over an hour. As I picked up my jog to a run again, I was more determined than ever to prove to her how much I loved her. I just needed to keep telling myself that she'd stopped him. She'd stopped him because she still loved me, even when she'd thought I had done the worst thing imaginable.

Our love is too strong to let some little pretty boy prick tear it apart.

As I walked up the stairs to the deck, I saw Jessie sleeping in one of the chairs. I smiled, looking at her all wrapped up in a blanket. *Damn…she's so beautiful with that blonde hair.* There wasn't a thing I wouldn't do for her, and now…now, it wasn't just her. *It's our unborn child also.*

I dropped to my knees and gently pushed her hair back. She looked like an angel while she was sleeping so peacefully. My heart began hurting when I pictured her standing here, crying, as I'd walked away from her earlier.

"I'll never leave you, baby. I promise, I'll never leave you. It's me and you, always and forever."

She moved a little and opened her eyes. She smiled. "How much do you love me?"

I let out a small laugh and kissed her nose. "To the moon and back, then back to the moon, and back again."

"That's a lot," she said with a giggle.

I gave her wink. "Yeah, it is."

"Scott…"

I shook my head and put my finger up to her lips. "I love you, Jessie, and I'll always love you. You're my whole world, and there is no way I'm going to let this thing come between us. I want to make love to you, baby. I just want to hold you in my arms."

She nodded and started to get up.

"Not here though. I want to get you home. I just want to leave and go home."

She bit down on her lower lip. "Me, too," she whispered.

111

"Lark has got some girl with him, but he should be ready in about forty-five minutes or so," I said as I rolled my eyes.

"Okay. Can we just sit here for a bit? Will you just hold me for a while, Scott?"

I stood, and she started to slide over. I crawled into the chair next to her. I pulled her close to me and silently thanked God for bringing us back together.

"Scott?"

"Yeah, baby?"

She turned and looked at me, tears filling her eyes. "I love you. I'm so sorry I hurt you."

My heart broke in two. The last thing I wanted was for her to be stressed or worried, especially with her being pregnant. I kissed her forehead and pulled her closer to me.

"I love you, too, baby, and I'm sorry for getting angry earlier. I need to be honest with you as well, baby."

She looked up at me, and I saw the fear in her eyes.

"At the bar one night, I kissed another girl, and I touched her breasts when I was drunk, but that was all I did. I swear to you…all I could see was your face, baby, and I couldn't do it."

She swallowed and gave me a weak smile. "Can we just forget that the last five weeks ever happened?"

I kissed her forehead. "Let's just get home and share our good news with everyone, okay?"

She gave me a weak smile and nodded as she snuggled in closer to me. As I looked out over the ocean, I thought about Trey and what he'd said. I was pretty sure that was not going to be the last time I ever saw him.

As we got closer to Austin, I looked down at a sleeping Jessie in my arms.

Lark had been on the radio with someone, talking about a mission or something. When I realized he was talking about a girl and not his job, I rolled my eyes. He glanced back at me and winked. I couldn't help but laugh. I'd met Lark in college, and we had quickly become friends. I swore that we'd done everything together. Lark's father was in the Secret Service, and Lark seemed to have followed in his footprints. Whatever Lark did for a living, it sure as hell was a secret.

I woke Jessie up when Lark said we were about fifteen minutes out.

"Are we stopping for fuel again?" Jessie asked.

"Nah, we're fixin' to land in Austin, baby."

Her eyes lit up, and she smiled so big that it caused me to laugh.

"Glad to be almost home?" I asked.

She nodded her head and put her hand on her stomach. "I'll be glad to land, too. I feel sick."

Lark snapped his head around and looked at Jessie. "There's a puke bag, doll, right there if ya need it," he said with a wink.

By the time we landed and made it through customs and all that bullshit, Jessie was practically running to the restroom. I felt so bad. I watched her as she almost plowed over a poor old lady.

Lark came walking up and slapped me on the back. "Thanks for the mini vacation, dude," he said with a grin.

"Pesh, I paid you good enough for that quick little trip."

His crooked smiled spread across his face, and he nodded his head. "Yeah, ya did. Boss man said anytime you need the use of the helicopter again, just let him know." Lark threw his head back and laughed.

"Dude, I paid you to go to Belize and pretty much get laid," I said as I glanced back toward the restroom.

Lark's smile faded. "Shit, I can get laid anywhere, dude. Perks of being single…and a pilot. Ain't gonna lie though, the strawberry-blonde was a good fuck."

"Lark, don't you want to settle down? Think about a family, maybe? I mean, I get the lure of traveling, and it seems like you have a pretty good paying job," I said as I rolled my eyes again, "but don't you want someone to wake up to every morning? Someone to say 'I love you' to or have her say it back to you?"

His eyes filled with sadness before he quickly snapped out of it. He watched a girl in a pair of tight jeans and cowboy boots walk by. "Are you fucking kidding me? No, thanks. I know what being in love brings—heartache. No, thank you, I'll pass. I like my life, Scott. I wouldn't change one goddamn thing about it."

I let out a sigh. "Are you going to be in town for New Year's?"

He looked around and then back at me. "Probably."

"Come on out to Mason for a few days, dude. Take in the country air. My parents would love to see you. Plus, you can celebrate with Jessie and me—new year, new baby, new beginnings."

He stood there, thinking for a minute, before he nodded his head. "Alright, I think some fresh country air might be just what I need. Since I'm not heading home to the ranch, I think it would do me some good."

I smiled and hit him on the back as I watched Jessie coming out of the restroom. "Perfect. It will do you good, buddy."

Jessie walked right into my arms, and I held her for a second before she pulled back and smiled.

"Can we stop and buy me a new cell phone? Mine is in a field somewhere in Mason." She scrunched up her nose.

We made plans with Lark to come out and stay with us for a few days, and then we said our good-byes.

Jessie and I headed out of the airport and to my truck. The cool December evening felt amazing.

After a quick stop for a new cell phone, we were on our way to Mason. Jessie was asleep before we were even out of the Austin city limits. I grabbed my cell phone and hit Gunner's number. After giving him a quick rundown, I asked him to let everyone know we were back in Texas, and we would probably be locking ourselves away for a few days.

I hit End and then peeked over at my sleeping beauty.

A father—I can't believe I'm going to be a father.

For the first time in the last five weeks, I finally felt happy. I turned and glanced at my bag in the backseat, knowing that I had Jessie's engagement ring in there. My heart started pounding in my chest. I was so glad I hadn't asked her to marry me last night in Belize.

As we drove down the driveway, Jessie woke up. She stretched and made the cutest noise. I couldn't wait to get her in the house and strip off her clothes. I wanted to do nothing but make love to her.

She looked over at me, and the passion in her eyes told me she was thinking the same thing. "I'm so glad to be home!"

"Me, too, baby. I'm gonna make love to you all night long."

She smiled and nodded her head. "I like that plan—a lot. Maybe I should start undressing now."

My dick jumped in my pants, and I laughed as I watched her pull her T-shirt over her head. I looked back ahead and slammed on the brakes.

"Shit! Jesus, Scott, why did you—" Jessie quickly put her shirt back on and started laughing. "Oh my god! Are you kidding me?"

I pulled up next to Drake's truck and took a deep breath. I looked at Jessie. "Looks like you're in trouble."

She slowly smiled and gave me the sexiest look I'd ever seen. "I guess you might have to spank me then after they leave." She opened the door and jumped out of the truck.

"Wait! What?" I yelled out after her.

I instantly imagined Jessie naked with me spanking her. *Holy fuck. Talk about an instant hard-on.*

I opened the truck door and jumped out. I tried to adjust my dick. As I walked around and grabbed her hand, she looked up at me and giggled.

"For that, I think you maybe deserve two spankings," I said with a wink.

Her eyes filled with lust, and she bit down on her lower lip.

"You ready for the wrath of your father and brothers?" I said as I glanced over at Drake, Aaron, and Dewey all standing on my porch.

I guess I should have told Gunner not to call Drake.

As we got closer, Jessie began squeezing the hell out of my hand.

I leaned over and said, "Baby, I need that hand for later."

She snapped her head over and looked at me. A blush quickly swept over her cheeks, and I couldn't help but laugh.

"It's gonna be fine. Don't worry," I said.

When we reached the top of the porch, Aaron walked up and hugged Jessie. "Jesus, don't ever do that to us again, you little brat," Aaron said as he pushed Jessie back and gave her a quick once-over.

He stepped aside and Dewey strolled up to her. His eyes were filled with tears.

"Dew, are you about to cry, dude?" I asked with a laugh.

He shot me a look that made me instantly stop laughing.

"I can still kick your damn ass, pretty boy," Dewey said as he grabbed Jessie and pulled him to her. "My god, Tiny…don't ever leave like that again without calling one of us. We were going crazy."

Jessie wiped a tear away. She leaned back and gave Dewey a weak smile. "I'm so sorry I worried you. I really am."

Dewey put his arm around her and turned her to face Drake. I had noticed the small smile on Drake's face when his sons were hugging their sister, but the moment Dewey moved, Drake's smile was replaced with a look of anger.

"You think you can just run away like that with no word to anyone, and then just walk back in like nothing ever happened?"

"Daddy, I—"

"No. You don't get to *Daddy* me. You left the goddamn country, Jessie. You didn't tell anyone. Then, you were holed up with some stranger while we all went insane."

Jessie sucked in a breath of air and quickly wiped her tears away.

"Drake, I think maybe you need to calm down before you—"

"No, Scott. I don't need to calm down, and if I were you, I'd be so pissed-off at this girl right now that I don't think I'd be walking up, holding her hand. You left him without so much as a reason why."

"I thought he—"

"Well, he didn't cheat on you, Jessie. You would have known that if you hadn't run away. How in the hell did you pay for this little trip to Belize?"

I saw her as she started wringing her hands together. She looked down at the ground and then up at her father.

"Oh my god. You didn't use your savings for the vet clinic, did you?"

Savings? What savings? I hadn't wanted to ask Jessie, but I was wondering how she'd paid to stay in Belize for so long. When I'd checked her out of the hotel, they had said she didn't have a balance due. She had paid in full through the end of the month…in cash.

"At the time, I guess I wasn't thinking clearly. Daddy, everything has changed, and I don't think I want to buy the clinic anymore."

"Damn straight, everything has changed. You left with no good-byes or explanations, and Doc sold his practice to another person."

Jessie let out a gasp and put her hand up to her mouth. "What?"

Drake shook his head. "Did you really think everyone would put their lives on hold while you were gone?"

Dewey let out a laugh. "Hell, Scott did. Bastard lost out on a—"

I cleared my throat and shook my head. "Dew…" I said.

Jessie glanced back and forth between Dewey and me. I saw the sadness in her eyes, and it about gutted me.

"People moved on, Jessica, and you lost out on your dream," Drake said, his voice filled with disappointment.

Jessie looked at her father. "I have a new dream, Daddy."

Drake let out a chuckle. "Oh, really? Did you graduate high school early and finish up college in record time for this new dream?"

I knew Jessie wanted to tell her father about the baby, but I also knew she wanted to make it special. "Jessie, baby, I don't think now is the time to—"

"No…Scott, he's right." Jessie stood up straighter and squared off her shoulders. "Dad, you're right, and I'm not going to argue with you. What I did was wrong, and I regret it more than you'll ever know."

She quickly looked at me and gave me a weak smile. I smiled back and winked at her. I didn't want her stressing over what had happened between her and Trey. It was over, and we were together.

"But…it happened, and there is nothing I can do about it now. I made a mistake, Daddy, and you've always said that some of life's best lessons are made through our mistakes." She took a deep breath and slowly let it out. "Yes, I used my savings to pay for the trip to Belize."

Drake shook his head and whispered, "Damn it."

"But, Daddy, I don't think I want to be a vet...at least not right now. There's something else I'd much rather be, and I would like to do it full-time."

She looked at me, and I smiled and nodded.

Drake folded his arms and glared at Jessie. "Oh yeah? Well, what is it, Jessica? I'm waiting with anticipation to hear about this new job."

I saw the tears building in her eyes, so I walked up to her. I grabbed her hand and kissed the back of it.

"I'd like to be a full-time mother," Jessie practically whispered.

I saw the smile spread across Aaron's face. I glanced over at Dewey, and he was smiling and shaking his head. When I looked at Drake, he seemed confused for a second before it hit him.

Drake dropped his arms to his side. "What? Jessica...are you..."

She nodded.

Both Aaron and Dewey let out a yell.

"Oh, hell yeah!" Dewey yelled as he walked up and grabbed Jessie. He started spinning her around.

As soon as he put her down, Aaron repeated the whole show. "Holy shit! Tiny is gonna have a baby! Our kids are going to grow up together, Jess." Aaron kissed her on the cheeks.

Aaron set her down, and then he reached over and shook my hand. "Jesus, dude, congratulations. I couldn't be more happy for y'all."

Dewey walked up and shook my hand. Then, he pulled me close to him and said in my ear, "You hurt her or this baby...and I *will* kill you and bury your body in your own backyard."

I pulled back and looked at him with a shocked look. "My own backyard? What the hell is wrong with you, Dewey?" I asked.

Aaron let out a laugh. I looked up to see Drake just staring at Jessie. I couldn't really read his expression, and I was sure Jessie couldn't either.

"Daddy...please say something," Jessie said.

Drake turned and started to walk away, and Jessie's body just slumped.

"Daddy..." Jessie whispered.

She glanced back at me, and the look in her eyes about killed me. She slowly walked into my arms, and I looked up at Drake. He was standing at the end of the porch, looking out.

In that moment, I vowed that this girl in my arms would never have that look in her eyes again.

Ever.

The moment my father turned and walked away from me, it all hit me—the hurt I caused him, my brothers, and especially Scott.

I let everyone down. I hurt the only people I truly love.

Scott pulled back and looked into my eyes. The love that was pouring out of him took my breath away.

"I love you," he whispered.

My heart dropped to my stomach. After everything that I had told him about Trey, he was still standing here, making me feel so loved and so cherished.

I tried my best to smile at him, but when he put his hand on my stomach, I felt the tears building.

"Go talk to him, baby."

I nodded and turned to see my brothers both looking at me.

"It's okay, Tiny. He's just probably in shock, and he was really pissed-off at you," Dewey said with a sweet smile on his face.

I let out a small laugh and started to walk over toward my father. I stopped right behind him. I looked down at my shaking hands and closed my eyes.

"Daddy," I said as my voice cracked.

He turned around and looked at me. He had tears in eyes, and I sucked in a breath of air.

Am I that much of a disappointment to him?

"I…I'm so sorry if I'm a disappointment to you." I began to cry.

He looked at me with a shocked expression on his face. "*What?* Why would you ever think you were a disappointment to me?"

"You just seem…well, you walked away from me, and…"

He reached out, grabbed me, and pulled me to him. "Oh, baby girl, you could never be a disappointment to me. *Ever.* I'm really upset with you for running away like you did. You about killed me, Jessica. Don't you ever do that to me again. You're my girl…my baby girl."

I slowly nodded my head. "Oh, Daddy, I promise I won't, and if I could take it all back…"

He pulled back and smiled as he wiped away the tears from my eyes. "I'm gonna be a grandfather, huh?"

I smiled. "Yes."

"When did you find out?"

I took a deep breath as I thought back to that night. The idea of crawling onto Trey's lap and sleeping somehow made me feel sick to my stomach. *I should have been with Scott...not another man.*

"Christmas Eve."

My father looked up and over at Scott. I turned and saw him smiling at something Aaron was saying to him. When I turned back to my father, he seemed conflicted.

"Daddy, are you not happy about the baby?"

"Oh, sweetheart, I'm very happy. It's just...I don't know how to ask you this..."

I looked at him, confused. "Ask me, what?"

He quickly looked at Scott and then back at me. "Is the baby, um...is the baby Scott's?"

I sucked in a breath of air. *Oh my god. Does everyone think I was with another man?*

You were with another man.

I quickly shook my head to erase the thoughts running through my head.

"Yes! Of course it is."

"I'm sorry. It's just that your one postcard made it sound like...well, it sounded like you were with someone."

I put my hand up to my mouth and started crying. Daddy pulled me to him and kept telling me it was okay.

"Oh god...I almost made the biggest mistake of my life, Dad. I can't..." I started sobbing again.

He put his arm around me as we walked around the porch and started down the steps. Once we got far enough away from Scott, Aaron, and Dewey, all he had to do was look at me.

"What happened?"

I just let it all out. "I met this guy. Nothing happened, but we did...we...oh god."

I wanted to scream every time I thought about what had happened between Trey and me.

"Stop with the guilt, Jessie. You thought something happened with Scott and Chelsea. You were hurting."

I started shaking my head as I dropped it back and looked up. "I know, Dad...I know. But if I hadn't run away, if I had just stayed and confronted my fear, I would have seen within five seconds that it wasn't Scott. I think a part of me knew it wasn't him, but I've always had this fear that he was going to leave me like he did the first time."

My dad snapped his head at Scott and then over to me. "First time?"

"No, nothing like that. In high school, he kissed me, and...oh god, Dad, that was so long ago. It doesn't matter." I started walking back and forth. "I think the thing that kills me the most is that I was carrying Scott's child when I let another man touch me. It almost makes my skin crawl, but at the same time, I feel something for Trey."

"Wait—what do you mean you feel something for Trey? Jessie...you're not in love with him, are you?"

I shook my head. "No! I mean, I care about him. He was a great friend, and we really grew close during those five weeks. I honestly don't think I could have made it through that time without him."

"Would you have come home sooner if you hadn't met him?" my father asked.

I stopped walking. It hit me like a ton of bricks. *My god...did I stay away out of fear? Or did I stay away because I was enjoying my time with Trey?*

"I...I don't know. Maybe."

My dad tilted his head and gave me a look. "Maybe?"

My heart started pounding, and I felt like it was all happening again. "I think so. I was only going to stay for two weeks."

"And it's over a month later," my father said as he walked up to me. "Scott loves you, and I've never seen a man so destroyed as he was when you were gone."

I felt the tears falling again. This crying thing was starting to be a pain in the ass.

"Jessie...you need to make sure you don't have any feelings for this Trey guy. You need to make sure you are one hundred percent with Scott and not just because you are pregnant."

All the air left my body. "Daddy...I love Scott more than anything. I only love him, and I'll only ever love him. I called him before I knew I was pregnant, and..." I stopped talking. I felt like I couldn't breathe. I put my hands on my chest. It felt like someone was sitting on it. "Do you think Scott thinks I picked him over Trey because I'm pregnant? Oh my god...Dad, if you thought that..."

"Now, Jessie, settle down. Take a deep breath, baby girl. It's not good to be this upset when you're pregnant. I'm sure Scott knows how much you love him, and no, I don't think he thinks that."

I took a few deep breaths to try to calm myself down. Then, I heard his voice.

"Jessie?"

I closed my eyes and felt the warmth take over my body just from the sound of his voice. I opened my eyes and looked into my dad's eyes. My dad must have noticed how I'd calmed down almost instantly.

"Daddy, if y'all don't mind, I really would like to spend some time with Scott."

My father laughed and took a step around me. He walked up to Scott, and as I turned around, I saw him shake Scott's hand.

"Congratulations, son. I'm very happy for you and Jessie. I still can't believe it—a grandchild."

The smile that spread across Scott's face caused me to smile. He was so happy about this baby, and it just made my heart swell even more.

"Aaron and Dewey had to leave, but they said to let you know they'll see you later, Jessie," Scott said.

"Okay, well, that's my sign to take off as well." My father looked at me and winked. "Call me later?"

"Yes…I promise," I said.

He gave me a hug. After I watched my father walk away, I turned my attention to Scott. He was just staring at me.

"I take it that he's happy about the baby?" he asked with a smile.

I let out a giggle. "Yeah, he's really happy."

Scott started to walk my way with that drop-me-to-my-knees, sexy-ass look of his. I instantly felt myself longing for him.

"So, where were we?" Scott raised his eyebrows up at me.

I let out a laugh. "I do believe you mentioned something about making love to me all night long. And what else was it?" I put my index finger up to my lips and looked up, like I was thinking. I snapped my head back and looked into his eyes. "Two spankings for bad behavior, I believe," I said as I licked my lips on purpose.

"Ah hell," Scott said. He reached for me and threw me over his shoulder.

I let out a scream as I pushed myself up off his back. As soon as his hand hit my ass, I felt the throbbing between my legs.

My god…I've never been so turned-on in my life.

Scott carried me into the house and straight to his bedroom. After he walked in, he slowly let me down. As soon as my feet hit the ground, he began kissing me as he reached for my jeans and started to unbutton them. I moved my hands to his pants and did the same thing.

"My god…I want you so badly," I practically panted.

He lifted up my T-shirt and pulled it over my head. Then, he pushed my bra up and over my breasts. He lifted it above my head. I didn't know how he had done it, but he'd quickly used my bra to pull my hands behind my back. He gently cupped my breast, and I threw my head back and moaned. He dropped to his knees and kissed my stomach. I felt a million different sensations run through my body.

Oh yes…I love this man and only this man.

He was still holding my hands behind my back as he put his mouth up to my clit and blew through my panties.

"Scott…oh god. *Please.*"

He let go of my bra and hands. I instantly put my hands in his hair and pulled him closer to me. I needed to feel him as close to me as possible. I needed his love to pour into my body in every way possible.

"God, Jessie, I've missed you so damn much, baby."

"I missed you, Scott, more than you'll ever know."

He slid his finger along my panty line, and the next thing I knew, he was taking them off and putting my leg over his shoulder. The moment his tongue brushed against my overly sensitive body, I let out a whimper.

"Jesus…" I whispered as I ran my hand through his hair.

"Jessie…" he whispered against me.

He placed his fingers inside me. The moment he began his assault on my clit, I was done. I began calling out his name as I threw my head back and got lost in the pleasure. I wasn't even down from the high when I felt Scott pick me up and carry me over to the bed. It didn't take me long to notice it was a new bed.

I sat up and looked around. "You got a new bed?"

Scott looked at me like I was crazy. "Fuck yeah, I did. My brother screwed my ex in my other bed. Gross!"

I let out a laugh and fell back onto the bed. My eyes caught his, and our gazes locked. I couldn't tear away from the look in his eyes. They were filled with passion and so much love. He began kissing me softly on my hips first, and then he moved over to my stomach. He stopped and peeked up at me with that smile.

Then, he looked back to my stomach and whispered to it, "Hey, baby…I absolutely cannot wait to lay my eyes on your precious face."

I felt the tears building in my eyes. I closed them and smiled. He moved up to my breasts where he gave each nipple equal attention.

"Oh god…they're so sensitive." I arched my back.

"You're so beautiful, Jessie, so damn beautiful." Scott began kissing my neck.

"Scott, I love you so much," I whispered.

He was moving his lips all along my neck, and he kept repeating how much he loved me. He bit down on my earlobe, and I let out a whimper. His lovemaking was so slow and intense. It was almost like he couldn't get close enough to me.

"I. Love. You. Baby." He placed kisses down the side of my face. He pulled back and looked into my eyes before he leaned down and grazed his lips against mine.

As he slowly pushed himself into me, I felt tears burning my eyes, and I fought to hold them back.

"Oh…god…Jessie," he whispered against my lips.

I grabbed his arms and deepened the kiss. I needed him. I needed to feel his love pouring into me. He pulled back and smiled at me as he made love to me while repeating over and over how much he loved me.

My heart was pounding in my chest as I felt my orgasm slowly building. The feeling was incredible, and I never wanted this to end. I wanted to stay right here with Scott, alone and together.

"Jessie…please, baby…I can't hold off any longer."

The moment he whispered that in my ear, my whole body exploded. I began calling out his name as the orgasm took over. Somewhere in my cries of pleasure, I heard Scott call out my name as he began to slow down, gently kissing my neck and telling me he loved me.

Scott rolled off of me and pulled me up next to him. "God, I'm so tired," he said.

He kissed my back as I snuggled up and smiled. I closed my eyes. *Home…I'm finally home.*

"Jess?"

"Hmm?"

The last few days were finally catching up to me, and I was exhausted.

"Are you still going to move in with me?" Scott asked as his voice cracked.

My eyes snapped open, and I rolled over and looked into his eyes. "Of course I am. Why wouldn't I?"

He smiled slightly and shook his head. "Just making sure you still want to."

I placed my hand on the side of his face and leaned over. I kissed him gently on the lips. "We're having a baby. I want to experience everything together. Scott, why would you think I wouldn't still want to move in?"

I watched as the hurt moved into his eyes.

"I want you to be one hundred percent sure that this is what you want…that I'm what you want."

My heart slammed in my chest, and I almost felt sick. *He doubts my love for him? Oh god.*

My mind went back to Belize, and I thought of Trey. I thought of how he'd made me feel, but it was nothing like how Scott made me feel. I knew that one hundred percent.

I went to say something, but Scott started talking again. "I saw the way you looked at him, Jessie. Lark also told me that when he'd gone to see if you needed help packing, you had been with him. You kissed him good-bye."

I sat up quickly, instantly feeling defensive. "What? Did you have Lark follow me or something?"

Scott's face fell. "No, of course not. He told me he was going to help you while I checked you out of the room."

I spun around and sat on the edge of the bed. I pulled the sheet up and around me. I wasn't sure if I was pissed at the idea of Lark spying on me or the fact that Scott knew I had kissed Trey good-bye.

Did Lark tell him it was a friendly kiss? Or did Lark tell him I called out after Trey and kissed him? Oh god. My head is spinning.

Scott went to touch me, and I pulled away. I wasn't really sure why I had, but I regretted it instantly. I was so angry at myself for kissing Trey good-bye the way I had. The guilt had been eating me alive for the last two days.

"Fine. Maybe we should talk about this later," Scott said.

I felt him get out of bed. I turned and watched as he walked to the bathroom.

"Scott, wait, please. There is nothing to talk about. Of course, I want to move in here with you. I love you. I love *you*, Scott."

He turned and looked at me. "I need you to tell me right now, Jessie. Do you love him? In any way…do you have feelings for him?"

I jumped up and immediately said, "No! I mean…I care about him…but only as a friend." I looked down and away from Scott.

I thought about Trey touching me…the way he'd made me feel. I could almost feel his lips on my skin. *Oh my god. What is wrong with me? I do not want Trey in any way!*

"You can't even look at me when you say that," Scott said with hurt in his voice.

I quickly looked up and into his eyes. "What?" I whispered.

He shook his head as he turned and walked slowly into the bathroom. He shut the door, and I stood there, stunned.

What just happened?

We had made beautiful love to each other, and then a minute later, this…

I shook my head and sat back down on the bed.

I didn't love Trey. *I don't.* I knew that. But…I had strong feelings for him that were starting to confuse me. I closed my eyes and wished I could talk to the girls. I needed to talk to someone about this. I was so confused…but not confused at the same time.

The bathroom door opened, and Scott walked out…dressed. I jumped up and moved closer to him.

"Where are you going?" I asked, panic in my voice.

"I need to get some fresh air. I won't be gone long," he said with a weak smile.

I grabbed his arm. "Scott…" I stopped in my tracks when I saw the tear roll down his face.

"The first time I knew I loved you, I pushed you away. I hurt you because I was afraid of my own feelings. I vowed to myself I would never hurt you again. This whole time we've been together, I feel like I've been trying to prove to you how much I love you. When you walked in and saw Chelsea and Bryce, you automatically assumed it was me. I never wanted that to ever happen. I never wanted you to ever think that I would do that to you. I wanted you to trust me and know in your heart how much I love you. I would never in a million years want to hurt you ever again."

I shook my head. "I didn't know it wasn't you," I said as a sob escaped my lips.

"But if I had just been able to show you how much I love you and that you are my whole world, you would have never had that doubt in your mind. You wouldn't have run away, and you would have never met…him."

I frantically shook my head, panic building in my body. "Scott! Please…I made a mistake by letting him touch me, and I swear to you, I was just confused and heartbroken. I thought you had…I thought you had…put yourself in my shoes! What would you have done if you'd walked into my bedroom and seen two people having sex?" I wiped the tears away quickly. "I love you. I've always loved you."

He smiled at me and wiped away the tears still rolling down my face. "I won't be the one who makes you hurt again. I won't. I need you to be sure you are with me for the right reasons and not because we're expecting a child together."

I started crying harder. "I'm not. I didn't even know about the baby before I called you. I love you…I love *you*."

"I know you do, baby. But I think you need to make sure you don't love him as well." He turned and walked away from me.

I slowly felt myself falling to the floor. I buried my head in my hands and cried. In one moment, my whole world had changed. It wasn't even the moment when I'd walked in on Chelsea in this very bedroom.

It was the one moment when I'd let another man into my heart.

"Make it stop!" Josh said as he reached for my phone and tossed it at me.

I let out a giggle and didn't even pay attention to who was calling.

"Hello?" I said, trying not to sound like I'd just woken up.

Of all the mornings when the twins actually sleep in, someone calls and wakes us up.

"Heather?"

I sat up quickly. "Jessie!" I practically screamed. "Is Scott with you? Where are you?"

I heard her sniffle. *Oh no. She's crying.* I flew up out of bed and went straight for the closet. I started getting dressed.

"I'm, um...home...at Scott's house. I need to talk to you, Heather."

"Yes! Oh my god, of course. Want me to come there?"

There was silence for a few minutes.

"I don't want Scott to think I've left. Can you come here?"

"I'm on my way. It might be closer to an hour though."

"That's fine. Heather?"

I stopped getting dressed. "Yeah?"

"Please be careful, and thank you."

"Always, sweets. See you in a few."

I hit End and pulled a sweatshirt over my head. I ran back out into the bedroom and sat down on the bed.

"What's going on? Jessie is back? Scott is with her, right?"

I quickly looked at Josh. My heart skipped a beat at how handsome he was, sitting there with his messy hair. I wanted to run my hands through it and crawl on top of him. I shook my wayward thoughts away.

"I'm guessing so since she's at Scott's house, but she's upset. Do you mind?"

"Of course not. I think Will, Libby, and I will head out and get some breakfast with Mom and Dad."

I smiled and crawled across the bed. I moved my lips along his neck. "Hmm...what I wouldn't do to have your parents take the kids for a few hours."

He pulled back and smiled. His dimple caught my eye.

"I might be able to arrange that," he said with a wink.

"Perfect. I've got to brush my teeth and then get on the road."

I kissed Josh good-bye and ran downstairs. I peeked into the twins' room, and they were both still sound asleep.

As I made my way out to my car, I hit Ari's number.

"Bitch, you better have a good reason for calling me so goddamn early, especially on the one day the kids sleep in."

I let out a giggle. "Ari, code blue. Jessie. Scott's house."

Ari let out a gasp. "Motherfucker. I'm getting up and dressed. I'll call Ells. What's going on? Oh my god, I'm gonna kick Jessie's damn ass when I see her."

"I'm not sure. She was crying. Mentioned something about she needed me to come there because she didn't want Scott to think she'd left him."

Silence.

"Ari?"

"Um…Scott's here. I hear Jeff talking to him," Ari whispered.

"What?"

"Let me get dressed. I'll find out what's going on, and I'll call you back. Be careful driving. See you in a little bit." Ari hung up on me.

It had never taken me so damn long to get to Mason as it had this morning. I was about ten minutes from Scott's house when my cell rang. I hit Answer on my screen.

"Hello?"

"Heather," Ari said, her voice coming through my car speakers.

"What did you find out?"

"Ells is with me right now. We're at Scott's gate, waiting on you, but this is what I got from Scott. So, Jessie was in Belize, but we all knew that. I guess while she was there, she met some guy named Trey."

My stomach dropped.

"He was there because his fiancée had left him at the altar. They were supposed to go to Belize for their honeymoon or some bullshit like that. I guess Jessie and this Trey guy became friends. They hung out the entire time she was on the island."

"Doesn't he work? Didn't he have a job to go back to?" I asked.

"I don't know. I didn't ask. Scott was a mess. He just kept telling Jeff over and over that he thought Jessie loved this guy."

"Oh no," I whispered.

"Anyway, long story short, they messed around. They didn't have sex, but I guess the guy felt on her. Here is the kicker though—Jess is pregnant."

"What?" both Ellie and I said at the same time.

Ari must have waited to fill Ellie in until she got me on the phone. "Scott's?" I asked.

"Yes. Jessie just found out on Christmas Eve. Scott thought he could put it all behind him. I mean, he knows Jessie thought he'd cheated and all, but then his friend, Lark, went to go help Jessie pack. He walked up on her kissing this Trey bastard…after she had told Scott about the baby."

"Oh. My. God. No wonder she's crying." I pulled up behind Ari in Scott's driveway. "I'm confused. Did Jessie want to come back with Scott?"

I saw Ari look at me in her rearview mirror. "According to Scott, yes. They've been together since then. Scott asked her if she was sure she wanted to move in with him, and then he asked if she had feelings for Trey. She couldn't look him in the eye and say no."

"Holy shit. Okay, well…let's get Jessie's side, and then we'll see what we can do."

"Okay. Let's do this."

Ari hung up on me again before I could hang up on her first. I rolled my eyes and followed her down the long driveway. As we pulled up, I saw Jessie standing on the front porch. She had clearly been crying. She was dressed in a pair of Scott's sweatpants and one of his shirts. Her hair was pulled up in a ponytail. I quickly got out of the car and walked up behind Ari and Ellie.

"Oh, Jessie, sweets…don't cry," Ellie said as she took Jessie into her arms.

Ari followed and wrapped her arms around both Jessie and Ellie, and I did the same. Ari and I exchanged looks, and she made a sad face at me and then pointed to Jessie's stomach. I knew what she was saying. All this stress wasn't good for Jessie or the baby.

"I've missed y'all so much," Jessie said as she broke down into tears.

Ellie grabbed her arm and started walking into the house. We made our way to the kitchen, and Ari started making tea since Jessie was the only one out of all of us who didn't drink coffee. I opened up the refrigerator and took out some fruit. Honestly, I was surprised Scott had any food in here at all. I made up a platter and set it on the table as Ari began putting down the mugs with hot tea in them. The whole time, Ellie had just held on to Jessie as she cried.

Ari looked at Ellie, then me, and then back at Jessie. "Scott is at my house."

Jessie snapped her head up. "Oh, thank God. I had no idea where he went, and I was so worried."

Ellie smiled slightly. "Jessie, we kind of know what's going on. Scott told Jeff a little bit of what had happened. Sweets, what in the hell is going on? And why did you stay away without talking to anyone?"

Wow. Ellie just went right for it.

Jessie threw her head back and let out a long sigh. "Oh god...if I could go back in time, I swear..." She moved her head back down and looked at each of us before taking a deep breath. "That night when I walked in and saw Chelsea...I think a part of me knew it wasn't Scott, but I had struggled for so long with letting myself fully trust him a hundred percent."

"Why? Did Scott ever give you the idea that he might leave or cheat?" Ari asked.

Ellie and Jessie looked at each other.

Jessie shook her head. "No, at least not since we've been together. But in high school, he, um...well, long story short, he kissed me, and let me tell you, I'd been in love with him for years before that. The moment he pulled away, we looked into each other's eyes, and I swore I thought he felt the same thing. Then, Chelsea walked by, and he pretty much just thanked me for the kiss and moved on. After we got together, he told me he had felt so scared of his feelings for me then, so he'd run away. Yes, I know we were young and all, but..."

"But..." I said, pressing her to keep talking.

"That fear was still there for me. Anyway...me running away was just me hiding from the truth. I couldn't take being hurt like that again or seeing him with Chelsea...or seeing Chelsea, period. They were the whole reason I finished up high school early and busted my ass to get through college in record time. I hardly ever came back to Mason because I couldn't stand the thought of seeing them together."

Ari nodded. "Okay, I get your reasons for leaving. I really do, but not calling anyone for the past five weeks, Jess? Then, sending the postcard saying you met someone else?"

Jessie shook her head. "I didn't mean for that to come across like it did. I meant that I had met a friend, and I did. I met Trey the first day I got there, and we connected and helped each other through the pain and hurt. I had fun with him, and yes...being with him helped me forget about Scott."

"I take it y'all were together a lot?" Ellie asked.

Jessie closed her eyes and nodded. "Every day. He was set to go home, but he decided to stay until New Year's...with me. He didn't want to go home and face questions with everyone telling him how sorry they were about what had happened."

"So, basically, you both hid like cowards," Ari said matter-of-factly.

My mouth dropped open, and I just looked at Ari. "Ari! Oh my god!" I said.

Ari just looked at me and shrugged her shoulders. "They did." She turned back to face Jessie. "I'm sorry, Jessie, but you left behind everyone who cares about you. For over a month, we went out of our goddamn minds, wondering where in the fuck you were. I thought Scott was going to lose everything."

Jessie looked at Ari with a questioning look. "What do you mean?"

Ellie grabbed Ari's arm. "Ari, maybe now is not the time—"

"No, now is the time. Scott went into a deep depression. He let his business go, and Jeff had to start taking all of Scott's business calls. They almost lost out on a racehorse they had been trying to get for the last few months. Scott pretty much gave up on everything…but his love for you."

I watched as the tears began to roll down Jessie's face. I looked at Ari and shook my head.

Ari shook her head and kept talking. "I'm sorry, Jessie. You know I adore you. There isn't a damn thing I wouldn't do for you, but what you did, not even calling anyone…it was just wrong."

Jessie sucked in a breath of air. "I know. I know it was, but at the time, I wasn't thinking clearly, and it was just easier to forget everything."

Ari rolled her eyes and looked away. I reached for Jessie's hand, and she looked at me.

I smiled. "Jessie, do you have feelings for this Trey guy?"

She shook her head and started crying. "No! I mean…yes…I care about him, and we became friends. He…he…helped me forget."

"Okay, I understand that," I said. "But Scott seems to think you might be in love with him, Jessie. Are you in love with him?"

She shook her head. "No. I love Scott, and we're having a baby, and…" She broke down in tears again. "Oh my god," she cried out as she rocked back and forth in the chair. "I let Trey touch me. I let him kiss me, and the whole time, it felt so wrong, but at the same time, it felt so right. I don't love him…I don't love him!" she yelled.

I glanced up at Ari and Ellie. They both had tears in their eyes. I noticed Ellie rubbing her stomach. I closed my eyes and felt sick to my stomach. The idea of finding out I was pregnant with the love of my life's child and knowing another man had touched me…

Oh god, poor Jessie.

"Jessie…did you have sex with Trey?" I asked.

She snapped her eyes over at me. "No! I didn't even let him give me an orgasm. I made him stop. Even though I thought Scott had cheated on me, I was still in love with him, and it felt wrong."

Ellie took a deep breath and started to rub Jessie's back. "Jessie, honey, take a deep breath and calm down."

Jessie sucked in a ragged breath and tried to calm her breathing down. She looked at Ellie and gave her a weak smile.

"Now…what happened between you and Scott that has Scott at Jeff and Ari's place and you here, crying?" Ellie asked.

Jessie took a deep breath and quickly let it out. "Everything seemed perfect. We just shared one of the most amazing nights of my life. Then, Scott said that Lark—Scott's friend who had brought him to Belize and then took us back home—had come to see if I needed help packing up while Scott had checked me out of the hotel. Lark saw me talking to Trey, and he saw…he saw…"

Ari, Ellie, and I all leaned forward and said at the same time, "He saw, what?"

"He saw me kiss Trey good-bye," Jessie said as she closed her eyes.

"Like, what kind of a good-bye kiss? A peck or a kiss-kiss?" Ari asked.

Jessie opened her eyes. "A kiss-kiss."

Ellie put her hands up to her mouth. "Why, Jessie?"

She began shaking her head. "I don't know! I guess I felt bad for him because I was just leaving him so suddenly. He seemed so hurt, and he wanted something more than friendship. It started out as just a friendly kiss, but Trey quickly made it into something more, and I stopped it immediately. I'm not sure what all Lark saw."

"Whoa…wait. He wanted to be more than friends?" Ari asked.

"Yes, but I kept telling him I wasn't ready. Then, I started to figure out that maybe it wasn't Scott who was with Chelsea. Like I said, I think a part of me always knew. Anyway, that was the day I called Scott and my dad when the storm came in. I called Scott first and told him I needed to talk to him. When I called him again later, I told him where I was. Then, everything started falling into place—how I had been feeling so bad and I hadn't had my period. I took a test in the middle of the damn tropical storm, and that was when I found out I was pregnant—on Christmas Eve. I told Trey, and he tried to tell me he would take care of the baby and me if Scott didn't want to. It was a terrible night because the phones had gone out, and I couldn't get a hold of Scott. I ended up sleeping in Trey's lap the whole night, and—"

"What?" all three of us called out again.

Ari stood up. "Jesus H. Christ, Jessie. You say you don't have feelings for this guy, but when you find out you're pregnant with another man's child, you sleep in the guy's arms all night long, and then you lead him on even more by kissing him good-bye."

I looked at Ari as Ellie stood up.

"Ari, stop this. Stop yelling at her," I said.

"No, this is bullshit." Ari looked down at Jessie, who was crying again. "You need to figure this shit out and figure it out fast. You clearly have feelings for Trey."

Jessie started shaking her head.

"Yes…yes, Jessie, you do. What happened between you and Scott this morning?"

Jessie wiped the tears away. "He asked if I was sure I really wanted to move in, and then he brought up Lark seeing me kiss Trey. I got mad and asked if he had Lark spying on me. Then, the guilt from me kissing Trey good-bye hit me like a brick wall, and when Scott reached to touch me, I pulled away. I don't know why I pulled away." She began sobbing hysterically. "I just feel so dirty, knowing I kissed another man and let him touch me where only Scott should be touching. Oh my god, I'm so confused."

She looked up at me, and my heart broke.

I took a deep breath and slowly let it out. "Jessie, if you truly didn't have feelings for this Trey guy, you wouldn't be sitting here, saying you're confused."

"No! No! I want to be with Scott. *I love Scott.* I'm not sure what in the hell it is. I think I'm feeling guilty more than anything. I don't have feelings like that for Trey! I want to have this child with Scott. I want to move in here and raise her together. I don't want anyone else!" Jessie screamed out.

Then, she stopped suddenly. "Oh god." She put her hands down to her stomach.

I jumped up and looked at Ari and Ellie. "Jessie?" I said.

She slowly stood and then leaned over. "Oh my god…no…please, God, no," Jessie barely whispered.

Ellie bent over and looked at Jessie. "Jessie, tell us what's going on, honey."

"I have a pain…in my stomach." Jessie tried to take a deep breath.

I looked up at Ari. She was standing there, frozen.

"Ari, call Scott and have him meet us at the hospital. I'm taking her to the hospital here in Mason," I said.

"My mother is working there today," Ellie said as she took Jessie's arm and helped her out to my car.

After we put Jessie in the front passenger seat, I turned and looked at Ellie. "She's gonna be fine. She's probably just experiencing cramps."

Ellie looked white as a ghost, and Ari was crying.

"Ari, you know this. You know you can have cramps early on in the pregnancy," I said. I looked at Ellie and touched her arm, causing her to jump. "Ellie…I need you to drive. Ari can't drive, sweetheart. Can you drive, Ells? Follow me to the hospital, okay?"

Ellie turned and looked at Ari. She looked back at me and nodded her head. I quickly walked to the driver's side of my car and got in. I looked at Jessie, who looked scared to death.

"Heather…what's wrong? Am I going to lose the baby?" She began to cry.

"No, you're not." I took off and headed to the hospital.

The whole way, I prayed to God that I hadn't just lied to Jessie.

21 Scott

I burst through the hospital doors and began looking around for one of the girls. Jeff was right behind me. We had stopped at Garrett and Emma's place to drop off Luke and Grace, and then we'd headed straight to the hospital.

My hands were shaking, and I didn't see Ari, Ellie, or Heather anywhere. I walked up to the nurses' station. I was just about to ask for information when I heard Heather's voice.

"Scott."

I turned and looked at her. I tried to read her face for any signs. I was so scared that Jessie had lost the baby. Heather smiled that sweet smile of hers and walked up to me.

"She's fine," Heather said.

"The baby?" I felt tears building in my eyes.

"The baby is fine also."

I let out the breath I had been holding and collapsed into Heather's arms. "Oh, thank God. Oh, thank you, God."

Heather pulled back and looked at me. "She just had some cramping, which is normal."

I looked at Heather, confused. "Cramping?"

She nodded her head. "Just think of it as her body's way of trying to get ready for what all is about to happen. Her hormones are in overdrive, and then add in the stress of everything on top of that. She just needs to try to de-stress."

My face fell, and my knees felt weak. *I caused this…oh my god.*

Heather must have read my face. "You didn't cause this, Scott. Please, just calm down, and try to relax before you go in the room. Ellie, Ari, and Sharon are in there."

I nodded and took a few deep breaths. "Where is she?"

"Come on, I'll take you to her room. They aren't planning on keeping her in the hospital, but they wanted to get some fluids into her."

I stopped outside the door. I couldn't move. I was frozen in place. Heather took my hands in hers and smiled.

"What if she leaves me for him?" I whispered.

I saw the tears in Heather's eyes as she shook her head.

"She won't because she loves you so much, Scott. *She. Loves. You,*" Heather said, stressing each word.

"But she cares about him, Heather. How do I know she's not going to be thinking about him, wondering what if she hadn't gotten pregnant?"

"Oh no, Scott, don't think that way." Heather wiped a tear away.

I smiled and took another deep breath as I opened the door. Everyone looked up, but the only person I saw was Jessie. The moment her eyes met mine, I wanted to run to her, to grab her in my arms and tell her how much I loved her. But I couldn't.

Sharon smiled and nodded. "Well…looks like dad is here now. Come on, girls. Let's give them some time alone. I'll be back, Jessie, in a few minutes. The IV drip is almost done, and then I'll get that out of your hand. Then, we can get you ready to head home."

As they all walked by, they each gave me a strange look.

Was that pity I saw in their eyes?

The moment the door shut, Jessie smiled at me. "I'm sorry if you were scared. The doctor said it's normal to feel cramping, and some experience it more than others. Hopefully, it won't last long."

I looked at the IV bag.

"I guess they thought I was dehydrated or something," she said with a weak smile.

I came and sat down on the bed. She reached for my hand, and when she touched me, I felt that familiar zap run through my body.

"I was so scared, Jessie. I don't know what I would have done if…" I couldn't even finish my sentence.

"I know. I was scared, too, but everything is okay."

I looked her in the eyes. "It will always be in the back of my head, Jessie, and I'm always going to wonder."

I watched as a single tear rolled down her cheek.

"I don't love him," she whispered.

I nodded. "Well, I guess you'll find out soon enough."

She looked at me, confused. "What do you mean?"

"He's heading to Mason."

"Who's heading to Mason?"

"Trey," I whispered.

"What? Why? How do you know this? Oh my god, did you ask him to come here?" She tried to sit up.

I just looked at her. "No, I didn't fucking ask him to come here. He said he got my number from the hotel clerk, the one you borrowed the phone from to call me. He called me and said he was coming to Mason."

She shook her head. "Why?"

I stood up and ran my hands through my hair. I walked to the window and looked out. "Because he said he loves you, and he thinks you love him, too. He's not giving up unless he knows this is what you want."

"Scott, you have to know I love you," she said as her voice broke off.

I turned and smiled at her as I nodded. "I know you do, baby. I know you do. I love you, too, and I'll do...I'll walk away if..."

I felt a tear run down my face as her eyes widened in surprise.

"If you decide that you need time...I'll wait for you. I'll always wait for you."

"Need time for what?" she asked.

"Jessie, I know you're confused. I could tell by your reaction this morning when I went to reach out for you. You have feelings for this guy, and you need to figure out just what they are before we can even talk about our future together."

She began shaking her head. "No...no, Scott. I don't need to figure out anything. I know what I want and whom I want. I just need time to forget about him, and—"

I sucked in a breath of air.

"No! Wait...that's not what I meant."

I walked up to her, leaned down, and gently kissed her on the lips. She reached up and went to grab on to the back of my neck, but I pulled away.

"I love you, Jessie."

She was crying, and a part of me was dying inside, knowing that I was the reason she was crying.

"I love you, too, Scott."

Sharon walked back in the room and started to take the IV out of Jessie's hand. Sharon began to give Jessie some paperwork on prenatal care, a prescription for prenatal vitamins, and her discharge papers.

Sharon smiled and said, "Now, go home and get some rest. Just take it easy for a few days. Eat some fruit and veggies and drink lots of water."

Jessie smiled and nodded her head.

We walked out of the room and into the lobby. Ari, Ellie, Heather, and Jeff all jumped up.

Ari walked up and gave Jessie a kiss on the cheek. She whispered, "I'm sorry for being such a bitch."

Jessie smiled. "No. You were being honest."

Ellie and Heather each gave Jessie and then me a kiss on the cheek. We all walked out together, and Jeff and I talked a little bit about the New Year's Eve party we were throwing at Gunner's place.

I got into the car and looked over at Jessie. "Do you want to stop and get the vitamins now or later?"

She looked at me and gave me a weak smile. "Later? I'm just so tired."

I nodded, and I started driving.

As Aaron and Jenny's house came into view, I noticed Jessie sit up a bit straighter.

She looked at me. "Why are you bringing me to my brother's? I don't want to go there. I want to go home. I just want to go home and go to sleep." Then, her face dropped. "Do you not want me at your house?"

"What? Of course I do. I just thought you might want to be at Aaron's, especially if…if *he's* coming to town to see you and all."

She turned and looked out the window. "I would rather stay with you, and I don't care that he's coming to town."

"Okay," I said as I pulled out of Aaron's driveway and headed home.

The short drive to my house was a silent one. When we got to the house, I got out, and by the time I got around to the passenger side, Jessie had already gotten out of the truck. She was making her way to the front door.

We walked in, and I set my keys on the table. I took my wallet and phone out and set them down as well.

She looked at me and smiled. "Will you lie down with me? Please?"

As much as I wanted to, I couldn't. *What if Trey comes to town and talks her into leaving with him? I'll be alone…again.*

"I, um…I have a ton of work I need to catch up on, and then there's this party we're planning, so I need to take care of some things for that."

Her smile faded as she nodded her head. "Of course. I understand." Then, she turned and headed for my bedroom.

Two hours later, and I was still sitting at my desk…with nothing done. I got up and walked outside and down to the barn. I walked up to the stall where the new filly was. I smiled as I looked at her name on the door—*Jessie Girl.*

I turned and sat down on a hay bale, and then I put my head in my hands. I'd never felt so torn in my life. *Does she love him?* Her eyes had told me that she didn't, but she had feelings for him. That much I could see in her eyes.

"What are you doing out here?"

I looked up and saw Gunner standing there, leaning up against the barn door.

"Thinking."

I'd forgotten Gunner had mentioned that he was going to come by and pick up a horse today.

He slowly nodded and started walking toward me. "About what?"

"If I'm doing the right thing," I said as I watched him take a seat across from me.

He took a deep breath and slowly let it out. "Talk to me, Scott."

I let a small laugh come out as I shook my head. "He had the fucking nerve to call me and tell me he's coming here…to fight for her. That motherfucker. She's pregnant with my child, and he thinks he's going to take her from me."

"What are you planning on doing?" Gunner asked.

I looked over at him. "I'm going to let her make the decision on her own. I'm not going to force her into anything…even if it kills me in the end. I won't hurt her again…ever."

"She loves you. You have to know that."

"I do," I said as my voice cracked.

"Don't just give up on her, Scott. Don't push her away again by thinking that what you're doing is helping her because it might end up hurting her. She needs to know that you will fight for her and your child. Don't let this prick just come walking in here, so he can try to convince her what happened on the island is worth walking away from the love of her life. From what Ellie and Heather told me, Jessie is scared to death that you'll walk away from her again. She is filled with guilt about what she did with this character. Don't let her think, even for a minute, that you're pushing her away. Because she just might find her way back into this guy's arms." Gunner raised his eyebrow.

I stood up and thought about how sad she'd looked when we pulled up to Aaron's and then when I didn't go lay down with her. She'd looked almost…devastated.

"Where is she now?" Gunner asked.

"Sleeping." I thought about how she must have felt as she walked back to the bedroom alone. I turned and looked at Gunner.

He stood up. "When will he be here?"

"Not sure. I'm assuming he's on his way."

Gunner walked up to me and put his hands on my shoulders as he looked me in the eyes. "Go to her, Scott, right now. Don't even let that fucker put a single doubt in her mind. Ellie truly believes that Jessie only cares for Trey as a friend. Don't push her away."

I thought about Jessie telling me about the day Trey had touched her…kissed her body in places where only I should be kissing. I felt the anger build up inside me, but then I remembered her telling him to stop, telling him she loved me and how it'd felt wrong. She thought I'd cheated, and she hadn't given up on our love.

I won't give up on our love either.

"Sorry, Gun…but I have to leave you to fend for yourself." I turned and walked away from Gunner.

I started to make my way back up to the house. I found myself jogging, and then I burst into a full-on run. I ran up the back steps and into the house. I stopped and took a minute or two to catch my breath. That was when I heard Jessie talking to someone. I slowly walked down the hall that led to my room and stopped to listen.

"I'm not really sure why you felt the need to come here, Trey. No…there is nothing to talk about. I care about you, I won't deny that, but only as a friend. At first, I was confused because that day…that day, I think a part of you captured my heart, but it was for all the wrong reasons. I wanted you to make me forget about the pain and hurt I was feeling. We weren't going to make love, Trey. We were going to fuck the hurt away."

I closed my eyes as I listened to her talk about that day. I balled my hands into fists, and I wanted to hit the wall.

"I love him…from the very beginning, I told you that I loved him. I never gave you any reason to think I didn't love him. Yes, I know. Okay."

Fuck! What are they talking about?

"Meet me at Willow Creek Café at seven thirty. That gives me thirty minutes to meet you. I need to let Scott know. Yes, I will."

She's going to meet him? I leaned my head up against the wall and tried to take deep breaths. *Why is she going to meet him?*

"Yes, that's the place. Okay, I'll be there as soon as I can find Scott and let him know. See you in a few."

I turned and quickly walked to my office where I sat down behind my desk. I felt like I was going to throw up. When Jessie walked in, I stood and walked over to her. I pulled her to me and kissed the living shit out of her. She instantly brought her hands up and pulled on my hair as she let out a sweet, long moan.

God, I love her so much. Please don't leave me, Jessie. Please.

I was just about to say something to her when she said, "Scott…please make love to me."

"What? Right now?" I asked, knowing she had to meet the fucker.

She smiled and nodded her head. I reached down and picked her up. I carried her over to my desk where I sat her down on it. She had a skirt on, and the sight of her beautiful legs about drove me mad. I sat down in my chair and placed my hands on her legs. I slowly moved them up toward her panties. She threw her head back and let out a moan.

I hooked my fingers in her panties and whispered, "Lift up, baby."

She lifted herself off the desk, so I could take off her panties. I set them aside as I stood, and then I started to take off my jeans. She smiled when she saw I had no underwear on. I sat back down in my chair and watched as she licked her lips and made her way onto my lap.

"Fuck…" I whispered as she slowly sank down onto me.

I threw my head back and let out a moan as she ran her tongue along my neck and then up to my ear.

"I love you," she said as she started to ride me fast and hard.

I grabbed on to her and looked into her eyes. In that moment, I knew what she was doing. She was proving to me how much she loved me and who was number one in her world. She had no idea that I knew she would be late for meeting that fucker, and I didn't even care at this point. All I knew was that the girl I loved more than life itself was making love to me in my office while whispering over and over how much she loved me.

"Oh god...Scott!" she called out as she held on to the armrest of the chair and leaned back.

I could almost feel her tighten on my dick as she began to come.

"Yes...oh god, yes." She snapped her head forward and looked into my eyes.

That was when I lost it. "Jessie..." was all I could manage to get out.

She leaned over and began kissing me. I moaned into her mouth while every ounce of my love poured into her body. She rested her forehead against mine as she tried to steady her breathing.

"Baby, I missed you so much."

"I missed you, too," she said, still trying to catch her breath.

I thought she would get up and move, but she stayed there. I was still inside her, and she let out a small moan as she moved her hips against me.

"I don't want to leave. I want to stay this way forever," she whispered against my neck.

I let out a laugh. "It would be kind of hard to deliver a baby with my penis in the way."

She giggled. "I hate the word *penis*," she said as she looked at me and winked.

"Then, maybe we should come up with a list of different words for penis," I said, raising my eyebrows. *That could be a fun evening.*

Her smile dropped, and she looked at me with tears building in her eyes. "Scott, I don't want you to ever again doubt my love for you. My whole heart belongs to you and only you. It always has, and it always will."

I love her so damn much. "Jessie," I said softly, "baby, I love you so much. You have no idea how much I love you, and I will fight for you until the day I die."

She took a deep breath and slowly let it out. "You don't have to fight for me. You already have me," she said with a smile.

I leaned up and gently kissed her.

She looked into my eyes and said, "I need you to go somewhere with me."

I nodded. "Okay. Where?"

"I need you to go with me to Willow Creek Café."
Holy shit. I wasn't expecting that.

The look on Scott's face was hard to read. He seemed shocked when I asked him to go with me to the café. I was almost scared to tell him that Trey was in town and would be there. I wasn't afraid to meet Trey alone at all. Lying in bed earlier, alone in Scott's room, it had all become so clear to me. I knew I didn't love Trey, and I was letting the guilt take over my emotions.

"Scott, Trey called the house. He said you were listed. I answered and agreed to meet him at the café."

Scott sat there, just staring at me.

"Being alone in the bedroom for those few hours, I really had time to think. That day when Trey had…well, when he touched me like he did…"

Scott closed his eyes, and I felt his grip tighten on my hips before he let go.

"That whole night, all I wanted to do was go back to my room and shower. I felt like I had been violated somehow even though I had asked him…to make me forget."

I saw the tears building in his eyes, and it was killing me, knowing that this conversation was hurting him.

"You don't feel that way about someone if you love him…or have feelings for him. I know now that it was my guilt that was eating away at me. It was playing with my emotions. Scott, I. Love. You. Only you."

Scott cleared his throat. "Why did you kiss him good-bye?"

"Guilt. I felt so bad for leaving him. I guess, in a sense, I formed a friendship with him because I knew he was hurting like I was. He knew how it felt to hurt so deeply. Once I started thinking more and more about that night when I'd walked in and seen Chelsea, the more and more I started to try to pull away from Trey…until one day, it just hit me. I needed you. I needed to talk to you, and I had to talk to you right then. I freaked out the night the storm hit because I couldn't get a hold of you, and I was so afraid. That next morning…when I said good-bye to him…I just didn't want to break his heart again. Does that make sense? He tried to deepen the kiss, but I pushed him away. I don't have those feelings for him. I care about him but only as a friend."

Scott looked into my eyes and then looked away. He stared down at the floor for a good two minutes before he glanced back at me. "Yeah…that makes sense. I get what you're saying. But why do you need me to go to the café with you? Are you afraid to see him alone? Afraid of what you might feel when you see him?"

I smiled and shook my head. "No. I want you there because I love you. I want Trey to see that I have no secrets with you, and I want to do this together. I don't want to be away from you for another minute."

The smile that spread across his face caused me to giggle. He reached up and ran his hand along my jawline, and I felt the butterflies in my stomach.

"Are you feeling okay, baby? You don't want to meet him tomorrow?" Scott asked.

"No. I'd rather just do this now, so he understands once and for all that he was only ever just a friend."

Scott nodded. "Well then, let's go."

I slowly got up, and I instantly missed the warmth of Scott's body up against mine. I put my panties on while I watched Scott pull up his pants. I wanted him again. I glanced over at the clock, and we were already late for meeting Trey as it was. Scott reached out for my hand, and we walked through the house and out to the truck.

He pulled me closer to him and said, "Love muscle."

I looked at him, surprised. "Huh?"

Scott smiled that drop-me-to-my-knees smile. "My first suggestion for a word other than *penis*—love muscle."

I tossed my head back and laughed. "I've got one," I said.

He held open the truck door and helped me up into his truck.

"Baby maker," I said as I wiggled my eyebrows up and down.

"Hell yeah, it is!" Scott said with a laugh.

By the time we walked into the café, we were almost an hour late. I looked around for Trey, and my heart sank. He was talking to Chelsea.

Good god. My worst nightmares are coming true all at once.

"Shit," Scott whispered. He leaned down and said, "What do you want me to do?"

I watched as Trey talked and laughed with Chelsea. A part of me was bothered by seeing him talking to her, but it wasn't jealousy. It was hate. I had nothing but pure hate for this woman who clearly was going to do everything she could to try to hurt me.

Well, no more. I'm done.

I smiled and looked at Scott. "Nothing. Let's go say hi."

I walked up to the table, and the moment Chelsea saw Scott and me, the smile from her face vanished. Trey turned, and his smile vanished just as fast.

I stopped right in front of them. "Chelsea, last time I saw ya, you were riding Bryce pretty good. Whose bed are you hitting tonight? Or are you taking the evening off from whoring?"

Trey choked on his food, and Scott let out a small laugh. Chelsea just glared at me.

I leaned down and put my hands on the table as I got right in her face. "You lost, bitch. I love him, and he loves me. Nothing…and no one," I said as I turned and looked at Trey, "will ever come between our love—especially now that we're having a baby."

Her eyes darted down to my stomach and then back up. She opened her mouth to say something, but then she shut it again.

I stood back up and felt Scott wrap his arms around me. I leaned back into him. I wanted nothing more than to just turn around, leave, go park somewhere, and make out.

Chelsea slowly stood up. She looked down at Trey and smiled as she reached into her purse. She pulled out her business card. "Give me a call sometime, Trey," she said with a wink. She looked back at Scott and then me and let out a laugh. "Honestly, you two are made for each other. Scott, Bryce was a much better fuck than you." She leaned closer to me. "Have fun with my sloppy seconds."

"Oh, we've already had fun—in his office, in our new bed, the shower, the kitchen table, the sofa, in both living rooms…oh, and I can't forget the pool table. The only place we still have to hit is"—I turned and looked at Scott with a smile on my face—"his truck."

His crooked smile instantly made me want to move my hand and touch myself to relieve the aching pulse between my legs. *I want him. I want him to show me how much he wants me.* I didn't care if we walked out of here right now and just left Trey sitting with Chelsea.

Chelsea stood there with her mouth hanging open. "I'm out of here." She pushed past both of us, hitting Scott in the shoulder as she walked by.

I watched her walk out of the café, and then I looked around quickly at everyone staring at us. I smiled and said, "Sorry, y'all."

I grabbed Scott's hand, and we both sat down at the table. I smiled at Trey. The sight of him sitting there did nothing to me. I was happy to see him, but other than wishing him the best, he had no effect on me whatsoever.

"Sorry, we're late," I said.

Scott reached his hand across the table, and Trey slowly extended his hand. They shook hands quickly.

Trey looked between the two of us. "Um...I assumed you would be coming alone."

"Why?" I asked.

Trey tilted his head and glared at Scott. He leaned back and put his napkin on the table. "I'm going to guess the reason you're late is the pool table, perhaps?"

I couldn't even believe that Trey had just said that. I sat there, stunned. Scott laughed and said, "Nope, my office."

I felt my cheeks turning hotter by the second.

Trey snapped his head over and looked at me. "Fine. You want to do this here in front of him, then so be it. So, you're going to forgive him—just like that? Like nothing ever happened?"

"Nothing did happen, Trey. Did you know that Chelsea was the girl I'd walked in on?" I asked as I looked him straight in the eye.

He shook his head and looked at Scott.

"Well, Scott was over at our friend's house. He was passed out cold, and Chelsea hatched a little plan. She texted me from Scott's phone and then got Bryce to sleep with her. It wasn't ever Scott, just like I thought."

Trey sat back. "What about us?"

I stared at him, stunned. "There is no *us*, Trey, and there never was. We were two people with broken hearts who found a kinship with each other, a place to forget the hurt for a while."

Trey took a deep breath and let it out quickly. "So, that's all I was to you, Jessie? A means to forget about your guy here." He jerked his head toward Scott. He leaned forward and looked into my eyes. "What about that time we shared together? You were ready to make love to me. Or have you forgotten that?"

The next thing I knew, Scott had grabbed Trey by the shirt and was about to punch him.

"Scott! Please don't! Please let me handle this. *Please*," I pleaded as I put my hand on his arm.

Scott pushed Trey back, and he slammed into the seat.

I grabbed Scott's hand and cleared my throat. "Trey, you know that was a mistake, and I asked you to stop. Why did I tell you to stop?"

Trey looked away.

"Trey?"

He never looked at me as he said, "Because you said you still loved him."

I slowly let out the breath I'd been holding in. I wasn't sure why I had been holding my breath. I guessed I was worried Trey would lie. He could have easily lied and said we had made love, but then I would have really never talked or even looked his way again.

"Jessie, I'm not going to lie to you and say I don't have feelings for you because I do. That month was probably some of the best days of my life."

I shook my head. "No, they weren't, Trey. We were hiding from the world. We were just two people who didn't want to face reality, and we got lost in a make-believe world. You don't love me, Trey. You love the idea of me. You need to go home, get back to work, and move on with your life. Someday, you're going to meet a girl who is going to fall head over heels in love with you. You're going to ask her to marry you, and things will work out this time."

Trey looked me in the eyes and then turned to Scott. He shut his eyes and shook his head. "I do love you, Jessie. That much I know is true, but I also know you've loved Scott from the first moment I saw you. As much as I want to try to convince you that you have feelings for me...I know deep down inside that you don't."

I could almost feel Scott's entire body relaxing.

I gave Trey a small smile. "I'll always care about you as a friend. You really helped me through a rough time, and I'd like to think I helped you as well. But as far as loving you...I love Scott. I'll always love Scott."

Trey nodded his head slowly and let a small smile play across his face. "Well then, I guess that means I'm heading home to face the family and the million questions I'll be answering." He stood, reached for his wallet, and took out a twenty. He threw it down on the table, and then he extended his hand to Scott.

Scott stood and shook it.

"You're one lucky son of a bitch. I hope you know that," Trey said as he gestured toward me.

Scott turned and smiled down at me. "Yeah, I know. I'm not lucky though...I'm blessed." He winked at me.

Trey looked at me and smiled. "I guess this is it then, huh? This is where I wish you the best of luck and hope that you find happiness forever...even if it's not with me."

I let out a small laugh and nodded. "I guess so. Have a safe trip to Dallas, Trey."

I stuck my hand out to shake his, and he just looked at me before glancing down at my hand. Then, he slowly turned and walked away. I watched as he left the café.

I looked at Scott, and his eyes were no longer filled with hurt or doubt. They were filled with nothing but happiness and love.

He pulled me close to him and moved his lips oh-so slowly to my ear where he nipped on my earlobe. "How about we go and break in the truck?"

I pulled back just a little and gave him the sexiest smile I possibly could. "Let me go to the restroom first. I need to ditch my panties," I whispered.

As I began walking away, I turned to see Scott standing there. His mouth was dropped open, and he was just frozen. I winked, and then I turned back around and went into the ladies' room.

I quickly used the restroom, which seemed to be a normal thing now. I swore I had to pee every five minutes. I slipped off my panties, and as I was walking out the door, I dumped them into the trash. I giggled as I walked out. I felt so naughty, going without panties, and it was turning me on even more.

I looked around for Scott for a few seconds before realizing he had already left and gone out to the truck. As I walked out of the café, I looked over to a small car where a girl was leaning against it. There was a guy with his hands on the car…kissing the girl. The closer I got, I was able to make out the girl. I sucked in a breath of air when I noticed it was Chelsea and some guy.

I shook my head and made a beeline right toward the love of my life. As he helped me into the truck, he moved his hand up my leg, under my skirt, and over to my sensitive lips. I instinctively opened my legs to him as he brushed his fingers across me.

I threw my head back and whispered, "Oh, sweet Jesus."

He let out a small laugh and then pulled my legs open more as he placed a finger inside me. He slowly moved it around and then pulled it out. Lifting my head, I watched him put the finger into his mouth and then slowly pull it out.

Holy shit. I've never in my life felt like I could have an orgasm without being touched. I couldn't pull my eyes away from his lips.

"Fuck, you taste good," he said.

"Oh god…I think I might have just had an orgasm," I barely said.

He jumped up and kissed me, his tongue moving so beautifully with mine. We both let out a moan together.

He pulled back just a bit and said, "Trust me, baby, you'll know when you're having an orgasm because you won't be able to stop calling out my name."

"Scott…I need you. Right now." I reached down and rubbed my hand on his hard dick.

He jumped down, shut the door, and headed to the driver's side of the truck.

I hadn't even been paying attention to where Scott was going. I just kept talking a mile a minute. The next thing I knew, we were in a field and in the backseat of his truck where he had taken me to heaven and back twice.

As we lay there, panting for air, I slowly moved my fingertips up and down his back. I smiled, knowing that I was happy again for the first time in weeks. Everything felt so right. It felt even better than before.

"So, did we break the truck in good?" he asked in a sleepy voice.

"Yes," I said before kissing his shoulder.

"Good, 'cause my deep V-diver is exhausted."

I let out a laugh and rolled my eyes. "Oh. My. God. Please…let's just go back to calling it a penis, shall we?"

He laughed as he looked at me and reached over to kiss me. "I love you so much, Jessie."

"How much do you love me?" I asked with a smile.

"I love you to the moon and back."

I moved in and began running my tongue along his lips. I wanted him again, but I knew he was tired. I was exhausted myself, and I was so ready to get home.

"I think I'm ready to go home and just snuggle up. I can hardly keep my eyes open," I said with a yawn.

"Well, we could always knock on the door of the owner of this place and ask to spend the night."

Scott got up and started to get dressed as I looked around in the dark.

"Wait—where are we?" I asked.

Scott laughed. "Gunner's place. Right behind your dad's place."

"Oh my god! Scott, you did not bring me to my dad's place to have sex with me."

He started to chuckle. "I sure as shit did. I've always wanted to make love to you right under your damn dad's nose ever since I first laid eyes on you."

"Why?" I asked, stunned.

Scott shrugged his shoulders. "I don't know. The thrill of getting caught, maybe?"

I couldn't help it. I lost it and started laughing. Scott began laughing because I was laughing.

"What's so funny?" he asked.

"What's my dad gonna do? Ground us? I'm pregnant with your child, for Christ's sake."

"Hey…don't blow this moment for me. Come on."

He opened the back door and helped me get my dress on. Then, he helped me out and into the front seat of the truck. As he pulled the seat belt around me, he smiled at me. I smiled back, and he reached up and kissed me on the nose.

I put my hand on the side of his face and said, "Please take me home to our house."

Scott smiled and said, "With pleasure."

23 Josh

Heather was due to be home any minute, so I rushed around and lit all the candles. Mom and Dad had taken the twins for the night, giving Heather and me some much-needed time together.

I walked into the kitchen, and the smell of the lasagna caused me to stop and inhale. *Damn, I love my mom's lasagna.*

I glanced up and looked out the back window. When I saw Heather walking up, I quickly lit the last two candles on the table and leaned up against the island. The door opened, and her beautiful face lit up like Christmas morning.

"Oh wow! What's all this?" she asked with a giggle.

I ran my hand through my hair and gave her the smile I knew drove her crazy. "Well, Mom and Dad took the kids for the night, and before they left, Mom made lasagna for dinner."

I watched as Heather looked around the room. I had put candles everywhere. The table was set with dishes, a salad I'd made with my dad, and a bottle of Heather's favorite Shiraz wine, The Stump Jump.

She licked her lips and turned back to me as she raised her eyebrows. "The whole night? Alone with no kids?" she asked as her eyes lit up.

I felt my dick jump, and I quickly looked to see how much time the lasagna had left. I looked back at her and nodded. The next thing I knew, she slammed her body into mine and frantically began taking off my clothes. It wasn't long before I joined in and had her down to her black lace bra and gray boy shorts with a black lace edge. I pushed her back and took in the sight of her beautiful body.

"Damn…sometimes, I still can't believe you're mine," I whispered.

She smiled and took a step back as she reached behind her back and unclasped her bra before letting it fall to the floor. Then, she hooked her thumbs in her panties, slowly shimmied out of them, and kicked them off to the side.

"Heather," I whispered.

She walked up to me and placed her hands on my bare chest. "I've always been yours." She brushed her lips softly against mine.

"Oh god, baby." I pulled her closer to me and deepened the kiss.

I moved my hand down her body and could feel her shudder in my arms. I lightly brushed my fingers over her and barely touched her clit when she let out a moan.

"Josh…I want you to make love to me all night, but right now…I really need you to just fuck me," she whispered against my neck.

My heart slammed in my chest. Something about my sweet princess asking me to fuck her drove me out of my goddamn mind. I picked her up, and she wrapped her legs around me. Our kissing had turned so passionate that it was like we needed each other's air to breathe.

I walked up to the kitchen table and set her down on it. I pulled my lips from hers and asked, "How much do you like these plates?"

She smiled. "I never did care for them too much."

I quickly took the salad and wine and put them on the island.

"Oh wait! The wine glasses…those were from your parents!" Heather said as she let out a giggle.

I grabbed those and the salt and pepper shakers that Gunner and Ellie had bought for us. Then, in one movement, I knocked everything else off the table. The sound of the dishes hitting the floor and breaking did something to me. I grabbed Heather and pulled her closer to me as I slammed my dick into her as fast and hard as I could.

"Yes! Oh god, yes, Josh."

I watched while I moved in and out of her, her breasts bouncing and turning me on even more, as she held on to the table.

"Ah…Heather," was all I could get out as I tried to hold off.

"Faster…oh god, go harder, Josh…harder!" she called out.

The moment she snapped her head up and looked at me, I felt her tightening, and I almost lost it.

"Oh god…I'm gonna come…yes…Josh, yes!" she cried out.

Watching Heather have an orgasm and call out my name was the hottest fucking thing in the word. I couldn't hold off any longer, and I let myself go as I called out her name. She threw her head back and repeated my name over and over again.

When I finally came to a stop, she looked into my eyes, her chest heaving up and down. I tried to steady my breathing as we both just got lost in each other's eyes.

Then, the timer went off for the lasagna.

"Damn, I'm good," I said.

Heather started laughing. She wrapped her legs around me tighter as I lifted her up and carried her over to the stove. I hit Off on the timer and turned the oven to warm. Then, I carried my princess upstairs and to our shower.

As the warm water ran over our bodies, I took a washcloth and slowly started to wash every surface of her body. I moved the washcloth over each breast, and when I kissed each cleaned nipple, she let out a moan.

"Josh," she whispered.

"Put your leg up on the ledge, princess," I said against her ear.

I moved my hand along the inside of her leg and slowly put two fingers inside her, then three, and then I began to move them in and out as I kissed one nipple and then the other.

"Jesus…" Heather said as she placed her hands on the walls of the shower.

I glanced up and saw she had her eyes closed. I quickly dropped to my knees and began kissing her clit. When I moved my tongue in and out of her, her hands were in my hair, grabbing and pushing me harder into her.

"Yes…oh god, yes!" she cried out in pleasure as she began to move her hips faster. "Josh…oh my god, that feels amazing…Josh!"

I smiled, listening to her say my name. She must have really needed these orgasms because I'd never heard her scream out so loud before. When she finally stopped moving her hips and calling out, I felt her body slowly starting to give out. I quickly stood up and grabbed on to her.

"My god." She was panting for air. "That was…that was amazing."

I smiled and pushed a stray piece of hair away from her face. "Did you need those, baby?"

She nodded her head. "More than you know."

I turned the shower off and stepped outside, holding on to her hand the whole time. I dried her off first and wrapped a towel around her. Then, I quickly dried myself off before putting a towel around my waist. I picked her up and carried her over to the bed where I gently placed her down.

"What about dinner? I'm starving now," she said with a giggle.

I smiled as I walked over to the dresser. I pulled out a pair of boxer shorts and slipped them on. "You just relax, princess. I'll bring dinner up to you."

She smiled, and I just about dropped to my knees.

"Really?"

I laughed and nodded my head. I turned to head back downstairs.

"Don't forget the wine!" she called out.

After we ate and had two glasses of wine each, we lay there in silence as I held on to the love of my life.

"What happened today?" I finally asked.

She sucked in a long breath and slowly let it out. "Oh, Josh." She sat up and pulled the sheet with her. She shook her head. "Jessie was confused because of this guy she'd met in Belize, and then Ari jumped all over her and got her even more upset."

"Is that when y'all had to take Jessie to the hospital? You said it was just cramping and nothing was wrong, right?" I slipped my hand under the sheet and moved my fingers up and down her thigh.

"Yeah, it was right after she got upset, but everything is fine. It breaks my heart because if she had only just stayed and not run away…"

I let out a breath and nodded my head. "I know, but I also know how much Scott loves her, and he's not going to let anything come between them. I mean, look at how he beat the shit out of his brother. I know a lot of that was anger toward Chelsea, but damn. If Gunner and Jeff hadn't pulled him off Bryce, I'd hate to see what would have happened."

She gave me a weak smile. "Yeah. I just hope Jessie and Scott can work everything out with the baby coming and all. They love each other so much and…" Her eyes filled with tears.

"Baby, don't worry. They're gonna work it out. I know they will."

Just then, Heather's cell phone went off. I had brought our phones upstairs in case my mom and dad needed us for anything.

Heather grabbed her phone and looked at me. "It's from Jessie."

I glanced at the clock. It was almost ten. "This late?" I asked.

I watched Heather's face light up as she read the text message. She turned to me and jumped up. Then, she leaned down and kissed the shit out of me.

"Gesh…read it again!" I said with a laugh.

"Oh, Josh! They worked everything out! Jessie said she would fill me in tomorrow, but she said everything is perfect. They are home, and Scott is snuggled up next to her, sleeping with his hand on her stomach!"

I had to laugh at how excited Heather was. I knew how much she cared about both Scott and Jessie, and she just wanted everyone to find the same kind of love and happiness we had found.

The look on her face turned, and she bit down on her lower lip. She placed her hands on my chest and gently pushed me onto my back. "Now, what's this about making love to me all night long, Mr. Hayes?"

She leaned down and kissed me gently on the lips as she slowly sank down on me. The moment I filled her body, she let out the sexiest moan I'd ever heard. I rolled her over and slowly began to make love to her.

"Josh, I love you. I love you so much," she whispered.

I watched a tear roll down her face. I used my thumb to wipe it away as I said, "I love you more times infinity."

24 Scott

I hit End on my cell phone and looked over at Jessie, who was sitting on a hay bale with her knees tucked up under her chin.

"I don't want to go," she whined.

I let out a laugh. "Baby, we have to. We've told everyone but them."

She threw her head back and let out a frustrated moan. "Ugh, Scott, they already don't like me. Now, add me running off for five weeks, causing their baby boy heartache, on top of me not being the girl they wanted you to marry."

"I don't give a fuck who they wanted me to marry. I want to marry you, the love of my life and the woman who is having my child."

She stood up and pouted. "But they've *never* liked me. Amanda has told me horror stories about her in-laws. What if that's how this is going to be? I mean, I don't come from money, and my name is Jessie, not Chelsea."

I walked over to her and used my finger to pull up her chin. I looked into her eyes, and they sparkled when I smiled at her.

"I. Don't. Care." I leaned down and kissed her.

She opened her mouth, and our tongues immediately began to explore each other. I was so lost in the kiss that I didn't want to hear the person clearing his throat behind me.

Jessie pulled slightly away and smiled. "Someone's here, babe."

"Go away," I said, without bothering to turn around to see whom it was.

"Fuck you, asshole," Lark said from behind me.

I smiled and looked over my shoulder. "I'm glad you changed your mind and showed up a day earlier." I walked up to him and reached my hand out to shake his hand.

He shook it and then tipped his cowboy hat at Jessie.

"My god…I would have never imagined you as a cowboy, Lark," Jessie said with a chuckle.

Lark grinned and slammed his right hand over his heart. "Oh, Jessie, you wound me. I grew up on a sixteen-section ranch in south Texas. I put the meaning in the word *cowboy*."

"Wow. What is that? Like, ten-thousand acres?" Jessie asked.

I wrapped my arms around her and rested my chin on top of her head. *Shit, the smell of her shampoo drives me crazy. I can't seem to get enough of her.*

"Ten thousand two hundred and forty, if you want to get down to the nuts of it."

I rolled my eyes and laughed. "Lark's dad owns one of the biggest and best hunting ranches in Texas."

"Ah, so I bet your house is probably loaded with dead animals," Jessie said with a laugh.

Lark shook his head. "Nope. I live in a condo in downtown Austin."

"Yeah, except when his crazier-than-rich boss calls him to duty. Communications, my ass. You better not be into anything illegal, Lark."

Lark let out a sigh. "Scott, Skip works for the U.S. government. He's sort of like a…contractor. That's how I got the job with him."

"And what do you do besides fly his helicopter?" Jessie asked.

Lark gave her that smile that would melt any girl's heart. "Oh, I help out in areas of expertise. I learned a lot during the short amount of time I was in the Marines," he said with a wink.

"Fair enough," Jessie said. She turned and looked at me as she whispered, "All secretive and shit. I can see why he's a ladies' man."

Lark laughed. "Shit. Speaking of…any new chicks since the last time I was here?"

"Damn it, Lark. You need to stow your dick for just a few days. I promise, it won't kill ya." I grabbed Jessie's hand, and we made our way back toward the house.

"Bullshit. Country ass is the best kind of ass…sorry, Jessie."

I just looked at him. "You'll never change."

Jessie laughed. "Oh, he'll change the moment he meets the love of his life."

Lark let out a loud laugh. "Well then, Scott is right. I ain't ever gonna change 'cause there is no way in hell this boy is settling down with just one pu—ah…um, girl. No way I'm just settling with one girl for the rest of my life."

Jessie smiled and turned. She walked backward and faced both Lark and me. "We'll see. I'll make ya a bet—by this time next year, you'll be head over heels in love with a girl, and you'll want to ask her to spend the rest of her life with you. Yep…that's right, Lark. You're gonna be a one-pussy kind of guy by next Christmas."

She turned and walked into the house as Lark and I both stopped dead in our tracks. I glanced over at Lark.

He had his mouth hanging open as he slowly turned his head and looked at me. "Jesus, dude. I think I'm in love with your girl."

I smacked him on the shoulder and made my way into the house. I walked up to Jessie, who was now filling up three glasses with tea.

I leaned down and whispered in her ear, "I want to be inside you…right now."

She smiled as she poured the last glass of tea and then turned to face me. "Can't. We have to go to your parents' house. Remember?"

I closed my eyes and silently cursed my own parents. I whispered, "Fuck."

Jessie giggled as she shook her head and looked toward Lark. "So, you get to pick which guest room you want to stay in. I have a friend from college who's coming to spend a week with us also."

Lark raised his eyebrows and smiled. "Oh yeah?"

"Oh no…no way. You are not allowed anywhere near her. She is pure. And when I say pure, I mean, P.U.R.E. Lark, don't even think about it," Jessie said as she put her hands on her hips.

"Wait—she's a virgin?" Lark asked with a Cheshire cat smile on his face. "I haven't popped a cherry in a while."

"Ugh. Oh my god. You are just…ugh." Jessie rolled her eyes and shook her head. "Scott, control your friend!" She looked at me. "Make sure he stays away from Azurdee."

I couldn't help it. I had to laugh. This was just Lark. He had always been this way, ever since I'd met him our sophomore year of college. The only thing I really knew about his life before then was that his high school girlfriend had died right after his freshman year of college. His brother had told me how much Lark had changed. He'd basically become the opposite of what he had been before she'd passed away.

"Azurdee? Huh, it's about as interesting as Lark," Lark said with a smile.

Jessie rolled her eyes again. "Is that your real name?"

Lark smiled and leaned against the counter. "Lark is my middle name. I don't like my first name, so I go by my middle name."

"What's your first name?" Jessie asked.

"Michael," Lark said as sadness filled his eyes.

"I like that name. Why don't you like it?" Jessie asked as she quickly glanced at me.

I shook my head. Lark had told me once when he was drunk that the idea of another girl saying Michael while they had sex made him sick to his stomach, so he had gone by Lark ever since his girlfriend had passed away.

I started to make my way out of the kitchen. "Dude, let's go and get you settled in your room. I'll make sure there is at least one room between him and Azurdee, babe." I gave Jessie a quick smile.

She gave me a weak smile. She seemed to understand what had just happened.

As I helped Lark bring his stuff up to his room, he set his rifle case down next to the bed. I smiled, and he smiled back.

"What? I thought maybe we could get some target shooting in while I'm here. Brought my bow, too. Maybe I can get a buck and show my dad that they do grow 'em big in the hill country."

I nodded my head. "Hell yeah, we do. I can't wait for you to meet Jeff, Gunner, Brad, and Josh. I have a feeling you and Jeff will hit it off the most," I said with a gruff laugh.

"So, which one is having the big New Year's party?" Lark asked as he put his suitcase on the bed.

"Gunner. They're going to build a huge bonfire with all the Christmas trees. It's pretty cool. Just know that they all have kids. Gunner has a little girl, who just turned one, and they're expecting another one in May. Jeff has a little boy, year and a half, and a four-month-old little girl. Josh has twins, four months old also. Brad has a little girl, nine months old."

"Jesus Christ. What in the hell is in the water here? Remind me not to drink it. What about you and Jessie? How far along is she?"

"We have to go to the doctor, but Jessie thinks she is a little over two months," I said with a smile plastered on my face. "Speaking of, we were heading to my folks' house to break the news to them before you showed up." I rolled my eyes.

"Ah hell, Scott, please let me come. I really want to see the look on your mom's face. She's gonna piss her pants. First, her baby boy did not marry the richest girl in the state of Texas. Then, you go off and knock up a simple country girl, and you're not even married. You're going to hell, you bastard," Lark said as he gave me a sad face.

I punched him in the arm. "Fuck off, asshole. Make yourself at home. We'll be back in a few hours. Sorry to leave you hanging like this, but we just went to the store, so everything is stocked up in the kitchen."

Lark stood up and smiled. "My fault for showing up a day early."

I said good-bye and headed back downstairs. Jessie was sitting on the sofa, pouting.

"Baby, pouting just makes you look sexy as hell."

She stood and stomped her feet. "Scott, I don't want to go. Can't you just tell them yourself?"

I walked up and grabbed her hand. "Come on, we have one stop before we head to my folks' place."

My heart had been pounding since Scott had pulled out of the driveway. The idea of going to see his parents always made me feel sick, but now…I really felt sick. I already knew what was going to happen. They would look at me like I was something to be stomped on, and then they'd pull Scott to the side and question the hell out of him.

Scott turned in the opposite direction of his parents' house and started driving toward the river. They owned the ranch that butted up to Scott's ranch. I was guessing that they'd probably bought more land near the river.

Scott and his parents pretty much owned most of the land around here. Garrett…well, actually, Gunner and Jeff now owned the second-largest chunk of land. With Scott taking over his family's breeding business so that his dad could focus on his partnership in an oil company, his parents were hardly ever in Mason anymore. And that was fine by me.

"Where are we going?" I asked.

"I need to show you something before we go to my parents' place. I already told Mom we were running late because Lark had shown up a day early."

I let out a huff. "Great, she'll just blame me for making us late."

I looked out the window and put my hand on my stomach. I smiled, thinking about our child growing inside me. *Not even Mr. and Mrs. Tight-Ass Reynolds can spoil this for me.*

Scott pulled down a dirt road that ran along the backside of his property and his parents'. It led down to the river, and it was one of the first spots where he had taken me on a date. I smiled, remembering back to that day. I remembered Heather telling me about how Josh and she had made love by the river for the first time, and it always made me swoon.

How romantic.

I couldn't help but smile, thinking about that date with Scott. He had come down a few hours before and set up an old quilt, picnic basket, and a bottle of wine for dinner by the river. By the time we had shown up, ants had been all over the place, and I remembered standing there, looking down at the old quilt covered in ants, and laughing.

I let out a giggle. Scott reached over and grabbed my hand. I instantly felt that jolt of electricity, and my stomach took a dive.

"What's so funny?" he asked.

"I was thinking about when we started dating, and you brought me to the river to have dinner, but then we found ants everywhere."

Scott shook his head. "Oh my god, that pissed me off so bad. Fuckin' ants."

I laughed harder and kissed the back of his hand. I looked over at him and almost couldn't believe that he was mine, that I was actually going to have his child. The feeling of love just engulfed my whole body, and I had to look away because it felt like I was going to cry.

As Scott turned down the same little road as on our first date, I noticed he sat up a little straighter. I peeked over at him, and he was smiling from ear to ear. I looked out the front window to see what he was smiling at, and I sucked in a breath of air.

"Oh my word. What's going on?" I asked in almost a whisper.

There was a white tent set up right next to the riverbank with a small black wrought iron table. There were four people walking back and forth from the tent to a trailer that said *Bon Vie Chef Services*.

Scott parked the truck and jumped out. I watched as he walked up to one of the men in white and shook his hand. For some reason, I was frozen in the truck. Scott turned and walked to the passenger side of the truck. He opened the door and held out his hand for me.

I looked down at him and said, "What's going on?"

The moment he gave me that panty-melting smile of his, I knew this was his way of making up for our first failed attempt at a picnic here. I couldn't help but smile back at him as I held my hand out and hopped out of the truck.

"We're celebrating," he simply said.

I giggled. "The baby?"

He stopped and turned me toward him. He leaned down and kissed the tip of my nose. He let out a small laugh. "Among other things."

Scott grabbed my hand and walked us over toward the table. One of the gentlemen pulled the chair out for me, and I thanked him. He poured me a glass of spring water and then one for Scott.

"Good afternoon, Mr. Reynolds, Ms. Rhodes. We will start off with butternut squash bisque since there is a bit of a chill in the air today. That will be followed by your main course of roasted lemon chicken with sage, thyme, and rosemary along with roasted root vegetables in a walnut dressing. For dessert, Mr. Reynolds has chosen the blueberry crumb cake. Mr. Reynolds, would you like a glass of wine?"

Scott looked up and smiled as he shook his head. "No, thank you. I'll stick with water." He looked back at me and smiled.

I knew he wasn't drinking wine because I couldn't have a glass.

"Scott, oh my god, this is all way too much!" I said.

"I don't think it's enough. We have a lot to celebrate," he said with a wink as he reached for my hand.

When they brought out the soup, it hit me how hungry I really was. I practically devoured it in two bites. Scott grinned and seemed very pleased by my healthy appetite.

I took my last bite of chicken and leaned back in the chair. "Oh wow. That was probably some of the best food I've ever eaten. Scott, I don't think I could eat dessert. I mean, it sounds so yummy, but I'm stuffed."

Scott looked up, and one of the servers came over.

"Yes, sir."

"Would you mind boxing up the dessert? My girl here is full."

I blushed as Scott looked at me. I wasn't sure why I'd blushed. Maybe it was the look of pure passion in his eyes. He had been watching me eat the whole time, and he almost seemed nervous. Maybe telling his parents right now about us being pregnant wasn't such a good idea. I glanced over, and the sun was slowly starting to go down. I was glad I had a long-sleeved shirt on as I started to feel chilly.

Scott stood up and reached for my hand. I smiled as I got up and placed my hand in his.

"Let's go for a walk," he whispered.

He leaned down and skimmed his lips against mine. I turned back and looked at the table, feeling guilty.

"Don't worry, baby. That's what they get paid to do. Come on, the sun is fixin' to set soon."

As we walked for a little bit, we talked about the baby and the plans to make the guest bedroom downstairs the nursery since I couldn't bear the idea of the baby being upstairs and so far away from us.

"Do you want to find out if it's a boy or a girl?" I asked.

Scott came to a stop and turned as he took both of my hands in his. "Do you?" he asked.

I giggled. "Yes! I don't think I could stand the wait. Plus, we can decorate the room either for a boy or a girl."

Scott grinned. "Then, it looks like we'll be finding out."

I looked out over the river. It was breathtakingly beautiful. The sun still had a good thirty minutes before it would set, giving us plenty of time to walk back to Scott's truck.

"It's beautiful," I whispered as I watched the sunrays dance along the top of the water.

"Yeah, it is," Scott replied back.

Then, I turned to see him getting down on one knee as he reached into his pocket. He took out a small blue velvet jewelry box, and my mouth dropped open as I instantly began crying.

"Oh, Scott…" I put my hand up to my mouth to hold back the sobs.

He let go of my other hand and opened up the ring box.

I let out a gasp. *Oh…it's the most beautiful ring I've ever seen.*

"Jessie, I think I've known that I wanted you to be my wife from the first moment you smiled at me. I want to have kids with you, grow old with you, fight and make up with you."

He wiggled his eyebrows up and down, and I let out a giggle.

"I want to be able to tell you every day that I love you. I want to prove to you every day that I've never loved and cherished anything in my life like I do you. I love you to the moon and back, baby. I always have, and I always will."

I couldn't control my sobs. *Damn hormones.* I smiled and wiped the tears away as he took the ring out and held it up.

"This was my grandmother's ring, and I know she would have loved you, Jessie. You would have captivated her, just like you have me."

He took my left hand and went to put the ring on my finger, but he stopped and looked back up at me with tears building in his eyes.

Scott tried to talk, but his voice cracked. He cleared it and smiled. "I know the last few months haven't been exactly how we would have liked, but if I had the choice of whether or not to do it over again, knowing it would put me right here in front of you, I would do it again. I'd rather die than ever lose you. You will always be mine. *Forever.* Jessica Ann Rhodes, would you do me the honor of becoming my wife?"

I could hardly see him through my tears as I nodded. "Yes…oh, Scott, yes."

He stood, and I threw myself into his arms. He picked me up, and I wrapped my legs around him. I pulled my head back and slammed my lips against his.

Then, I kept repeating, "Yes," over and over again.

We kissed each other like crazy fools. I had dreamed of this day for so long, and I'd never imagined it would make me as happy as I was.

"Baby, I love you so much," Scott said.

"I love you…oh god, I love you so much it hurts," I said in between kisses.

After we kissed for what felt like forever, he slowly let me down. I felt his erection, and I wanted nothing more than to strip down and tell him to take me up against a tree. I wanted him so badly.

"I've been so damn nervous about asking you," he said with a small laugh. "I've been carrying that ring around with me for a few months now."

I sucked in a breath of air. "You were going to ask me before the baby?"

He gave me that crooked smile of his and nodded his head. "I was going to ask you on Christmas Eve, but…well, shit happened, and then I remembered that day we came down here. I thought it would be kind of cool to do it here."

I smiled so big that it almost felt like my cheeks were going to cramp. "It was beyond cool. It was the most romantic thing ever, and I will never forget this moment for as long as I live."

He put his hand on the side of my face and winked at me. "Good. That makes my heart happy."

He pulled me into a hug, and we stood there for a few minutes.

"Scott, your parents are going to be *pissed*. We are really, really late."

He laughed and threw his arm over my shoulder as we made our way back to his truck. I kept glancing down at the ring on my finger. It was breathtaking, and knowing it was his grandmother's made my heart swell even more.

The platinum filigree ring was stunning. The princess cut diamond was huge and had to be over a carat. It sat atop two smaller princess cut diamonds flanking the main diamond. Then, it tapered down to baguettes. Scott had mentioned before that his grandmother's platinum engagement ring was the most beautiful ring he'd ever seen and how he would never be able to find a ring as beautiful as it was.

He was right. It is breathtaking. The engraving on the band was exquisite.

"Scott, did your grandmother give you this ring before she passed away?" I asked.

Scott looked at me and smiled. "Nope," was all he said as we walked up to where we had just spent the most amazing few hours of my life.

I was shocked to see everything had been cleaned up, and the catering company trailer was pulling away.

"Holy crap. They're fast," I said.

"Come on, Mom and Dad are waiting for us," Scott said.

My heart dropped just a little. I really wanted to go home and celebrate being engaged, not go see his parents who hated me.

As we stood at the door, waiting for someone to answer it, a strong urge to break free of Scott's grip and make a run for the woods hit me. Anything else would be better than facing his mom's constant stares of disgust.

Melody threw open the door and was wearing the biggest smile on her face. "Well…it's about time y'all showed up!"

She walked into Scott's arms and told him how much she loved him and then she turned to me. When she pulled me into her arms, I was momentarily worried she might try to squeeze me to death.

She whispered in my ear, "I was so worried about you, sweetheart. I'm so glad you're back." When she pulled back from me, she shook her head. "When I found out what that little evil bitch did to my two boys and how she hurt you…well, let me tell you, it took every ounce of my Southern manners to hold myself back from going and giving her a piece of my mind."

I just stood there, stunned. *Who is this person? Where did Mrs. Tight-Ass Reynolds go?* I gave her a weak smile and nodded my head. I quickly glanced over her shoulder, only to see Scott's dad, Scott, Senior walking up.

He pushed his wife out of the way and took me in his arms as he spun me around. "Jesus, darlin'. Don't you ever do that to us again." He put me down and kissed the side of my cheek. "Come on, I've got a fire going in the pit on the back patio."

They both turned and walked into the house. Scott started to walk in, and I grabbed his arm.

"Did you pay them?" I asked in a whisper.

"What?"

"You had to have paid them…or promised them something in return for acting that way toward me." I looked back into the house.

Scott threw his head back and laughed. "Nope. No promises and no money have been exchanged. It looks like they've liked you all along. I told you they liked you." He shrugged his shoulders and headed into the house, making his way out to the back patio.

I followed closely behind with my guard up. I was ready for what was sure to be an ambush attack from either one or both of them.

We sat for a few minutes, catching up on what had been going on. I felt like I was in the twilight zone. I noticed Melody glance down at my hand. She brought her hand up to her mouth, and tears started forming.

Oh shit!

Scott and I seemed to be so shocked by their behavior toward me that we'd totally forgotten about our engagement.

Scott must have noticed at the same time because he cleared his throat and started to talk. "Um…Mom and Dad, I asked Jessie to marry me earlier. Well, really, it was right before we got here. Obviously, she said yes," he said with an awkward laugh.

I peeked over at him and smiled before looking back at Melody and then Scott, Senior. The smile that spread across Scott's dad's face caused me to giggle. Melody then jumped up and started making these goofy sounds.

Okay, clearly, she's drunk or something.

They both hugged Scott and then me.

Melody said, "Oh, Jessie, sweetheart, welcome to the family!"

Shocked—there is no other word for what is happening. She must be in a state of shock. I know I am.

I smiled and nodded. "Thank you so much, Mrs. Reynolds."

"Pesh! Good heavens, don't call me that. I always felt so funny having you call me that. It's Melody or...or..." Her eyes filled up with tears again. "Mom. You can call me Mom, if you want, sweetheart."

I felt my stomach drop, and now, it was my turn to have tears in my eyes. I didn't know what to say. I'd always dreamed of having a mother figure in my life. I'd longed for it really, and now, with the baby...

"Uh...Mom, Dad, that's not the only news we have for you," Scott said. "You might want to sit down for this one."

They both looked at Scott and then me. "Okay," they said at the same time.

"Well..."

Scott reached over and grabbed me. He pulled me to him and sat me down on his lap. I felt so strange, sitting there on his lap, but at the same time, I felt all the tension just melt away with his hands touching my body.

"Jessie is pregnant. We think she's a little over two months and—" Scott didn't even get to finish.

Melody jumped up, screaming, and Scott, Senior stood up. They both threw themselves into each other's arms.

My mouth dropped open, and I looked at Scott. "What in the hell happened to your parents? These are not your parents," I whispered.

"Um...I, um...I don't..." Scott shook his head as if he was trying to clear his thoughts.

After about two minutes of Melody and Scott, Senior hugging and dancing around, they reached for me and pulled me off of Scott's lap. They each took a turn hugging me, and then Melody wrapped her arm in mine as we started to walk back into the house.

"Oh Lord, we have a wedding to plan and a birth to plan. Oh! Scout's honor, I promise not to be one of those overbearing mother-in-laws who tries to plan everything...but we need to get cracking."

I turned and looked at Scott. He was standing there, shocked.

He turned to his dad, and I heard him ask, "How much have you and Mom had to drink today, Dad?"

His father laughed and pulled Scott in for another hug.

The next thing I knew, I was sitting in front of a computer, laughing my ass off and sipping sweet tea, as I began to plan my wedding…with Scott and my future in-laws.

Either I was dreaming, or the pregnancy hormones were affecting Melody and Scott, Senior. Whatever it was, I didn't want it to stop.

I'd never in my life felt so much love.

26 Lark

"Skip, don't worry. I'll take care of it when I get back to Austin. Just let me enjoy my vacation, please. Yep. I know it's back to work on January fourth. Yes, I know our work doesn't take a vacation. January fourth, we are heading to Columbia at oh five hundred. I'll make sure everything is ready to go."

I heard the buzzer for Scott's gate go off.

"Listen, Skip, I've got to run. If anything comes up, I'm just a few hours away from Austin, and I can get things up within a matter of hours."

The gate buzzed again.

"Have to run. Stop stressing. Fuck, in our line of work, how have you not had a heart attack yet? Talk to ya later."

I walked up to the intercom and pushed a button. "Talk to me."

"Hey, Scott! It's Azurdee. I'm so sorry that I'm a day early."

I smiled and shook my head. I glanced at the clock. It was nearly nine, and I was pretty sure that Scott and Jessie were going to be home soon.

"Come on up. I'll meet you on the front porch."

"Okay!"

I quickly walked to the front door and out onto the porch. I perched myself up against the post and waited to lay my sights on the P.U.R.E. Azurdee.

How in the hell does a girl in her early twenties stay a virgin these days?

As I saw her Toyota Camry pull up and park, I couldn't help but smile when I saw it was a Hybrid. The moment she stepped out of the car, she stretched, and my knees about buckled. I grabbed on to the railing.

Holy fucking shit. That hasn't happened in a long time. Get a grip, for Christ's sake, Williams. She's just another pussy. You've seen one, you've seen them all.

I watched her as she took her hair down from her ponytail. She had long, wavy dark brown hair that went down to the middle of her back. She pulled it back up into a ponytail as she turned and saw me standing there. I followed her eyes as they moved up and down my body. When her eyes caught mine, she smiled.

Jesus Christ.

"You most certainly are not Scott," she said with a smile.

It took me all of thirty seconds to get my wits about me. "No, ma'am, I am not. You must be Azurdee," I said as I made my way down to her car.

I put my hand out, and she shook it. I was pretty damn sure she just felt the same thing I did when we touched.

She looked away quickly before glancing back at me and focusing in on my lips. "You have an advantage on me, it seems. Mister..."

"Lark Williams, old college friend of Scott's. Going to be staying for a few days."

I purposely licked my lips and bit down on my bottom lip. She sucked in a small breath as her caramel eyes darkened. They were breathtaking, and I swore they sparkled.

Those are the most beautiful brown eyes I've ever seen. I wonder what they would look like when fucking her.

"It's a pleasure to meet you, Mr. Williams," she said with the cutest damn smile I'd ever seen.

"Lark, please call me Lark."

She nodded and looked around. "Azurdee Emerson. Are Jessie and Scott here?"

She seemed nervous as hell, and I couldn't help but let out a laugh.

"I promise I won't bite, sweetheart," I said with a wink.

"Azurdee."

I tilted my head at her. *Feisty.* "You don't like the word *sweetheart?*" I asked.

Now, it was her turn to lick her lips before biting down on her bottom lip. She tilted her head back as she said, "Oh, I love the word *sweetheart.* I just don't like it coming from a guy who probably bags at least two girls a week."

My mouth dropped open as she pushed past me. She opened her trunk and started to pull out her suitcase. Then, she stopped and looked at me.

Pure, my fucking ass.

I walked over and took the suitcase from her. I made my way into the house and up the stairs as she pulled out her cell phone and called Jessie. From the sound of it, Jessie was freaking out that Azurdee was here alone with me.

"Honestly, Jess, I'm fine. It was my fault for coming in a day early. I finished up work, and I was so excited to see you that I didn't even think of calling."

I made a beeline straight to the bedroom next to mine. Before I walked into the room, she cleared her throat. I stopped and turned around to see her standing outside the bedroom at the end of the hall. She smiled and pointed into the room.

Fuckin' A.

"Yep, and Lark is being such a gentleman by carrying my suitcase."

She let out a laugh, and when I walked by, my arm brushed up against hers.

Shit! What in the hell is with the weird feelings every time I touch this girl?

I put her suitcase down on the bed, turned, and ran my hand through my hair. I didn't like the way I felt when I was around her, and I'd only been around her for about ten minutes. When I looked up, I saw she was staring at me.

"Oh, um…what did you say, Jessie?" She quickly looked away. "Okay, I probably will because I am starving. Okay, see y'all soon." She hit End and looked at me again. She gave me the sweetest smile. "They're, um…they're going to be heading back soon. Have you eaten dinner?"

My heart dropped to my stomach, and I was starting to get pissed-off at how my body was betraying me. I just needed to either fuck this girl or completely ignore her.

"Nope," I said, cursing myself the moment the word came out of my mouth.

She nodded as she set down the two bags she'd carried up with her. Then, she turned and walked out of the bedroom. I followed her out and down the stairs to the kitchen. I sat down as I watched her open the refrigerator. She took a quick look, and then she went to the pantry and looked around. She pulled out powdered sugar, cinnamon, vanilla, and the bread. She walked back over to the refrigerator and pulled out some eggs.

"Do you like French toast? I've been craving it so bad the last few days." She pulled out a bowl and began cracking eggs into it.

I had to swallow the lump in my throat before I could talk. "I love French toast." *Nikki used to make me French toast all the time. I miss her so much.*

"Hey, are you okay?" Azurdee asked as she placed her hand on top of mine.

I instantly pulled it away. "Yeah. Why the fuck wouldn't I be?" I snapped.

The hurt in her eyes made me instantly regret snapping at her. She took a deep breath and went back to mixing everything in the bowl. She got out a frying pan and put some butter in it.

"Jesus, you sure do know where everything is. Do you come here often?" I asked, trying to make up for being short with her.

She gave me a weak smile and began dipping the bread into the egg mixture.

"I've only been here a couple of times. I made Scott and Jessie dinner a few times. I love to cook, and I've been told I make a pretty damn good fettuccine alfredo," she said as she wiggled her eyebrows. "All from scratch, I might add."

I let out a small laugh as I shook my head. "I think maybe I need to be the judge of that."

She flipped the toast in the pan. "You got it. I'll make it while we're here. When are you leaving? I'm staying until the third and then heading back to Austin."

The feeling of disappointment washed over me. I wanted both of us to stay longer. I wanted to leave my world behind just for a few days more, so I could get to know this girl better.

"I'll probably leave on the third." I got up and took out two glasses from the cabinet. I grabbed the orange juice and poured us each a glass. I glanced over and noticed her watching me.

Yeah, I just need to stay away from her as much as possible.

I sat down and watched her whip out the French toast in record time.

"Will you get out some plates, please?" she asked without even looking at me as she reached and stretched to put the syrup in the microwave.

I stood up, took out two plates, and set them on the island. She put French toast on each plate, and then she took a spoonful of powdered sugar and sprinkled it on top. She turned and stood on her tippy toes to get the syrup out of the microwave.

I smiled as I looked down at her tight-ass jeans. *Motherfucker, she has a nice body. No way is this girl still a virgin.*

I made my way over toward her. I leaned against her as I reached up and grabbed the syrup. When I pushed myself into her, she turned around quickly.

"I never understood why they placed that microwave so damn high," she said as a flush spread across her cheeks.

I couldn't help myself. I reached up and pushed a piece of hair that had fallen out of her ponytail behind her ear. She quickly touched the side of her face.

"You're just short," I said with a wink.

I backed away when I noticed her chest was heaving up and down quickly.

Yep, she felt it, too.

She let out an awkward laugh. "I guess so. Anyway, um…dig in!"

We sat down on the bar stools and ate at the kitchen island.

"Damn girl, this is the best French toast I've ever had." I shoved another bite into my mouth.

She giggled. "Thank you. I've always loved to cook. I get to do a lot of baking with my business," she said before taking a bite.

"What do you do for a living?"

She smiled, and my breath was taken away when her beautiful eyes lit up.

"I own a coffee shop called Rise and Grind. It's right outside of Austin in Wimberley."

I laughed. "I like it. Cute name."

She smiled. "Thank you. It's been a dream come true…well, at least for me, it has. My father, on the other hand, is still upset with me for not coming and working for him. He keeps telling me that my degree was a waste of his money—even though the coffee shop has done so well this last year. This is the first time I've left it. My mother has a business degree, so she has been helping me out with it."

For a moment, she almost looked sad.

What is it about this girl that is getting to me?

"What is your degree in?" I asked.

"Ocean engineering," she said with a weak smile. "My father is a petroleum engineer, and he owns his own company."

I let out a small laugh. "Well, hell, why open a coffee shop when you could be building dikes and flood control systems? If you worked for your dad though, I guess you would be exploring offshore gas and oil fields," I said.

Her mouth dropped open.

"What's wrong?" I asked with a smirk.

"No one ever knows what an ocean engineer does. I always have to tell them," she said with a small smile.

I smiled and gave her a wink. "Well, you've finally met someone who knows."

I heard Jessie and Scott come in, and I turned to see Jessie barreling through the door. She stopped the moment she saw us. She smiled when she saw Azurdee, and Jessie immediately walked over to her. She took Azurdee in her arms and hugged her.

Jessie turned to me and gave me a look. She put her two fingers up to her eyes and then pointed at me as if to say that she'd be watching me. I was just about to take a bite, but I stopped my fork right at my mouth. I couldn't help but laugh. I shook my head and winked at her.

Scott walked up, hit me on the back, and sat down. "You behaving, Lark?" he asked with a cocky smile.

"Yes, I am. Isn't that right, Azurdee? I've asked her to sleep with me only three times."

"What?" Jessie yelled out.

Azurdee laughed and shook her head. "He has not. He's really been a gentleman."

She looked at me, and I gave her my signature smile that I knew drove all the girls crazy—except it didn't seem to faze Azurdee at all. Her smile dropped, and then she turned away as Jessie held up her ring finger. They both started screaming and jumping up and down. I threw my hands up to my ears and looked at Scott, who was laughing.

Holy hell, why must girls scream when they're happy? The only time I want a woman screaming is when I'm giving her an orgasm.

"Jesus, make them stop, Scott," I said.

I peeked over at Azurdee. She was talking a mile a minute as she kept bouncing up and down.

Fuck, she has nice breasts.

Ugh, I need to get the fuck out of here.

I got up, walked over to the sink, washed off my plate, and put it in the dishwasher. I leaned against the sink and looked at Scott. "Is the Wild Coyote Bar still open?"

He nodded, and I noticed Azurdee look over at me.

I pushed off the counter and started to walk out of the kitchen but not before I said, "Good. I need to get laid."

"Oh, really nice, Lark. Do *not* bring a girl back here!" Jessie called after me.

I took the steps two at a time and quickly changed before heading back downstairs. Jessie and Azurdee were engaged in a conversation as they sat together on the sofa. I looked over at Scott, and he shook his head. He must have known I was going to ask if he wanted to come.

I shrugged and said, "Well, thank you, Azurdee, for dinner. Y'all have fun tonight."

Scott stood and walked me to the door. "Dude, are you sure you want to go out? Why don't you stay here? We'll grab a few beers, head down to the barn, and catch up."

I smiled and put my hand on his shoulder. "Dude, I haven't had a piece of ass since Belize. Don't wait up for me," I said with a wink.

I glanced over his shoulder and saw Azurdee looking at me. Our eyes caught, and then she rolled her eyes and looked away.

He slapped my back and laughed. "Yeah, 'cause Belize was *so* long ago."

As I walked out, I made a vow that I would not let this girl get under my skin. I sat down in my truck and threw my head back against the seat. *I haven't felt this way ever since Nikki. One good fuck, and I'll get over it.*

I spotted the beautiful blonde the moment I walked into the bar.

After three drinks, a few spins around the dance floor, and one shot, I was pulling up her dress and ripping off her panties in the backseat of her car. All thoughts of Azurdee vanished when the blonde told me to fuck her hard.

"My pleasure, sweetheart," I said as I slammed my dick into her. Blocking everything and everyone out, I only focused on her calling out my name.

27 Scott

I walked into the kitchen, and Jessie, Azurdee, and my mom were all sitting at the kitchen island, looking at paint samples.

I stood there, shocked. "Mom? What are you doing here at eight in the morning?"

The fact that my mother and father had done a complete one-eighty with Jessie had freaked me out enough, and now, she was in my kitchen looking at paint colors.

"Well, we have to paint the baby's room—the sooner, the better," she said with a wink.

I looked over at Jessie, who shrugged her shoulders and smiled. I still couldn't believe she was pregnant, and we were getting married. All thoughts of Trey were gone, and she seemed to be happy with the idea of staying home and raising our child.

I glanced at my watch as I walked over to pour a cup of coffee. "I'm going to head over to Gunner's place and see if they need any help with the New Year's Eve party. Is Lark around?"

Jessie motioned for me to walk out back with her.

"He went for a ride. I have to show you something outside. It looks like maybe one of the horses might have gotten out and made his way up to the house," Jessie said.

My mother looked up at Jessie and giggled. Even she knew that Jessie was using a lame excuse to get me outside.

I followed Jessie outside. She smiled as she reached up and wrapped her arms around my neck. I leaned down and gently kissed her soft lips.

"Hmm..." she said as she grabbed my lower lip between her teeth. "Thank you for last night," she whispered.

I smiled. "No, baby...thank you for this morning."

She put her finger in her mouth and barely bit down on it.

My dick was hard instantly. "Fuck, Jessie."

"I'd like that," she said with a wink. "Oh god, Scott, the moment you walked into the kitchen, something happened...and...and I..."

"What? You, what? Are you okay?" I asked as I put my hands on either side of her face.

"I don't know if it's because we were apart for so long or if it's because I'm pregnant, but I'm so horny, and I just want you," she said as she closed her eyes.

My stomach did all kinds of weird things. I grabbed her from behind her neck and pulled her lips to mine. I kissed her like I wasn't going to kiss her ever again. I moved my hand up her shirt and felt on her breasts.

"Your mother is right inside."

"I don't care." I picked her up and carried her around to the side of the house.

"Scott…" she whispered.

I put her down, and she pulled off her panties. I unbuttoned my pants and pulled them down. Then, I lifted up her skirt and slipped a finger inside her.

Jesus Christ…she is soaked. "Motherfucker, you're so wet." I removed my finger, picked her up, and slowly slid into her.

She threw her head back and whispered, "Oh god, yes. Scott, it feels like heaven. You feel so good."

I didn't know if it was because we could get caught at any minute or if it was the way she was whispering to me, but this was so fucking hot. I moved fast and hard, and I knew I wasn't going to last much longer.

"Jessie, I'm not gonna last very long, baby."

"Almost…oh god, it's right there!"

I lifted her higher and pushed in harder. She threw her head into my shoulder and tried like hell to be quiet.

"Oh, baby, I'm coming. Ah, yeah, that feels so damn good," I said as I poured myself into her.

I leaned her against the side of the house, my dick still pulsing inside her, as I tried to catch my breath.

"Scott? Jessie? Are you out here?" my mother called out.

Jessie brought her hand up to her mouth as her eyes widened. I smiled and put my finger up to my lips.

"Mrs. Reynolds! Oh, you have to see this crib! I think it's perfect," Azurdee called out.

We stood there for a few minutes before I put Jessie back down.

"Have I told you how much I like Azurdee?" I said with a wink.

Jessie giggled and picked up her panties. She shoved them into my pocket as she gave me a wicked grin. "Now, I have to go back in there with no panties on and try to make it to our room to clean up!" she said as she hit me on the shoulder.

I pulled the panties out of my pocket and bent down. I lifted her dress and used her panties to clean her up. I looked up at her, and her eyes caught mine as she chewed on her bottom lip.

I let out a laugh. "Again?"

She nodded, and I stood up and shoved the panties back into my pocket. I grabbed her hand and walked us around to the back porch.

I kissed her quickly as I dropped her hand. "I'm heading to the barn, baby. Be good!"

I walked backward with a smile as she smiled and blew me a kiss before she turned and walked back into the house.

God, I love that girl.

I walked into the barn and saw Lark taking a saddle off of a horse.

"I thought I might find you in here." I walked up to him.

He looked at me and grinned as he shook his head. "Damn, dude. I only have one thing to say to you." He set the saddle down.

"What's that?" I asked as I grabbed a brush.

"Look the fuck around before you take your bride-to-be outside!

I let out a laugh and shook my head. "Ah hell, I don't know what came over us. My mother is in the house, too."

Lark rolled his eyes. "Ugh...that makes it hot, I guess, but damn...I like Jessie, and I didn't need to see that shit. I've never turned a horse around so fucking fast in my life."

I threw my head back and laughed harder. As I stopped laughing, I looked at Lark. "Shit, don't tell Jessie you saw us. She'd never be able to look at you again."

"Trust me, I'd rather forget what I just saw."

I slapped him on the back. "Did you have fun last night? You got home late."

He turned and looked at me. "Yep, I had a good time. Met some girl named Monica. Well, I think that was her name." He stopped and thought about it.

I rolled my eyes. "Tell me you didn't..."

He smiled as he opened the stall door to lead the horse back in. "Fuck yeah, I did. Let me tell you, that girl probably gave the best head I've ever had."

I let out a sigh. "Lark. Dude, aren't you afraid you're going to get a girl pregnant one day?"

He just looked at me like I was an idiot. "I've never in my life had sex without a condom. *Ever.* That is my number one rule. No condom? Then, she can give me head, and if she's good, I return the favor."

"My god...you talk about it like it's nothing, like it's meaningless."

He shrugged his shoulders. "It is."

"What if it's not to them? What if they actually don't want a one-night stand?"

"I never make any promises. They know that all I'm looking for is a fuck. I make that pretty damn clear, and so far, I haven't had any problems."

I shook my head. "Lark, don't you want to settle down? Get married and raise a family?"

He looked at me with sadness in his eyes. "There was only one girl I wanted to do that with, and she's dead."

"If you just opened up your heart, dude…"

He put his hand up and smiled. "I don't need a lecture. I got one from Miss Goody Two-Shoes last night when I got home," he said with a laugh.

"Azurdee?" I asked.

"Yeah. She was up, reading. She came into my room and asked if I got laid. When I said yeah, she sat on my bed and began to tell me how dangerous it was."

I smiled and nodded. "Sounds like her. She has a good heart and means well."

"Well, I already have a mother. I don't need another one. And that's exactly what I told her. She got pissed and walked out. So, really, Scott, I'm good. I know you're happy and all that shit, but I don't want the same things you want. Plus, my job would never allow for me to be in a relationship. I travel too much."

I rolled my eyes and pulled out my phone. "You ready to go meet Gunner and Jeff?"

He smiled. "Let's do it."

As we walked back toward the house, I smirked and said, "Dude, bring your gun."

Lark looked at me and smiled. "Why?"

"I want you to fuck around with Jeff. He is always bragging about how good he can shoot."

Lark shook his head and laughed. "Hell, this ought to be fun."

I pulled up behind Josh's truck and smiled. "Awesome. Josh is here, too. You're going to like him. Down-to-earth guy and good with his hands. He made the desk in my office."

"No shit? He's the one with the twins, right?"

I snapped my head and looked at Lark. "You were actually listening to what I said?"

"Of course I was, dickhead." He opened the door and got out.

I walked around the truck as Ellie came out and smiled at us.

"That's Ellie, Gunner's wife."

"She's beautiful. Lucky bastard," Lark said.

Ellie made her way down to us. She gave me a hug and a kiss on the cheek.

She turned and held out her hand to Lark. "Hi, you must be Lark. It's a pleasure. I'm Ellie."

Lark smiled and took her hand. "Ellie, the pleasure is all mine."

Ellie looked back at me. "Gunner, Jeff, and Josh are all out back. I don't know which one of them is the most excited. They actually went into town and took trees from the recycle pile," she said with a giggle.

I would never get over how sweet and innocent Ellie was. I glanced down at her stomach and smiled. Ellie and Jessie were probably going to give birth within a month or so of each other.

"How are you feeling, Ells?" I asked.

She smiled bigger and put her hand on her stomach. "Wonderful."

"Congratulations, Ellie," Lark said.

"Thank you so much! Now, y'all go around back. I have to get to my garden before Alex wakes up."

"Yes, ma'am." I tipped my hat.

Lark and I walked around back.

Josh looked up and smiled. He walked up and reached out for my hand. "Congratulations, dude. I couldn't be happier for you and Jessie." Josh flashed me that smile of his.

"Thanks, Josh. I've never been happier in my life. Hey, this is my buddy from college, Lark. Lark, this is Josh Hayes."

They both shook hands as Lark said, "Lark Williams. It's a pleasure."

We repeated the process with Gunner and Jeff. We stood around for a few minutes, shooting the shit, and then Lark went in for the kill.

"Are those targets back there?" He glanced around Gunner's shoulder.

Gunner turned and then looked back at Lark. "Yep."

Jeff smiled and said, "You like to shoot?"

Lark nodded. "Love it. I even brought my gun, hoping to get some target shooting in."

Jeff took the bait. "Hell yeah, dude. Go and grab it. Let's see how good you are."

I felt kind of shitty. Gunner shook his head as he smiled and made his way into his house to get a gun. Gunner had never met Lark, but Gunner knew Lark had been in the Marines and was a sharpshooter.

Lark walked out to my truck to get his gun as Gunner came out with his Remington Model 700.

Then, Jeff started talking shit. "Damn, dude, I hope I don't embarrass your friend. You probably should have told him that I kick your asses in target shooting every time," he said with a wink and a smile.

It took everything out of me not to start laughing. I smiled and looked at Gunner as he busted out laughing.

"Jeff, you might want to pull back on the smack talk," I said.

Lark came walking up and put his gun case down. He glanced up at the targets. "Three hundred yards?"

Gunner nodded. "Give or take."

Josh took Gunner's Remington and shot first. He was about three inches left of the center. Gunner went next. He shot just a bit better than Josh, but then again, it was his gun.

I smiled as I stood there and watched Jeff. *God, I love fucking with him.* He glanced over at me and winked, and I just smiled back at him. *Cocky bastard.*

Jeff was next. I had to admit that Jeff could shoot a gun. He was probably the best I'd seen since Lark. Jeff shot and was about one inch to the left of the center.

He smiled and looked at Lark. "Don't know if you can get any better than that, dude."

Lark smiled as he bent down and opened up his case. He pulled out a custom Nemo Omen .300 Winchester Magnum.

"Jesus H. Christ, that is one bad-ass gun," Josh said.

Jeff just looked at me. I shrugged my shoulders and smiled at him.

Lark glanced at Josh and smiled. "Thanks, dude. She's my baby."

Lark got settled and started shooting. I peeked over and watched Jeff's face fall. When I turned back and looked at the target, Lark's grouping was tight, and it looked like one bullet was inside the other in the dead center of the target. He was barely nicking the hole, making it bigger. He took a step to his left and started shooting the next target with the same results.

When he stopped, he looked over at Jeff. "I think that's better, dude. This was baby's play. I'm used to shooting at a thousand yards."

"Motherfucker. Where in the hell did you learn to shoot like that?" Jeff asked.

Josh and Gunner both started laughing.

Lark let out a small laugh. "My father owns a hunting lease in south Texas. I think I had a gun in my hand as soon as I turned five."

"Holy hell, I'm impressed," Gunner said.

Lark smiled as he put his gun back in the case. He closed it and stood up. "I was also in the MSOR, Marine Special Operations Regiment."

Jeff quickly looked at me. "You motherfucker, you set me up."

I laughed and held up my hands. "Hey, you were the one talking shit."

Jeff just shook his head. "Fucker."

Lark laughed as he turned and headed back to my truck to put his gun away.

We spent the rest of the afternoon setting up for the party and just having a good time while hanging out. Ellie brought out a few beers and set them down before going back in. We took them to the barn and talked for another hour.

I looked around at my friends. I'd be lost without them. They were more like brothers than friends.

I finished off my beer and stood up. "Alright, I guess I better get back."

Gunner stood and reached out for Lark's hand. "You're staying for tomorrow night, right?"

"Hell yeah. It's the only reason I'm here. Scott went on and on about the New Year's Eve parties y'all throw. I'm not due to go back to work until the fourth, so I'll probably be leaving on the third."

Josh and Jeff both stood and shook Lark's hand and then mine.

"It was great meeting you, Lark. You'll have to come out more often to target shoot," Jeff said with a smile.

"Damn, I wish I could. I travel a lot for my job," Lark said.

"You still in the Marines?" Josh asked.

Lark shook his head. "Nah, medical discharge."

Gunner looked at me and then back at Lark. "What do you do?"

Lark smirked. "Contract work for the government among other things. My boss dabbles in a few different things—all legal." He glanced at me and winked.

Gunner laughed. "Fair enough."

Lark hadn't uttered a word ever since we left Gunner's place.

"What's on your mind, Lark?" I asked.

He smiled. "I like your friends. They are a good group of guys. They seem really happy."

I nodded. "Yeah, they are a good bunch, and yeah, they're all pretty happy."

He nodded as he looked out the window. I knew Lark wanted what we all had—someone to wake up to every morning and lie down with every night.

"You ever think of changing jobs?" I asked.

"Fuck no. I love my job. I live for my job," Lark said quickly.

I sucked in a deep breath and slowly let it out. "You don't ever think about settling down, Lark? Ever?"

He shook his head and smiled as he looked at me. "Nope. It would have to take an act of God to get me to settle down with one person."

I nodded my head. As we drove down the driveway, I saw Jessie and Azurdee both riding horses. They were walking along the road. I pulled to a stop and rolled down the window.

"Damn, girl. You sure look good sitting up there on my horse," I said with a chuckle.

Jessie smiled and let out a small laugh. "Your mother wouldn't leave. She went from paint to baby furniture to wedding plans. I think I liked it better when she didn't like me and never talked to me," she said as she made a funny face.

Azurdee laughed, and I heard Lark suck in a breath of air.

"How about we go out for dinner tonight?" I asked.

"Azurdee has plans for a home-cooked meal tonight," Jessie said as she looked over at Azurdee.

"Yep, pasta," Azurdee said as she ducked her head down and peeked into the truck at Lark.

"Pasta, it is. Y'all need help with the horses?" I asked.

"Nope. We're enjoying our girl time. We won't be long, I promise," Jessie said.

I slowly drove away and glanced over toward Lark. He was looking out the window as I smiled to myself.

Azurdee Emerson could very well be the act of God Lark was talking about.

28 Jeff

I walked into the kitchen, and Ari was bent over, wiping off the counter. I snuck up, grabbed her hips, and began pumping the shit out of her.

"Oh yeah, baby! Feels so good!" I said.

Ari laughed and tried to stand up. "Jesus, Mary, and Joseph. Give me fucking whiplash, why don't you?"

"You know you want me, baby," I said as I let her go.

She turned to face me. "Actually, I'm so damn tired. I've been cleaning all day on top of studying. I will be so glad when these online classes are over."

I looked around. The house was so quiet.

"Where are Luke and Grace?"

Ari smiled. "Sleeping."

"At the same time?"

She nodded her head and smiled. I grabbed her hand and pulled her into our bedroom before she could argue. I shut the door and pushed her against it. I cupped her breast in my hand as I leaned in and licked her bottom lip.

"Jeff...we can't. Luke is going to wake up any minute."

"I'll go fast. Baby, this is for you." I dropped to my knees and started to pull down her sweatpants and panties.

She looked down at me and giggled as she lifted each foot before kicking off her clothing. "For me, huh? How is this for me?"

"You're stressed. You need relief." I lifted her leg and put her foot on my shoulder.

"Jeff, no! I've been cleaning for the last two hours. I'm all sweaty and—"

I buried my face between her legs and gently began sucking on her clit.

"Oh god, holy shit!" she shouted.

I slowly slipped two fingers in, and she began moving her hips as she grabbed on to my hair.

"Yes...oh god...mother of God, that feels so...oh god." She began grinding her hips faster.

I moved my tongue as fast as I could against her clit, and she began to fall apart.

The sounds she was making were driving me mad. I reached down and unbuttoned my pants. I kept sucking gently on her clit as she called out my name. I pulled my fingers out of her and stood up. After I kicked off my pants, I picked her up and brought her over to the bed. I crawled on top of her and slowly put the tip of my dick barely inside her.

She thrashed her head back and forth. "More!" she called out.

I smiled and shook my head. "My greedy, greedy girl."

She rolled over and got on her hands and knees. She backed her ass up against me. "More..." she whispered.

I pulled her to me and slammed my dick into her.

She let out a whimper. "Harder...touch me, Jeff."

I moved my hands around to her front and began playing with her clit. "No...not there..." she said.

I slowed down and looked at her ass. *Motherfucker.*

I slid my hand along her body and watched as she shuddered. I moved my finger and barely touched her ass.

"Oh god...yes."

My heart started pounding. *If I put my finger in her ass, I'm not gonna last.*

"Ari..." I said.

She pushed herself against me as she grabbed on to the sheets. I slowly moved my finger into her ass just a bit, and she let out a moan.

"Oh...god..." she said.

I held on to her hip with my other hand and began going faster and harder.

"Jeff...please..."

I pushed my finger into her more, and she began calling out my name.

"Jeff...oh god...that feels amazing!"

I lost it. "Jesus, baby...I'm gonna come."

"Yes! Jeff, yes!"

I was so out of breath that I rested on top of her as she fell to the bed.

"Holy hell! Why have we not tried that before?" she asked in between pants.

I was still trying to recover from one of the most intense orgasms of my life. I moved and fell to the side of her. She rolled over and looked at me. Her eyes were filled with love and passion.

"Ari, I think you just about killed me. Where in the hell did that come from?"

She laughed. "I don't know. I've been wanting to try some back door action. I guess the moment just hit me."

I just looked at her. "The moment just hit you? Do you realize that when you told me to touch you there, I almost came on the spot?"

She smiled bigger and shook her head. "You liked that?"

"Uh-huh...hell yeah, I did."

"Want to play around more with it?" She bit down on her bottom lip and began abusing the hell out of it.

"I think you just made me the happiest man on Earth," I said as I pulled her closer to me.

She moved to sit on top of me and began grinding against me.

"Baby, I'm not Superman. There's no way."

She threw her head back and started feeling her breasts.

She's trying to kill me.

"Hmm…you feel so good up against my body," she whispered.

Then, we heard Grace over the baby monitor. Ari snapped her head down and looked at me.

"Later tonight? Back door?" she asked with a wink.

I can't breathe. "Yes. Most certainly yes."

She smiled as she crawled off of me, and then she began putting her panties and sweatpants back on. I looked her body up and down, and I had the most intense feeling run through my body.

"I love you, Ari."

She stopped and smiled as she looked at me. "I love you, too."

She turned and walked out of the bedroom. I lay there for a few minutes and thought about how blessed I was.

I heard Ari talking to Grace and Luke in the kitchen, so I got up and headed to the bathroom to wash up. I got dressed and made my way out to join them.

As I walked into the kitchen, I stopped and watched my beautiful wife with my precious kids. Luke was helping Ari put Grace into her high chair.

"I don't know what I would do without my big man here to help me. Huh, Grace?" Ari said.

Grace let out a giggle as Luke ran over to the refrigerator and tried to open it.

Ari picked him up and opened the door. "What do you want, little man? Want some yogurt?"

"Yes, peeze," Luke said.

I smiled and walked into the kitchen. Grace started kicking as soon as she saw me.

I leaned down and kissed her. "Hey, baby girl."

"Daddy!" Luke yelled. He fought like hell to get out of Ari's arms.

She set him down, and I squatted, so he could run into my arms for a hug.

"Alwex?" Luke asked.

"You want to see Alex, buddy?" I asked.

He began nodding his head. I looked up at Ari, who smiled.

"I've been promising him a playdate with Alex all day," she said.

I looked back down at Luke. "You get to see Alex tomorrow. You're spending the night with Gramps and Grams—both of y'all."

Luke started jumping up and down when he saw Ari setting his yogurt on the table. He pointed to his seat, so I picked him up and set him in it as I glanced at Ari. She was smiling as she made cereal for Grace.

"Are you happy, baby?" I asked her.

The sexy smile that spread across her face was all I needed to see to know her answer.

"Yes. I've never been so happy in my life," she said with a wink. "Are you?"

I walked over to her and took her in my arms. I gently brushed my lips back and forth across hers. "Everything I've dreamed of and wanted is in this very room right now. You've made me the happiest man on Earth, Ari. I love you so much that it hurts. If I didn't have you, Luke, and Grace…I'd be so lost. I love y'all so much. Nothing can ever come between us, Ari. Nothing."

She smiled as I pulled her closer to me and kissed her. I was beginning to get lost in the kiss when the doorbell rang. I pulled away, and she laughed.

"Damn it, Johnson. You sure know how to make a girl horny, you know that?"

I laughed as I turned and headed to the front door. I wasn't sure who in the hell it could be since our front gate buzzer hadn't gone off. I smiled and opened the door, expecting it to be Gunner or Gramps, and then I instantly felt sick to my stomach.

"What in the hell are you doing here?" I looked him up and down.

He smiled and shook his head. "Now, Jefferson, is that any way to greet your father?"

When I heard what the man at the door had said, I almost dropped the jar of baby food.

Jeff's dad is here? What in the hell is he doing here? How did he get through the gate?

I stood there, frozen. I quickly looked at Grace and then Luke. Luke was eating his yogurt and lost in his food. I grabbed the bowl of cereal and set it in front of Grace.

Oh Jesus, I'm setting myself up for a mess.

I walked around the corner and saw Jeff still standing at the door. He hadn't asked his dad to come in.

"How did you get through the gate?" Jeff asked.

His dad let out a small laugh. "Well, it was open, and I just drove down the driveway."

Oh my god. I put my hand up to my mouth as I thought about Sharon calling earlier and asking if she could stop by. I'd opened the gate, so she could just drive in. I'd totally forgotten.

Shit! Sharon's coming over! I looked over at the clock. *Jesus H. Christ, she'll be here any minute.*

I peeked in on the kids. Grace was dipping her finger in the cereal and looking at it, and Luke was eating his yogurt, still in heaven.

I walked up behind Jeff and put my hand on his shoulder. He didn't bother to turn around.

"What do you want? Why are you here?" Jeff asked.

His father took a deep breath and slowly let it out. "I know I'm probably the last person you want to see, but I wanted to talk to you and Ellie. Your mother—"

"She's moved on and has finally gotten over you. She's getting married, and I seriously doubt she wants to see you."

The sadness in Jeff's father's eyes almost made me feel sorry for him.

He nodded his head. "Your mother was my first love, Jefferson. I loved her with all my heart, and I still do."

"Did you let Angie know how much you loved Mom while you fucked her behind Mom's back?"

"Jeff," I whispered.

His dad looked down. "It's just...we had you when we were so young, and I was so scared. I felt like I had so much more in life to do, and I felt…trapped. Angie was my only way out. I never loved her like I loved your mother."

Jeff let out a gruff laugh. "You sure have a funny way of showing your love."

Just then, Luke came running out. "Daddy!" he screamed as he ran and grabbed on to Jeff's leg.

The look on Jeff's father's face when he saw Luke made me so sad. I silently thanked God for my parents and their unconditional love.

"Your son?" Jeff's dad said as his voice cracked.

Jeff turned and looked at me. I could see the confusion in his eyes.

He slowly turned back to his father. "Yes. I also have a daughter."

Shit! Grace! I spun around and ran back into the kitchen.

As soon as I saw her, I busted out laughing. She had cereal everywhere, and she gave me the biggest smile ever.

I walked over to her and smiled down at her. "If I didn't love you so much…"

I began cleaning her up as I heard Jeff talking to his father in the living room.

He needs to leave—like right now!

"Jeff, I need your help in here… now, please," I called out.

Jeff came walking into the kitchen, holding Luke in his arms, and he just looked at me. "What in the fuck?" he said.

I knew it wasn't because Grace was covered in baby food.

"I know, but listen, your mom is going to be here any minute. You need to get him out of here, Jeff—like now!"

Then, the doorbell rang.

Jeff closed his eyes. "Fuck. Me." He turned and walked out of the kitchen.

I moved with lightning speed to clean up Grace. I heard Jeff telling his dad that he shouldn't have just shown up like this. Then, I heard Jeff opening the front door. I grabbed Grace and practically ran out into the hallway to the front door.

I stopped in my tracks when I saw Sharon, Ellie, and Alex. "Oh no," I whispered. *We're about to have a little family reunion.*

"Um…Mom, Ells…can I talk to you outside?" Jeff asked.

I glanced over to his father sitting on the sofa. I couldn't help but notice how sad he was. *Serves his ass right for what he did to all three of them.*

"Why? What's wrong?" Ellie asked.

Ellie could always tell when Jeff was upset or worried. Nothing got by her as far as he was concerned.

"Ells…let's just…"

Sharon looked at him as she tilted her head. "Jeff, what's going on? Your face is white as a ghost." She peeked over Jeff's shoulder and saw me standing there. She smiled when she saw Grace kicking and holding her arms out for her. She pushed Jeff out of the way and started to walk in.

"Mom…really, I think it's best if we step outside for a minute."

"Nonsense. I want to see my grandchildren and…" Her voice trailed off as she looked into the living room. "Brian? Is everything alright?" she asked in a whispered voice.

"Sharon, I'm so sorry. I had no idea you would be here," Brian said as he slowly stood and started wringing his hands together.

Ellie came barreling in and stopped right behind Sharon. She stood there and just stared at her father. He smiled when he saw her, and when he looked down at Alex, he smiled bigger.

"Why are you here? How dare you come back into our lives! Haven't you caused us all enough trouble? You need to go…right now!" Ellie shouted, scaring both Grace and Alex.

Sharon turned around and shook her head. She took a crying Alex out of Ellie's arms. "Shh…baby girl, it's okay. Ellie, please, honey, calm down."

Jeff walked in and set Luke down.

He immediately ran up to Sharon. "Alwex! Alwex!"

Sharon put Alex down, and Alex and Luke both hugged each other. I quickly looked up at Brian, who seemed to have tears in his eyes. I glanced over to Jeff, and he looked more confused than angry.

"Luke, Alex…come on, y'all. Let's go into Luke's room and play!" I said, trying to be all cheery and shit.

Luke and Alex took off for the playroom, and I followed behind them. As I looked back, I saw Sharon turn toward Jeff and Ellie.

"Kids, your father and I need to tell you something."

Holy shit. Sharon wasn't at all surprised to see Jeff's dad. Shit! Why can't it be nap time?

30 Ellie

I stood there and just stared at my mother. *Why is she not surprised to see my father?*

I glanced over at him, and he looked exactly like I remembered…but older…and sadder. His eyes were filled with sadness.

Good, I hope his life has been miserable—that bastard!

"Mom…why are you not surprised to see him?" Jeff asked.

My mother walked over and stood next to our father.

Oh god…she's not leaving Philip for our father, is she?

"Ellie, sweetheart, calm the thoughts in your head. I see you thinking a mile a minute."

I shook my head. "Mom…are you leaving Philip for…for him?" I pointed to the man standing in front of me.

I didn't even want to call him my father. It was his fault that my mother had treated us so badly all those years. He had been the reason for her sadness and bitterness.

"What? No! My god, no, Ellie. Jeff…Ellie, baby…please sit down," my mother said with a weak smile. She turned and looked at my father. "You couldn't wait for a few days longer until I talked to them?" she asked in a soft…almost caring voice.

He shook his head as he sat down. My mother took a seat next to him.

"Okay…can I just say that this is fucking weird?" Jefferson said as we both sat down.

They both gave us a slight smile, and then I almost fell out of my chair when my mother reached for my father's hand.

I stood up quickly. "What is going on?" I practically shouted.

Jefferson reached up and pulled me back down. "Calm down, Ells…let Mom talk."

My head was spinning. *This is not happening. Are they friends now? Did he get in touch with her? Or did she get in touch with him?*

"About three months ago, your father contacted me. I agreed to meet him—with Philip."

I felt sick to my stomach. I put my hand on my swollen stomach, and right at that moment, the baby moved. I'd felt her move this morning, and I thought Gunner would have come out of his skin because he'd wanted to feel it so bad.

"Mom, why would you open up that hurt again?" Jefferson asked.

I watched as my father looked down and then up at my mom. She looked at him and smiled.

"Jefferson, Ellie, I will always love your father. He was my first love. He was probably the love of my life."

My father reached up and wiped a tear away from his cheek. My heart jumped a beat, and I grabbed Jefferson's hand.

"But I am also deeply in love with Philip, and I plan on spending the rest of my life with him. He gives me unconditional love, and I can't imagine my life without him."

I was finally able to open my mouth and say something. "Are you still with Angie?"

My father snapped his eyes up at me, and the moment his blue eyes caught mine, I wanted to cry. I remembered those eyes looking into mine while he'd told me stories. I used to dream I would marry someone like him.

"No. We divorced a few years ago. She left me and said she couldn't live in the shadow of another woman."

I shook my head, the anger building. "What in the hell does that mean?"

He took a deep breath and let it out slowly. "Ellie…your mother was my first love. She's probably the only woman I've ever truly loved in my life."

I went to say something, but Jefferson squeezed my hand.

"I had all these plans for us…and when we went to college, I sort of freaked out. I was leaving town for games, and all I could do was think about her. What was she doing? Who was she with? Did she miss me? My mind was consumed with thoughts of your mother."

I began shaking. "Why did you cheat on her then?" I spat out with as much hate as I could.

My mother looked down and away.

Oh god…hearing him say this must be tearing her apart inside!

"I wish I could answer that, but there really is no answer. I was scared…scared of the feelings I had for her. A part of me wanted to push her away, so I wouldn't have to worry about anything. I just wanted to worry about football and taking over my father's business. The other part of me wanted her so much that I could hardly stand it."

He looked over at my mom, who just gave him a weak smile.

"One day, your mother saw me kissing Angie at a game. I ran after your mom, and I promised myself that I would never see that look in her eyes again. I would never hurt her again."

"But you didn't keep that promise," I said, my voice cracking.

My mother gave me a weak smile.

"Mom…are you okay?" I asked.

She smiled bigger as she tilted her head and slowly shook it. "Ellie, darling, your heart is so pure and sweet. Yes, sweetheart, I'm okay. Your father and I have been talking during the last few months about a lot of things. I think I have come to a place where I am able to forgive him. I needed this to happen, so I could have closure and move on with my life. So do you kids."

I sat there, stunned. "Why didn't you tell us you were talking to him?" I looked at my father. "Why didn't you try to contact us? Why did you leave when we all needed you?" I finally lost it and broke down, crying.

Jefferson took me in his arms and held me while I cried uncontrollably from all the emotions surfacing all at once. The next thing I knew, I felt a hand on my knee. I pulled my face away from Jefferson to see my father kneeling down on the floor with tears streaming down his face. One quick look at my mother revealed that she was also crying.

"I'm so sorry, pumpkin eater," he whispered.

"What did you call me?" I asked in a whispered voice.

"Pumpkin eater—it's what I called you the first time I ever saw you." He smiled.

I slowly shook my head. "But you didn't want me. I was a mistake."

His mouth dropped open, and he pulled back slightly. "Don't ever say that Ellie. *Ever.* I did want you. I loved you and still do. I love you very much. You did nothing wrong."

He looked up at Jefferson. "And neither did you, son. This is entirely my fault. All the pain and hurt I'd put the three of you through was all my fault. I have no excuse for what I did. I walked away from three of the most important people of my life because I was a scared, selfish bastard. I wanted that free life of partying and traveling that I didn't get to have. If I had a wife and family, I couldn't do that." He dropped his head and began sobbing. "I was a stupid fool, such a stupid fool."

I slowly looked at my mother, who was wiping away her tears. I was so confused, and my head was spinning.

"Why Angie though? You kissed her before you even knew Mom was pregnant with Jeff." I said.

He looked up at me, and his eyes caught mine. "Because I was an asshole, Ellie. I don't have any other reason than that. I was a cheating bastard. I loved your mother more than anything, but there was a side of me that just wanted to…I don't know." He shook his head. "Angie gave me attention like I'd never had before, and I…I liked it."

I peeked over at my mother as she sat there so calmly while she dabbed her eyes. She'd come so far, and I just prayed that this wouldn't have a negative effect on her.

"Were you happy with Angie?" I asked.

He looked away and then back into my eyes. "No."

"Why didn't you come back to us then?" I asked as the anger continued building inside me.

"I tried a few times. I'd go and visit your mom, and I would just end up…well, I would—"

"You'd fuck her and leave," Jefferson said.

"Jefferson Johnson!" my mother said.

Jefferson looked at Mom. "Sorry, Mom. It just…it makes me so angry. Dad, you have no idea how angry I am."

My father put his hand on Jefferson's knee and nodded his head. "Yes, I do. I do know how angry you are because I've been angry for the last twenty-something years. I'm angry at myself, at Angie, at my father, who encouraged me to leave your mother."

I sucked in a breath of air. "What? *Why?*"

He took a deep breath and let it out very slowly. "Your grandfather didn't like your mom very much."

He looked over and winked at her, and she smiled.

"He always thought I should have married someone who came from money. He threatened me when he found out that your mother was pregnant with you, Ellie. He told me he was going to take everything away from me. He was going to disown me for getting her pregnant again. He said I'd never run the family business. My mother though…she loved Sharon and you kids, and it broke her heart when I left. My father wouldn't allow her to talk or even see Sharon or you two."

"Oh my god. How could someone have so much hate in his heart?" I asked.

"I don't know, but I let his hate guide my life. I can't do anything about it now, but the last few years, I've been trying to think of a way to tell your mother and you kids how sorry I am. I never had children with Angie. The idea of having kids with her turned my stomach, so I ended up having a vasectomy right after I left your mother."

My mouth dropped open, and at first, I couldn't speak. "So, you spent all those years with a woman you didn't love, away from the love of your life and your kids…to please your father?"

His eyes looked so sad, and my heart actually began to hurt for him. I no longer felt anger toward him…only sadness.

"Yes," he barely said.

My mother stood up and walked over to us. She held out her hand, and my father took it as he slowly stood. They walked back over to the sofa and sat down together.

My mom took a deep breath. "When your father contacted me a few months back, I wasn't sure how to feel. When he told me how he felt…I won't lie…a part of me wanted nothing more than to fall into his arms and pick up where we'd left off all those years ago." She looked at him and smiled, and then she looked back at Jefferson and me. "But I love Philip with all my heart, and your father and I have talked about this. He certainly didn't expect me to just fall back into his arms."

"I wished it though," he said with a weak smile.

I couldn't help but smile at their easy banter with each other, and I looked at Jefferson, who was also smiling.

"We talked about him coming and talking to you kids—when we both thought it was time." She quickly glanced at him and then back at us.

My father cleared his throat and nodded his head. "I wanted to see you both...to tell you how sorry I am for what I did...for leaving you and causing your mother to fall into such a deep depression. I don't expect your forgiveness, but I certainly would love it," he said with a small smile. "I want you each to know that the days you were born were the happiest days of my life. And to see how you've each turned out to be such caring, loving, and successful..." He stopped talking as his voice cracked. "I'm so very proud of each of you. So very proud." He smiled at Jefferson and then me. "Your mother and I decided to wait until after the New Year, but I don't think I have...I don't...I..." His voice trailed off as he looked down at the floor.

My mother grabbed his hand and held on to it as she wiped a tear away with her free hand. "Jeff, Ellie...your father has stage two lung cancer. It has spread to his lymph nodes. He has had surgery, and he is about to start a combined chemotherapy and radiation treatment. The doctors are very optimistic though."

I put my hand up to my mouth. Just when I thought I was getting my father back, it felt like he was leaving again. I slowly shook my head. "No...you just came back to us."

My father's eyes captured mine, and I felt like I was looking into my own soul.

"Pumpkin eater..." he whispered.

I stood up as he did the same, and I walked into his arms. I began crying, and then Jeff took us both into his embrace.

"I love you both so much. Please know that I've always loved you both," our father said in between sobs.

"Daddy...you just came back to us. Please don't leave us again," I said. Jeff hugged us both harder.

I wasn't sure how long we stood there...wrapped up in our embrace. My heart was slowly feeling whole, but at the same time, it was breaking in two.

As we all sat back down, our father began telling us how he used to come to our school events and how he almost approached us each time.

"Did you see any of my games at UT, Dad?" Jefferson asked with a cracked voice.

My father smiled so big that I couldn't help but laugh.

"Hell yes, I did. You were an amazing football player. *That* you did get from your old man," he said with a wink.

I heard Ari clear her throat behind us, and we all turned and looked at her. She was holding Grace while Alex and Luke were holding hands as they stood next to her. I got up and walked over. I took both their hands and led them to my father.

I sat down on the floor and looked at Alex and Luke. "Alex, Luke…this is my daddy, your grandfather."

Jefferson sat on the floor and pulled Luke onto his lap. Luke immediately started laughing.

Jefferson glanced up at our dad and asked, "What would you like them to call you, Dad?"

My father quickly wiped away the tear from his cheek. He looked at my mom before turning back to Jefferson. "Grandpa would be a dream come true."

Jefferson smiled and said to Luke, "Can you go say hi to your grandpa? He's my daddy."

Luke turned to Jefferson. "Daddy's daddy?"

Everyone laughed.

Jefferson said, "Yeah, buddy, my daddy."

Luke jumped up and went right up to my father. "Bandpa."

My father smiled and reached out his arms, and Luke fell right into them.

"Bandpa, it is," he whispered.

Alex giggled and yelled out, "Bandpa!"

He took them both in his arms, and before I knew it, they were all over both my mother and father. I sat there and watched the whole thing play out as tears slid down my face. I felt Jefferson reach over and wipe them off my face. I looked over at him, and we both smiled.

"I love you, Ells," he said.

I threw myself into his arms. I tried so hard not to choke up on my words. I managed to whisper in his ear, "I love you, too, Jefferson. I love you, too."

31 Scott

I stumbled out of my bedroom and followed the heavenly smells of coffee and breakfast. *Azurdee must be cooking.*

I walked into the kitchen and saw Azurdee at the stove, Jessie sitting at the table, and Lark sitting across from her. I glanced at Jessie, and her smile instantly made my head feel better. One look at Lark, and I felt like shit again. He gave me that smile and looked down at his coffee.

"Motherfucker," I whispered.

Jessie and Azurdee giggled as I barely walked over to the coffee pot and poured a cup of coffee. I turned and sat down next to Jessie, but not before I leaned down and gave her a kiss.

"I swear I didn't have that much to drink last night, but I feel like total shit." I took a quick look at Lark.

He shrugged his shoulders. "Dude, you weren't even drunk. You just took two shots, and I think if I remember right, you can't handle shots—at all."

I took a drink of my coffee and then nodded my head. The last time I'd felt this bad was the morning I'd woken up to find Jessie had left. I thought back to that party. *Did I have any shots? Yep. Jeff and I did a few shots—a few as in, like, ten of them.*

"I think I'm going to give up drinking for a while." I winked at Jessie.

We had all gone out last night since Azurdee and Lark were both leaving today.

Between Gunner's New Year's Eve party and then last night...I am done with alcohol. Done.

"It's not like college anymore, old man. Your impending fatherhood has made you a lightweight," Lark said as he let out laugh.

"Fuck you, Lark," I said.

Azurdee began setting plates in front of us. I looked down at the plate, and I almost didn't want to touch it. There were two crepes filled with cinnamon apples on the plate. The top of the crepes had a scoop of vanilla yogurt with a strawberry and a mint leaf. Dulce de leche sauce was drizzled all over it. It looked heavenly.

Lark looked up at me as I peeked over at him. We both turned and watched as Azurdee sat down and started eating.

She glanced up and stopped. "What? What's wrong? Do you not like crepes?" she asked.

I looked at Jessie, and she was digging in.

"Oh…oh my god! Oh, Azurdee. These are so good. My god, I've missed your cooking. How I didn't gain a ton of weight in college is beyond me. Hmm…oh…yes…"

"My god, Jessie. Make love to the damn thing, why don't you?" I said.

Jessie snapped her head up and looked at me. "I've been craving these so much. They. Are. Heaven."

Lark laughed, and then he took a bite. "Holy shit. These are delicious."

Azurdee smiled and started eating again.

The moment I took a bite, I wanted to say how good they were, but I held back. Instead, I simply said, "Azurdee, these are the best crepes I've ever had."

"Thank you. I make them for the coffee shop all the time. If we run out, our regulars get so mad," she said with a giggle.

I peeked over and saw Lark staring at Azurdee. He could deny it all he wanted, but he liked her. Last night, he'd done everything in his power not to dance with her until he'd broken down and finally asked her to dance. The moment Keith Urban's "We Were Us" had come on, they had both taken off dancing. I hadn't seen Lark smile and laugh like that in a long time. The song had ended, and then they'd danced to "Don't Let Me Be Lonely" by The Band Perry. Jessie had mentioned how sad Lark had looked. I'd been sure he had been thinking of Nikki.

"So, are you sure you need to leave today? You were planning on staying till the third," I said before taking another bite.

Lark was snapped out of his trance and went back to eating.

Azurdee rolled her eyes. "Ugh, as much as I have loved being here, I have to get back. I left my mother in charge of the coffee shop, and if I didn't lose any employees, it will be a miracle. I do wish I could stay longer though. I've really enjoyed myself," she said with a smile as she looked over at Lark.

He was concentrating on clearing off his plate.

"Lark, you sure you have to leave?" I asked.

He looked up at me and smiled. "Dude, this was the longest Skip has let me off in a long time. I need to get back to work." He stood up and looked around the table. "Speaking of, I probably need to get ready to leave soon."

I quickly looked at Azurdee. Her whole body sagged in her seat, and she tried to smile, but it looked forced and weak. I stood up with my plate, grabbed Lark's and Azurdee's, and then I reached for Jessie's. I practically had to pull the plate out of Jessie's hands. I was ready for her to start licking it.

"Hey, I thought you were going to go look at that filly I bought. Didn't you say you were interested in her?" I asked, knowing Lark really wanted that filly.

I also knew Azurdee loved going to the stable. She loved the horses.

"Shit. Yeah, I do want to take a look at her." Lark ran his hand through his hair.

"Well, let's go take a peek at her. Azurdee, would you like to go with us? I know how much you love the horses."

She jumped up and clapped her hands. "Yes! I'd love to."

Jessie laughed. "Y'all go ahead. I'm going to stay here and clean up."

Azurdee's smile faded. "No, Jessie, I cooked. I will stay and clean it up."

"Nonsense, Azurdee. Go see the horses. You cook, I clean, remember?" Jessie said with a wink.

Azurdee smiled and nodded her head.

After we left the house and made our way to the ranch Jeep, Lark jumped in the back to let Azurdee sit up in the passenger seat. We were at the stable five minutes later. Azurdee jumped out of the Jeep before I even came to a stop. When she began skipping up to the stable, I smiled and looked over at Lark.

"She likes horses, I take it," he said with a laugh and a shake of his head.

I chuckled. "Yeah, she loves them. She grew up in the city and has always dreamed of having a ranch or marrying a rancher."

Lark's smile faded for a brief second before it returned again. "Well, with the way that girl cooks, she's gonna make some rancher one happy and fat guy."

I laughed and nodded my head.

We got out of the Jeep and headed into the stable. As Lark and I talked about the filly, he kept looking at Azurdee. She was moving from horse to horse—talking to them, scratching them, and hugging them.

He looked back at me and said, "What did you say?"

I threw my head back and laughed. "Distracted?"

He rolled his eyes. "Fuck. I can't hear you with her going on and on about the horses." He turned and glared at Azurdee.

She just stopped and looked at Lark.

"Jesus Christ, they are just horses. Do you have to make such a production over them?" Lark snapped at Azurdee.

I watched as she slowly smiled a weak smile.

She said, "I'm sorry. I guess I just get excited when it comes to the horses. I'll wait in the Jeep for y'all."

She began walking out, and I just stared at Lark. He closed his eyes and threw his head back as he let out a breath of air.

"Azurdee, wait, I didn't mean to snap at you like that. It's just that I can't hear what Scott is saying with you going on and on," Lark said.

Azurdee walked right past him. "No worries." She made her way out of the stable.

I narrowed my eyes and looked at my best friend. "You're a complete fucking asshole, do you know that?" I said.

He looked at me with a surprised expression on his face. "Why? 'Cause I asked her to calm the hell down?"

I shook my head. "She likes you, dickhead. I guess you haven't been able to figure that out the last few days. She's a sweet girl, and you just acted like a total douche toward her."

Lark looked over my shoulder at the filly and then back to where Azurdee had just walked out of the stable. "Well...I don't like her, and I'm not interested in any kind of a relationship." He walked over and began running his hand along the filly. "I'll take her. Can you arrange to have her delivered to my place?"

I just looked at him. "Your dad's ranch?"

"No, mine," Lark said.

"When in the hell did you buy a ranch? Where? How much land?" I asked.

Lark smiled. "Dude, I didn't tell you I bought some land?"

I shook my head. "No, you didn't."

"Yeah, about seven months ago. I bought three hundred acres between Johnson City and Marble Falls," Lark said with a smile. "I'm going to have a small ranch house built on it."

"No shit. I thought, for sure, you were going to settle in Austin," I said as I slapped his back.

"Fuck no. I was raised in the country, and I want to die in the country. Besides, I can build a shooting range. I could have Jeff come out and embarrass the shit out of him," Lark said with a wink.

I couldn't help but laugh as I shook my head. "Well, congrats, dude. Just make sure I have the address, and I'll have them bring her out in the next week or two."

Lark smiled at the filly. Then, he turned, and as he walked out, he said, "No rush. I'm leaving the country for about a week or so."

I followed Lark out of the stable and laughed. "You ever gonna tell me what it is you really do?"

Lark stopped and looked at me with a serious face. "If I did...I'd have to kill you."

He started to walk back to the Jeep as I just stood there.

"Wait. Are you kidding? Or are you being serious?" I called out.

He just shrugged his shoulders and began looking around. I glanced over and saw that Azurdee was gone.

Where in the hell did she go?

We both looked around for her, and then I saw her walking in a field behind the stable. The grass was at her waist, and she had her phone out, taking pictures. Lark and I walked up to her.

Lark said, "What in the hell are you doing?"

Azurdee was startled. "Taking pictures. What does it look like I'm doing?"

"You're lucky it's cool out today. You can't be walking around in stuff like this. What if a snake bit you?" Lark said.

Azurdee rolled her eyes. "Why would you care?"

She bumped into his shoulder on her way to the Jeep, and we followed. She hopped in, and Lark climbed into the back. That Jeep ride back to my house was one of the longest rides in my life. As soon as I parked, they both jumped out and headed into the house. No one had said a word since we left the stable.

I walked into the kitchen and noticed the dishes had not been cleaned yet. Jessie was nowhere around. I walked into our room, and she wasn't in there either.

Where in the hell is she?

I headed out onto the front porch and noticed her car was gone. I instantly began panicking. *She left again. Where did she go?* I quickly grabbed my cell phone out of my pocket and hit her number.

"Hello?" she answered.

"Where are you?" I asked, trying to stay calm.

"Um…don't be angry. Promise you won't be angry."

I took a deep breath and slowly blew it out. "Okay. I promise, I won't get angry."

She took a deep breath and slowly let it out. "I got a call from Trey. I didn't know what to do. He was so upset, and he started talking crazy. He hasn't gone back to Dallas yet, and he kept saying all this stuff about how he had nowhere to go, he couldn't go home, he was all alone, and he was going to do something to himself."

I instantly balled up my fists. *That motherfucker.* "Okay," I whispered.

"Well, he was just so upset, Scott, and I felt so bad. He told me he'd spent the holidays alone."

"And that's your problem, how, Jessie?" I snapped.

"Scott, he's still a friend," Jessie said.

"What are you going to do, Jessie? Comfort him?"

I regretted the words the moment they had come out of my mouth and even more when I heard her suck in a breath of air.

"Scott, he started saying all this crazy stuff about how he didn't want to live anymore and how he missed me. I just thought if I talked to him, he would—"

"He would, what? Feel better? He wants you, Jessie! He wants you to leave me and go with him. He told me himself that he wasn't going to give up on you. He is doing this to get you to go to him, to leave me again."

"I would *never* leave you again, Scott. *Ever.* You know this! We're getting married and having a baby. I'm just trying to be a friend to him."

I let out a breath and shook my head. "I don't have a good feeling about this guy, Jessie. Please just come back home. Please," I practically begged.

"Scott, you know I love you. I love you so much, but I have to make sure he is okay. Trey is a good guy, Scott. I got to really know him."

I let out a gruff laugh. "Yeah, I know you really got to know him, Jessie. He got to know you really good, too."

Silence.

"That's not fair, Scott," Jessie whispered.

"No, Jessie, what's not fair is that some fucker can call you on the phone, give you some sob story, and make you run to him without you even bothering to tell me where you are going. You didn't even give me a chance to offer to go with you. I would have gone with you if you were that worried about him. You didn't even give me the chance!"

I heard her crying.

"I…I guess I just panicked when he said he was wishing he wasn't even alive."

"Where are you meeting him? I'll meet you there. Don't go in until I get there. You can't be that far ahead of me."

"Don't go in? What do you mean? I have to wait for you? I'm not meeting him in his room. I told him to meet me in the lobby. He's staying at the Hampton Inn in Fredericksburg."

I was stunned into silence. *He's in Fredericksburg? He's been forty minutes away this whole time?*

"Jessie, turn around and come home now." I had the worst feeling in my gut.

"Scott, he was talking about hurting himself. I'm sorry…I just feel like I have to help him."

I tried to stay calm. "Jessie, you don't think it's strange that he's been staying in Fredericksburg?"

"I mean, I guess I was a little surprised he was there, but he is so afraid to go home and face his family, Scott. He said his dad kept telling him how much of a failure he was. He just needs a friend. I promise that we will sit in the lobby and talk until you get there."

I squeezed my cell phone as I lowered it. I just wanted to throw it. *Damn it!* I took a few deep breaths to calm myself and turned to walk back into the house.

I put the phone up to my ear again. "Jessie, I'm so fucking pissed-off at you right now. Don't go anywhere with him, and please don't go up to his room."

I ran up the steps two at a time and saw that Lark's bedroom door was open. He was zipping up his suitcase, and he just looked at me.

"I'm not going to go up to his room! My god, Scott."

"I really wish you would just come back and let me go with you," I said as I held up my finger to answer Lark's questioning look. My hands were shaking because I was so pissed-off…and worried.

"Just meet me at the hotel, and we can talk to him together."

"Fine. I'm leaving now. I'll call you when I get on the road," I said.

"Scott?"

I didn't say anything. The bad feeling in my stomach was growing stronger and stronger.

"Scott, please don't be mad at me. I love you, baby. I love you more than anything. I just felt so bad for him."

I slowly nodded my head even though she couldn't see me. "I'm calling Josh now. I don't want you meeting with him alone. I'm telling you, Jessie, I don't think this guy is who you think he is."

"If calling Josh will make you feel better, I'm totally fine with that until you get there."

"Jessie, let me know when you get there. I'm on my way."

"I will. Love you to the moon and back, baby," she said.

My heart broke in two. "I love you to the moon and back, too."

I hung up and immediately called Josh.

"What in the hell is going on, dude?" Lark asked.

"Give me two—"

"Josh! Are you in Fredericksburg? That fucker Trey called Jessie. Told her a bunch of shit that scared her, made her think he was going to hurt himself. She panicked and left while Lark and I were down at the stable. He's staying at the Hampton Inn there. Jessie is going to meet him in the lobby. I have a really bad feeling, and she won't wait until I get there. Can you hightail it over until I get there? Yeah. Okay. Thanks, Josh. I just don't have a good feeling about this. The fact that he is still around and staying in Fredericksburg just sits wrong with me. Thanks. I'll leave here as fast as I can."

I hit End and looked at Lark.

He nodded his head and said, "Let's go. I'll drive my truck."

As we walked down the hall, Azurdee came up the stairs.

"Where is Jessie?" she asked.

I couldn't even talk. The lump in my throat was so big. So many emotions were running through my body. I was so pissed that she'd left without telling me, and I was worried because I didn't trust this guy. *Fuck!*

"Short version—Trey called Jessie and told her he was going to hurt himself. She panicked and took off to talk to him. He's in Fredericksburg at the Hampton Inn," Lark said.

He made his way down the stairs, and I followed.

Azurdee said, "What? She left to go meet him by herself?"

Good. I'm glad I'm not the only one who thinks it's crazy.

Lark turned and looked back at Azurdee. "Yep. We need to get to Fredericksburg."

Azurdee grabbed her purse. "Oh, I'm going because that bitch left without even saying good-bye to me."

Twenty minutes later, my phone dinged, and I looked down at it.

> *Jessie: I'm here, and we are talking in the lobby. I think he is drunk. He's in bad shape, Scott…but all is well. Take your time.*

Take your time? Is she crazy?

I replied back.

> *Scott: Just sit there and wait for Josh. We are on our way.*

I kept glancing over at the speedometer. My foot was tapping a mile a minute. We were less than ten minutes out from the hotel.

"Lark, go faster," I said.

"Jesus, Scott, I'm going almost eighty."

My phone rang. I looked at the screen to see it was Josh calling.

"Scott?" Josh said.

"Yeah. Are you with them?" I asked in a panicked voice.

"You said the Hampton Inn, right?"

No. Oh god, no.

"Yeah, the Hampton Inn, Josh. In the lobby. She should be in the lobby with him. She said he seemed drunk. Is there a bar? Maybe they are in the bar."

"Let me go look, but I'm standing in the lobby, and I don't see Jessie anywhere."

Fuck! I fucking told her to wait.

"Josh, please find her. Please," I said, my voice cracking.

"Scott, I'm looking. I don't see her anywhere. She's not in the lobby or in the bar. What's Trey's last name?"

"Um…his last name is—"

"Walker," Lark said.

I snapped my head over and looked at Lark. *How in the hell did he remember Trey's last name? Did I even tell him Trey's last name?*

"Uh, it's Walker. Trey Walker."

"Give me a second to talk to the front desk."

I let out a shaky breath. "Okay."

I could hear Josh talking to a girl. "You saw him? Was he with a girl? What do you mean she seemed like she didn't want to go?"

My heart was pounding. *What is going on? What is she telling Josh?*

"Josh! What's she saying?"

He kept talking to the girl, ignoring me.

"Josh! What in the hell is going on? Where are they?"

I felt a hand on my shoulder.

"Scott, calm down, okay? Jessie wouldn't go with him anywhere. Maybe they walked outside to the pool or something." Azurdee said.

I looked at Lark as he took his phone out before hitting a number.

He looked at me and said, "Tell Josh to get the license plate Trey gave the hotel. Most hotels want a license plate number. Josh might have to charm the person he's asking."

"Josh…Josh…" I said.

"Yeah, sorry. I was trying to get information from the front desk."

"Get his license plate number!" I practically screamed through the phone.

I heard Josh asking the girl.

Then, I heard him tell her, "She might be in danger. I need that plate number."

I felt sick to my stomach. *Jessie. Oh god…if he puts a finger on her, I swear to God, I'll kill him.*

"I need a plate ran and tracked…hold for it," Lark said.

Josh said the plate number, and I repeated it to Lark. He gave the number to whomever he was talking to.

"Five…no, make it two." He hit End on his cell and set the phone down. He glanced at me and then quickly looked in the rearview mirror at Azurdee.

I turned to look at Azurdee, and she looked scared to death.

I gave her a weak smile. "Don't worry, Azurdee. I'm sure everything is fine."

She tried to smile back, but the single tear that slid down her face about killed me.

"You're a terrible liar, Scott," she said.

I turned back and looked out the window.

Lark's phone rang, and he quickly answered it. "Talk to me. Okay. Keep on it. Let me know if the direction changes." He hit End and punched the gas even more.

"Lark?" I asked.

"He's headed toward Austin."

"Wait. How do you know that?" Azurdee asked.

"It's part of my job to be able to find people," Lark said in a quiet voice.

"Oh," was all Azurdee said as she sat back in her seat.

I tried to calm my beating heart. *Dear Lord, please…I'll do anything you want. Please don't let him hurt or take her from me.*

"What else did Josh say, Scott?" Lark asked, snapping me out of my prayer.

"He told me the girl at the front desk said that she had noticed Jessie sitting there with Trey. She told Josh the only reason she was watching was because she had liked Trey, and he had taken her out a few times, so she was a bit jealous to see him talking to another girl. She heard Jessie telling Trey to stop this before he regretted doing it. She had a line of people checking in, but when she glanced up, she saw Trey had Jessie by the arm, and he was quickly guiding her out of the hotel. She said Jessie looked scared, but the girl didn't think anything of it at the time."

Lark slowly looked at me. "If you called the cops, we can't prove that she's been kidnapped."

"Kidnapped!" Azurdee called out from the backseat.

"We can't prove it unless the front desk girl saw something else. See if they have a security camera and if they will let Josh see it."

I called Josh back. "Josh, is there any way you can ask to see if they have a surveillance video of Trey and Jessie leaving? Buddy, you are awesome. Call me back as soon as you can."

I looked at Lark. "Josh had his mother come up to the hotel and start talking legal bullshit. They are both about to watch the video now."

"Oh god. Oh my god. What if he…the baby…" Azurdee said.

I hadn't even thought of the baby up to this point. "I'll fucking kill him," I whispered.

My cell phone rang, and I answered to hear Josh saying something to his mother.

"Josh? What's going on?" I asked.

"He had a gun. He had a gun pointed at her side the whole time they walked out of the hotel. Mom is on the phone with the Austin police department right now. You said they were heading to Austin, right?"

I couldn't talk. My whole world flashed in front of my eyes—Jessie at our wedding and giving birth to our child and sitting on the back porch together in our rocking chairs. *She's my whole world.*

"Scott? Scott? Scott!"

I heard Josh, but I couldn't answer him.

The next thing I knew, Lark took my phone and started talking to Josh. Everything went quiet, and all I could see was Jessie when she had woken up this morning and leaned over to rest her chin on my chest.

"Sometimes, I think I'm dreaming," I whispered as Jessie looked into my eyes.

The smile that spread across her face caused my stomach to drop just a bit.

"Same here. I can't believe how happy I am. The wedding, the baby— everything is just falling into place for us...*finally!*" she said with a laugh.

I ran my hand through her hair, and every now and then, she would let out a soft moan that moved through my whole body.

"Do you want a boy or a girl?" I asked her.

"I want a girl. I mean, a healthy baby would be perfect, boy or girl, but...I would love a little girl. What about you?"

I sat there for a minute or two and thought about it. "A boy would be pretty cool. I could teach him about hunting, riding, the business, how to smile at a girl and melt her panties," I said, laughing as Jessie hit me in the side. "But a girl...oh man. I'd love to have a little girl to do all that with and just spoil her. I'd make her feel special and always let her know how cherished she is, just like her mama."

Jessie smiled. "I like that for a name."

I looked at her funny. "Cherished?"

She giggled. "No. Cherish."

"Hell no! My child is *not* going to have one of those hipster names. No way."

Jessie giggled as she reached under the covers and began stroking my dick. I looked down at her lips as she licked them.

"I want you, Jessie, but my head is killing me," I whispered.

She bit down on her lower lip, and before I knew what was happening, she had me in her mouth and was moving up and down, making moans that vibrated my dick. I put my hands in her hair and tried like hell to hold off. The way she was moving her tongue was driving me nuts. She traced her finger across my ass, and that was it. I couldn't hold back.

"Jessie...baby, I'm going to come."

She started going faster, and she let out a low moan as I poured myself into her mouth. My eyes about rolled back into my head. It felt so fucking good.

"Fucking hell, Jessie...ah...feels...so good."

She sat up and leaned back against her heels as she wiped her mouth and then smiled. "I think that was the best one yet, and I got all of it down!"

She was so proud of herself that I couldn't help but laugh. She winked at me before getting off the bed and making her way into the bathroom. It didn't take long before I heard her throwing up. I flew up out of bed and ran into the bathroom to see her sitting on the floor.

She looked up at me. "Oh god, I tried. I swallowed, but…it tastes so fucking gross. You need to eat kiwi!"

I busted out laughing and sat down next to her. "I love you, Jessie, and what you just did felt fucking amazing, but I don't want to feel good if it makes you feel sick."

She nodded and gave me a small smile. "I did a pretty good job though, didn't I?"

I smiled and pulled her onto my lap. "Yeah, baby. Yeah, you did."

"Scott…Scott! Snap out of it," Lark said.

I turned and looked at him.

"I just got another call. We're catching up to him. I need you to open the glove box."

I reached over and opened the glove box to see a handgun. *Fuck.*

"Be careful. It's loaded. Hang on to it, and if I tell you I need it, don't waste a second. Do you hear me?"

I slowly nodded my head as I heard Azurdee crying in the backseat.

"Trey, will you please just pull over, and let's talk about this, okay? Your driving is really making me sick, and—"

"Jessie, I just need you to be quiet. Just be quiet. I need to think," Trey said, his voice cracking.

I sat there, looking down at my purse. *Scott. Why didn't I listen to him? What if we never see him again?*

I began crying, and Trey looked over at me.

"Why are you crying?" he asked.

I just stared at him. "*Really?* Are you really asking me that? Why are you kidnapping me?" I practically shouted.

"I'm not. We belong together, Jessie. I knew it the moment I sank my fingers into your body. You belong to me."

Oh god, I feel sick. I let this man touch me. I let him kiss me and—

I shook my head, and more tears began to fall. "No, we don't, Trey. That was a mistake. I was lonely and scared. I wanted Scott that day, and I just used you to help me forget, but it didn't work because I love him and only him. I'm having his child, Trey. This baby is his."

Trey looked at me and smiled. He went to put his hand on my stomach, and I knocked it away. He looked stunned and looked back at the road.

"I can raise the baby just fine. We don't even have to tell the baby about Scott. Our kid will never know about Scott."

I sat there, in shock. I couldn't even talk. "Have you lost your mind? What in the hell makes you think I would *ever* do that?"

I noticed Trey's jaw tighten up. *I need to get out of this car, and I need out fast.*

"Trey, please stop the car. I don't want to go with you. I don't love you."

"You do, Jessie. I know you do, deep down inside."

Jesus Christ. No wonder his fiancée left him at the altar. She was smart.

"Trey, I don't love you, and I'm so sorry if I ever gave you the impression that I did. I thought we were two friends just trying to help each other through a hard time."

"You sat and slept on my lap that whole night. Even after you found out you were pregnant, you held on to me all night." He smiled.

I slowly shook my head and whispered, "No."

He nodded and let out a laugh. "Yes! Yes…you love me."

"No, I was scared, and it was in the middle of a damn storm, Trey! I thought you were my friend. You're acting crazy."

He slammed his hand down on the steering wheel, causing me to jump. "No! Friends don't fucking crawl onto their friends' laps and hang on to them all night. They don't kiss their *friends* good-bye, like you kissed me. You want me, Jessie. You're just scared, but once you feel what it's like to have me inside your body, you will see how much I love you. You will feel how much we love each other."

My heart began beating faster. *Oh god. Please, God, don't let this happen. The baby…*

"I'm not having sex with you," I barely said as I began sobbing. *Scott…please come get me. Please…find…me.*

Trey slowly turned and looked at me. He grabbed my arm and pulled me toward him. "Yes. You. Will. And you're going to see how much you like it, you bitch. You dick-teased me for weeks, Jessie, with all your fucking *friends* bullshit. I thought I could be patient and let you realize on your own how that damn pussy isn't meant for you. *I'm* meant for you."

I tried to pull away from him, but he was holding on to my arm so tight.

"Trey…you're hurting me!" I said.

"Kiss me, Jessie. Lean over here and kiss me. Feel the love from my body as it goes into yours."

I tried to pull away harder. "No. Trey, please…oh god, please don't do this. Why are you doing this? This is not the Trey I came to know and care about in Belize."

He let out a gruff laugh. "Care about? Care about? Is that what you call it, Jessie? You know…that other girl…what was her name? Chelsea. I bet if I called her right now, she'd fuck me again. Want to watch us, Jessie? It was pretty hot with her."

I sucked in a breath of air. "What?"

I pushed my arm away from him, and he let it go. He threw his head back and laughed.

"Yeah, I called her up and told her I was going to be hanging around for a few extra weeks. She came to Fredericksburg, and it didn't take much to get the bitch up to my hotel room. She's a kinky bitch, too."

I put my hand up to mouth. I felt like I was going to be sick from the way Trey was swerving.

"What's wrong, baby? The idea of me fucking Scott's ex make you sick?" he said with a laugh.

"No, you asshole. It's your driving," I said.

He slammed on the brakes, and I felt the seat belt jam into my stomach.

The baby!

"Trey! I'm pregnant, and your driving is scaring me. Please…please just stop this craziness now."

He held up his hand as he gunned it. "We're being followed."

What? "What? Why in the world would you think we are being—"

Lark…Lark is still with Scott. Maybe they found out that Trey had forced me out of the hotel, and they figured out a way to track him.

I tried to turn around, but Trey reached over and pushed me back. He swerved into the other lane, and I let out a scream as he whipped the car back into our lane.

"Shit! Trey…oh god, please…I'm begging you to just pull over. *Please* think of the baby I'm carrying. This isn't her fault. Please just pull over. You can just drop me off, and I promise, I won't press charges or anything."

I began crying harder as he pressed on the gas. I glanced over to see that he was going over ninety miles an hour.

"Shut up, Jessie! I need to concentrate. I think that's your fucking boyfriend behind us."

My heart dropped to my stomach. *Scott!* I closed my eyes and just prayed to God that Trey would stop.

"Oh, he thinks he can track me down and bully me…fuck no. You're mine, and I'm not giving you up."

As I cried uncontrollably, all I kept thinking of was that this was my fault…again. I was going to lose the baby, and it was all because I had gotten on that damn plane, running away from my own fears.

Trey turned and looked behind him. I turned, too, and I could see that Lark was driving…and I saw Scott. They were so close behind us.

"Scott!" I called out. For some reason, I turned back around. "Trey!" I screamed.

He was drifting into the other lane, and a truck was coming right toward us. Trey turned the steering wheel so fast and hard that we spun around as he lost control of the car. All I heard were horns and screeching tires, and then it felt like I was in the air.

I closed my eyes, thinking of only two things—Scott and the baby.

33 Scott

Lark slammed on the brakes as we watched Trey's car flip over twice before it came to a stop up against another car. For a good fifteen seconds, I couldn't move. I heard Azurdee scream out Jessie's name, and I saw Lark get out of the car and start running.

I snapped out of it and yelled for Azurdee to call 911. I jumped out of Lark's truck and started running behind him. The car was in an upright position, and as I got closer, I saw Jessie.

No...God, please no.

Lark was trying to open up Jessie's door as I heard someone behind me yelling not to move her and that an ambulance was on the way.

Lark kept repeating, "Fuck," over and over as he tried to open the door.

I pushed him out of the way and tried. I took one look at the blood covering Jessie's face, and I almost fell to the ground.

"Jessie!" I screamed out as I tried harder to open the door.

The next thing I knew, I was being pulled away from the car.

"Let me go! That's my fiancée, and she's pregnant. Let me go!" I yelled out as I fought to get back to the door.

Then, I saw firefighters everywhere. I tried harder to get out of the hold I was in. Lark stood in front of me, blocking me from seeing them cut out Jessie's door.

"Scott, you need to calm down, dude. Please...calm down," Lark said as he grabbed my face to look at him. "Scott, they are going to arrest you if you hit a cop. Dude...please calm down."

I looked around, and two police officers were holding on to me.

I shook my head and began sobbing. "I just want to be with her."

Then, I felt my legs going out. Lark reached out and grabbed me.

"What hospital will they take her to?" Lark asked as he walked me over to a police car.

"Please," I whispered, "just let me be with her."

"Sir, please let the paramedics get to her first, and then you can go to her. Please just try to stay calm."

I slowly nodded my head as Azurdee walked up to me. She threw herself into my body, but I couldn't even get the strength to hug her back. She was crying so hard. She pulled back and looked at me. Then, she turned and looked like she was going to pass out. Lark reached for her and held on to her as she cried harder.

She kept saying, "Lark…please tell me she is okay. Is she okay?"

As he looked me in the eyes, he began stroking her hair as he said, "Shh…it's okay, honey…she's going to be fine. I promise, she'll be fine."

I watched as they removed Jessie from the car. Two paramedics were on Trey's side of the car, but then they came around and started helping with Jessie.

Is Trey awake? I am going to kill that motherfucker.

I got up and started to make my way over when I felt someone grab on to my arm. I turned and looked at the police officer. "He kidnapped my fiancée, and she's pregnant. I'm going to kill that motherfucker, and if you want to arrest me, go ahead, but I'm going to get to him even if I have to fight off ten of y'all."

He looked toward the car and then back at me. When he shook his head, I just stared at him.

"I don't think we will have to do that. The driver is…he's dead, sir," the officer said.

All the air left my body at once. "What?" I snapped my head back toward the car and then back at the officer. "Jessie…is she…"

"Sir, she is breathing, and they are about to get her on a stretcher and into an ambulance. You will be able to ride with her if you stay out of the way while the paramedics attend to her."

I nodded my head. "Yes, of course. Can you let them know she is pregnant and…" I felt tears burning my eyes as I looked back at the paramedics lifting her onto the stretcher. "I feel sick," I whispered.

The officer grabbed my arm and practically dragged me to the other side of his patrol car. I felt like I was about to throw up my spleen.

"God, please don't take the baby. Please don't…please…"

I leaned against the car and tried to stay calm, but the moment I heard Azurdee's voice, I lost it and started crying.

She grabbed on to me and hugged me. Now, it was her turn to comfort me. "Scott, she's going to be okay because she is the strongest person I know. She's going to be okay…Lark promised."

I couldn't help but let out a small laugh when she said that. I pulled back and smiled. "So, because Lark promised, it makes it so?"

She nodded and barely grinned. "He seems to know everything…so I'm going with it."

The officer called for me to follow him, and the next thing I knew, I was sitting next to Jessie in the ambulance. I held her hand and just stared at her.

I looked up at one of the paramedics and whispered, "The baby?"

She didn't answer me, but she gave me a weak smile. I slowly looked back at Jessie and thought about Trey.

The driver is…he's dead, sir.

"The driver, did he…instantly?"

Fuck me. Why would he try to take her? What in the hell was he thinking?

"I'm not sure, sir," she said.

I shook my head and held on to Jessie's hand as the ambulance raced to the hospital. I closed my eyes and prayed like I'd never prayed before.

The moment her hand moved through my hair, I felt that familiar feeling zip through my body. *She'll always have this effect on me. Even when we are eighty, I'll still feel this way when she touches me.*

I slowly lifted my head and smiled when her stunningly beautiful green eyes met mine.

"The baby?" she whispered.

"She's perfect. I got to see her," I said. My smile grew bigger.

"You did?" she gasped. "That is *so* not fair!" She went to move and grimaced. "Oh god…I'm so sore everywhere." She lifted each arm and then wiggled her toes. "I feel sore, but…I'm not in a whole lot of pain."

I smiled. "Yeah, you were so incredibly lucky, baby. You didn't break anything. You're just battered and bruised."

I watched as a tear rolled down her beautiful face. I reached up and wiped it away.

"I'm so sorry I didn't listen to you. I should have turned around or waited for you to get there before I met him. I just…I just never imagined Trey would ever hurt me…but…" She began to cry harder.

I grabbed her hand and kissed the back of it. "Shh…baby, it's okay. Please don't be upset. You need to relax and try not to get stressed out, okay? Just take a deep breath and blow it out. You couldn't have known he would do something like that."

She quickly wiped away her tears.

I reached for a Kleenex and wiped her nose. "I'm practicing. Ari said I'm going to have to wipe a lot of runny noses," I said with a wink.

She let out a giggle and shook her head. "Where am I?"

"Brackenridge, but I think they said you could go home tomorrow if you felt good and got some fluids in you."

"Tomorrow? Oh, I want to go home now, Scott. Can't I go home now?" she said in that cute whiny voice that drove me mad with love.

There was a small knock on the door, and it slowly opened. I turned to see Azurdee and Lark both walking in.

"How are you feeling, honey?" Azurdee asked with a smile.

"I'm okay…just really sore," Jessie said.

Azurdee walked to the other side of the bed and took Jessie's other hand. I glanced up at Lark and shook my head, letting Lark know Jessie didn't know about Trey yet.

"I'm glad you're okay, Jessie," Lark said.

Jessie flashed that smile of hers at him, and I knew what was about to come.

"So, now, are you going to tell us what you do? Because I would love to know how in the hell you caught up to us like that. How did you know where we were?"

Lark shrugged his shoulders. "I just needed the license plate number, and after one phone call to a friend at the Department of Public Safety to check the traffic cameras, bam, there ya go."

"I'm never going to get it out of you, am I?" Jessie asked.

I peeked over at Azurdee, who was looking at Lark.

"Nope. Nothing really to tell," Lark said as he quickly looked at Azurdee and then back at Jessie before he turned and sat down.

"We just wanted to make sure you were okay before Lark and I took off. We left all our stuff back in Mason," Azurdee said as she pushed a piece of Jessie's hair behind her ear.

Jessie tried to sit up, but she stopped when she realized how sore she really was. "Oh no. I'm so sorry y'all have to drive back to Mason and then turn around and come back to Austin."

"No big deal, honey. It just gives me more time to grill Mr. Tight Lips here," Azurdee said as she gestured toward Lark.

Jessie let out a small laugh and then looked back at me. Her smile faded a bit as she took a deep breath and slowly let it out. "Is Trey okay? Did they arrest him?" she asked.

I looked up at Azurdee and then quickly back at Jessie. "Baby, um…Trey died in the car accident. He broke his neck and died instantly," I said.

I watched the tears build in her eyes before she closed them.

"So stupid. Oh my god. If I had just waited for you, none of this would have happened, and…and…maybe you could have just talked him into leaving, and he would…" Jessie began crying.

Azurdee said, "No, Jessica, this is *not* your fault. You had no idea that Trey would do something like this. You can't sit here and play what-if. It doesn't do anybody any good. What happened, happened. There is nothing you can do about it."

Jessie looked at me, and my heart broke at the hurt I saw in her eyes.

"I'm so sorry that I didn't listen to you, Scott. I'm so sorry I didn't just wait for you."

She began sobbing, so I crawled onto the bed and took her in my arms. I saw Azurdee wipe a tear away from Jessie's face. I closed my eyes and just held the woman I loved more than the air I breathed.

Once she finally stopped crying, I gently laid her back down and kissed her lips. I whispered, "I love you, Jessie. I love you so much."

She looked into my eyes, and I had to catch my breath.

"Scott," she whispered, "I love you so much, and I don't deserve your love after the stupid shit I've done."

I laughed and kissed her nose. "Get some rest, baby. I'm going to walk Lark and Azurdee out."

I got up as I looked over at Lark and winked.

Azurdee gave Jessie a hug and kissed her on the cheek. "Call me if you need anything. I'm just a couple of hours away."

Jessie smiled. "Okay, will do. Thank you so much, Azurdee, for coming to visit and for all the yummy food. The baby is going to miss your French toast."

Lark laughed. "Shit, I already miss it!"

I walked Lark and Azurdee outside. I shook Lark's hand, and then I hugged and kissed Azurdee.

"Lark, I don't even know how to thank you, dude," I said.

"I'm just glad that we were able to catch up to them and that Jessie is okay. That wreck scared the shit out of me. It's a miracle that she's just sore and didn't get hurt."

I nodded my head and looked at Azurdee. "She's going to miss you."

She grinned. "I'll come visit more often. The coffee shop just keeps me so busy, but I want to help with the baby's room and the wedding," she said with a wink.

"Sounds like a plan."

"You're sure that y'all got a ride home tomorrow?" Lark asked.

I nodded my head. "Yep. My parents are already in Austin. They were on their way to the hospital earlier, so they should be here any minute."

"Alright. I'll be out of town for a bit, but you know how to get a hold of me if you need me, right?"

I laughed. "Yeah, I know. Thanks, Lark, for everything. I'll talk to you soon."

"Later, dude."

I watched as Lark and Azurdee walked into the parking garage. I smiled, wondering how the two of them were going to get along by themselves during the drive back to Mason. Lark would never admit it, but I knew he liked Azurdee.

I turned and headed back into the hospital. When I walked into Jessie's room, she was sleeping peacefully. I quietly sat down and watched her sleep as I said a silent prayer, thanking God that Jessie and the baby were okay. I leaned back in the chair and closed my eyes as I thought about Trey. I thought about his family and how devastated they would be about his death.

Senseless…it was all just so senseless.

I felt myself drifting off into sleep. Images of Jessie standing before me with her hands on her swollen belly filled my body with a warm sensation.

I will always love, cherish, and protect them both until the day I die. Always.

34 Gunner

I watched as Alex walked up ahead of me and stopped every five minutes to bend down and look at either an ant or a flower. I smiled, thinking how she was about to become a big sister to Colt. The moment I'd found out I was having a son, I'd wanted to shout for joy.

Alex watched a butterfly as she sat down on the ground and laughed. My heart couldn't be filled with any more love right now. I looked over toward the garden and saw a very pregnant Ellie with Grams. Ellie took to country life like she had grown up on a ranch her whole life.

It was May seventh, and Ellie was four days past her due date. I knew she was miserable as hell in this heat. She glanced over and smiled at Alex, and then our eyes met. My heart melted every time this girl looked at me with that smile. I would never get tired of seeing her look at me with so much love.

Alex squealed as Brian, Ellie's father, came walking up to her. He bent down, picked her up, and spun her around. I noticed Ellie as she watched her father playing with our daughter.

Brian had been battling lung cancer, and things finally seemed to be going well with him. His health was improving more and more every day, and Jeff, Ellie, and Sharon were well on their way to healing completely. Brian had retired from his position of CEO of his company, and he'd bought a little house in Mason. At first, Ellie had felt upset about it since her mother and Philip had just moved here. She had been terrified that her mother would slip into old habits, but when Sharon and Philip got married on Valentine's Day, that had put all of Ellie's fears to rest.

Then, of course, there was the fact that Brian had met Carol here in town, and they had gone out on a few dates. That had helped to put Ellie's mind at ease even more. Brian was being careful though as he didn't want to fall in love with someone, knowing what his situation was, but Carol was a sweetheart, and she loved Alex, Luke, and Grace.

"Gunner, how are you today?" Brian asked as he held Alex in his arms while she hugged him around his neck.

"I'm doing good. Did you talk to my dad about that horse?" I asked.

He nodded his head and laughed. "I sure did. Looks like I'm going to be taking some roping lessons from your old man. He wasn't kidding when he said he wanted this ranch to be run by family and only family."

I let out a laugh. My father and Brian had really hit it off, and they had become good friends over the last few months.

I thought back to the other night in the barn up by Grams and Gramps's house. Just me, my father, Gramps, Drake, Brian, Jeff, Josh, and Greg had all been sitting there—drinking while talking about cows and horses and the women who made up our world. It had been like a dream come true. Even Jeff had seemed to be so happy and content. It had been months since we'd had any drama, and I was planning on keeping it that way.

"Gunner?"

I glanced over toward Ellie, who was standing next to the garden gate with her hand on her stomach. I slowly walked up to her, and leaning down, I gently kissed her on the lips.

"You look so beautiful, do you know that?" I asked with a wink.

She smiled and then grimaced.

"What's wrong?" I asked.

Then, I saw Grams walking up to Brian and Alex. She put her hand on Brian's arm and said something to him that caused him to look up at Ellie in a panicked way.

I slowly turned and looked at my breathtakingly gorgeous wife. "Ells?"

She smiled. "My water just broke."

I shouted out, "Yes! Finally!"

I took her arm and looked back at Grams and Brian. "Do we all know what to do?" I asked.

Brian let out a laugh. "My god, Gunner. Just get her suitcase and take her to the hospital. Emma and I clearly know our roles."

"Daddy?" Alex called out.

I stopped and turned back to look at her. She was staring at me with those beautiful blue eyes of hers.

Damn. She is going to break a lot of hearts.

"Hey, Little Bear, Mommy is going to have your little brother, Colt. Bandpa is going to get Grammy, okay?"

When she nodded, her little pigtails moved back and forth, and my heart swelled up with so much love.

I looked at Brian, and before I could even say it, he said, "I'll call your parents right after I call Sharon."

Grams laughed as she walked by me. She had her cell phone in her hand and was texting Gramps. "I'm going to warn Garrett not to share the story of the last time Ellie went into labor." She threw her head back and laughed.

Ellie giggled and peeked up at me. She shrugged her shoulders and said, "You gave them the cell phones and showed them how to text."

After I helped Ellie into my truck, I turned and gave Alex a kiss good-bye. "I love you. Be a good girl for Grammy and Bandpa, okay, pumpkin?"

She nodded her head and reached out for me. She grabbed around my neck so tightly that I almost found it hard to breathe for a second. The hold this little girl had on my heart sometimes scared the shit out of me.

She pulled back and said, "Ice cream?"

I laughed and looked at Brian. "Good luck!"

When I ran around the front of the truck, I looked over and could tell Ellie was having a contraction. I jumped in and looked at her. "Deep breaths in and—"

"Gunner! That shit doesn't work. Just get me to the hospital, so they can give me an epidural, and we can get this kicker out of me."

I smiled as I started the truck and made my way down the driveway.

I knew better than to talk to Ellie, so I just stayed quiet until we got to the hospital. Her contractions were getting closer together. By the time they got Ellie into her room, I thought she was going to pull her hair out and then go after mine.

"Where is Pete?" Ellie asked the nurse.

"Dr. Johnson will be in at any moment, Mrs. Mathews."

"Gunner, Ellie, how are y'all?" Pete asked as he walked in. He shook my hand and then turned to look at Ellie. "Ellie, how are you feeling?"

Ellie shot him the dirtiest look. "I'm in pain—a lot of pain. I want an epidural—like yesterday."

Pete laughed as he began to examine Ellie, and then he quickly looked over at me.

"Ugh!" Ellie called out as she grabbed on to the sheets and threw her head back.

I knew by the look in Pete's eyes that Ellie wasn't going to get an epidural.

"Um…if you'll excuse me, I think I need to use the restroom," I said as I started to make my way out of the room.

He quickly stood up in front of me and laughed. "Oh no." He leaned in and said quietly, "You bastard, you are *not* leaving me alone to tell her."

"Damn it, come on, Pete. We've become good friends. Do a guy a favor. I've invited you to my house on numerous occasions. You know how strong these pregnant women are. She's not going to take it out on you. It's going to be me who will pay for this!" I whispered.

"What in the hell are you two whispering about over there? I want this baby out! It feels like he's coming out!" Ellie yelled.

Pete grabbed me and pushed me over toward the nurse. "Get him ready."

I heard Pete talking to Ellie. "Ellie, honey, you're at ten centimeters, and the baby is about to start crowning—"

"What?" Ellie called out.

"Uh...Dr. Johnson..." one of the nurses said.

The other nurse was putting a gown on me. She smiled and nodded at me when she was done, and I turned back to hold Ellie's hand.

"Ellie—" Pete started to say.

Ellie cut him off with another contraction.

I'd never seen Pete move so fast, not even in our flag football games. The next thing I knew, he was telling Ellie to push, and she was squeezing the hell out of my hand.

"Um...Ells, can you let up just a little bit, baby? It's kind of hurting," I said.

She snapped her head over to me, and her eyes turned dark gray.

Holy shit.

"You. You did *this* to me. You want to know what hurts? Oh god!"

Another contraction hit her as Pete told her to give him a good push.

Ellie flopped back down and started shaking her head. "I can't...I can't do it anymore. I'm so tired, and it hurts so bad, Gunner. Just...just cut him out."

Pete chuckled, and I looked at him. He shrugged and smiled at me.

He said, "Come on, Ellie. I see his head. Just a little bit more, honey, and then I promise, you can rest."

Ellie looked at me, and the tears rolling down her face about dropped me to the ground.

"Gunner..." she whispered.

"Oh, baby, I know. Squeeze the hell out of my hand. Break it if you have to. Baby, just one more time. I know you can do it."

Ellie pushed two more times before the cries of our baby filled the room. The nurse took him, cleaned him up, and did a few things with him before she wrapped in a blanket, brought him over, and placed him in Ellie's arms.

"Meet your healthy eight-pound-two-ounces baby boy," the nurse said.

Ellie looked up at me as the tears flowed down cheeks, and she smiled. Her eyes lit up, and I couldn't help it. I let the tears fall as I looked at how happy she was.

I leaned down and kissed her. "Good job, sweetheart. I'm so proud of you."

She laughed. "Thank you." Then, she looked down at our baby boy. "Hey, big boy," she whispered as she gently moved her index finger along his face.

She glanced up at me and wiped a tear away from my cheek. I grabbed her hand and kissed her palm.

"He's beautiful," I said. "Just like his mother and sister."

Ellie grinned so big and looked back down at him. "I've been waiting a long time to meet you, Colt Hunter Mathews, my precious baby boy."

After Ellie and I spent some time alone with Colt, everyone started coming in. First, it was Jeff and Ari, then Heather and Josh, and then Scott and Jessie. I swore Jessie was getting bigger every time I saw her. She was due in July, and she looked beautiful.

"Brad and Amanda are on their way, sweets," Ari said.

I smiled as I watched Ellie. She couldn't take her eyes off of Colt.

I leaned over and asked, "Are you hungry, baby?"

She laughed. "Yes! I want a chopped beef sandwich and sweet tea."

I went to kiss her but stopped short of her lips as I smiled at her. "Are you happy, Mrs. Mathews?"

The love in her eyes told me her answer even before she opened her mouth. "Drew, I can't even begin to tell you how I'm feeling right now. I love you so much, and…I feel…" Her voice cracked, and she closed her eyes briefly. When she opened them again, she looked into my eyes like she was looking into my soul. "I've never been so happy in my life. Everything just feels so right. It all feels…perfect." A single tear moved slowly down her face.

I kissed her gently on the lips and then whispered, "Yeah, sweetheart, I know how you feel because I feel the same way. I'll never be able to tell you how happy you've made me, how much I'm in love with you, Ellie, and how that love grows more and more every day."

"Drew…" she whispered as she reached up and wiped away a tear from my cheek.

"You've made me so happy by just loving me, Ells…and by…by giving me Alex and Colt…" My voice cracked as I tried to hold back the overwhelming love I was feeling for this woman. I smiled at her as I pushed a strand of loose hair behind her ear. "It's…it's everything I've ever dreamed of and wanted."

"Why. Does. It. Have. To. Be. So. Hot? I hate Texas in July," I said as I kicked my feet in Jeff and Ari's new pool.

Ari was sitting on the edge with Grace, who was splashing and laughing.

"I can't believe that Grace, Will, and Libby are going to be one next month," I said as I tried to lean over and splash water on my face.

"I know. It goes by so fast. I still can't believe Luke is two," Ari said as she smiled a soft, sweet smile.

I dropped my head back and felt the hot sun on my face. The baby had been moving all over the place today. I felt a funny pain and put my hand on my stomach.

Luke and Alex both came running out of the house and started jumping around in the pool. Grace immediately began crying, and Ari picked her up and put her on her lap.

"Luke, you know better than to run around the pool and splash Grace. She's smaller than you. You have to protect her, not hurt her."

Luke tilted his head and peeked at Ari with his beautiful long lashes.

Oh…he melts my heart in an instant.

"Don't fall for it, Jessie. They learn early how to work you," Ari said. She turned back toward Luke and said, "Well?"

Luke walked up to Grace, gave her a kiss on the head, and quickly said, "Sorry," before turning and playing with Alex.

I felt Scott come and sit behind me. He moved his body up against me and put his legs on the outside of mine, dipping his feet into the pool water.

"Damn that feels good. What is it outside? A hundred degrees?" Scott asked as he lifted my ponytail. He began kissing my neck.

"Oh, that feels good," I whispered.

"Knock it off, you horny bitch. My kids are right here," Ari said as she winked at me.

I let out a laugh as I watched Gunner pull up a chair for Ellie and Colt. Ellie looked exhausted but so happy. She glanced over and smiled at me. Then, she looked at my stomach and let out a giggle.

"Jessie, you have to be having a boy. You are all belly," Ellie said.

Ari's dog, Scarlet, came up to me and began nudging my arm. I picked up my arm and began petting her softly. I closed my eyes, and an image of Trey popped into my head. I hadn't thought about him in months. I still felt like the accident was entirely my fault. If I had just waited for Scott, Trey wouldn't have tried to force me to leave, and the accident would never have happened.

When I'd met Trey's mother and father, they'd told me that Trey had been having some emotional problems. That had been one of the reasons his fiancée had left him and he'd stayed in Belize for so long. He had been hiding from a life he didn't want to go back to.

Would things have been different for him if he hadn't met me? Would he have gone home and led a different life? A happy life?

I opened my eyes and looked over at Ari, who was staring at me.

She has some kind of sixth sense, I swear.

She always seemed to know when I was feeling guilty.

She gave me a slight smile and shook her head. "Stop," was all she had to say.

I did just that. I quickly pushed all thoughts of Trey from my mind.

I felt the pain in my stomach again, and I quickly looked around. Jeff was now leaning down, kissing Ari, as Grace was reaching out for him. Alex and Luke were pouring water over each other. Josh and Heather were in the water with Will and Libby. Ellie was talking to Heather while Scott was in a deep conversation with Josh about making a bench for the end of our bed. He wanted Josh to help him make it. Gunner walked around, holding a sleeping Colt. Matthew was sitting in one of the lounge chairs, playing a video game.

I turned and looked at all of our parents. They were all sitting under the covered pavilion that Scott, Jeff, and Gunner had made. Sharon, Grace, Elizabeth, and Sue were all sitting together, laughing at something Emma was saying. Jack, Brian, Philip, Mark, Greg, and my father were all listening to a story Garrett was telling.

I tilted my head and looked around at four generations of friends.

Gunner started humming, and Alex must have heard him because she got out of the pool and ran up to him. She started asking him to put the baby down and hold her. I giggled at how jealous she was of Colt getting attention from her daddy.

Gunner smiled down at her. "You miss your daddy's cuddle straps?"

"What?" Josh, Jeff, and Scott all said at once.

Gunner smiled as he handed Colt to Ellie. "Yeah, my cuddle straps," he said as he flexed his arms.

Ellie rolled her eyes.

Ari said, "Oh, for the love of all things good, Gunner."

Jeff, Josh, and Scott all looked at each other and then back at Gunner as they started laughing.

Jeff shook his head. "Pussy."

Ari smacked Jeff. "Jeff! The kids, for Christ's sake."

Jeff turned and looked at Ari. "See! See, this is why your dad gets pissed at me when the kids swear. You get mad at me when I swear, but you swear at me for swearing. Why can you swear at me, but I can't swear? How is that fair, Ari?"

She took a sip of water and smiled as she shrugged her shoulders. "Don't know, but in my father's eyes, it's fair."

Jeff just looked at Ari and smiled as Luke dumped water over Ari's head. She screamed and jumped up. She grabbed Luke and gave him a tickle attack.

"Are Brad and Amanda still planning on coming out?" Heather asked Josh.

"Nope. I think the move into the new house is taking its toll on them all. Amanda wasn't feeling good, and Maegan has strep throat," Josh said.

Everyone let out a gasp. We all looked at each other and laughed.

"Jesus H. Christ, look at us," Ari said as she glanced around.

Everyone took a good look around and then turned back at Ari.

"We're old. I mean, we act old. It's like we're our..." Ari looked over at where Garrett was still telling his story to everyone. Then, she turned back to us and scrunched up her nose. "We're consumed by the fear of sickness because, my god, if our kids get sick, then that's it for our perfectly planned days. Germs and running snot noses for a week. We plan a Fourth of July get-together *with our parents* instead of going to some country bar where we can take a few spins around the dance floor while getting drunk. It's like we've grown up and become..." She turned and looked over at the older group of friends all talking and laughing with each other. She slowly smiled. "Them. We've become our parents."

"Ari? Why do you say you are Mom and Dad?" Matt asked.

Ari laughed. "It's just that we act like them, Matt, 'cause we are all older now and have kids."

Matt nodded his head. "Will I ever have kids, Ari?"

I saw the sadness instantly fill Ari's eyes as her smile faded for just one brief second.

"Would you like to have kids someday, Matt?" Ari asked.

Matt looked around at each of us. He was really taking in the sight of everyone before he looked back at Ari. "Hell no, I want to be a motherfucking cowboy."

Jeff jumped up and down as he did a fist pump, and then he walked up to Matt. "Yes! Buddy, you said it right this time! Motherfucker!"

"Jeff!" Ellie and Ari both called out.

Matt stood up. "Jeff, I'm going to hug you!" He slammed into Jeff, clearly pleased that he had just made Jeff so happy.

Ari shook her head. "Wait till my father hears this one."

I let out laugh, and then I felt the same pain, but this time, it was stronger, like the baby had kicked the shit out of me.

Scott had his hands on my stomach. "Damn, that was a big kick, and your stomach is getting hard."

I had to take a deep breath. *Wow, that really hurt.*

Ellie stood up and walked over to me. "Jess, how long have you been having pains?"

Scott jumped up. "What? Pains? When did you start having pains? How long have you had them for? Why didn't you tell me you were having pains? I'm supposed to time them!"

Josh said, "Damn, our only job, and it seems like we all mess that part up."

"Right?" Jeff and Gunner both said at the same time.

Heather started to push Libby on the float as she made her way to the edge of the pool. "Jessie, oh my god, is it time?" She picked up Libby and walked out of the pool.

I shrugged my shoulders. "I, um…I don't know. I mean, they feel like Braxton Hicks contractions…but harder."

"Jesus, Mary, and Joseph…Jess, those are contractions. How long have you been feeling them?" Ari asked.

"Uh…"

"The suitcase! I don't think I packed it in the truck! Shit!" Scott said as he took off running toward the truck.

"Jessie, did they just start, sweets?" Ellie asked me.

"Well, I felt the first one right about when Scott came out with y'all."

"How many have you felt since then?" Heather asked as she dried off Libby.

"I think that was the third one?" I said as I watched Scott running like an idiot over to his truck.

The next thing I knew, my father was walking up. "Is it time?"

I honestly didn't know what to say. *Am I in labor? Is this it?* "I don't—"

"I've got it!" Scott yelled.

I looked past my father and saw Scott running back up. He had a huge smile on his face. The next thing I saw was Scott tripping over Scarlet, who had run in front of him and cut him off, while he was trying to hurdle the lounge chair, and then he landed in an awkward position.

The moment I heard him cry out in pain, my heart dropped to my stomach…and then I had a contraction.

"Oh my god!" I screamed out.

Ari and Heather were running toward Scott, but then they stopped and ran back to me.

"What?" Ari skidded to a stop in front of me.

I started shaking my head frantically. "I-I don't know! Oh my god! Is he hurt? Ah...motherfucker!"

"Motherfucker, I want to be a motherfucking cowboy!" Matthew called out.

Sue and Mark walked up to him and started to tell him not to say that.

"But Jeff and Jessie said it," Matt said.

Mark smiled. "At least we moved on from mudderfucker."

Sue just looked at Mark, and I glanced back over toward Scott. Jeff and Gunner both ran into each other, trying to turn and go into the house, each saying something about getting ice. Jeff yelled out in pain, and Gunner tripped. He lost his balance, and he started to fall backward.

Oh no...this is not going to be good.

"Gunner! Watch out!" Ellie called.

Gunner reached for Jack, who reached for Greg, who reached for Mark...who saw what was about to happen and took a step back before Greg could grab a hold of him.

The next thing I knew, Gunner, Jack, and Greg were in the pool. Mark walked up behind Jeff and gave him a good push. Jeff ended up going into the water as well.

"Daddy!" Ari called out.

"What? He has a swimsuit on," Mark said.

I couldn't help but giggle at Jeff's expression when he was getting out of the pool. I glanced up at my father, who was standing there, shaking his head along with Garrett.

"What in the hell is wrong with you group of people? My daughter is in labor, and you're playing around!" Drake said.

I turned my head to see Scott sitting on the ground while Josh had ice on Scott's ankle. I made my way to Scott and tried to get down, but I was so damn big that I could hardly move.

"Scott, are you okay?" I asked as I attempted to sit down on the lounge chair.

"Don't sit. We're going right now. We have to get you to the hospital." Scott said in a panicked voice.

Josh helped Scott up as Matt came walking over.

"Scott, you assmole, you made me laugh with how you danced in the air," Matt said with a laugh.

That caused everyone else to start laughing, including me.

Then, another contraction hit, and I started to panic. *Shit, they're not that far apart.*

"Come on, I'll drive," Josh said. He turned back to Heather and said, "Babe, can you get the twins on your own?"

Elizabeth was standing next to Heather. "I'll help her with Libby and Will. Just get Scott and Jessie to the hospital," Elizabeth said as she picked up Will before giving him a big kiss.

I turned and looked at Scott. Panic had taken over in his eyes. My heart was breaking because I knew how he'd wanted everything to go so smoothly.

I smiled and walked up to him. I put my hands on his face and reached up to kiss him. "You ready, baby?" I asked in a whispered voice.

He smiled, and his eyes lit up, causing me to smile bigger.

"Never been more ready, but, um…Jessie?"

"Yeah, Scott?"

"I think I might have broken my ankle."

36 Scott

After Josh pulled up to the emergency room doors, I hopped out of the backseat and attempted to help Jessie out of the truck. Her contractions were not getting any closer together, and I was thanking God because I was almost a hundred percent sure I'd broken my ankle. Josh ran inside, and the next thing I knew, there were two wheelchairs.

The nurse walking up to us giggled. "Well, we haven't seen this in a while."

"Seen what?" Jessie asked as I helped her sit down in the wheelchair.

"The pregnant wife with the husband who broke something while frantically trying to get the wife to the hospital." The nurse winked at me.

She started to push Jessie in as Josh pushed me in while he was laughing. Just the nurse referring to Jessie as my wife caused my heart to beat faster.

"I wasn't frantic. I was jumping over a stupid lounge chair, and Ari's damn dog ran in front of me," I said, folding my arms. I was pretty sure if I could see myself, my face would be pouting.

Josh stopped at the nurses' station and slapped me on the back. "Dude, I've got to park your truck. Jessie, I'll bring your suitcase in." He looked at me and shook his head. Then, he turned and walked off, still laughing.

Bastard. I'm sure he panicked even more when Heather went into labor.

The nurse mentioned something to Jessie about how we had preregistered, so we had to sign only a few things. Then, she turned to me and asked for my insurance card.

"What?" I asked, confused. "Don't worry about me. My fiancée is in labor!"

The nurse smiled sweetly. "Mr. Reynolds, we need to get you down to X-ray, so we can see if your ankle is broken. Then, we will take care of it from there."

I went to stand up and felt a hand on my shoulder. I turned and saw my father standing there.

"Scott, just let them do this, so you can get it done and get back to Jessie. Your mother and I are here."

"Who called you?" I asked, confused as hell.

"Garrett. Now, go on. Just let them get you fixed up, son. I promise, you won't miss anything."

I turned and looked at Jessie, who was holding my mother's hand. I smiled when I looked at the two most important women in my life. They had both grown to love each other so much, and I loved that Jessie called her mom. She was the mother that Jessie had never had, and my mother adored Jessie so much. I felt tears building in my eyes as I looked up at my mother. She nodded her head, and I knew they were right.

I reached out my hand for Jessie's. "I'm so, so sorry I did this."

She let out a giggle. "I love you, Scott. I'll hold the baby off for as long as I can."

As the nurse began taking me down to get an X-ray, I turned around and saw Jessie staring at me. She lifted her hand and waved, and I blew her a kiss. I watched as the smile spread across her beautiful face.

I turned back around and cursed all lounge chairs and dogs.

We are never getting a pool. Ever!

I was impressed that the doctor in the emergency room had worked so fast to get me fixed up. The X-ray had shown a small fracture, so the doctor put a cast on and gave me crutches. He told me to follow-up in a few days with my doctor.

I swore Jeff was having a grand ole time, pushing me in the wheelchair as fast as he could, as I held on to my crutches while telling him to hurry the hell up.

By the time we got up to the labor and delivery area, my heart was pounding so hard that I was beginning to have a hard time breathing. I saw our family and friends in the waiting room and smiled. *I have the best group of friends ever.*

"Where are all the kids?" I asked, looking at Heather, Ari, Ellie, Gunner, and Josh all sitting around, drinking coffee.

Ari laughed. "That's the best part of having the grandparents over for a party. If we all need to leave, we've got built-in babysitters!"

"Ellie, you left Colt?" I asked, knowing Ellie had yet to leave Colt with anyone.

She smiled and nodded her head. "Well, I figured five grandparents could take care of him and Alex."

"Mr. Reynolds? Your fiancée is getting closer," the nurse said.

I jumped up and out of the wheelchair with my crutches. "Shit! Shit, this it!"

Everyone let out a laugh. Jeff, Josh, and Gunner walked me to the door.

Before I went in, I turned and looked at them. "I don't know what to say, but thank you. Thank you for being more than just a friend. Y'all are like my brothers, and I...I..."

Gunner put his hand on my shoulder and smiled. "We know what you're saying, dude. Go welcome your baby into the world, and don't forget to tell Jessie what a great job she did."

"And tell her she looks beautiful," Jeff said with a wink.

I looked at Josh, and he smiled. "Oh man, dude...take it all in because it will be one of the most amazing moments in your life. Just make sure she knows how happy you are, Scott."

I nodded as I looked at all three of them. I opened the door and heard Jessie cry out in pain. I quickly shut it and turned back around to them.

"Holy fuck, I can't do it." I started to hobble away.

Gunner grabbed me and opened the door. He turned me around and gently guided me into the room.

The moment her eyes caught mine, I didn't need any help. I needed to get to her. She looked down at my ankle in a cast, and she started crying.

"No...no, baby, don't cry." I tried my best to make my way to her side.

My mother was standing on the other side of Jessie, and she smiled at me when I finally made it to Jessie's side.

"Honey, I'm going to step outside now that Scott is here," my mother said.

Jessie reached for her. "No! Mom, please stay with us. Please," she said as her voice cracked.

My mother smiled and pushed Jessie's sweat-dampened hair away from her eyes. I saw tears building in my mother's eyes as she nodded her head.

"Of course I will stay with y'all, baby girl," my mother said.

My heart felt like it was going to burst. I was so happy.

My mother looked at me. "You have one very strong and brave young woman here. She is doing this with no drugs."

I instantly felt like shit, remembering how I had just begged the ER doctor to give me something strong to take away the pain. *Some cowboy I am.*

"Looks like you made it right on time, Scott. I think a few more pushes, Jessie, and we will get to meet this baby of yours," Pete said.

The next few minutes felt like a lifetime, yet it all happened so fast. Jessie pushed about five more times, and she never once complained about the pain. She cried out in pain each time, but I could tell she was trying to be so strong. I leaned down after each push and told her how proud of her I was and how much I loved her.

Then, it happened. Jessie let out a long and loud scream with the last push.

Pete looked up at us and smiled. "You have a beautiful and healthy baby girl."

I busted out in tears and looked at our baby girl as Pete held her up.

"Oh my god! She's the most breathtaking thing I've ever seen," Jessie said.

Pete handed the baby to the nurse, who moved our girl to a table. I watched the nurse do all kinds of weird-ass shit to the poor little thing. She was crying away, and my heart had never felt like this before. I thought loving Jessie was amazing, but this…this was beyond amazing, just like Josh had said.

I glanced down at Jessie as she cried and tried to see what the nurse was doing to the baby.

I leaned down, placed my finger under her chin, and moved her face over to look at me. "I love you more than anything. I never in my life thought that I could feel so much love in my heart, and you just proved me wrong…again. You amaze me. I'm in awe of you right now, and you…you've made me the happiest man on Earth. Thank you for loving me."

I gently kissed her, and she moved her hand to the back of my neck, pulling me in for a deeper kiss.

When we parted our lips, she smiled and looked me in the eyes as she said, "I love you to the moon and back."

She began crying again, and I wiped the tears from her cheeks.

"And I just want you to know…I'm *never* doing that again," she said.

My mother busted out laughing. I smiled and nodded my head as I looked up at my mother, who winked at me.

"Are you ready to meet baby girl Reynolds?" the nurse asked.

She walked up to me and gently put my daughter in my arms. The moment I held her, she immediately stopped crying.

"Hey…look at that. Already a Daddy's girl," Pete said.

He walked over to the sink and did a few things with the nurses, and then they slowly sat Jessie back up.

Looking down at this beautiful miracle in my arms, I couldn't help but smile. When she yawned, my knees about gave out.

"I promise to always love and protect you and your mommy. You two are my whole life now, baby girl."

I turned to see Jessie watching me. The smile on her face was like nothing I'd ever seen before in my life. I carefully took our baby and placed her into the arms of the woman I'd loved since before I could remember.

I would lay my life down for this woman and for our daughter.

I watched as Jessie brought our baby girl up to her lips, and she began kissing our daughter all over her little face. One peek at my mother, and I saw she was crying like mad. I smiled and wiped a tear away.

"I'm so, so happy to finally meet you. I've waited so long to hold you, and I thought for sure with how much you kicked and punched me, baby girl, that you were going to be a boy!"

We all laughed.

My mother lightly brushed her hand across the baby's head. "Do we have a name?" she asked as she looked at Jessie and then at me.

I looked down, and we both nodded.

"Lauren Ashley. Her name is Lauren Ashley Reynolds," Jessie said with a smile.

"It's perfect. She's perfect. Let me give y'all a few minutes. Before I go, Scott, would you like to go tell your friends it's a girl?"

I quickly looked up at my mother. "Oh yeah! Let me go real quick, Mom…on my crutches and all."

I made my way out of the room and down the hall. Everyone stood up at once. I knew the moment I opened my mouth, I was going to start crying again, and Jeff would probably call me a pussy. I looked at each of them standing there with smiles on their faces. These were my six friends who had stood by me through everything. I knew there wasn't a damn thing we wouldn't do for each other. My life would be empty without them in it. I knew this wouldn't be the last time we were all going to be waiting to hear the news of another new baby. Our lives were just starting. So many more happy memories were waiting for all of us.

"Well?" Ari said. "Are you going to tell us, dickwad? Or make us all stand here and guess?"

I let out a laugh. Only Ari could make me laugh when all I wanted to do was cry.

"It's a girl—Lauren Ashley," I barely said.

They all made their way over to me. With every handshake and hug, my heart grew bigger and bigger, and my love for my friends grew tenfold.

"Congratulations, dude," Gunner said as he took me in for a hug.

Each of the girls took turns giving me a kiss and wiping away my tears.

Josh smiled as he gave me a hug. "I told you, didn't I?"

I nodded my head. "Yeah. You weren't kidding either."

When Jeff walked up to me, I braced myself for what I was sure was going to be an onslaught of snarky comments.

"Welcome to fatherhood, dude. It's one of the coolest things ever. I'm glad you had a girl because if you had a boy, I would have to worry about him going after my Grace. If your son were anything like you…"

I started laughing and shook my head. "Thanks, Jeff."

He smiled, and to my surprise, he brought me in for a quick hug and slap on the back. "I'm really happy for you and Jessie."

As everyone stepped back, I saw my father walking down the hall with Starbucks coffees, and Bryce was following behind him with more coffees.

Dad stopped and smiled as he looked at me.

"A girl—Lauren Ashley," I said.

He handed Josh the coffees, walked up to me, and pulled me in for a hug. "Son of a bitch. Well done, son. Well done. I'm so damn proud of you and Jessie."

I smiled, and Bryce reached out and shook my hand. Things hadn't been the same with us ever since the whole Chelsea incident, but we were trying to work on it.

"So, I'm an uncle. Pretty damn cool."

"Dad, would you like to see her?" I asked.

"Do horses shit?"

I laughed and shook my head. I turned and made my way back into the room as I listened to my father talk about all the things he was going to teach Lauren.

I never want this feeling to end.

As I held my daughter in my arms, I glanced over at Scott sleeping away in the recliner next to the bed. I smiled and slowly shook my head.

"Your daddy seems to be tired, sweet baby girl."

I looked at the cast on his ankle, and my heart broke for him. He was supposed to be training a horse next week, and now, he couldn't, and he was so upset about it. When he'd asked Ari if she would do it, I'd thought she was going to jump through the roof because she had been so happy.

Lauren yawned while I used the tip of my index finger to gently trace a pattern along her face. She smelled so good, and she was so precious. Every time I looked at her, my heart wanted to burst open.

"You know, I remember the first time I felt you move. I was standing outside, and at first, I thought it was like a nervous feeling, but then Ellie told me it was you moving around. I also remember the first time I saw your little body move across my stomach." I let out a little chuckle. "Your daddy cried the first time he felt you move. I'm going to let you in on a little secret. I'm pretty sure you are going to be spoiled beyond belief. Between your daddy and your two grandpas, you will be one tough little girl. Don't worry though—your grandmother will be sure to keep you dressed to the nines in pink ribbons and bows."

Lauren opened her eyes, and I could swear that we were looking into each other's souls. The strangest feeling moved over me, and I couldn't pull my eyes away from hers.

As she slowly closed her eyes and drifted off into sleep, I thanked God for the blessings in my life. I had been feeling so sorry for myself the last few weeks—wishing my mother could have been here to see the birth of my child or to watch me marry the love of my life. I knew though that she was with me. In some strange way, it almost felt like she was letting me know she was here.

I slowly moved to get up when I heard the door open. I looked and saw Melody walking in.

"Hey," she whispered.

"Hey! What are you doing here? I thought you had a lunch you had to go to today?" I asked as I tried to stand up. I was so sore that all I really wanted to do was soak in a hot bath.

She walked up to me, took Lauren from my arms, and took her over to the bassinet.

Oh, thank God. I don't have to get up and move now.

"Are you still going home today?" she asked in a whispered voice.

I nodded my head and grinned like a fool. Scott and I had put Lauren's bassinet in the sitting room off of our master bedroom, and I couldn't wait to get home and start working on her room. We'd held off until we knew if it was a boy or a girl, and I had so many ideas.

Melody walked up to me and held out her hand. "Come on, you need to walk around. Trust me, it will help with the pain."

I rolled my eyes, and she put her hands on her hips.

"Did you just roll your eyes at me, young lady?"

"Uh…"

"You're in deep shit now," Scott said from behind me.

I turned to see him looking at us with that panty-melting smile of his. *Oh Lord…*

I instantly wanted him, but after I was split open from giving birth to his child, I had made a vow never to have sex with him again. I slowly licked my lips, and his smile faded for one brief second. Then, it was quickly there again, but this time, he raised an eyebrow. He always could tell when I was turned-on, which turned me on even more.

"Come on, up you go. I see you are dressed and ready to go, so I think a walk around will do you a bit of good," Melody said.

I slowly stood and felt every single pain.

As we made our way down the hallway, arm in arm, we chose to remain silent.

"Let's get a bit of fresh air, shall we go outside?" Melody asked with a smile as big as the Texas sky.

I couldn't help but smile back.

As we walked over to a bench and sat down, I took a deep breath of air in and slowly let it out.

"Jessie, I wanted to apologize to you."

I snapped my head over and looked at her. "For what?"

She shook her head, and then she looked up toward the sky. "For the way I treated you when you first started dating Scott. I know I was nothing but a bitch to you."

I pulled my head back and widened my eyes. *Where is this coming from?* "Melody, you don't—"

She held up her hand. "No, please let me get this all out. I sat down today at brunch, and I looked around at all these women who were sitting there. They are the best of the best, I guess you could say. Then, I saw Chelsea take a seat, and my stomach turned. Just thinking about what she did, using brother against brother just to hurt you, and how I-I…" She quickly shook her head as if she were clearing a memory or thought from her mind. "I just let her do it. I knew she didn't want Scott. I knew that. I

236

knew they were never meant to be together, and when I heard her say she was going to win him back, I chose to do nothing. Now, Scott and Bryce barely talk to each other. What if…what if you had never come back? Scott's heart would have been devastated."

I felt tears stinging my eyes, but I tried desperately not to cry. "I did come back though because what Scott and I have is real, Melody. I love him with all my heart, and I have loved him for so long. What happened is in the past and doesn't matter anymore. It really does no good to keep thinking about it. We have an amazing future ahead of us, and I want to focus all my energy on loving and taking care of Scott and Lauren. And I might add that we have a wedding to plan."

She nodded her head and looked at an older couple walking by as they held hands and laughed. When she looked back at me, our eyes met, and I saw the sadness.

"I just need you to forgive me for acting like such a snobby-ass bitch because, really, I'm not. When you and Scott came over and I saw his grandmother's ring on your finger, I was so happy. Then, you said you were pregnant, and I thought Scott, Senior and I were going to have heart failure because we were so excited. I just want you to know that you are like the daughter I never had, and I'm so happy that you are a part of this family."

That was when I lost it. The battle to hold back the tears was now over and done. I began sobbing, and Melody pulled me into her arms and began rocking me.

A lone memory of my mother holding me while she sang to me entered my mind. I could almost smell her perfume and hear her voice. Everything hit me at once—the loss of my mother, the guilt I felt about leaving Scott and being with Trey in Belize, and the guilt I felt about Trey's death. All of it crashed down in that one moment, and I cried like I'd never cried before.

I wasn't sure how long we sat there as I cried, but by the time I was done, I couldn't believe how much better I felt.

Melody pulled back and looked into my eyes. "Listen to me because I'm only going to say this once. It was not your fault. No one blames you for leaving. I would have probably done the same thing if I had walked in and seen what you did. No one blames you or judges you for staying away for so long, and it is not your fault that Trey died. He made the decision to do the things he did. Okay? So, I don't want you to ever have those thoughts in your mind again."

I nodded my head and wiped at my tear-soaked cheeks.

"Now, I know I could never, ever replace your mother, but I will do the best I can to be like a mother to you. I always wanted a girl." She smiled as she gave me a wink. "I can't dress you up in pink ribbons and bows, but I sure as hell can do that with Lauren."

I busted out laughing, thinking about how I'd had the same thought earlier.

She laughed and shook her head. "You know I'm going to spoil the hell out of her, don't you?"

"Yes, I know," I said.

We both stood up and started to head back to the room.

"Let's talk wedding. Do we have a date in mind?" she asked as she slipped her arm through mine again.

I peeked over at her. "Scott wants to get married on Halloween."

I cringed at how she was going to react. I was pretty sure she wanted a huge wedding where we would have to invite everyone in town, but Scott and I wanted something with just family and our closest friends.

She let out a gasp, and then she threw her head back and laughed. "Oh Lord! Halloween was always his favorite holiday besides Christmas, so I'm not surprised in the least bit."

I slowly let out the air I had been holding in. "Wait—you're not upset? I mean, if we decided to get married on Halloween and only have family and our closest friends attend, you would be okay with that?"

She stopped and looked at me. Her whole body seemed to straighten up more. "Jessie, I'm already thinking of the decorations…and what I want to wear! Oh, please say the guests can come dressed up. I have the perfect costume in mind!"

My jaw dropped to the ground, and I just stared at her. *Who is this woman? And where did the Melody I thought I knew go?*

"You're looking at me like I have two heads, Jessica. I can get my party on just like the rest of them. Come on, let's get y'all home. We have only a little over three months to plan this! Oh, we can set up games for the kids, too. My mind is racing with ideas."

As we walked back to the room, Melody kept coming up with all these wonderful plans for the wedding.

"Damn it, I wish I had a pen and paper, so we could write this all down," I said as I pushed the door open. Then, I stopped dead in my tracks.

Scott was holding Lauren and dancing with her in the middle of the room as he hummed a song. He was totally lost in the moment with her. My knees began to wobble, and I had to reach for the wall to hold myself up. I felt Melody steady me with her hands.

She let out a giggle. She whispered to me, "I remember the first time I saw his father holding him just like this. I was so swept away that I thought I couldn't breathe. When you get angry with him…think of this moment. Always remember this moment, sweetheart." She kissed me on the cheek and turned to leave. "Call me when y'all get home."

I couldn't even answer her. I just nodded my head. I was captivated by what was happening in front of me. I was falling in love with him all over again.

I walked into the room and just stood there. He finally looked up and saw me. He had a single tear rolling down his cheek, and there it was. I couldn't breathe. This man standing in front of me, holding our child and loving her, just took my breath away.

"I've never wanted to have sex with you so badly than I do right now in my entire life," I blurted out.

Scott's eyes widened, and he slowly smiled. "I thought you said you were never having sex with me again."

I walked up to him and looked at my sweet angel sleeping. I gently kissed her on the cheek. I reached up and gently brushed my lips against his. I tugged on his bottom lip with my teeth and then let it go. I slowly slid my hand down his stomach until I felt the evidence of his desire for me.

I winked and said, "I lied."

38 Jeff

I turned and glanced at the clock. It was two thirty in the morning. I rolled onto my back and attempted to go back to sleep. I could hear Ari breathing next to me, and the sounds she made while she slept drove me insane with lust. I turned my head and looked at her. I gently moved to my side and watched her sleep for the next five minutes.

I love her so damn much.

I placed my lips against her neck, right under her ear, where I gently kissed her.

"Mmm..." she said as she moved slightly.

Son of a bitch, I just have to look at this girl, and I want her so much.

I slowly slid my hand down her side and into her panties. I lightly brushed my fingers against her, and she pushed her hips into my hand.

"Jeff..." she whispered.

"Baby, I want you."

She opened her eyes and looked at me. The smile that spread across her face was my green light. Before I knew it, I was pulling off my boxers and crawling on top of her already naked body.

I slowly pushed myself against her while she let out the softest, sweetest moan. Her fingertips moved lightly up and down my back, causing a million and one jolts of electricity to move through my body.

"Jeff...please go slow." She pulled me closer to her.

I gently sank into her and let out a moan. I started moving in and out of her oh-so slowly. "Baby, you feel so good," I whispered against her neck.

"Oh god...what a wonderful way to wake up!" Ari said as she moved her hips in perfect rhythm with mine.

This had to be my favorite thing to do—being buried inside the woman I was so desperately in love with, taking my time in making love to her, giving her nothing but pleasure and pure love.

I moved my lips up to hers, and she gently took my lower lip in her teeth. When she lowered her hands down and grabbed my ass, I almost felt like I was going to come.

"Don't stop, Jeff. Please don't stop," Ari said against my lips.

"I'm trying not to come, baby...but you feel so fucking good."

She smiled and let out a small giggle. "Mmm...it does feel good...so, so good."

I moved again, slowly in and out, trying to take in every sensation that was traveling through my body.

"Jeff?"

"Yeah, baby?"

"Will you please go faster?"

I smiled as I buried my face into her neck. "Faster, huh?"

She bucked her hips against me. "And harder."

"Harder, you say?" I continued to move slowly, up and down and then in a slow circle.

"Ah…Jeff, please…I need you to go faster," Ari pleaded.

"What do you want me to do, Ari? How do you want me to make love to you?"

She grabbed my face with her hands and gave me the sexiest damn smile ever. "I want you to fuck me, Mr. Johnson. Fast and hard, please."

I winked. "Anything for my beautiful wife."

It didn't take long before Ari was throwing her head farther back while calling out my name. Every time with Ari felt like the first time. I wasn't sure how she did it, but she made me feel like I was taking her to heaven and back every single time we made love.

The smell of bacon was calling me into the kitchen even though I was running late this morning. I needed to go help Gunner with a few fence repairs, and then we were going to head into town for a few errands.

When I rounded the corner, I couldn't help but smile at what I saw. Luke and Ari were both dancing to Keith Urban's "Even the Stars Fall for You." Grace was busy eating, and she couldn't have cared less about what Ari and Luke were doing. The second Grace saw me, she smiled and held out her arms for me. I walked up and took her out of the high chair. Then, I began dancing with her to the music. Grace started laughing, and Ari rolled her eyes.

"Oh, sure. For you, she drops her food and gets into it. For me and Luke, she ignores us for Cheerios."

I laughed as I leaned over and kissed Ari. I bent down and got a big hug and kiss from Luke.

"I love ya, Daddy!" Luke yelled over the music.

"I love you, too, buddy."

After the song was over, Ari turned off the music and helped Luke up into his seat. I put Grace back in her high chair, and she wasted no time in shoveling the little Os into her mouth.

"Where in the hell does that girl get her appetite?" I asked with a chuckle.

Ari shrugged her shoulders. "Beats me. Your mom said Ellie used to eat the same way up until she was about two."

I grabbed the orange juice out of the refrigerator and started pouring Luke, Ari, and me a glass each. I glanced over at Ari scrambling eggs and humming.

"Ari, are you happy?" I asked her as I set the orange juice down.

She stopped everything and turned to look at me. At first, her face was serious, but then she gave me that smile that I'd do anything for.

"I've never been so happy in my entire life. Are you happy?" she asked with a wink.

I walked over to her and pulled her close to me. I placed my hand on the side of her face and gently brushed my thumb back and forth over her soft skin.

"I'm so happy I could burst with joy, baby. I swear, every morning I wake up, I have to pinch myself because I can't believe this is my life. You amaze me, do you know that? The fact that you finished school online with two kids while helping me with our business and Ellie with the cattle business and spending time with my mother and father...I'm just in awe of you. I can't wait to spend the rest of my life waking you up in the middle of the night to make love to you. When I'm near you, Ari, I feel like I'm walking on a cloud. Your love is amazing. You are amazing."

She smiled bigger, and I saw tears building in her eyes. I thought back to that day when she'd come to me as I'd sat against the oak tree.

"Jeff..." she whispered.

I kissed the tear from her cheek, and then I leaned down and kissed her lips. Our kiss quickly turned from sweet and innocent to passionate and full of need. More than anything, I wanted to make love to her right then and there.

When we finally broke away from each other, she gave me the sweetest smile.

"I love you so much, and the way you make me feel...I..." The tears rolled down her face, and she quickly wiped them away. "You make me feel so loved, Jeff, so very loved and needed, and I would never want to spend a single day in this life without you."

I brushed my lips against hers and whispered, "Arianna...thank you, baby, so much for loving me and for giving me two of the most precious gifts I could have asked for. Thank you for saving me."

I stood outside and watched Jeff drive off toward Gunner and Ellie's place. My stomach was still quivering from what Jeff had said to me this morning. I touched my lips with my fingertips and smiled. He said I'd saved him, but he'd saved me.

I glanced down at Luke, who was attempting to help Grace walk. I chuckled as I bent down and brought them both in for a hug.

"Do you want to take a nap, y'all?" I asked.

Luke made a face and quickly shook his head. "Too old for naps, Mommy," Luke said.

I pulled my head back and gave him a shocked look. "A person is never too old for a nap, son."

I picked up Grace and looked toward the driveway. Ellie was pulling up. I grabbed a hold of Luke. He was ready to bolt out to greet Ellie, and I was sure he was hoping Alex was with her.

Ellie jumped out of the truck and smiled as I let Luke run up to her.

"Mellie!" he screamed. "Alwex?"

"She's with her grandma and grandpa, baby boy."

Luke pushed Ellie away, turned, and stomped into the house. Ellie looked at me and laughed.

"I wonder where he gets that attitude from?" she said with a wink.

"Not from his loving mother, that's for sure."

Ellie shook her head as she walked up to me and took Grace from my arms. "Oh, baby girl, you're getting so big!"

"Where's Colt?"

Ellie smiled. "Grace and Jack begged me to let them watch both of them. Who am I to argue? Besides, we have a bachelorette party to plan for tonight."

I rolled my eyes and turned to walk into the house. I pulled out the little rolling walker, and Ells put Grace in it. Grace took off and started going around the kitchen island.

"Gesh. I take it she likes that thing?" Ellie let out a giggle.

Luke came walking in with his cars and started setting up shop under the kitchen table. He knew to stay away from the threat of a speeding walker.

"Okay, so we have a problem," I said as I grabbed a Diet Coke for Ellie and a water bottle for me.

"With what? The bachelorette party?"

I nodded my head. "Yep, Jessie is being a pain in my goddamn ass."

Ellie smiled slightly. "What's she doing?"

"She doesn't want a stripper, and she won't stop threatening me. She said that if one is there, she wouldn't go tonight!"

Ellie choked on her Diet Coke.

"Huh…Jessie had the same reaction you just did, Ells."

Ellie looked shocked. "A stripper? Oh my god, Ari! Don't you think we're all past that? I mean, we all have kids now. We can't do that stuff anymore! Amanda just had Taylor, for god's sake, Ari."

I rolled my eyes at her again and put my hands on my hips. "Would you just pull your granny panties back up, you pussy?"

Ellie dropped her mouth open. "I don't wear granny panties, you bitch."

I raised my eyebrow up at her. "Really? Prove it."

"What?"

"Pull your pants down. I want to see what type of undies you have on."

Ellie's mouth dropped open, and she shook her head. "Are you insane? I'm not pulling my pants down to show you what kind of panties I'm wearing."

I turned and walked toward the pantry to get Luke and Grace a snack. "Because you got granny panties on."

Ellie stood up and stomped her feet. "I do not!"

I tried like hell to hold my laughter in.

"Fine, you bitch. You want to know what kind of underwear I have on?" She began unbuckling her belt and then her pants.

The next thing I knew, she turned around and pulled down her jeans to expose her very nice pink lace cheekini panties.

She looked back at me and said, "Happy?"

"Nice…very nice, sweets," I said with a chuckle.

"What in the hell are you two doing?"

I quickly looked up to see Josh and Heather standing there, each holding one of the twins. Heather was trying to hold in her laughter, and Josh was standing there, waiting for his question to be answered.

Ellie jumped and pulled up her pants as she called me every name under the sun.

"Really, Ells! The kids' innocent ears don't want to hear your filth," I said with a wink.

"You are too much, do you know that? You got me to do that." Ellie pointed to me, and then she turned to Josh and Heather. "She was accusing me of wearing granny panties."

Josh let out a laugh. "And you wanted to prove to her that she was wrong? Why?" he asked, stressing *wrong* and *why*.

Ellie grabbed her Diet Coke and took a quick drink. "It doesn't matter," she said as she sat down on the bar stool with a thud.

I couldn't help it at that point. I lost it and started laughing my ass off. Luke jumped up and started laughing, too.

"Luke, you don't even know why you're laughing, bud," Ellie said with a smile.

"Mommy is laughing!"

Good enough reason for me.

"Well, hell, girls, I'd love to stand here and talk about your granny panties…or lack thereof…but I was supposed to be at Gunner's place to help with some stuff thirty minutes ago."

Josh put Will down, and he took off, walking over toward Luke. They both started playing with the cars, and I caught Josh's smile as he watched them.

He leaned over and kissed Libby and then Heather good-bye. "I don't think we will be long, baby."

"Take your time 'cause y'all are watching the kids tonight," Heather called out over her shoulder.

As soon as Josh shut the door, Heather put Libby down. She also took off walking—a little wobbly but still walking—toward the boys.

"Is Grace walking yet?" Heather asked.

"She took three steps last night and fell on her ass. She must have cried for a solid fifteen minutes. Now, she won't even attempt it. She's in her safety net right now," I said as I pointed to Grace whizzing in her walker past Heather.

Grace saw that Libby was out, and she stopped, looked up at Heather, and put her hands up for Heather to take her out. Heather reached down, took her out, and set her down. Then, Grace started walking up to Libby, and I almost died.

At the same time, Heather, Ellie, and I all screamed, "She's walking!"

Poor Grace got scared and jumped, causing her to fall again on her bottom.

"Oh shit!" I said as I walked up to her and bent down. "Yay, Grace! You walked like a big girl." I clapped my hands.

The next thing I knew, Heather and Ellie were right next to me. Grace pushed herself up and took off. This time, she went off at full speed out toward the living room.

I stood up and smiled. Then, my smile faded briefly. "Oh hell…now, I'm going to have two of them loose and crazy."

"Welcome to my world!" Heather patted me on the back.

"A stripper? Are you crazy?" Heather asked as she placed a bowl full of noodles in front of Will.

Ellie pointed at me and said, "See, I'm not the only one."

"I thought Jessie said no strippers, no way. Why are you planning on having one, Ari, if she doesn't want one?" Heather asked as she placed Libby into the portable high chair she had brought.

I let out a sigh. "Okay, listen, you prudes…just trust me, will you? Now, what time are we going to head into Austin?"

Heather shook her head. "Ari, if Josh finds out there's a stripper…well, hell, never mind Josh. When Jessie finds out, she's gonna freak!"

"Agreed," Ellie said before taking a bite of noodles.

"Bitches, just stop with your whining, my god. After all, we're almost twenty-two. It's not like we can't still have fun just because we've pushed out a few pups."

"Jessie is older, and I'm pretty sure she said no strippers," Heather said.

I stood up and placed Luke's dish into the sink. I took a deep breath before I turned around. "Listen, we're going out tonight, and we're going to have fun. I *need* fun. I *need* to drink a little, not get drunk but pretty damn close to it. I need to laugh and just have a good time, and I know you two need to do the same. I just want one night for all of us to have a good time. I promise y'all, I'm not going to do anything that the guys wouldn't like or that Jessie wouldn't want. Okay?"

Ellie and Heather looked at each other and then back at me. "Okay," they both said.

I smiled and nodded my head. "Okay, the limo will pick us up at Scott and Jessie's. Amanda is going to Jessie's house, and I believe they are spending the night there, so Brad will be there with Maegan and Taylor. Scott's mom will be there to help them get the kids to bed. Ellie, are Jack and Grace watching both kids?"

Ellie shook her head. "Only Alex. Gunner is keeping Colt."

Heather smiled. "Josh and I are staying at Ellie and Gunner's place tonight. Josh brought the portable cribs for the twins, and he's watched them plenty of times alone. Plus, I think Sharon is going to stop by, right, Ells?"

Ellie nodded.

"Fine. Now that we have all of our kids taken care of, we can decide who's not going to get drunk," I said.

Ellie grinned. "Well, since Jessie's getting married in two days, I think we need to make sure she takes it easy. Amanda won't drink 'cause she's still breast-feeding Taylor. Oh my god, did you see the cute picture of her that Amanda sent last night?"

Heather smiled. "Oh, I know! She is the cutest baby!"

I tilted my head and looked between the two of them. "Really, y'all? Can we please stop with all the baby and kid talk? Before we need to start putting the kids down for a nap, we have to talk about getting ready."

"Fine…let's talk about how we are going to have a clean, fun night tonight." Ellie looked at me and raised her eyebrow.

"Hey, I said I wouldn't do anything that would upset Jessie or the guys." I crossed my heart with my index finger and smiled. "I cross my heart," I said as I looked at both of them.

"Good. Now, what are y'all wearing?" Heather asked with a clap.

After we made all the arrangements and talked about who was driving over to Jessie and Scott's, Ellie and Heather headed over to Ellie's house.

I put Grace and Luke both down for a nap and headed back downstairs.

Now, I just have to call the stripper and make sure he has the plans down for tonight.

The evening had been a blast so far. I couldn't help but worry about Lauren though, and Ari was getting frustrated with me because I kept trying to call Scott.

"If you try to call him one more time, I swear to God, Jessie, I'm gonna smack you!" Ari yelled over the music.

Ellie came bouncing back over from the DJ. "Oh my god, I'm having so much fun! He's gonna play a song for us, y'all!"

I glanced over at Amanda and Azurdee dancing on the dance floor. Two guys were trying desperately to dance with them.

When Katy Perry's "This Is How We Do" started playing, Ellie let out an, "Eeeep!"

She grabbed Ari and me and dragged us out to where Amanda and Azurdee were. I couldn't help but laugh at all of them. They were having a blast, and all I wanted to do was go home to Scott and Lauren. Scott and I weren't going to be spending the night together tomorrow since the wedding would be the next day, so tonight was our last night together before we got married—and I was out dancing.

A few friends of mine from college had met us at the club, and they were dancing right along with us. A guy walked up to Ari and said something to her. She smiled big and looked at me. She tapped on a few of the girls' shoulders before she grabbed me, and then we took off, following the guy. We walked down a hallway and then into another room that had a giant glass window with tables all around.

"We get our own private room?" Ellie asked with a smile. She looked over at the pole in the middle of the room and smiled. "Oh god, I want to take pole dance lessons!"

Okay, she's had too much to drink.

"Just take lessons from freaky-fresh Heather over there. She knows how to get her groove on," Ari said as she jerked her head over toward Heather, who was on her way to being drunk also.

"Hell yeah!" Heather grabbed Ellie's arm and dragged her over to the pole.

I looked up and saw a DJ in a booth. He started laughing, and then Eminem's "Shake That" started playing. I couldn't believe how Heather could move her body. I just stood there and stared at her and Ellie dancing.

"Years of dance lessons and getting nasty in the bedroom will do that for ya," Ari said as she hit me in the arm.

I snapped my head over at Ari and busted out laughing. "My god…she could make serious money doing that," I said as I shook my head. "What are we doing in here anyway?" I yelled over the music.

Ari smiled. "I have a surprise for you." She pulled out two pieces of red satin and wiggled her eyebrows up and down.

"What is that for?" I asked as the music stopped.

Heather and Ellie were laughing their asses off as they walked back over toward us. Ari reached for my hands and pulled me over to a chair that someone had put in the middle of the room.

Oh, hell no! She did not…

"Sit down, Jessie," Ari said with a wicked smile.

"No! Oh my god, no, you didn't, Ari. I said no strippers."

Azurdee jumped up and down. "Stripper? Yes!"

I quickly looked at her, and my mouth dropped. "Azurdee!"

She shrugged her shoulders. "What? Do you know how long it's been since a man has touched me? The least you could do is let me touch a hot guy dancing."

Heather, Ellie, Amanda, and the rest of the girls all started laughing.

"For me, Jess?" Azurdee practically pleaded with a smile.

"No!"

Ari pushed me down in the seat and grabbed my hands. She pulled them behind me and quickly tied them.

"Ari, so help me God, if a strange dick comes anywhere near me, I will never talk to you again!" I yelled at her.

"Ari, you promised us no strippers," Ellie said.

"Stop whining, Ellie, and just trust me," Ari said with a wink.

I looked up at Ari. "Ari…please. I don't want to do this, so please…"

Ari put the red satin cloth over my eyes, and I instantly started panicking.

Oh my god. Scott is gonna find out, and I'm not going to get married. He won't marry me!

Def Leppard's "Pour Some Sugar on Me" started playing.

"No! Absolutely not, Ari. Scott loves that song!" I yelled out.

Then, I heard all the girls start yelling and hollering.

What in the hell is wrong with them? Is that Ellie yelling? Ellie, of all people, is going crazy over a stripper! Oh, I am so going to have a talk with her after this. Gunner would be devastated!

Oh god…he's in front of me. The moment I felt him near me, I wanted to puke. I tried hopping back in the chair, but I was getting nowhere.

"Take it off, cowboy!" Heather yelled out.

"What?" I screamed. "Oh my god, Heather! What is wrong with y'all?" I tried to figure out where he was. "Just stay back, stripper cowboy."

Then, I felt him straddle me. He must have taken off his shirt because I felt something wrap around my neck, and Ellie screamed something about how hot his abs were.

"Um...no...I'm not happy with this at all. Really, go dance with one of the horny drunks."

Then, I felt his breath on my neck. *Oh god...he smells like Scott.* For about ten seconds, I lost my wits.

"Please...I really don't want..."

I felt someone untying my hands.

Fuck. Fuck. Fuck.

"You have got to feel his abs, Jessie!" Azurdee said with a laugh as someone grabbed my hands.

"Azurdee! If that is you grabbing my hands, you are no longer my maid of honor. I'm stripping you of the title."

The only girl I couldn't hear was Amanda.

"Amanda! You're my new maid of honor!" I yelled out.

Ari started laughing. "Sorry, sweets. Amanda is busy making out with one of the stripper's friends."

What. In. The. Hell?

"*What?* She's not even drinking. Ari, please...you're gonna get everyone divorced and—"

The minute my hands touched the stripper's chest, I felt a funny feeling zap through my body. I froze for two seconds until he straddled me again. I moved my hands across his chest and then slowly down to his abs.

I'd know this body anywhere.

I slowly smiled and then felt his lips against my neck. My body instantly jumped to attention, and every sensation kick-started. He slowly kissed along my neck and up to the side of my face.

"Wait," I said.

He stopped moving, but he kept his lips against my face. He was now putting more pressure on my legs, and I could feel his hard-on.

"I'd like to take off this blindfold, so I can see my future husband strip for me," I said.

Scott started laughing as I reached up and pulled the silk cloth up and over my head. He didn't even give me time to say anything before he started kissing me. All I heard was everyone whooping and hollering. His kiss felt like heaven, and I wanted nothing more than for him to pick me up and just take me out of this stupid club.

"For a second there, baby, I was getting worried that you might be liking this a little too much," he spoke softly against my lips.

I smiled. "The moment I touched you, I knew it was you."

I glanced over and saw Brad and Amanda making out like they hadn't in years. Gunner was hugging Ellie and whispering something in her ear. Josh looked like he wanted to rip Heather's clothes off her body, and Jeff had Ari in his arms while he was talking to her. Lark was talking to a few of my college friends, and Azurdee was standing there, looking really pissed-off.

I turned back to Scott. "What in the world are y'all doing here?"

"Ari planned it all. I know I told you I didn't want to have a bachelor party, but we've pretty much been following y'all around all night. Josh and Lark are well on their way to being trashed with Jeff and Gunner running a close third and fourth. All I've wanted to do was get this part over with, so I can take you back to the hotel and have my wicked way with you."

I shook my head. "Is that why all the moms were at the houses because y'all had planned on going out the whole time?"

He looked down into my eyes, and I swore they were piercing into my very soul. I would never get tired of how he looked at me with so much passion.

He tilted my chin up with his finger and slowly leaned in to kiss me. "I. Want. You," he whispered after each kiss.

"Yes," was all I could manage to get out.

This was the first time we were out and away from Lauren for so long, but we both needed it.

"Scott?" I asked as I quickly looked around.

"Yeah, baby?"

"Please save me from this bachelorette party. Take me to the hotel and love me."

The way his body moved when he turned around and walked over to Gunner turned me on. I loved his walk. It was confident and sexy as hell.

Gunner nodded his head and said something back to Scott. Lark walked over with Cassie, a friend from college, on his arm, and when I looked over toward Azurdee, she was standing at the window of the club, looking out. I walked over to her and put my arm around her.

"Why does he do this to me?" she asked.

I shrugged my shoulder and pulled her closer to me. "I don't know. Defense mechanism, maybe?"

She turned around and rolled her eyes, and then she glanced back out the window. "He's probably going to take Cassie back to her hotel."

"Azurdee, go tell him how you feel. I know y'all like each other. I think everyone can feel it when the two of you are together."

Azurdee let out a small chuckle. "Everyone but Lark. It doesn't matter. I'm not going to force someone to like me if he doesn't. I think I'm going to ask my friend Paul to the wedding. I sure don't want to be the only one there without a date."

I looked down at the ground and then back up at her. "I don't blame you."

"Um…do you know if Lark is bringing anyone?"

I shook my head. "Nah, he told Scott that it would just be him."

I saw the slight smile move across Azurdee's face. My heart slightly broke at the idea of Lark just planning on hooking up with one of our college friends, but I didn't dare say anything to Azurdee.

I felt Scott's arms wrap around me as he pulled me closer to him. He had put his shirt back on, and he looked so damn handsome in his cowboy boots, jeans, tight-ass T-shirt, and cowboy hat.

"Are you ready to go?" he asked as he raised his eyebrows.

I looked at Azurdee. "Will you be okay?"

She nodded her head. "Oh yeah, the limo is big enough for all of us to fit in and head back to Mason."

"I don't think y'all are going to Mason tonight. Gunner made hotel reservations for everyone at The Driskill Hotel."

"Oh, okay." Azurdee quickly glanced over toward Lark.

I followed her eyes, and Lark was now talking to Brad and Amanda. They had finally pulled their lips apart from each other. Cassie was now back with the rest of our college friends. When she turned and walked up to us, I held my breath.

"Hey, Jess. Azurdee, we are going to head back to our hotel. It's been a blast, but I need to get back and give my boyfriend a call before he starts worrying. I can't wait to see you at the wedding. If you need any help, Azurdee, please give me a call."

I saw Azurdee's whole body instantly relax.

"Will do!" she said a little too excitedly.

Scott grabbed my hand. "If you'll excuse us, I have to finish my strip show in private."

I immediately felt my cheeks turn red as everyone laughed.

As we walked outside, Scott called for a cab, and my stomach started doing flip-flops. I had no idea why I was feeling the way I was, but the idea of Scott stripping for me had my body aching even more for him.

As he held open the door to the cab for me, he said, "I'm about to make this a night you won't forget, baby."

I smiled. "Bring it on, stripper boy."

41 Josh

I couldn't wait to get Heather back to the hotel and just be alone with her. I couldn't shake the image of her dancing on the damn pole for the last hour. The girls had had no idea that we had been there as we had stood on the other side of a two-way mirror, watching them. I was sure Gunner had felt the same reaction I had. The whole time that damn song had played, I'd even thought about putting a pole in our bedroom.

I followed as Heather walked through the door and into our hotel room. The second the door shut, I grabbed her and pushed her against the wall. She let out the sweetest moan, and I couldn't get her clothes off fast enough.

"Jesus, Heather, do you know how turned-on I've been since I saw you dancing?"

"Wait—when did you see us dancing?" Heather asked.

I smiled and pushed myself into her. "There was a two-way mirror, and we were standing behind it, waiting for y'all to get Jessie seated. We had no idea that you and Ellie would start, um…dancing like that. I thought someone was going to have to hold Gunner back from busting in and taking Ellie right then and there."

Heather laughed as she put her hands under my shirt and pushed it up and over my head. She bit down on her lip as she looked me up and down. "I want you so much, Josh. I never get tired of looking at your body."

I picked her up, and she wrapped her legs around me.

"Back at ya, baby."

I walked over to the bed, and I gently laid her down on it. Then, I took off her shoes before making my way up to her pants. As I pulled them off of her, I took her body in.

So beautiful and all mine.

My eyes landed on her black lace push-up bra that clasped in the front. I reached over, and with one flip of my fingers, her breasts sprung free, and my pants grew tighter. I crawled on top of her and cupped each breast in my hands as I leaned down and began sucking on one and then the other.

"Oh god…Josh."

"Heather…you are so damn beautiful, baby."

"I love you. Please make love to me, Josh."

As I moved my hand down her side, I felt her whole body shiver. I smiled, knowing that even now, I could still cause her to shudder with just a touch. When I slipped my hand into her panties, I thought she was going to come off the bed. One slip of my finger inside her told me she wanted me badly.

"You're always so wet for me, Heather."

"Yes…" she whispered as she pulled my face to hers.

We began kissing, and then I pulled away just long enough to take her panties off before I crawled on top of her and teased her with my tip.

"Ugh! Josh…*please*. Please don't tease me."

I slowly pushed myself into her warm, wet body. I let out a long moan as I buried myself as deep in her as I could. I took her hands in mine and laced our fingers as I pushed them over her head. As I moved in and out of her, I kissed her gently on the lips over and over again and whispered how much I loved her.

I could feel when she was about to come because it felt like she was squeezing my dick.

"Oh…Josh…yes…I'm going to come," Heather whispered in my ear.

I moved a little faster, and when she began to softly call out my name, I gently kissed her lips. There was nothing else on this Earth that I loved more than coming at the same time with Heather. Feeling our bodies react to each other was one of the most amazing things I'd ever experienced. I rolled over, pulled her to me, and listened to her breathing. Her body fit so perfectly with mine.

I thought back to the first time I'd ever seen her. She'd walked into Jeff and Gunner's house, and I'd never had that feeling before—the feeling of all the air being taken from my body, my knees going weak, and that sensation in my stomach that I still got when she would unexpectedly touch my body.

"Heather," I whispered.

"Mmm…"

"I just want you to know how much I love you," I said, my voice cracking.

She turned over and looked into my eyes. "I do know. I love you so much, too," she said with a smile that melted my heart.

"You know I'd do anything for you and the kids, right?"

She nodded her head. "Josh, is everything okay?"

I pushed her hair back and grinned. "Everything is perfect. It just scares me sometimes. I don't ever want to lose you, Will, and Libby. I'll do whatever it takes to make the three of you happy. Everything I do…it's all for you."

I watched as a single tear rolled down her face.

"Oh, Josh…you make me so happy every single second of the day. I'd be completely lost without you. I'll love you forever."

I laughed. "That's a long time."

She nodded her head and winked. "Yes, it is, but I think I'm up for the challenge."

"You better be because I intend on making love to you as much as possible for the rest of our lives."

She pushed me onto my back and crawled on top of me. As she slowly sat down on me, she smiled. "I'm going to hold you to that, Mr. Hayes. You're my everything, Josh, and I love you so much."

I pulled her body closer to me and placed my hands on the sides of her face as I looked into her beautiful blue eyes. *I will love this girl forever with everything in my heart and soul.*

"I love you more times infinity. I'll forever be faithful to our love, princess."

42 Scott

The Wedding—October Thirty-First

I stood there like an idiot, just watching everyone run around as they set up things for the wedding. I turned around and looked at our bedroom window. I smiled, imagining her getting ready. *What will her dress look like? Is she going to wear her hair up or down?* I took in a cleansing deep breath and blew it out as I felt someone slap my back. I turned to see Lark there.

"So, I believe it's the best man's responsibility to make sure the groom is at the wedding on time. I've got that covered. I also need to make sure he is dressed and ready to go." He looked me up and down and smiled. "That's covered. Now, I see what my real hurdle is going to be."

I chuckled. "What's your hurdle?"

"Keeping you away from the bride before the wedding," he said with a wink.

I threw my head back and laughed. "That is going to be a hurdle because all I want to do is see her."

"Tough shit. Come on, let's go get a beer. I know a place where we can get away from all this wedding bullshit."

He started to head down toward the barn. I looked at the tables that were being set up. Jessie was going to be so happy when she could see how everything was coming together. I glanced over and saw my mom talking to Jenny. The two of them planning this wedding was just what they both had needed. They worked amazingly well together, and Jenny had asked my mother if she'd ever thought of going into wedding planning. As of three weeks ago, they had become business partners, and this wedding was their first as partners.

I looked to my left and saw my father ordering around the guys who were setting up the bar and putting out the kegs. I chuckled and shook my head. *Leave it to him to be in charge of the booze.*

I turned the corner and walked into the barn. Jeff, Gunner, Josh, and Brad were all kicked back and sitting around a small table. Everyone, except Brad, had a beer in his hands.

"So, this is where my groomsmen have been, huh?" I walked around and grabbed a beer out of a—

Pumpkin?

"What in the fuck is this?" I asked as I sat down.

They all laughed.

Brad said, "This was Amanda's job—carve out pumpkins for little mini ice chests."

They all looked at me, but no one said a word.

"What?" I asked.

"You nervous?" Jeff took a drink of his beer.

"Pft, no. I'm not nervous at all," I said, trying to keep my hands from shaking. They'd been shaking ever since I'd woken up this morning.

Gunner and Josh both laughed.

Brad smiled at me. "Dude, we've all been in your shoes—well, everyone but Lark here."

"The only one with brains, I guess," Lark said before downing his beer.

Brad laughed and rolled his eyes. "We've all been in your shoes. We know you're nervous."

I dropped my head and shook it. "I don't understand what's wrong with me. I mean, I want to marry her more than anything. I'm not having doubts at all, but my stomach is in fucking knots. I feel sick, my hands won't stop shaking, and…and I'm…I'm…"

"You're afraid she is going to change her mind? Wonder why in the hell she is marrying you? Does that sound about right?" Josh asked.

"Yes! That is exactly it. I have this fear that she's going to decide at the last minute that she doesn't want to get married."

"Trust me, she's just as nervous, if not more, than you are, Scott. Don't worry, dude. That girl has been in love with you since we were kids," Gunner said.

Lark held up his hand. "So, let me ask y'all something. Every single one of you is happy. No desire to be with another woman? You're…content?"

We all let out a laugh.

"Fuck, you couldn't pay me to be back in the dating world. Ari literally saved my ass. If it wasn't for her, Luke, and Grace…" Jeff slowly shook his head and looked at Lark. "I wouldn't want to live without Ari in my life."

Josh leaned forward and nodded his head. "I feel the same way. Heather is the air I breathe. She's my life, and then you add in Will and Libby…" He smiled bigger. "I wouldn't trade my life for anything. One day, you'll find the one girl who will make you lose your train of thought just by her smile. When she walks by you, her smell will about drop you to your knees. Her kiss will cause your body to go insane with desire, and the sound of her voice will make you feel all fucking giddy inside. Yeah…once you find that, you won't ever want anything else but that."

"Amen, brother," Brad and Gunner both said.

Gunner lifted his beer bottle to Josh. They clicked bottles together and then did some hand gesture that they always did. It was something from college, and I'd never understood it or cared to.

"I should take all your damn man cards away," Lark said with a smile.

"Are you hiding in here?" Drake asked.

We all turned to see Drake and Garrett walking in.

"Gramps, Drake. Y'all want a beer from our very own pumpkin cooler?" Gunner asked. He got up, walked up to them, and shook their hands.

I stood up and also shook their hands. "Nah, I'm just trying to avoid your sons. Dewey keeps making threats to me, and honestly, I don't think he's kidding anymore," I said with a wink.

Drake laughed and nodded. "Don't piss that boy off, let me tell you. I think he and your daddy are about to go at it over where the Bud Light keg should go."

We all laughed as I gestured for them to sit down.

Drake shook his head. "We only came down to ask that y'all stay in here. Your mama wants Jessie to take a peek at everything before she gets dressed."

I perked up. "She's going out?"

Then, I felt a hand on my shoulder.

"Don't even think about it. I haven't forgotten about that day when I came back to the barn from a ride," Lark said.

He winked, and I felt my face instantly blush. I knew he was referring to the day I had taken Jessie on the side of the house while my mother and Azurdee were inside.

"Right. Um…yeah, Drake, we won't budge from this spot until my mother or Jenny comes and gets us." I nodded and smiled at him.

"Don't ruin this for my baby girl. This is her day, not yours. Do you understand me? Just because you got a baby with her doesn't mean I won't kill you if you hurt her," Drake said.

And then, I saw Dew and Aaron walk in behind him.

I swallowed hard and nodded my head. "Yes, um…yes, sir."

We all watched as Drake turned and walked out of the barn with Dewey and Aaron following right behind him.

I let out the breath I had been holding, and I felt my whole body relax. "Holy shit, that man scares the piss out of me," I said.

Josh laughed. "I guess I'm the only one who has never had to deal with the father-in-law."

Jeff, Brad, Gunner, and I all said at the same time, "Lucky bastard."

43 Jessie

I smiled as I looked down at Lauren sleeping peacefully in my arms. "This day couldn't be any more perfect," I said.

I felt Jenny put her hand on my back. She guided me out of the house and into the backyard. I sucked in a breath of air as I looked around.

"Oh, wow," was all I could get out.

To my left were about ten high-top tables set up around where the DJ would be. On the opposite side of the DJ was the bar. I chuckled when I saw Scott, Senior and Dewey directing the guys with all the beer and wine. My eyes moved to the right where there was a huge dance floor.

"My god. Why is the dance floor so big?" I asked.

Ari and Ellie started laughing.

"So all the kids have room to run around, but it still leaves space for the adults to dance. I just want to do a little bit of two-steppin', damn it," Ari said with a sigh.

I laughed and walked up to the tables. "Oh, Mom, Jenny…y'all, these are perfect. It's exactly what I wanted!"

The round tables had white linen draped down to the ground, and a dark silver satin cloth was draped over and pinned up to make the scalloped edges. It looked beautiful.

Each table had a pumpkin that Ari, Ellie, and I had carved out, soaked in bleach, and then sprayed down with some preservative that Jenny had made, so they wouldn't mold. Inside each pumpkin were beautiful fall flowers. Light brown and ivy-colored candles were set in hurricane glasses on either side of the flower centerpiece. The seats were all labeled with mini pumpkins that had a little sign stuck in it with each guest's name written in chalk.

"I thought we were going with plastic dishware?" I asked as I went to pick up one of the silver plates. As soon as I picked it up, I realized it was plastic. "Holy hell. They look like real plates!"

Jenny nodded her head.

Melody picked up the pumpkin-shaped cookies. "These are to die for. Wait until you taste them! A girl in Fredericksburg made them."

I looked around at each table setting, and there were cookies in every shape, including pumpkins, ghosts, bats, and witches. Each cookie was in a darling clear bag tied with black and silver ribbons.

"The tables are perfect," I said with a smile.

"Want to see the cakes?" Melody asked as she clapped her hands.

I nodded my head as I looked at Jenny, who rolled her eyes and smiled. Jenny was so used to all of this, but this was Melody's first job. Not to mention, it was her son's wedding.

We walked up to the dessert table, and I had to stop.

Oh. My. God. They went crazy!

In the middle of the table was a beautiful three-tiered white cake with black and silver scrolls on it. It was the exact cake I'd had in my mind brought to life. On either side of the cake were two huge five-layered plates of cupcakes. The various decorations—ghosts, witches, bats, gravestones, black cats, and little spiders—were all so cute.

"The kids are going to go crazy over these," Ellie said with a giggle.

"Good god, look at the candied apples," Ari said before licking her lips. "Cake pops? Jesus H. Christ, there are cake pops. Luke and Jeff are gonna be up all night. Oh my god! Look at those cupcakes. They look like brains! Luke is going to be in heaven." Ari turned to me and said, "This is going to be the best wedding ever!"

I tried not to laugh, so I didn't wake up Lauren, but I almost busted out laughing at how excited Ari was.

"Melody, I think there are more desserts than there is food!" I said.

"Speaking of food…" Jenny turned.

We all followed her.

Ellie leaned into me and whispered, "Holy hell…you have cake, cupcakes, cake pops, brownies, cookies, candied and caramel apples, and I'm pretty sure I saw chocolate-covered strawberries."

"Melody kind of thinks Scott has a sweet tooth," I whispered back.

Ellie pulled her head back and looked at me. "I don't think I've ever seen him eat a single sweet thing," she said with a confused look on her face.

I held back a laugh. "He hates sweets. His mother had them in the house all the time. He got so sick of eating them, so he won't eat them anymore."

"Shit, I wish I felt that way about sweets," Ellie said.

We walked up to the table, and I couldn't help it. I let out a squeal. They had written each food item on small tan pumpkins.

"Mac and cheese," I said. I laughed out loud and then began rocking Lauren who had woken up during my moment of insanity. "That is the cutest thing I've ever seen."

Melody smiled and pointed at Jenny.

"I love it. I love it all. Thank you, Mom. Thank you, Jenny. You've truly made this a dream wedding. Not only are the adults going to love everything, but the kids are also going to have so much fun." I hugged each of them the best I could with Lauren in my arms.

Melody took Lauren from me and gently kissed her as she turned and started walking away with my crying baby. "I'm going to go feed her. It's almost showtime, and you need to get dressed," she called over her shoulder.

I looked at Ellie and Ari. "I'm so nervous."

They each linked their arms in mine, and we made our way back to the house, following Jenny as she barked orders to people while we walked by them. We headed into my bedroom, and I took one look at Amanda and busted out crying.

"What? Oh god. Do I have the wrong dress on or something? Shit, it's the baby weight, isn't it?" Amanda said as she began jumping up and down, vigorously shaking her hands.

"Don't be silly, Amanda. You have the right dress on, and, bitch, you don't even look like you just had a baby. Jessie is just happy to see it on you," Ari said as she just began getting undressed in front of all of us.

I dropped my mouth open as I looked at her and instantly stopped crying. "Fuck me. How do you look like that after two kids?" I looked her up and down.

The smile that spread across her face was priceless. "Lots and lots of sex." She raised her eyebrows.

"Ugh…really? Gag me," Ellie said as she took off the sweatpants and T-shirt I had made for each of them.

They were both wearing black corsets with matching lace panties.

Azurdee came walking out of the bathroom, cursing. "Shit…how in the hell do you get these bastards on?"

Ari whistled and looked at Azurdee. "Damn, girl. You might give Heather a run for her money in the boob area."

Heather laughed as she looked up from where she was sitting and putting on makeup. "You look beautiful, Azurdee. Here, turn around and let me help."

Ellie giggled.

"Will you zip me up, please?" Ari asked me.

I zipped her up, and then she turned around.

"Well? You still like them?" Ari asked.

I glanced up at Heather, who was now helping Azurdee into her dress. I shook my head, looking around at each of them. They each had on black chiffon ruched dresses that were strapless and knee-length. They were all so damn beautiful and doing nothing but bickering with each other.

They all came and stood next to one another. I made my way down the line, looking at each one. Azurdee was my best friend and maid of honor. Lark was going to shit his pants when he saw her. Heather was the sweetest one of the bunch but the first to admit that she liked to play in the bedroom. Ellie had her innocence that just poured off her as she stood there with that sweet smile of hers. Ari was all spit and fire in a beautiful package but one of the kindest people I'd ever known. Amanda was the person who would drop everything in order to help out one of her friends.

I felt the tears building as I looked at each of them. They had started off being my friends, but over the last few years, they had become my sisters.

"Oh no, honey…don't cry. You're gonna ruin your makeup," Heather said as she walked up and took me in her arms. She let me go as she stepped back and winked at me. "It's your turn."

Ellie let out an, "Eeeep," as she quickly got my dress that was hanging up. She brought it over and laid it down on the bed.

I slowly started taking my sweatpants and T-shirt off.

"Holy hell," Ari said.

I stood there in my white corset, lace thong panties, and garter belt that Ellie had helped put on before we had gone outside.

"And you just had a baby a few months ago. What are *you* doing?" Ari said with a wicked grin.

"Sex…lots and lots of sex. I actually think the sex is better now after the baby than before. God…I swear he just has to whisper my name, and it seems like I'll orgasm," I said with my own wicked smile as I raised my eyebrows up and down.

When Ari quickly shook her head at me, I instantly knew who was standing behind me. I spun around to see Melody.

Oh Lord…where is the closest rock for me to crawl my ass under?

I slammed my hand over my mouth and felt my cheeks turn warm. I closed my eyes and wanted to die. My future mother-in-law had just heard me talking about sex with her son—while I stood there in a thong, for Christ's sake.

She slowly let a small smile spread across her face as she nodded her head. "Nice to know my husband taught him something right." She walked up to me and took the white thigh-high stockings from my hand. Then, she bent down, gently taking my foot, and started sliding them on.

I quickly looked up at Ari and the rest of the girls as they all just laughed.

I smiled as I started to step into my beautiful wedding gown. As Melody and Azurdee helped me, I thought back to the day when I'd bought it.

I stared at myself in the mirror. Tears were rolling down my face as Ari, Azurdee, and Ellie all went on and on about the dress I had on. I looked over at Melody. I thought she knew how sad I was that I was doing this without my mother. Heather wasn't able to come with us, and I was really hoping she would since she'd done this before. When Melody had asked if she could come, I'd almost wanted to scream yes.

She quickly wiped the single tear away and smiled at me. I raised my eyebrows at her in my silent way of asking what she thought. She smiled bigger and nodded her head. I smiled and looked back at myself in the mirror.

The dress had a sweetheart neckline with a slim A-line cut. The intricate lace was stunning as was the hand-beaded bodice. The removable cap sleeve bolero jacket added such a sweet and innocent look. The functional corset back just made the dress feel sexier, and the chapel-length train added just the right touch of elegance. The straps were removable, making the dress even more elegant. It would be perfect for the reception.

"You look beautiful," Ari said with a wink.

I was surprised at how good I looked in it, considering I'd just had a baby a few weeks ago.

I looked back at Melody. "Do you think Scott will like it?"

She smiled and started crying harder. She nodded her head. "Yes. He's going to piss his pants when he sees you walking down the aisle."

Everyone laughed as I stepped down and hugged her. She held on to me probably a little bit longer than needed.

Before she let me go, she whispered in my ear, "You look beautiful, baby girl. Just beautiful."

I felt a hand on my shoulder.

"Thinking about the day you bought it?" Melody asked as she looked at my reflection in the mirror.

"How did you know?" I asked.

She let out a small laugh. "I've stood right where you are. I also stared at myself in the mirror, praying that I wasn't dreaming."

I turned to face her. I was sure she could see the fear in my eyes. "Why am I so scared? It's not like we don't love each other…I mean, we are living together, and we have a baby. So, why am I shaking from head to toe?"

She shook her head and laughed. "I don't know. I wish I had the answer for you, but I don't, sweetheart. Let me ask you something. Do you love Scott?"

I sucked in a breath of air. I couldn't believe she was even asking me this. "Of course I do—with all my heart."

"And do you want to spend the rest of your life with him and only him?"

"Yes!" I said, not even having to think about it.

She smiled bigger. "Then, you have nothing to be scared of because I asked him the very same questions, and I do believe you both answered back in record-breaking time. He loves you so much, Jessie. And I know you love him. The moment you see each other, I promise your nerves are going to disappear, and nothing but love will replace them."

I pulled Melody into my arms and hugged her as tight as I could. "Thank you. Thank you so much for everything you've done and for welcoming me into your family with open arms."

She pulled back slightly. "Oh, Jessie, thank you. Thank you for making my son the happiest I've ever seen him. Thank you for my beautiful granddaughter in the other room, who already has her grandpa wrapped around his finger. Thank you for loving my son like you do. I couldn't have asked for a better daughter if I had planned it myself."

I dabbed at the tears in my eyes.

Ellie came running over with tissues and makeup in her hands. "Don't cry! Your makeup!"

44 Scott

The Wedding

"Scott, take a deep breath, dude. I can practically hear your heart beating," Lark whispered.

It was finally here. The moment I'd been dreaming of since I could remember. I was marrying the girl of my dreams, the only girl I'd ever truly loved.

"I'm fine," I said.

Gunner leaned over and laughed. "If you keep rocking back and forth, we're all going to get motion sickness."

I looked over at him and smiled. I had been rocking back and forth, and if I dug my fingers into my hands any more, they were going to start bleeding.

"Were you this nervous?" I asked no one in particular.

They all answered, "Yes," with the exception of Lark, who laughed.

I laughed and shook my head. I looked down the line at my friends. These guys were more than friends. They were like brothers to me. It wasn't lost on me how all the female guests were looking us up and down. We each had on black tuxes with silver vests and silver ties. Jessie had insisted we all wear our cowboy boots, and not one of us had argued with her. It had been decided that we would be allowed to change into jeans and just keep the white shirts, vests, and ties on for the reception.

Then, the music began playing, and I instantly felt sick. Then, Lark put his hand on my shoulder.

He squeezed it and said, "Scott, the moment you see her, it will all go away. Every fear will vanish when she smiles at you, dude."

I nodded my head, knowing he was right. "I just want to make her happy, Lark. I just want her to know how much I love her."

He slapped my back lightly. "I don't think you have to worry about that. I see the way y'all look at each other, Scott. Just speak from your heart."

The first couple down the aisle was Alex and Luke. They were walking together, holding hands, and it was probably the cutest damn thing I'd ever seen.

I glanced at Lark, who had a smile from ear to ear.

"My god, if that isn't the cutest damn thing I've ever seen," he whispered.

I chuckled since I had just thought the same thing.

"Stick around for a while, Lark. There's something in our water if you want one," Gunner said.

Lark's smile never faltered. He didn't even make a smart-ass comment about how happy he was being single.

Alex immediately walked up to Gunner and hugged him, but Luke pulled her away to where he had been told they needed to stand. I had a feeling that Alex was going to have a very hard time dating when she got older with Gunner, Jeff, *and* Luke to watch over her.

Then, Amanda started down the aisle, followed by Heather, Ari, and then Ellie. They looked breathtaking. I smiled at each of them as they walked up and winked at me.

Damn, I love those girls like sisters.

Then, Azurdee appeared, and I heard Lark let out a gasp next to me. One quick look at him told me everything I'd already known. He was head over heels for her. During the few times they had been together out at our place, it was obvious that they both liked each other, but Lark was being a stubborn ass about it.

Then, the wedding march began playing. I closed my eyes and prayed to God that I wouldn't cry. If I did, Jeff would never let me live it down.

As I opened my eyes, I saw her. It felt like all the air had been sucked from my body as our eyes met. I looked her up and down, and I was pretty sure I felt my knees wobble. I felt like I was about to pass out when she smiled that big beautiful smile of hers. I smiled back, and it was like a million sensations traveled through my body.

I never took my eyes off of her as she made her way closer to me on her father's arm. She was carrying a huge bouquet of flowers that matched all the flowers on the tables and the flowers that the girls were carrying. Jessie's bouquet was bigger and wrapped in silver silk with a runner.

Right before she got to me, she stopped and turned toward my mother, who stood up. She was holding Lauren, who was sleeping like the little angel she was. My mother handed something to Jessie and then kissed her on the cheek. Jessie leaned down and kissed Lauren before turning back toward me and walking up.

The pastor took a step forward and smiled. "We are gathered here today in the presence of God and Scott and Jessica's family and friends, so that they may be united in holy matrimony. Who gives this woman to be married to this man?"

Drake wiped a tear from his eye. "I do." He placed Jessie's hand in mine and looked at me as he said, "I'm giving you my life. I'm trusting you to love her, take care of her, and never hurt her."

I smiled as I reached out and shook Drake's hand. "I promise you, I'll spend the rest of my life loving her and taking care of her. She's my everything."

He gave me a weak smile and turned to Jessie. He wiped a tear from her cheek and gave her a kiss. My heart was beating a mile a minute, and all I could think of was that I would be doing the same with my Lauren one day.

Jessie and I turned and both took a few steps closer to the pastor.

I looked at Jessie. "I've never seen anyone so beautiful in my entire life. You take my breath away."

She let out a small sob and tried to hold the tears back. "I love you," she whispered.

I used my thumbs to wipe away her tears. "I love you, too."

We decided to say our own vows, and I had been panicking the whole night and morning about it. I knew what I wanted to say, but the moment it was my turn to talk, I just stood there, frozen. I couldn't open my mouth until Lark gave me a nudge from behind.

Jessie smiled, and I knew exactly what I wanted to say. I smiled and shook my head as I gently squeezed her hands in mine.

"The very moment I knew I loved you, I ran away from you. I was nothing but a scared and stupid boy fighting his feelings. The moment you showed up in my world again, I knew I would never run away from you ever. I knew I would fight every day for the rest of my life to show you how much I loved you, how much I needed you.

"Every morning when I wake up and look at you, I realize how much I love you more with each passing day. When you walk into a room, I swear it feels like I can't breathe from just the sight of you. When you smile at me, I feel your love pouring out, and I thank God that he blessed me with that love.

"The day you said yes to me, I thought that was the happiest day of my life, but I was so wrong. The day our daughter was born, I just knew *that* was the happiest day of my life. But I was wrong again.

"Today, standing here in front of you, knowing that you're about to become my wife and that I get to wake up every day to your beautiful smile for the rest of my life…*today* is the happiest day of my life because I know it's me and you, forever and always. Without you, I'd be nothing, Jessie. You're my *entire* world. My reason for being is to love you, protect you, and make you feel nothing but…cherished," I vowed, my voice cracking. I barely got out the word *cherished* before I felt the tears running down my face.

Jessie was smiling at me as tears rolled down her cheeks in what looked like one endless stream.

She wiped the tears away and gave my hands a quick squeeze. She took a deep breath and slowly let it out before she began talking.

The Wedding

I knew my hands were shaking, and I was still trying to recover from what Scott had just said to me. When his voice had cracked, it had been my breaking point, and I couldn't hold back my tears any longer.

Now, it was my turn to try and express to him how much he meant to me, how he made me feel every day of our lives.

I took a deep breath and slowly let it out. "Scott, since the first day you ever smiled at me, I knew my heart would always belong to you. Then, you kissed me, and I really knew I was yours. The road we traveled to get to where we are today was not an easy one. We both took a few wrong turns and had some pretty big hills to climb, but we did it. I can't imagine my life without you in it. You are the air that I breathe, the light in my darkness, and the hope of my future. I never in my life imagined that you could make me as happy as you have or make me feel as loved as you do. I love you, and I'll always love you with every ounce of my being. Thank you for loving me and never giving up on our love."

I reached up and lightly brushed the tear away that was slowly moving down his cheek.

Everyone let out an, "Aww…"

Scott grabbed my hand and kissed my wrist. "I love you to the moon and back, baby."

I laughed. "I love you to the moon and back and then to the moon and back again."

"One-upper," he whispered.

Everyone laughed.

When the pastor said it was time to kiss the bride, I couldn't wait to feel his lips on mine. I would never get tired of him kissing me. I longed for his touch twenty-four hours a day.

The kiss was sweet yet passionate.

Before he pulled away, he whispered against my lips, "You look breathtaking in that dress, baby, but damn, I can't wait to get you out of it."

I moved my lips to his ear. "Neither can I. Wait till you see what I have underneath the dress."

He pulled back and looked at me. His eyes became filled with nothing but passion. I had to bite down on my lip to distract myself from the aching pulse between my legs.

The pastor pulled us both out of our trance by announcing us as husband and wife. "Ladies and gentlemen, I give you Mr. and Mrs. Scott Reynolds."

As we began walking down the aisle, we both stopped and kissed Melody and Scott, Senior. Then, we walked over to my father, Dew, and Aaron. I kissed each of them. I was still upset that my brothers hadn't wanted to be a part of the wedding party, but I understood their reasons. They had known Scott wanted his friends, and they hadn't wanted us to have a huge wedding party. I smiled and punched Dewey in the arm. I quickly smiled and said hello to his new girlfriend, Rachael.

As we walked down the aisle, I couldn't help but feel like I was walking on cloud nine. I never thought the birth of my child could ever be topped, but I did believe this day just tied for first place.

As the night went on, kids ran around on nothing but sugar highs. Games were played, new memories were made, and lots of dancing happened. One by one, the kids crashed throughout the house in beds, sofas, and portable cribs.

I'd never laughed so hard in my life, and being surrounded by our family and friends just made it all the more special. Melody had a blast playing hostess, and Jenny kept everything moving along.

When it came time for the bride-and-groom dance, I started shaking. Scott had left it up to me to pick the song, and I couldn't pick just one. I had narrowed it down to Mark Wills's "I Do" and Kenny Chesney's "Me and You." I had been stressing about it for two weeks until Ellie and I had gone out for a ride one morning.

She had said, "Play each song by yourself with no one around. Whichever song moves you the most is the right song."

That evening, I'd asked Scott for a few minutes alone. I'd grabbed my iPod and made my way to the main barn right behind the house. I'd sat there and listened to both songs, and one of them had clearly spoken to me. Every word in it had screamed Scott and me.

I closed my eyes and prayed that he would agree with the song choice. As we made our way to the dance floor, Dewey and Aaron each took turns saying a little something. It mostly consisted of threatening poor Scott with bodily harm if he ever hurt Lauren or me.

Scott had taken it like a trooper, but as he took me in his arms, he said, "Jesus H. Christ…I don't know who to be more scared of—your father or your brothers."

I laughed as I kissed him quickly on the lips.

The DJ announced we were about to dance our first dance as a married couple.

I looked into Scott's eyes and smiled. "I love you, Scott," I said with a shaky voice.

He placed his hand on the side of my face and brushed his thumb across my cheek. I leaned my head into his hand and closed my eyes. He slowly moved his hand to the back of my neck and pulled me to him for a kiss.

Kenny Chesney's "Me and You" began playing, and I felt him smile against my lips.

He barely pulled away. "How did you know?" he asked me.

I shook my head. "How did I know, what?"

"The first time I ever heard this song, I thought of you. I thought if we ever got married, this would be our song. I used to have dreams of dancing with you to this song."

I sucked in a breath of air and began crying as I buried my head into his chest. The way he was running his hand up and down my back while softly singing the words to me only caused me to cry harder.

Any doubts and bad memories I ever had about our relationship completely melted away with every word he sang to me. I had no doubt in my mind that this man would always love and be faithful to both Lauren and me with everything he had.

I looked up into his beautiful blue eyes and smiled. "Scott, I've never in my life felt so incredibly loved and cherished. Thank you for making this one of the happiest days of my life."

The smile that spread across his face caused me to smile.

"Baby, I plan on making you feel that way every day for the rest of your life."

I placed my hand on the side of his face as he brought his lips down to mine.

Right before he kissed me, I said, "Sounds like a good plan."

45 Scott

The Honeymoon

"Baby, we have to go." I tried to pull Jessie away from my mother and Lauren.

"I don't know. Scott, she's only three months old! I can't leave her," Jessie said with pleading eyes.

"Baby, she's almost four months old, and yes, you can. She's in good hands. We are only going to be a few hours away. I promise you, my mother has done this before."

My mother let out a chuckle and winked at me. "Jessie, you wouldn't let the boy take you to Hawaii because you said it was too far away. South Padre Island is only a few hours away, and I promise you, I will take extra special care of her."

Jessie nodded her head and kissed Lauren on the forehead. She turned to Azurdee and gave her a hug.

After kissing Azurdee on the cheek, Jessie said, "Thank you so much for staying at the house while we're gone. I didn't have the heart to board the new kitten we just got."

Azurdee rolled her eyes. "Uh-huh…that's why Lark is staying there, too?"

I let out a laugh. "He's only staying for the night, but y'all have the whole house to yourselves." I winked at her.

The blush that crossed her face was the cutest thing ever.

"Go on back outside, and enjoy the party, Azurdee. I love you, and thank you for everything. It was a beautiful wedding," Jessie said with one last hug.

"Y'all be careful driving down, and text me when you get there," Azurdee said.

Jessie and I both nodded.

"Will do. Go party. I think all the kids left with their grandparents, so go have fun," I said with a smile.

Azurdee smiled. "Yeah, the only ones left are Brad and Amanda with Taylor and Maegan."

Jessie and Azurdee hugged yet again, and after this time, Azurdee turned and headed back outside.

I took Jessie's hand and began pulling her through the house and out to my truck.

"Bye, Mom. Take good care of my baby girl," I called over my shoulder.

"Oh! Mom, remember to make sure to turn on her little music player when you put her down. She loves to go to sleep to music. Oh! And be sure to turn on her Pooh night-light. She sometimes will fight her afternoon nap, but don't pick her up! She will only cry for like two minutes, and then she's out."

I heard my mother laughing.

"Jessie...I have watched this child before, you know. Go enjoy your honeymoon!" she called out.

I opened the door and practically lifted Jessie up into the truck. I quickly shut it and ran around to the other side. I jumped in, started the truck, and took off down my driveway faster than I'd ever had before.

"Damn, why are you driving so fast?" Jessie asked.

I glanced at her quickly. "For fear of you being tempted to jump out of the truck and run back."

She giggled and shook her head. When she reached for my hand, I felt a jolt of electricity run through my body.

This would never get old.

"So...where are we going?" she asked.

I squeezed her hand. "The Four Seasons."

She made a little squeak sound. "On Town Lake?"

"Yep," I said as I popped my P.

"God, I just can't wait to get out of this dress. I wish you would have just taken it off at home, so I could be comfy."

I laughed as I brought her hand up and kissed the back of it. "If I had done that, we'd still be at home, and I'd be making passionate love to you, not caring who heard your screams of pleasure."

"Screams of pleasure? You're pretty sure about yourself, huh?"

I snapped my head over and looked at her little evil smile. "Baby, I've been saving some of my best stuff just for our honeymoon night."

She let out a laugh as she pulled her hand away. "What? Impossible. I don't think being with you could be any better than it is."

I smiled and thought about the little surprise I'd brought along with me. Jessie and I never played in the bedroom, and tonight, that was going to change. Just the idea of tying Jessie up and having my way with her caused my pants to get tighter. Of course, the idea had come from the one girl I'd never thought I'd have a conversation about bondage with—*ever*. But Heather had ended up giving me lots of exciting suggestions.

"What are you up to, Mr. Reynolds? That smile on your face is one I don't think I've ever seen before."

"You're gonna have to wait and found out, sweetheart, but I promise you, I'll make tonight a night you will never forget."

As I opened the door to the presidential suite on the ninth floor, Jessie let out a, "Oh my god!"

I smiled when I looked around. It was perfect with sliding glass doors all across the back wall and a private balcony.

"The décor in here is beautiful! I love the French country feel of everything," Jessie said.

I smiled and made my way into the bedroom. With one look at the massive wood headboard, I nodded and made a mental note. *Check that one off the list.*

I had made arrangements with the hotel to have the bedroom and bathroom covered in red roses and petals. The smell was amazing. Jessie walked in and threw her hands up to her mouth. Roses were everywhere. If there was counter space, there were bouquets of roses. The bed was covered in rose petals.

She slowly turned and looked at me. "How?"

I winked and pulled her to me. "Oh, I have my ways. Wait till you see the bathroom."

She quickly pulled away and made her way into the bathroom. She was like a kid running into a candy store. "Oh my god! There is more in here, and…the tub is huge!" She peeked her head around the corner and gave me a Cheshire cat grin. "I mean, like big enough for two people."

I used my index finger and motioned for her to come to me. As she began walking up to me, I took in her wedding gown yet again. It looked amazing on her, and I'd been fighting the urge to rip it off of her since I first saw her walking down the aisle.

"I'm going to slowly peel that dress off of you. Then, I'm going to fill up that tub with hot water and make love to you in it."

"Oh my…" Jessie whispered before licking her lips.

She stopped right in front of me. I placed both of my hands on her face and gently brought her in for a kiss. She let out a moan, and I had to concentrate hard on going slow.

I stepped back. "Turn around, Jess."

She immediately turned around, and the corset was begging to be untied. I slowly started to untie it, and as the dress became looser and looser, Jessie moaned a little bit more.

"Oh god…that feels so good." She threw her head back.

I pushed the dress slightly away from her right shoulder and gently placed a kiss on her soft, tender skin.

"Scott…"

"I know, baby. It's killing me, too, but I want to savor every moment with you."

I pushed the dress off her shoulders and watched as it pooled on the ground around her feet.

Motherfucker. I think my heart just stopped beating.

She had on a white lace bustier with matching white lace thong panties. The thigh-high white lace stockings looked amazing, and all I could think about was peeling them off of her. She turned slightly and held out her hand for me to help her step out of the dress around her ankles.

When she turned around and stood in front of me, it was my turn to let out a squeak…or more like a deep rumble.

"Did you just growl?"

I nodded my head. "I think I did. Holy shit, Jessie…you look…I've never…I mean, you are…" I greedily looked her body up and down. *No way this girl just had a baby four months ago.*

"I guess all that working out has paid off," she said with a giggle. "You seem to be speechless."

I snapped my eyes up to her lips that she was now licking.

"Fuck going slow. I want you now."

I pulled her to me and frantically began taking off the bustier as she tried desperately to get my shirt off. I stopped and ripped the damn thing open. Buttons went everywhere. She ran her hands all over my chest, and then she began kissing my nipples. When she gently bit down on one, I about lost it. I stepped back and quickly took off my jeans as she unsnapped the hooks holding up her stockings.

I grabbed her hands and said, "Leave those on."

The fire in her eyes lit up even more before she turned for me to unclasp the bustier. Once it was free of her body, I picked her up, and she wrapped her legs around my body. I pushed the thong panties out of the way as I backed her up against the wall, and then I entered her body in one swift move.

"Oh god, yes!" she called out. "Scott…"

"Jesus, you feel so good," I said as I moved in and out of her, fast and hard.

I needed more of her. I gently pulled out of her and moved us over to the bed. I laid her down and took off her panties as she put her finger in her mouth and began sucking on it.

"What the hell, Jessie? Are you trying to kill me?"

She smiled and lifted her hips up to me. I ran my hand down her leg and lifted it up. Her shoes and stockings were still on. I took her shoes off, and then I moved my hand up her leg. Goose bumps spread across her entire body.

"Your touch is driving me insane. Please hurry. I need to feel you inside me."

I pulled the stocking off and repeated the process with the other stocking. I held them both in my hands. I was going to use my own version on the whole tying-up thing.

"Move farther up the bed, Jessie."

She quickly slid up. I crawled on top of her and moved my body in the way that I knew drove her mad.

"Baby, put your hands above your head."

She didn't even ask why I was asking her to do this. She just did it. Passion filled her eyes, and she let out a whimper as I pushed myself down on her. I took one of the stockings and held it out in front of me. Her eyes grew bigger, and she bit down on her lip so hard that it was turning white.

"Scott...what...what are you going to do?"

I took both of her hands and put them together before tying her hands to the wood headboard.

"I'm going to play, Jessie."

"Oh god...I think I'm going to come."

I gave her a crooked grin. "I haven't even done anything yet."

"I know..." she said as her chest heaved up and down faster.

Hell, I'm not going to last a minute if this is how she is reacting.

I moved my hands all over her body, except where she wanted it most, and she arched her back off the bed.

"Touch me, damn it!" she called out.

I reached down and took a nipple into my mouth.

"Yes! Oh, Scott, please..."

I slowly started kissing down her chest to her stomach.

"Oh, please. Please, Scott, *please!*"

Jessie had never begged like this before. I moved farther down and kissed from one side of her hips to the other. Then, I gently blew on her clit.

Her whole body started to tremble. "I'm so close...fuck!"

"Oh, I will, baby. Just be patient."

I slipped two fingers inside her, and I used my tongue to give her one small lick. *Jesus H. Christ, she's soaking wet.*

"Ah!" she cried out.

I took my fingers out and moved my tongue away.

Her head was thrashing back and forth. "I...I can't take much more...Scott!"

I had never been so turned-on in my life. My dick was throbbing, and all I wanted to do was be inside her.

"What do you want me to do, baby?"

"Make. Me. Come. Now!"

"How?"

She lifted her head and looked at me. "What?"

"How do you want me to make you come, baby? I want you to tell me what you want."

"Um…"

I knew she wanted oral sex. I could see it in her eyes.

"With…um…oh fuck, Scott. Make me come with your mouth…please…"

With that, I buried my face into her, and the moment I pushed three fingers inside her, I could feel her pulsing around my fingers.

"Yes! Yes! Yes! Oh god…mother…fucker…ah…" Jessie cried out.

It felt like her orgasm was going on forever. She kept calling out my name over and over as I moved my tongue faster and sucked harder.

"Stop! Oh god…I can't take it anymore…please stop!"

I moaned against her, causing her to start calling out my name again. I didn't think she could squeeze my fingers any more than she was.

"Holy hell…please…can't…take…it…"

When I finally felt the pulsing come to an end, I pulled my mouth away. I gave her clit a small lick, and she about jumped off the bed. I looked up at her chest. She was breathing frantically. I began kissing her stomach, and then I made my way up her chest to her neck.

I moved my lips up against her ear and whispered, "How did that feel?"

"Oh. My. God," she said between breaths. "I. Can't. Catch. My. Breath. Amazing…I still feel…I still feel my body coming down."

I smiled as I moved more on top of her, and then I slowly buried myself into her body.

"Oh…oh god, no! Scott…"

"Again, baby?" I said as I began moving faster.

"Yes! Harder…Scott, harder."

I went as fast and as hard as I could before I couldn't hold off any longer. "Baby, I'm going to come."

She pulled on the restraints, and I quickly reached up and pulled it loose. She grabbed on to my ass and called out my name as I poured myself into her. She was moving her hips and keeping right up with me until I collapsed onto her body. I kept my weight off of her by lying on my elbows. I tried to catch my breath as I pulled up and looked into her eyes. What was filled with passion just seconds ago was now replaced with pure love.

"I love you so much," I whispered. "I'll always love you."

The single tear rolling down her face caught my attention. I leaned in and kissed it away. I moved my lips to hers.

She whispered, "To the moon and back…forever."

46 Jessie

I tried to catch my breath as Scott lay on top of me after what was probably the most intense, mind-blowing, toe-curling, sexiest moment of my life. Scott began kissing me gently, and the love pouring from his body brought me to tears.

He rubbed his lips against mine. "I love you so much. I'll always love you."

I felt a tear sliding down my cheek, and I saw him look at it. When he leaned in and kissed it, my heart stopped for a moment before I was able to say, "To the moon and back…forever."

He rolled off of me and pulled me into his body. "Holy shit…I'm exhausted," he said.

I laughed. It felt like I had just run a marathon. "So am I. I'm so sleepy. I can't keep my eyes open." I snuggled into his chest.

"Go to sleep, baby."

At some point, Scott had turned on the radio, but I just noticed the music. When Blake Shelton's "God Gave Me You" started playing, I smiled. Scott and I both pulled back and looked at each other for what seemed like forever.

Scott closed his eyes and whispered, "Thank you."

My heart began beating faster as I watched the expression on his face. He opened his eyes, and they were filled with tears.

"What are you thanking me for?" I asked.

He gave me the sweetest smile. "I wasn't thanking you, baby. I was thanking God for you and Lauren."

I immediately began crying as he rolled me over to my back. He gently began kissing away the tears as he slowly made love to me.

I stood on the balcony and felt the sun shining on my face. My whole body felt amazing. I couldn't believe how wonderful I felt, especially since I had gotten only about two hours of sleep. I smiled as I thought about him waking me up with kisses and then picking me up and carrying me into the bathroom. When he'd placed me into the hot bubble bath, I'd let out a long sigh. It had felt like heaven. Then, he'd crawled in and washed every inch of my body before he'd made love to me again.

"Feel good?" Scott asked as he wrapped his arms around my body and pulled me to him.

"Mmm," was all I could get out.

He kissed the top of my head. "Are you ready to leave?"

I shook my head. "I want to stay here forever and do what we did last night every day." I let out a small laugh.

"Baby, we can do that anywhere, anytime."

I turned, put my head on his chest, and took in a deep breath. He smelled like heaven.

"I miss Lauren so much, but at the same time, I just want to stay here with you. I just want to do nothing but lie in bed with you and touch you anytime I want."

"How does making love on the beach sound to you?" he asked.

I looked up at him and raised my eyebrows. "That sounds…amazing. With a fire?"

He nodded and pushed a piece of hair behind my ear. "If you want a fire, I'll build you a fire."

I nodded my head. "I want a fire."

"Then, a fire you will get."

He grabbed my hand and walked us back into the bedroom. I stopped at the end of the bed and watched as he got our suitcases and took them to the door.

I reached over and pinched my arm. *Nope…I'm not dreaming.*

He turned, looked at me, and smiled.

"Do you know how long I've loved you?" I asked.

He walked up to me. "For the same amount of time I've loved you."

I laughed. "How do you know that?"

"Because the first time I ever saw you…I knew I was going to love you for the rest of my life."

I let out a small laugh and nodded my head. *Yep. That was the same thing for me. I knew the moment I first saw him, I would love him forever.*

He held out his hand, and I placed my hand in his.

"Mrs. Reynolds, are you ready to spend the rest of your life with me?"

I put my finger up to my chin, looking like I was contemplating his question. I took a deep breath and let it out. "I don't know, Mr. Reynolds. Do you promise to always love Lauren and me? Oh! And always make me my favorite meal?"

He laughed. "Fettuccine alfredo?"

I nodded my head. "Yep. If you promise to always love both Lauren and me, make me your fettuccine at least twice a month, and tie me up at least once a week, then you've got yourself a deal."

He slowly shook his head. "I think we're going to get a late start to the coast."

"Why?" I purposely licked my lips…very slowly.

"Because I'm tying your ass up again."

I pulled my T-shirt up and over my head and began to take my jeans off as I watched him strip out of his clothes.

"I think this arrangement is going to work out just fine," I said.

I giggled as he pushed me down on the bed and began tickling me.

"So do I," he said. He kissed me and then pulled away quickly as he looked deep into my eyes and repeated, "So. Do. I."

Ten Years Later

I watched as Alex, Grace, Libby, and Lauren went running by.

"Where are you girls running to?" Ellie called out.

Alex stopped, turned around, and screamed, "Mom! Luke and Will have lizards, and they're trying to put them down our shirts!" She quickly turned and took off running again.

Heather laughed and shrugged her shoulders. Josh and Heather had sold their house in Fredericksburg and built a house on fifty acres just down the road from Gunner's and Jeff's ranches.

"Hey, don't look at me. Your child is the oldest, Ari, and according to Will, Luke comes up with all their plans," Heather said as she looked at Ari, who was flipping hamburgers on the grill.

Ari rolled her eyes. "Pesh. I can't even begin to argue with you on that one. That child is worse than his father with his grand ideas."

Ellie laughed and nodded toward the pool. "Look at those three."

I turned and saw Colt with Maegan and Taylor. He was showing them something that had both of their attentions.

"Good Lord, my son is a player at ten years old," Ellie said.

"That's my boy," Gunner said as he walked up behind Ellie and wrapped his arms around her. "Three boys up against six girls. I think he's doing pretty good since he has two all by himself."

Ellie slapped Gunner on the arm.

"Oh, come on, Ells…give me some sugar stamps."

"Go play with the other daddies." Ellie kissed Gunner quickly on the lips.

Scott, Jeff, Brad, and Josh were all walking up from the barn. Gunner grabbed a football and threw it to Josh, who jumped up and caught it.

"I want to play!" Will, Luke, and Colt all yelled as they ran up to the guys.

"Hey, we want to play, too," Grace said as she put her hands on her hips.

Alex walked up next to Grace and did the same thing. "Yeah. We want to play, too."

Will came up to Alex. "You can't. Alex, you're a girl, and you could get hurt."

"Aww…he's worried about her getting hurt," Ellie said as she looked at Heather.

Heather smiled and shook her head. "I swear, I think Will has a crush on Alex. She is all he talks about."

Gunner walked up. "Don't be silly, Will. Alex is my daughter, and she's as tough as any ole boy. Ain't that right, sweetheart?"

He held up his hand, and Alex slapped it.

"That's right, Daddy," Alex said with a smile.

Colt stomped his feet. "Dad, for once, can the girls please just sit out a game? Grace, Alex, and Libby are too good of players."

Josh and Jeff both smiled as Gunner let out a laugh.

"Well, son, you might actually learn something if the girls play," Gunner said.

Grace held up her hand. "No…it's fine, Uncle Gunner. If Colt is afraid of being beaten by a few girls, then we are more than happy to sit this one out."

"We are?" Libby, Alex, Lauren, and Taylor all said at once.

Maegan did a fist pump and started to walk away. "Yes! I hate football."

Amanda busted out laughing. "God, it kills Brad that Maegan hates football…that she hates any sport really."

"Oh, gesh, if Grace ever told Jeff no to football, I think he would curl up into a ball in the corner somewhere and cry his eyes out," Ari said as she put cheese on some of the burgers.

Ellie and Heather both laughed.

"Same here. Gunner would resort to bribing Alex in some way or another," Ells said.

Heather went back to cutting tomatoes. "I'm just glad I have a daughter who can throw a football, and she still stops to make sure her hair is pinned up to her expectations."

As the day went on, more football was played, and more screaming girls ran by as Colt chased them with a garden snake in his hands.

I saw Scott standing off to the side, leaning against a tree. I walked up to him and put my arms around his waist.

"What are you thinking about?" I asked.

He looked down at me and smiled. "How blessed we are."

I leaned my head against him. "Mmm…that we are. Very blessed indeed."

I looked out to each of our friends and smiled. Jeff was attempting to talk Ari into sneaking off somewhere to make out. Gunner had Ellie on his back while Josh carried Heather on his back as they ran after the kids in a race around the barn. Brad and Amanda were lost in their own little world, talking to each other.

When Scott brushed his hand up and down my arm, I felt that familiar tingle. Even after all these years, his touch affected me still.

"What are you thinking about, baby?" Scott asked as he pulled me closer to him.

I looked around again. Nine beautiful kids were all running around, playing and laughing, and each one was healthy and happy. We had eight amazing friends who had been there for each other through the good times and the bad times. Not once had any of us ever turned our backs on each other or ever stopped to ask questions. I felt the tears building in my eyes as I looked at each of them. They were more than friends. They were family.

I turned and faced Scott as I smiled. "I'm thinking how we each got everything we've ever wanted."

He smiled and nodded his head. He lifted my chin up and kissed me softly on the lips. He put his arm around me and led me back toward everyone. I watched Gunner and Josh attempt to grab a hold of Ellie and Heather.

Gunner yelled, "It's tickle-the-moms minute! Grab a mom and tickle them for a minute!"

Scott held me tighter. "You have a thirty-second head start."

I pushed him away as I began laughing, and then I took off running.

Nothing in this life made me happier than just being right where I was with the people I loved.

As I made my way to Ellie, Heather, Ari, and Amanda, we all formed a circle and tried to keep the rest of the crew away from us. The next thing I knew, we were all rolling around on the ground, laughing and tickling each other. When Ari threatened to pee on someone, the kids disappeared, and we all started laughing.

Ellie fell back and looked up at the sky, laughing. "Holy hell. I've never been so happy in my entire life."

Ari let out a sigh. "Well, my mother would kill me if she knew I wasn't quoting the great Katharine Hepburn, but I love this quote."

We all turned and looked at her as she continued to look up at the sky with a smile.

"I believe it was Ben Sweetland who said, 'Happiness is a journey…not a destination.'"

The End…almost.

WANTED
family tree

Seven Years Later
Alex

"Will, if my father catches us in here, he is going to be really upset," I said as I looked back at the barn door nervously.

"Lex, we're both leaving for college in a few months. Don't you think you need to let your dad know what school you picked?" Will asked as he reached for my hand.

My father had it all planned out. I was going to the University of Texas like he did and getting my degree in marketing, but I had other dreams. Will was going to Texas A&M to get his degree in agribusiness, so he could help Jeff and my father run the ranch. I'd been accepted into both schools, and my parents were just waiting on me to say yes to Texas.

It was Luke's, Colt's, and Will's dreams to take over the ranch someday, and I had no doubt in my mind that they would be great at running it.

If only Luke and Will would stop fighting...about me.

Luke hated that Will and I were sneaking around, seeing each other, and he'd threatened to tell my father on more than one occasion. The fights that Luke and Will had been in always drove me insane. Each time, one or the other would end up with a black eye and then would blame it on a football game.

It wasn't like my father didn't like Will. He loved Will...like a son. Daddy had dreams for me though, and those dreams didn't include a boy who would be working on a ranch. His dreams were of me moving to the city and getting to experience all that city-living would offer. Then, I could decide if I wanted to come back to Mason or not. Colt wasn't being told what he should do, and Luke was already at Texas A&M.

I didn't think it was fair. I wanted what my mother had. I wanted to live on the ranch, waking up every day to work in the garden. I wanted to see my husband off to work with a kiss every single morning. I wanted the life my parents had, and I couldn't figure out why my father didn't want me to have that life. He and my mother were so happy.

Will moved his lips to my neck, and his hot breath on my skin caused my stomach to drop.

God...just being around him makes my body do such crazy things.

Grace had said I was just horny and that Will and I needed to at least move on to a little bit more than kissing. She'd said we needed to cop feels here and there. Will was such a gentleman though, and he'd never once pushed me into doing anything I didn't want to do. There had been so many times I'd wanted to tell him to touch me, to just ease the tingling between my legs, but I'd known that wasn't what either one of us wanted…at least not yet.

I could hear Grace's voice in my head.

My god, you're eighteen. Stop piss-assing around about it, Alex. I swear, y'all have liked each other since, what…we were ten years old?

I was eighteen years old, and Will was seventeen. He would turn eighteen in August.

I had to smile though because Grace was all talk. She liked Michael Clark, but she was too damn afraid to even look at him.

"What are you smiling about, Lex?"

Will was the only one who called me Lex, and I liked it that way. It felt special, like it was something that was just between the two of us, something only we shared together, and we could do it in front of everyone. He had called me that since we were about ten years old.

"Us."

He pulled away and looked at me. "Us? What about *us?*"

I felt my cheeks turning red, and I was almost positive Will could feel the heat coming from them.

"You're blushing, Lex. Why, honey?"

I looked down and away, but he brought his finger up to my chin and forced me to look at him.

"Alex? What about us?"

"I'm tired of hiding. I want to tell our parents that we've been dating. I want to tell my dad that I've decided on A&M, and I want…I want…"

His smile was from ear to ear. "You want, what, sweetheart?"

Oh god. His voice alone sends me over the edge.

"I want more…" *Damn it. I can't bring myself to say it.*

"More of what?" he said with that stupid smile of his.

When he tilted his head and gave me that dimple smile, I knew he was teasing me.

I took a deep breath and quickly let it out. "I want to make love."

Will's smile faded, and he took a step back.

Oh no. What if he doesn't feel the same? What if my feelings for him are stronger than his feelings for me? Oh. My. God. What if that's the reason he's never pushed me into anything more?

I instantly felt like a fool. I pushed past him and started to walk away.

"Wait, Lex…please just wait a second." He reached for my arm.

I felt tears burning my eyes as I looked everywhere but at him. "I'm…I'm sorry. I should have just kept my mouth shut. Obviously, you don't feel the same way, so…"

I was cursing Grace inwardly for even planting this in my head, and I was already hatching a plan to bitch her out the next time I saw her.

Before I knew what was happening, Will was backing me up until I came to a stop against the wall of the barn. I looked up into his eyes. He had the most beautiful blue eyes. His hair was wavy and light brown.

I want to run my hand through his hair so bad.

He looked just like his father, and he was probably the sweetest guy I knew—besides Luke and Colt, who were both hopelessly romantic.

He ran the back of his fingers down my face and smiled. My cheek almost felt like it was burning where he'd touched me. He bent down like he was going to kiss me, but then he stopped just short of my lips. His eyes darted down to my lips and then back up to my eyes.

"Lex, I love you," he whispered.

I sucked in a breath of air and fought like hell to keep the tears from falling. It wasn't the first time he'd ever said it to me, but this time, it felt so...different. I felt a tear fall, and he quickly brushed it away with his lips.

He let out a low, soft moan. "You have no idea how hard it is for me not to make love to you every time I'm with you. I want nothing more than to be with you, but I want it to be right. I want it to be perfect for you, and we won't be sneaking into a barn or doing it in a car. You deserve so much more than that, honey. I want to make you feel special the first time we make love."

Wow. Oh...just wow. I felt my breathing getting faster. I looked at his lips as I licked mine.

He closed his eyes. "You drive me mad with desire, Alexandra. You have to know that."

Oh dear God...I think I might have my very first orgasm...right now...right here.

When he opened his eyes, they were filled with something I'd never seen before. The intense feeling of need I had for him grew about a hundred times.

I tried to talk but nothing would come out, except for a whispered, "Will..."

When his lips touched mine, I let out a moan. I opened my mouth to him, so our tongues could explore each other like we had done a hundred times before. I brought my hands up and ran them through his hair. When he pushed himself into me, I felt his erection, and I wanted to wrap my legs around him so badly. He pulled his body away some, but the kiss started to turn more passionate...until I heard someone clear his throat.

I snapped my eyes open right as Will moved back and scrunched up his face.

"Shit," he whispered low enough, so only I could hear. He took a few steps away from me as he ran his hand through his hair.

Lord, help me. I wanted this boy so badly, and even though I knew we had just been caught making out in my father's barn, my desire for him was so intense I wanted to cry.

I never took my eyes off of him. He winked at me, and then he turned to the side.

"Dad, Uncle Gunner, um…I mean, Mr. Mathews, um…I mean, sir…"

I closed my eyes and took in a deep breath. *Oh…holy…hell. My father.*

I tried to compose myself as I pushed myself off the wall. I turned to face my father and Uncle Josh. Even though Josh wasn't really my uncle and my father wasn't Will's uncle, we had always called them that. I'd wanted to giggle when Will had struggled on what to call my father, but when I looked into my dad's eyes, I knew that wouldn't be the smartest thing to do.

"So…" Uncle Josh started to say as he shook his head and smiled at Will. "Damn, boy…you picked the wrong girl to be caught making out with in her daddy's barn."

I glanced quickly over at Will, who looked at my father and then back at his dad. He smiled slightly, but then he quickly looked back at my father and swallowed hard.

My father cleared his throat and said, "Alex, Will, I think y'all need to head on up to the house and wait for us on the back porch."

Will and I looked at each other, and at the same time, we said, "Yes, sir."

As we walked out of the barn, Will grabbed my hand right in front of my father.

He looked at me, winked, and whispered, "I think that went well."

I just stared at him with my mouth hanging open. "You must have a death wish upon yourself."

WILL and Alex

Coming 2014

I wanted to say thank you so much for sharing this incredible journey with me. I will forever have Gunner, Ellie, Jeff, Ari, Josh, Heather, Brad, Amanda, Scott, and Jessie in my heart. I hope you feel the same.

A *sneak peek* AT THE BOOK

Unconditional LOVE

LARK *and* *Azurdee*

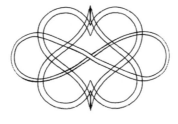

COMING *Spring* / *Summer* 2014

Azurdee

I walked back outside and looked around. Lark was sitting at a table, and two of my college friends were talking to him. He looked bored out of his mind, and I didn't think he was even listening to them.

Billy Currington's "Must Be Doin' Something Right" started playing, so I walked up to the table. I smiled at the girls and looked at Lark. "I think the best man and maid of honor should dance together at least once, don't you?"

He looked up at me and smiled. "Yep, I think so." He set his beer down, grabbed my hand, and practically dragged me to the dance floor. As he pulled me close to him, he said, "Thank God you showed up when you did."

I giggled as we started to two-step. "Why? You aren't enjoying yourself?"

"Sorry, but the girls you went to college with are either bitches or boring as hell."

I placed my head on his chest and closed my eyes. When I felt his chin rest on top of my head, the butterflies in my stomach went crazy.

I looked up at him. "So, what type of girl are you looking for anyway?"

The left corner of his mouth moved up just a bit further when he smiled. It almost felt like my knees might have wobbled for one quick second.

"What do you mean?"

I hit him in the stomach. "You know what I mean, Lark. What kind of girl is it going to take to get you to settle down? You know, for you to stop your man-whoring ways?" I asked with a wink.

"Why do you want to know? What makes you think I even want to settle down with someone?"

He instantly took the offensive approach. I shrugged my shoulder, wishing I hadn't even brought it up. I looked away and tried to act like his response hadn't bothered me.

"Are you wanting to apply for the position?" he asked as he pulled me closer to him.

"Um…I thought you just said you weren't looking for someone," I said, my voice sounding so small. I was kicking myself for letting him catch me off guard like that.

"If I was, you'd be my type, Azurdee. Your innocence just pours off of you, and it's sexy as hell," he said in almost a whisper.

I smiled even though I tried desperately not to. "Oh yeah?" I said, trying to be calm even though my heart was racing a hundred miles an hour.

He looked down at me as he gave me a slight smile, and then he looked away. "But I'm no good for you, Azurdee."

My smile faded. The anger started to build up inside me. "Don't you think I should be the judge of that?" I asked in an angry tone.

He looked back down at me and laughed. "You have no idea what you are saying. You know nothing about me, Azurdee. Why would you want to be involved with someone you know nothing about? I have secrets, and I've done things I'm not proud of."

I saw the hurt in his eyes, and all I wanted to do was make it go away. "I know everything I need to know about you. Everyone has secrets and has made mistakes in life."

"Is that so?" he asked in such a seductive way.

"Ah...yep. Isn't that what it's all about though? Getting to know each other. I would think that would be the best part of a relationship."

He threw his head back and laughed. "That is one of the best parts. Sex is the other."

I felt my face blush. If he ever knew I was a virgin, he would probably run away as fast as he could. He looked at me, and the look in his eyes caused goose bumps to pop up all over my body.

"Trust me, Azurdee, you need to just stay away from me. I'm no good for you."

I pushed him back. "I think you just say that because you're afraid of being in a relationship with someone."

He tightened his eyes as he glared at me. The hurt in his eyes was replaced by something else, but I couldn't figure out what it was.

Anger? Lust maybe?

He pulled me back into him. The song had changed at some point, but we were still dancing slowly.

"Do you want to be with me, Azurdee?"

Oh god. He just came out and asked it. What do I say? Do I tell him the truth?

I looked into his eyes and whispered, "Yes."

He closed his eyes and shook his head. "Azurdee, no, you don't."

"Yes. Yes, I do. I want to be with you, Lark. I want you to make love to me."

He opened his eyes, and the look in them caused me to suck in a breath of air.

He placed his hand on my face and whispered, "You don't know what you're saying, baby."

I put my hand on top of his. "Yes, I do. I want you, Lark. I want to get to know you...please let me."

He looked into my eyes for what seemed like forever before he finally gave me a small smile. "If I do this, Azurdee, you need to know what you're getting into. I'm...I'm not sure if I can be what you want me to be."

I swallowed and nodded my head. "I understand."

He's just scared. That's all. He needs someone to love him.

He pushed his hand into my hair and grabbed it. "Once you're mine, you're mine though, Azurdee. I won't share you with anyone."

I smiled. "I won't share either, just so you know."

He shook his head. "This is a dangerous game you're playing with me."

It felt like my heart dropped to my stomach. *What does he mean by that?*

"I'm not playing any games, Lark," I whispered.

Right then, Katy Perry's "Dark Horse" started playing. The smile that spread across his face shocked me. I wasn't sure if I should be turned-on or if I should turn around and run. He pulled my hair, making my head tilt back some, exposing my neck to him.

He leaned down and put his lips against my neck, and right before Katy started singing, he whispered, "Do you want me to make you mine, Azurdee?"

Chills ran up and down my body instantly. The moment the beat started, he pulled me to him and started dancing with me so seductively that I could feel my face blushing yet again. I didn't know if it was the way he was dancing with me or the song itself, but I felt like I was falling deeper and deeper into a trance, and he was in total control of every single one of my emotions.

I'd never danced like this before, and I had never felt so incredibly turned-on like I was. The way his body was grinding into mine had me going insane. If he were to tell me to strip down for him and make love to him right here in front of everyone, I would do it. His hand was moving up and down my body, and I was quickly falling faster and faster for him.

I want him more than ever.

He let go of my hair and moved both his hands over my body. Everywhere he touched, I felt like I had been zapped by tiny bolts of electricity. He placed both of his hands on my face and tilted my head up to him. Then, he just stopped moving. I had to hold on to something to keep my legs from going out underneath me. I grabbed on to his arms and stared into his eyes. He brought his lips barely up to mine and stopped just short of kissing me. I could feel his hot breath, and I was trying like hell not to seem desperate for his kiss.

"Who's the guy you're with?" he asked.

I shook my head to clear my thoughts. He had me pressed up against his hard-on, and I was going insane with lust.

"Um…just a friend. He's just a friend."

He smiled as he tilted his head and looked down at my lips. Then, he looked back up into my eyes and said, "What's your answer?"

"My answer?" I asked, confused as hell.

He lightly brushed his lips against mine, and I let out a moan. I was inwardly cursing myself for seeming so needy. He dropped his hands and took a few steps back from me.

No! I wanted to call out and reach for him to pull him back against my body. I needed to feel him close to me. I needed to feel his heat.

The farther he moved away, the colder I felt.

"If it's a yes, Azurdee, tell him he can leave anytime, and the sooner, the better because I really want to make love to you. *Now.*"

He turned and started toward the house. I stood there, just watching him walk away from me, as I tried to catch my breath. He turned back around and smiled at me right before he walked into the house.

Oh dear God. This is the moment I've been waiting for, dreaming about since the first time he ever looked into my eyes. He had been the one I was saving myself for.

I looked around to see if anyone had been watching us. I could feel the heat burning my cheeks. I took a deep breath in and slowly let it out. I looked around and found Paul, my date for the wedding.

As I walked over to tell Paul good-bye and to thank him for coming, I had the strangest feeling that I was about to give my heart and soul to someone who could possibly take it and crush it into a million pieces. I knew one thing for sure though. I was about to walk into something that both excited and scared me.

It was the perfect storm indeed.

Thank You

I'd like to first and foremost thank God for the many wonderful blessings in my life.

There are a few people who have been with me since the beginning of this journey, and without them, I don't think I could have done what I've done. So, I'd like to thank them first.

Darrin Elliott—I love you. I love that you support me. I love that you put up with my postings about you on Facebook, and I love that you inspire so many stories. I love that you love me.

Lauren Elliott—Thank you for putting up with the crazy world we have adapted to this last year. I'm so proud of you, Lauren, and I love watching and seeing the amazing person you are growing up to be. Now, if I could just get you to read! Damn it.

Ari Niknejadi—Thank you so much, sweets, for always believing in and me and being such a huge part of this series. You always kept me going and helped me so very much those first few months. I will forever be grateful to you for that. Thank you for your friendship!

Patricia Winn—You are not only my big sister but probably my biggest fan. You will never know how much it means to me that you stood by me when so many didn't. I love you and love your never-ending support. You are my very own personal cheerleader.

Elizabeth Bartell—Thank you for being such an incredible friend. Your help with *Wanted* will never be forgotten. I'm so blessed to have you in my life.

Molly McAdams—Oh, Molly. Molly, Molly, Molly, how I adore you and our friendship. You have been such an amazing force in my life this past year, and I hope you know that. You make me laugh…like ALL the time. If it wasn't for you, I think I would go insane. Thank you so much for all of your support, and most importantly, thank you for your friendship. I value it more than you know. #PeasAndCarrots

Heather Davenport—Heather, we have been through this from almost the very beginning. You were one of my very first supporters, and our friendship has grown so much this last year. I can't even begin to tell you how much I adore you and how thankful I am for everything you do for me. I hope you know how much I appreciate it.

Gary Taylor—I just don't even know what to say. As I type this, it will have been almost a year since you came into my world. It feels like we've known each other for a lifetime. Thank you for being the amazing friend that you are. Thank you for supporting this crazy dream of mine, and thank you for always making me laugh when I just want to cry. I hope you know how much that means to me. You truly are like a brother to me. Love you, cowboy!

Kristin Mayer—Thank you for the Magic 8 Ball. Thank you for your endless laughs each day. You keep me sane, I swear. Thank you for finding the picture that I used on this book. Your talents amaze me! I can't tell you how much I enjoy our banter each day. Love you, girl!

Jovana Shirley—*Holy hell.* You. Amaze. Me. These books would not be what they are if it wasn't for you and your editing talent. I don't think you realize how just your simple little notes off to the side where you say I made you laugh mean to me. You are incredibly good at your job, and if you ever gave it up, I very well might crawl into a hole and cry for weeks, possibly even months. Thank you for everything. Thank you for your friendship as well. I love you, girl!

Sarah Hansen—Thank you so much for the two amazing covers you did for me for *Wanted* and *Saved*. You truly are talented at what you do, and I feel honored to have had two of my book covers done by you.

Angie Fields—What can I say? You, my dear, are one talented lady. You have rocked out four of the most amazing book covers ever, and you are truly a joy to work with! Thank you so much for dropping everything for me to do the book cover for *Cherished*. I will never forget it.

To my street team, Kelly's Most Wanted—Y'all are an amazing group of people, and every day, I thank God for you and your support. I'm in awe of y'all, and I know that's not the first time I've said it.

To all my friends/readers—This journey would not be possible if it wasn't for y'all. I can never truly thank you enough. You've made my dreams come true on more than one occasion. I hope that I can continue to share with you the voices in my head.

To all my wonderful friends—I wish I could list each of you but know you are in my heart!

Playlist

"Wasting All These Tears" by Cassadee Pope—Jessie is on the plane heading to Belize.

"Cold as Stone" by Lady Antebellum—Scott finds out why Jessie thinks he cheated.

"Better" by Maggie Rose—Jessie spends the day with Trey.

"Baggage Claim" by Miranda Lambert—Gunner walks into the Wild Coyote Bar and sees Scott drunk.

"Trouble with Girls" by Scotty McCreery—Gunner, Jeff, and Scott talk about women.

"3" by Britney Spears—Trey and Jessie dance together on Christmas Eve.

"Don't Let Me Be Lonely" by The Band Perry—Jessie and Trey dance together at the club in Belize.

"Can't a Girl Change Her Mind" by Sarah Marince—Jessie realizes she was wrong about Scott and Chelsea and tries to call Scott.

"On My Way" by Boyce Avenue—Scott goes to Belize to get Jessie.

"When I Look at You" by Miley Cyrus—Josh and Heather make love on Christmas night.

"Come Back to Me" by Keith Urban—Scott walks along the beach after Jessie tells him about Trey touching her.

"Dare to Believe" by Boyce Avenue—Scott asks Jessie if she's still moving in with him.

"Stay" by Florida Georgia Line—Scott tells Jessie she needs to make sure she doesn't have feelings for Trey.

"Mine Would Be You" by Blake Shelton—Scott asks Jessie to marry him.

"Love Somebody" by Maroon 5—Lark fights his feelings for Azurdee.

"Echo" by Jason Walker—Ellie and Jeff's father tells them he has cancer and asks for their forgiveness.

"We Were Us by Keith Urban—Lark and Azurdee dance together for the first time.

"I Feel Like That" by Jason Walker—Gunner and Ellie's son, Colt, is born.

"Two Is Better Than One" by Boys Like Girls—Lauren is born, and Scott is dancing with her.

"My Girls" by Christina Aguilera—The girls are getting ready for Jessie's wedding.

"Even the Stars Fall 4 U" by Keith Urban—Ari and Luke dance in the kitchen while making breakfast.

"She's Amazing" by Love and Theft—Jeff tells Ari how happy he is with her.

"Shake That" by Eminem—Heather and Ellie dance on the pole.

"All for You" by Keith Urban—Josh and Heather make love at The Driskill Hotel.

"Me and You" by Kenny Chesney—Jessie and Scott dance to their wedding song.

"God Gave Me You" by Blake Shelton—Scott and Jessie make love on their honeymoon.

"Puzzle Pieces" by Justin Young with Colbie Caillat—Will and Alex are in the barn.

"Must Be Doin' Something Right" by Billy Currington—Azurdee asks Lark to dance.

"Dark Horse" by Katy Perry—Lark and Azurdee are dancing, and Lark tells Azurdee he wants to make love to her.

CPSIA information can be obtained at www.ICGtesting.com
Printed in the USA
LVOW05s1720060314

376324LV00014B/1099/P